"Brad Meltzer . . . won't have to make his living practicing law anytime soon."
Orlando Sentinel

"Riveting . . . The book zips along like a movie, and the character development is stunning. . . . The story line is full of unexpected twists. This is Meltzer's second book, and it is as good as his first. . . . The relationships . . . are so believable that they draw you in and don't let you go."
Albuquerque Journal

"Just when you thought there were no more changes to be rung on the legal thriller . . . Sleek, suspenseful . . . [A] compelling tale of legal and extralegal adventure."
Publishers Weekly

"Meltzer has mastered the art of baiting and hooking readers quickly into a fast-moving plot. . . . *Dead Even* succeeds. . . . Meltzer has a good ear and eye for capturing the sweaty insecurities and competitiveness of young lawyers."
USA Today

"[Meltzer's] writing skills are quite masterful."
Newport News Daily Press

"Dark humor . . . legal action like Grisham, and nail-biting suspense make this a thriller in the true sense of the word. Meltzer gives the reader well-rounded characters; demonizing neither prosecution nor defense, he shows both as human beings doing a job. Recommended."
Library Journal

ATTENTION: ORGANIZATIONS AND CORPORATIONS
Most Harper paperbacks are available at special quantity discounts
for bulk purchases for sales promotions, premiums, or fund-raising.
For information, please call or write:

Special Markets Department, HarperCollins Publishers,
10 East 53rd Street, New York, New York 10022-5299.
Telephone: (212) 207-7528.   Fax: (212) 207-7222.

BRAD MELTZER

DEAD EVEN

HARPER

An Imprint of HarperCollins*Publishers*

This book was originally published in hardcover May 1998 by William Morrow, an Imprint of HarperCollins Publishers, and in paperback March 1999 by Warner Books.

HARPER

An Imprint of HarperCollins*Publishers*
10 East 53rd Street
New York, New York 10022-5299

Copyright © 1998 by Forty-four Steps, Inc.
ISBN 978-0-06-197812-8

First Harper premium printing: November 2010
First William Morrow hardcover printing: May 1998

HarperCollins ® and Harper ® are registered trademarks of Harper-Collins Publishers.

Printed in the United States of America

Visit Harper paperbacks on the World Wide Web at
www.harpercollins.com

10 9 8 7 6 5 4 3 2 1

For Cori,
who couldn't possibly mean more to me
because she already means everything

And for my parents,
who showered me with love,
taught me how to laugh,
and always let me dream

ACKNOWLEDGMENTS

I'd like to thank the following people, who contributed their tremendous talents and energies to this book: my wife and favorite lawyer, Cori, without whom this book would not exist. When I decided to write about married attorneys, I knew I'd be drawing on personal experience. What I didn't realize was that I'd also be driving the two of us insane. From the very start, Cori kept it all together, and if this book is anything, it's a testament to the strength of our marriage and the love I have for my wife. (Thanks, C—you know I'd be lost without you.) Jill Kneerim, my agent, for her unfailing faith in me as a writer, her insightful advice, and, most of all, her treasured friendship; Elaine Rogers; Sharon Silva-Lamberson; Robin Chaykin; Ike Williams; and everyone else at The Palmer & Dodge Agency for their constant support and, most important, for never giving up on me.

I'd also like to thank my sister, Bari, who always stands in my corner and, as a result, provides me with more help than she'll ever realize; Noah

Kuttler, for his tireless attention to every detail and nuance of this book (Noah, I can't thank you enough; you really are incredible); Ethan Kline, for his discerning reaction to early drafts of the manuscript; Matt Oshinsky, Joel Rose, Chris Weiss, and Judd Winick, for their always perceptive suggestions and always valued friendship; Matthew Bogdanos, for inviting me into the world of prosecution and letting me see, up close, the vivid reality of what it really takes to fight crime—thank you for that trust; Maxine Rosenthal, for her extraordinary assistance; Dale Flam, Sandy Missakian, Barry Weisburg, Ronnie Aranoff, Alan Michaels, Bob Woodburn, and Eric Menoyo, for walking me through the details; Dr. Sam Snyder and Dr. Ronald K. Wright, for all the wonderful forensic and medical advice; Sara Emley, for the two words that appeared on the hardcover; Janice Doniger, for her keen understanding of what to wear and where to be seen; the helpful and extremely patient people at the Manhattan DA's public information office; and all my family and friends, whose names, as always, inhabit these pages.

Finally, I'd like to thank all the truly incredible people at Rob Weisbach Books and William Morrow: Bill Wright, Patricia Alvarez, Jacqueline Deval, Michael Murphy, Lisa Queen, Sharyn Rosenblum, Elizabeth Riley, Jeanette Zwart, Richard L. Aquan, Tom Nau, Colin Dickerman, David Szanto, and all the other amazingly nice folks at Weisbach/Morrow whose hard work made this book a reality. I'm honored to work with every one of them. I also owe a great deal of thanks to Larry Kirshbaum, Maureen Egen, Mel Parker, Airié Dekidjiev, and all the terrific people at Warner Books, who always make it a true pleasure. Finally, I'd like to thank my editor and publisher, Rob Weisbach. After close to a thousand pages together, I still have a hard time finding the perfect words for Rob. As an editor and publisher, there is no better—he pushed me to draw on reserves I didn't know existed, and his influence can be felt on every page. As a friend, he is someone I turn to without hesitation. So thank you, Rob, for your trust, for your enthusiasm, and, most of all, for your faith.

CHAPTER 1

hat if it's a disaster?" Sara asked as she got into bed.

"It's not going to be a disaster," Jared said. "You're going to be great."

"But what if I'm not? What if I'm just average? Maybe that's what they were trying to tell me. Maybe that's the lesson."

"There's no lesson, and you've never been average," Jared said, joining his wife under the covers. "It's just your first day of work. All you have to do is show up and be yourself." He shut off the lamp on his nightstand and reached for the nearby alarm clock. "What time do you want to wake up?"

"How about six-thirty?" Sara paused. "Actually, make it six-fifteen." She paused again. "Five forty-five. Just in case the train's running late."

"Shhhh, take a deep breath," Jared said. He propped himself up on his elbow. "It's okay to be nervous, but there's no reason to get nuts."

"I'm sorry. I just—"

"I know," he said, taking her hand. "I know

what's riding on this one—I remember what happened last time. I promise you, though, you're going to be great."

"You think so?"

"Absolutely."

"You really think so?"

"Sara, from this moment on, I'm choosing to ignore you."

"Is that a yes or a no?"

Jared pulled one of the pillows from behind his head and held it over Sara's face. "I refuse to acknowledge that question."

"Does that mean we're done talking about work?" Sara asked, her laughs muffled by the pillow.

"Yes, we're done talking about work." Jared straddled his wife, keeping the pillow on her face.

"Uh-oh, someone's getting kinky." Sara tried to pull the pillow away, but she felt Jared press down even harder. "C'mon, that's not funny," she said. "It's starting to hurt."

"Stop whining."

"What?" she asked.

He didn't respond.

"I'm serious, Jared. I can't breathe."

She felt him moving forward on her chest. Her left shoulder was suddenly pinned back by his knee. Then her right.

"Jared, what're you doing?" She grabbed his wrists and dug her nails into his arm.

He only pressed down harder.

"Jared, get off me! Get off me!" Her body was convulsing now, violently trying to knock him from his perch. As her nails tore at his arms and legs, her lungs lurched for air. But all he did was hold

tight. She wanted to stop fighting, but she couldn't. Choking on her own tears, she called out his name. *"Jaaared!"* she sobbed. *"Jaaared . . ."*

Jolted awake, Sara shot up in bed. Her face was covered in sweat and the room was silent. Jared was asleep next to her. Just a dream, she told herself, trying to stop her heart from racing. It's okay. But as she put her head back on the pillow, she couldn't let it go. Even more than the others, this one felt real. Her fears, his response, even his touch. All so real. It wasn't about Jared, though, she told herself. It was about work. To prove it to herself, she pressed her body up against her husband and wrapped an arm around his chest. He felt warm under the covers. Clearly, it was about work. She took a deep breath and squinted at the clock on Jared's nightstand. Two more hours, she realized. Only two more hours.

"Here's what I want," Jared said to the red-headed man behind the counter at Mike's Deli. "A sesame bagel with most, but not all, of the seeds scraped off, a light schmear of cream cheese, and a coffee—very light, with one spoon of sugar."

"That's nice, dear," Sara said. "While you're at it, why don't you just ask him to suck the nougat out of the Snickers?"

"Don't give him any ideas." The man behind the counter started on Jared's order. "In my whole life, I've never seen a man who gave more instructions for a stinking bagel and coffee. You'd think it was a work of art or something."

"Mikey, by the time you're done with it, it will be," Jared said with a wink.

"Don't suck up to me," Mikey said. He turned to Sara. "Now what does the normal half of the family want?"

"Whatever you want to get rid of. Just make it exciting—nothing plain."

"See, now that's why you're my favorite," Mikey sang. "No headache, no pain-in-the-ass demands, just normal, considerate—"

"Are you the manager?" a gray-haired woman with large glasses interrupted.

"That I am," Mikey said. "Can I help you?"

"I doubt it. I just want to register a complaint." She pulled a coupon from the pocket of her LOVE IS A PIANO TEACHER book bag and thrust it across the counter. "This coupon says that I get one dollar off a box of original flavor Cheerios. But when I checked the shelves, I saw that you're out of this item and that the coupon expires tomorrow."

"I'm sorry, ma'am, but we're a very small store with limited space. If you want, you're welcome to use the coupon on the other flavors of Cheerios. We have multigrain, and honey-nut, and—"

"I don't want any other Cheerios. I want *these* Cheerios!" the woman shouted, causing everyone in the small grocery store to turn and look. "And don't think I don't know what you're doing. When you print up these flyers with the coupons, you hide all the items in the back room. That way we can never redeem them."

"Actually, ma'am, we just don't have the space to—"

"I don't want to hear your excuses. What you're doing is false advertising! And that means it's illegal."

"No, it's not," Sara and Jared said simultaneously.

Surprised, the woman looked over at the couple, who were still waiting for their bagels. "Yes, it is," she insisted. "When he sends out those coupons he's making an offer for his products."

"Hate to break it to you, but an advertisement isn't an offer," Sara said.

"Unless it specifies an exact quantity or indicates exactly who can accept it," Jared added.

"Uh-oh," a man in line behind Sara and Jared said. "I smell lawyers."

"Why don't you both mind your own business?" the woman snapped.

"Then why don't you leave our friend alone?" Sara said.

"I didn't ask for your opinion."

"And our friend didn't ask to be talked down to like he was a piece of garbage," Sara shot back. "Now, as a Cheerios lover myself, I can appreciate your frustration, but we don't go for that kind of unpleasantness here. Instead, we've taken a new approach: It's called acting civilly to each other. I can understand if you don't want to participate, but that's the way we play it. So if you don't like it, why don't you make like a coupon and . . . and disappear."

As Jared fought to contain his laughter, the woman sneered at Mikey. "You'll never see me in this establishment again," she seethed.

"I'll live," Mikey said.

With a sniff, the woman turned and stormed out of the store. Mikey looked over at his two favorite customers. "Make like a coupon *and disappear*?"

"What can I say? I was under pressure."

"It did get her to leave," Jared pointed out.

"You're right about that," Mikey agreed. "Which means breakfast's on me."

* * *

Fifteen minutes later, Sara and Jared were crammed in the middle of a packed-to-capacity subway car. Sara was dressed in her best navy-blue pantsuit, while Jared wore a frayed Columbia Law sweatshirt and a pair of jogging shorts. A long-distance runner since his early years in high school, Jared still had his athletic build, although a small bald spot on the back of his head made him feel far older than he looked. With his suit packed neatly in a trifolding backpack, he began every Monday, Wednesday, and Friday with a half-hour run. "That's not a bad way to start the day," Jared said, pressed tightly against his wife. "Your first day on the job and you already have a victory."

"I don't know," Sara said as the train pulled away from the Fifty-ninth Street stop. "There's a big difference between cranky piano teachers and actual criminals. And if past performance is any indication, this job is going to be an even bigger loser than the last one."

"One stupid incident at one hotshot law firm means nothing about your value in the job market."

"But six months of looking—c'mon, Jared."

"I don't care, you're going to be great." Sara rolled her eyes. "Don't give me that look," Jared added. "I know what you're thinking and it's not true."

"Oh, so now you think you can read my mind?"

"I don't think I can read your mind—I *know* I can read your mind."

"Really?"

"Really."

"Okay, then, lover boy, take your best shot. What's going through my panicky little brain?"

Jared closed his eyes and rubbed his temples.

"I see great unrest. Great neurosis. No, wait—I see a handsome, brilliant, casually dressed husband. My, my, my, is he a good-looking one . . ."

"Jared . . ."

"That's his name—Jared! My God, we're sharing the same vision."

"I'm serious. What if this job doesn't work out? The article in the *Times* . . ."

"Forget about the *Times*. All it said was that the mayor was announcing budget cuts. Even if it leads to layoffs, that doesn't mean you're going to be fired. If you want to be safe, though, you can call Judge Flynn and—"

"I told you last night, I'm not calling him," Sara interrupted. "If I'm going to stay here, I want it to be because I deserve it, not because someone called in a favor."

Jared didn't argue the point further. Since they had first met, Sara never wanted special treatment—no professional favors, no help. Her independent streak ran deep: When Jared's uncle had offered to put in a good word so she could get an interview at his law firm, Sara had refused. To Jared, her logic was irrational and counterproductive. But Jared thrived on connections; Sara despised them. "I'm sorry I even brought it up," he finally said. "Besides, if this job doesn't work out, you can always find another."

"No. No way," she insisted. "My psyche's taken enough of a beating."

"That's exactly what I was about to say," Jared backpedaled. "No more psyche-beating for you. They're going to love you here, and they're going to realize you're a genius, and unlike Winick and Trudeau, they're never going to fire you. Starting today, they're going to fan you with giant feathers and baby-fresh-scent perfumes. You're not going to have to worry about the budget cuts and the butterflies will never swarm in your stomach."

"Let me ask you something," Sara said with an affectionate smile. "Do you really believe all the noise that comes out of your mouth?"

"I'm a defense attorney. That's my job."

"Yeah, well you're making the rest of us lawyers look bad."

"You're not a lawyer anymore—starting today, you're a DA."

"And that means I'm not a lawyer?"

"Once you go to the district attorney's office, you become a vampire. All you'll care about is arresting and convicting innocent people."

"Says the man who helps guilty criminals go free."

"Says the self-righteous DA."

"Says the man who will never again have sex with his wife."

Jared laughed as the train pulled into the Fiftieth Street stop. "Says the woman who is always right and never wrong and should never again be doubted."

"Thank you," Sara said.

He kissed her then—a lingering kiss. "You're going to miss your stop," she said, pulling away. The doors of the train closed.

"Don't worry," Jared said. "Today I'm taking it downtown."

"You have some work in court?"

"No," he said with a grin. "I just want to check out a new jogging path. I figure I'll start at the courthouse and work my way back to the office."

"Wait a minute. You're going to run an extra thirty blocks just so you can walk me to work?"

"It's your first day, isn't it?"

She couldn't help but smile. "You don't have to do that."

"I know," Jared said.

When the number nine train arrived at Franklin Street, Sara and Jared got off and joined the throngs of commuters who filled New York's overcrowded streets. The September morning was warm and bright and as close to sunny as the Manhattan skyline allowed. "All set?" Jared asked.

"All set," Sara said. "They have no idea what they're in for."

"There we go—that's what I like to hear."

"In fact, if I get any more excited, I may get in another fight just for fun."

"Okay, hon, but no more than two a day."

"I promise," she said. "That's my limit."

Jared gave his wife a quick kiss, then took one last look at the woman he loved. When they first met, he was captivated by her deep green eyes and expressive eyebrows—he thought they made her attractive in an understated way. He also loved the fact that she wore no makeup except for a stroke of blush. Remembering the moment, Jared turned away and started his jog to work. "Good luck!" he called out over his shoulder as he headed up West Broadway. "And don't forget: You're smarter than everyone!"

Watching her husband wave good-bye, Sara laughed at how goofy he was. And within a minute of leaving him, she also realized how wrong he was. Now Sara was alone. And the butterflies were swarming.

Tucking a stray curl behind her ear, Sara tried

to get her bearings. She was the only still point in a flood of people, all in dark suits, all with briefcases, all in a hurry. All lawyers, she thought. Steeling herself with a tightened jaw, she headed forcefully toward Centre Street. "Kill the butterflies. Kill the butterflies. Kill the butterflies," she whispered to herself.

At 80 Centre Street, the drab brick building that was home to the Manhattan District Attorney's Office, Sara followed her mental map toward the elevators at the back of the building. As she headed down the dark marble hallway, what seemed like an army of men and women in navy-blue suits pushed past her at a frantic pace. A man carrying an armful of files bumped into her and continued on his way. A woman in a pin-striped suit chased him. "Don't forget—we have the Schopf hearing at two!" she yelled. Another man, pushing a small cart full of files, wove his way through the morning crowd shouting, "Late for court! Late for court!" Frenzied and bleary-eyed, some of them looked like they hadn't slept in days. But if there was any doubt that being an assistant DA was one of the most sought-after jobs in the city, one needed only to look at the six-month waiting list to interview for the position.

Watching each of the tiny operas that played out around her, Sara felt her panic give way to excitement. After six long months, the law was once again animated and alive. This was why she wanted to work in the DA's office—her old law firm, with its rafts of blasé young associates in Italian suits, never had anything like this vitality. To some, it was chaos. But to Sara, it was the biggest lure of the job.

On the seventh floor, Sara passed through a metal detector and walked down a wide hallway with faded blue industrial carpet that reminded her of her old junior high school. Following the room numbers as she searched for her office, Sara couldn't help but notice that plastic dry-cleaning bags hung from every available hook and decorated almost every single coatrack in the twisting hallway. Not a good sign for free time, she thought as she reached room 727. The room number was painted on the translucent glass window of the heavy oak door, and no one was sitting at the desk outside the office. Feeling no need to wait, Sara opened the door and stepped inside.

Her office was exactly what she expected: a large metal desk; a Formica credenza that held an outdated computer; a Leatherette desk chair; two metal folding chairs; two large metal filing cabinets; a bookcase filled with New York statutes, sentencing guidelines, and other legal books; and a coatrack, with dry cleaning hanging on one of the hooks. Typical government office.

"Sara Tate, right?" A stocky young man entered the office.

"That's me," she said. "And you are . . ."

"I'm Alexander Guff—your TPA." Noticing the blank look on Sara's face, he added, "Trial prep assistant."

"Which means?"

"Which means I do whatever you need me to do. At the very least, I'm your secretary. But if you want to take me under your wing, I'm your assistant, your right-hand man, your boy Friday, the Jimmy Olsen to your Superman, the Watson to your Holmes . . ."

"The Captain to my Tennille?"

"Yeah, something like that," Guff said with a laugh. Guff was short and stocky, with bushy black hair that reminded Sara of a Brillo pad. His round face and pug nose were accentuated by his slouched posture, which made him look like he had a slight humpback. "I know what you're thinking," Guff said, stuffing his hands in his pockets. "No, I don't have a hump—this is just the way I stand. I'm a nervous kid and this is an outward symptom of my internal anxieties. And just so you know, I also like to stuff my hands in my pockets. It helps me think."

"Whatever makes you happy," Sara said with a shrug.

"See, I can already tell I like you," Guff said. "You see it, you say it, you let it rest. That's a good sign. We'll get along."

"Are you always this blunt?" Sara asked.

"This is just the way I am. Sometimes people like it, sometimes I creep people out."

"So that's the nutshell, huh?" Sara asked, taking a seat at her desk. "I'm the new boss and you're the witty assistant?"

"Do I look that obvious to you?" Guff asked, pulling out a chair and sitting down opposite her.

"I haven't decided yet. Keep talking." She wanted to ask him about the budget cuts, but she still wasn't sure if she could trust him. And she wasn't about to open up quite so fast. "How long have you lived in the city?" she added, trying to get more information.

"Only since I graduated from college, which makes a little over two years. Personally, I'd prefer living at home and saving some money, but I'm in the process of revolting against my suburban up-bringing."

"Oh, you are?" Sara asked doubtfully. "And you're doing this how? By working in the DA's office?"

"Of course not. I'm doing it by just existing. I mean, look at me. With this posture and this messy clump of hair, would you know that my father is a doctor? That my mom drives carpool?"

"Give me a break," Sara said. "You sound just like my husband."

"So the ring's for real, huh?" Guff asked.

"Real for six years." She tapped her platinum-and-gold wedding band against her desk.

"See, that's just my luck," Guff said. "All the good ones are taken. I can never meet someone who's on her own, who isn't a psycho, who doesn't want to set fire to my futon, who—"

"Who digs suburban anarchists who think they're much more rebellious than they are?"

Leaning back in his seat, Guff laughed.

"No offense, Guff, but the entire female population is not plotting against you."

"Tell that to my Beatles collection and my missing stereo. I mean, my life is proof to the contrary."

"Uh-oh, chronic paranoia. Does that mean you're also a conspiracy nut?"

"Depends how you define *nut*. I'm not a fan of the overused conspiracies that Hollywood keeps recycling, but I do believe there are some unexplained phenomena we can't answer. For example, take your typical deck of cards. If you add up the number of letters in the words *ace, two, three, four*, all the way up to *jack, queen*, and *king*, you get the number fifty-two—the same as the number of cards in every deck."

Sara paused a moment. "So?"

"Secret code, baby. Believe the hype." Sara shook her head, amused. "Don't blame me—it's all in the upbringing."

"With that, I actually agree."

"Of course you do—we're all the product of our families. That's why you have to tell me about yours. Do you have any brothers or sisters? Are your parents crazy-insane like mine—"

"My parents were both killed during my first year of law school," Sara interrupted, stopping Guff in mid-sentence. "They were on their way back from a day trip to Connecticut when they hit a patch of ice," Sara explained. "Their car slid across the road and plowed into an oncoming van. They died instantly."

"I'm really sorry. I didn't mean to—"

"It's okay," Sara said, forcing confidence into her voice. "You couldn't have known."

"But I—"

"Guff, please don't worry about it. Everyone on this planet has a memory they'd rather not recall. We just happened to hit mine early. Now let's move on—we were having a good time."

Noticing the embarrassed look in Guff's eyes, Sara realized he was genuinely upset. It was clear he felt awful that he'd hurt her. That was all Sara needed to see. This was a good guy. Now she could open up. Taking a deep breath, she continued. "Any word around the office about that article in yesterday's *Times*?"

"You saw that, huh?"

"It's not good, is it?"

Guff paused. "Maybe you should go see Monaghan," he said, referring to the district attorney.

"Don't do that, Guff. If you know something, tell me."

"All I know is the mayor's trying to shrink the number of city employees by announcing across-the-board budget cuts for all city offices."

"Does that mean I'm going to be fired?"

"I don't know about you specifically, but when layoffs hit in this office, the last ones in are always the first ones out. And since the moment I walked in this morning, the office rumor mill's been buzzing like crazy—according to a guy on the elevator, all the new hires are supposed to be automatically on notice."

"No one's told me a thing."

Guff pointed to the metal tray on Sara's desk. "That's why they call it an in-box. I'm sorry, Sara."

Sara snatched up the single sheet of paper and read through a memorandum addressed to the entire staff of the Manhattan District Attorney's Office. According to the memo, the mayor's recent announcement "will require us to reevaluate our current staff size. In keeping with the historical precedents of this office, decisions will be made proportionately among support staff, trial assistants, and attorneys. While these decisions will be difficult for all involved, we expect that this period of reorganization will not interfere with the day-to-day operations of this office."

"I can't believe this," Sara said, her voice cracking. "I can't lose this job."

"Are you okay?" Guff asked.

"I'm fine," she said, unconvincingly. "I just don't understand it. Why now?"

"Are you kidding? We have an election coming up next year. The mayor's no dummy—he knows big government is out. And by not favoring one department over another, he'll look efficient, fair, and industrious all in a day's work. It's a political coup."

Sara put her hands behind her neck, trying to massage away the tension. As she tried to organize her thoughts, her mind was reeling. This was even worse than she expected—a wrecking ball against her ego. Why is it happening again? she wondered. Why isn't it ever easy? Feeling self-pity wash over her, Sara remained silent.

"Sorry. I didn't mean to ruin your day so quickly."

For a long minute, Sara didn't say a word. But when she realized that she couldn't just sit there and sulk, self-pity slowly gave way to defiance. What would Jared do? she asked herself. No, don't do it like that. This isn't his. It's yours. It's yours and it's not so bad, she thought. You've been through worse. Much worse. At least here, it's not final. At least here you're not alone. At least here you can use your brain. That's what he said: You're smart. You're smarter than everyone. Looking up at Guff, Sara broke her silence. "When do you think Monaghan's going to take action on the memo?"

"Probably a week or two. Why?"

"I want to know how much time I have."

"Sounds like you have a plan."

"Not at all. But it took me six months to get this job, so I'm not losing it without a brawl."

Impressed by his boss's determination, Guff asked, "Then what do we do now?"

"You tell me," Sara said. "You're the one who works here."

"All I know is you have to be in orientation

until lunch, and I have a doctor's appointment this afternoon, so we probably can't get started on a solution until tomorrow."

"Terrific," she said, glancing at the clock on the wall. She looked back at Guff. "What do you think my chances are?"

"My honest opinion?"

"Of course."

"Then let me put it this way: If I were a betting man . . ." He paused.

"What? Tell me."

"I'd put my money on another horse."

It was only one in the afternoon when Sara arrived back at her office, but her face was already showing signs of exhaustion. Although the four-hour orientation session was supposed to be a simple and informative introduction to the DA's office, Sara spent every hour of it worrying about who would be the first to go. Still trying to figure out the answer, she collapsed in her seat. Before she could even catch her breath, the phone rang.

"This is Sara," she answered.

"Well?" Jared asked. "How is it? I've been calling all morning, but you haven't been there."

"That's because within my first hour of work, I found out I'm going to be fired."

"You were fired?"

"Not yet—but Monaghan announced layoffs this morning and everyone thinks I'll be the first to go."

"Says who?"

"Says my assistant . . ."

"What does your assistant know?"

". . . and my orientation leader," Sara continued,

"and the woman who helped me fill out my paper-work, and the attorney I had to cross-examine during my mock trial, and the four other lawyers I met in the . . ." Her voice broke and her eyes welled up with tears. "I'm not like you, Jared—it doesn't all work out for me. That's why people think I'm such a failure."

"Whoa, whoa, whoa," Jared interrupted. "No one thinks you're a failure. This isn't anything personal—it's a budget cut."

"But you know what comes next," Sara said. "More job searching, more interviews, more rejection letters . . ."

"Shhhhhh, calm down," Jared said. "You're going to be great."

"The only one who thinks that is you."

"That's not true. Pop called me first thing this morning to ask if you won your first case yet."

"Jared, you're talking about my grandfather. He's not exactly an unbiased source."

"It doesn't matter. You're still going to be fantastic."

"No, I'm not. I'm not prepared for—"

"Hunter College, magna cum laude."

"Big deal—it's a small city school."

"What about Columbia Law School?"

"My parents paid the dean to get me in."

"No, they didn't," Jared said. "And even if they did, didn't you do well there?"

"I guess." Sara shot from her seat and walked around to the front of her desk. "Damn, why am I feeling so sorry for myself? I sound like I'm in high school. Change the subject. What's going on there?"

"Nothing," Jared said. "I'll tell you about it later."

Sara raised an eyebrow. "Tell me about it now."

"It's not that important."

Something was wrong. "Jared, you better not be doing what I think you're doing."

"Which is what?"

"Which is hiding good news just because you're worried about me."

"I'm not hiding anything. It's not even that big a—"

"See, I knew it. I knew that's what you were doing. Now spill it."

Reluctantly, Jared gave in. "When I was coming back from lunch, Wayne came up to me and told me I was, quote, 'on the right track.'"

"Wayne?" Sara asked, excited. "As in Thomas Wayne? Did he say when they'd vote on you?"

"The general consensus is that I'll be up for partner within the next six months—depending on how much business I bring in."

"That's fantastic," Sara said.

Jared didn't respond.

"Don't tell me you're still worried about bringing in business," she added.

"That's why I didn't want to bring this up now. . . ."

"Jared, I appreciate what you're trying to do, but I can handle two things at once. Now stop hiding and start talking. What about the list we made? Who's left on that?"

"No one—I tried them all. Our alumni associations, the chamber of commerce, the synagogue, the church, the Ninety-second Street Y, the Democrats, the Republicans, the Kiwanis Club, the Rotary Club, the Toastmasters—if they have a newsletter, I've put an ad in it; if they have a meeting, I've sat in on it. I just don't understand why it's not working."

"Honey, I know you're not used to being human like the rest of us, but it's okay to admit that something's actually a challenge. That doesn't mean it's your fault."

"I disagree. There's got to be something I'm overlooking. Maybe I should dress a little more casually next time—just so they don't feel like it's a hard sell."

"You never stop, do you?"

"Not until I figure it out. There's always a solution."

"Now you're suddenly bold?"

"I'm always bold."

"Jared, the only reason you wear your slacks uncuffed is because your dad still does."

"That has nothing to do with a lack of boldness. The uncuffed look is elegant. It's flawless. It's in."

"No offense, dear, but you have no idea what's in. And if it wasn't for me, you'd be equal on all sides."

"Are you calling me a square?"

"All I'm saying is, we're no closer to solving the problem."

Just then, Guff entered her office. "Who wants to save their job today?" he sang.

"Give me one second," Sara said to Guff, putting her hand over the mouthpiece. "Jared, I really should run."

"Everything okay?"

"Yeah. Hopefully," she answered. "And by the way, thanks again for listening."

"Are you kidding? That's my pleasure."

Sara put down the phone and looked up at her assistant.

"I asked a question, campers: Who wants to save their job?"

"What're you doing here?" Sara asked. "I thought you had a doctor's appointment."

"I just heard Transportation's letting three hundred people go, so I decided to cancel it. If this thing is moving as quick as I think it is, I couldn't let you twist in the wind."

"And how'd you know I wouldn't be out at lunch?"

"Once again, I must thank that wicked queen I call deductive reasoning. I figured if you were serious about staying on board, you'd be back here, pulling your hair out. And judging by the redness of your eyes, I'm right."

"You're pretty smart for a suburban kid."

"All life's lessons can be learned at the mall. Now are you ready to start? I think I know how you can save your job."

"You do?" Sara asked.

"We'll never know if we sit here all day."

Sara threw Monaghan's memo in the garbage. "Guff, I really appreciate you canceling your appointment. You didn't have to do that."

"Listen, this morning you treated me like an equal, and that means a lot to me. Considering I usually get crapped on by most of the women I meet, that's enough to keep me loyal for life. Now let's get out of here."

Sara followed Guff to the door. "Where are we going?"

"To the courthouse across the street. If you want to be an ADA, you have to get a case."

CHAPTER 2

Sitting in his immaculate office, Jared stared at his state-of-the-art telephone. "C'mon, you bastard—ring already."

"That's not how it works," his assistant, Kathleen, said as she walked into the room clutching a series of files. "It doesn't ring until you look away from it." Three weeks ago, Kathleen had turned thirty-five, although a face full of freckles and poker-straight hair down to her waist made her look at least five years younger. She had started working at Wayne & Portnoy almost seven years ago, when an aversion to the sight of blood forced her to rethink her career in nursing. For the past four years, she'd worked for Jared. And while Jared's attention to neatness and organization made him a high-maintenance boss, Kathleen prided herself on being even more compulsive than he was. As the joke around the office went, Kathleen was so aggressively organized, she could alphabetize dust. Some thought her dedication to Jared was an expression of her own love of control, while others thought it was a clear indication of the small crush she had on her boss.

Jared's office reflected the tastes of his living room at home—comfortably elegant, handsome, and filled with old movie memorabilia. Jared had developed his fascination with pop artifacts while majoring in history and minoring in film. Then, as a graduation gift, his parents bought him an original movie poster for Humphrey Bogart's *The Big Sleep*. It was love at first sight. Today, two framed movie posters decorated his office walls: one of the Italian classic *The Bicycle Thief* and one of the French version of Woody Allen's *Manhattan*. On the credenza behind his mahogany desk was an old trophy from his years on the Yale cross-country team. Always the competitor, Jared had been obsessed with running for as long as he could remember. He didn't care about speed; he wasn't a sprinter. He was far more concerned with the pacing and planning that were required for long-distance races.

He had won the trophy during his junior year in college, when he was invited to an international race sponsored by the University of Madrid. Of the three hundred American competitors, Jared was the only one who did research on the terrain. After a few well-placed phone calls and a trip to a travel agency, he realized that city planners, in an attempt to bring the Summer Olympics to Spain, had recently torn up a once-smooth section of downtown and replaced it with more authentic and tourist-friendly cobblestone streets. Jared and his teammates trained for months in the rougher-paved sections of New Haven, and the Yale team swept the long-distance events.

Jared's approach to running was logical, rational,

pragmatic—a physical activity he used as a means to hone his cerebral skills. That intellectual challenge was what kept him competing, and that intellectual challenge was what attracted him to the law. By the time he graduated from law school, the racetrack had become the partnership track.

"Can I ask you a question?" Jared said, his eyes still glued to the phone. "When it comes to bringing in new clients, am I not good at it, or is it just plain hard?"

"What did Sara tell you?" Kathleen asked.

"She said it's hard."

"And what do you think?"

"I think I'm not good at it."

"That's all I need to hear—I refuse to answer."

Jared looked up. "Why do you always have to do that?"

"Jared, remember what happened last time I disagreed with you? You wanted to know what to buy your mom for her birthday—Sara and I said scented soaps and bubble bath; you said a bouquet of flowers. Then you drove us both completely insane by buying every women's fashion magazine and spending at least a week trying to prove us wrong. And then, when you were finally convinced that you could even prove something as silly as what to buy someone for their birthday, you still kept pushing until we both converted to your conclusion."

"I was right, though. Bubble bath was a passing fad. At least for that year."

"This isn't . . ." She stumbled. It wasn't her place to scold him. After a moment, she added, "When it comes to work, and the law, and an important case, I love watching you get caught up in the research. But when it comes to my very own personal opinions, I don't want to be on the receiving end of the inquisition."

"So you agree Sara's being—"

"Please, Jared, stop critiquing everyone's advice. Sara's good at facing hard problems. She knows what she's doing and she knows you."

"Okay, so that means you really think—"

"The only thing I really think is that your wife's a smart woman. And since I'm no dummy myself, I see no reason to get involved. Now can we please move past this and get back to the case?"

"No, you're right," Jared said, eyeing the phone one more time.

"What time did he say he'd call?" Kathleen asked.

"Twenty minutes ago. I don't care if he's late—I just want to make sure I have the information before Hartley gets here." Jerry Hartley was Jared's opposing counsel in a lawsuit accusing Rose Microsystems of sexual discrimination. Rose was one of Jared's biggest clients, and while Hartley's case was pretty weak, Jared knew discrimination cases were always dangerous territory.

"So what's the strategy?" Kathleen asked.

"In this situation, I do everything in my power to make sure the case never goes to trial. Negotiate or die."

"What if Hartley won't negotiate?"

"All lawyers negotiate. We just have to find Barrow."

"He may be your favorite private investigator, but the guy has dropped off the face of the planet," Kathleen said. "In the last fifteen minutes alone, I called him at the office, called him at home, called his cell phone, beeped him, and faxed him. I'd send out a carrier pigeon, but I need a destination first." Kathleen opened the file folder that she was holding. "Maybe we should contact a different private eye. On my list alone, I have fourteen other detectives, six moonlighting cops, and three low-life informants. All of them are up to the task."

"Barrow's already put in a week's worth of work. Trust me, I know him—he'll come through."

Before Kathleen could respond, Jared's phone rang.

"Jared Lynch," he answered. "Yeah. No. Bring him up." He hung up the phone and ran his hand through his neatly trimmed hair. "Ready or not, here comes Hartley."

"And you don't have jack," Kathleen added.

"And I don't have jack."

As she headed next door to 100 Centre Street, Sara struggled to match Guff's breakneck pace. Dodging through the stream of lawyers who regularly crisscrossed between the two buildings, Guff explained, "Not only is this where most of the courtrooms are, this is also the home of ECAB."

"*E*-CAB?" Sara asked.

"Don't worry, you'll see." Guff walked in the front entrance of the building. Once past security, they headed straight for the elevators. The elevator doors were about to close when someone jammed an arm between them. The doors opened wide and a tall man with pepper-gray hair and a military-style crew cut gave Sara a cursory glance and stepped inside.

"Good to see you, Victor," Guff said.

"Mmm," Victor said coldly. With a freshly pressed dark-blue suit and a perfectly knotted red-and-navy Hermès tie, Victor cut an imposing figure.

Hoping to break the tension, Guff tried again. "Victor, I want you to meet Sara Tate. Sara—this is Victor Stockwell." Sara and Victor nodded to each other. "Sara just started with us. I'm taking her to ECAB to show her the ropes."

"Better show them quick," Victor said. "As of now, they're letting sixty people go."

"Sixty?" Sara asked as the elevator doors opened on the second floor.

Sara and Guff followed Victor out of the elevator and into the middle of the hallway. "Where'd you get that number?" Guff asked.

"From Elaine," Victor said, referring to the district attorney's secretary. "Although that includes all staff, not just lawyers." He looked at Sara. "But if I were you, I wouldn't unpack my boxes just yet. Rookies die first."

"Thanks," Sara said, unnerved by Victor's warning.

"There's no way to sugarcoat it," Victor said. As he headed up the hallway, he added, "See you in there later."

When Victor was out of earshot, Sara said, "How long has he been captain of the cheerleaders?"

"Don't take it personally—that's just the way he is," Guff said. "He's a former marine, so he's always hard on the new recruits. It makes him feel like he's still in the military."

"Any chance he'll be fired instead of me?" Sara asked.

"Not one in a grillion. Victor's probably the best prosecutor in our office, if not the entire state."

"Mr. Tough Guy with the dark eyes? Juries buy it from him?"

"He may be a stone-cold hard-ass, but they adore him in the courtroom," Guff said. "Juries love him, witnesses love him, judges eat out of his hands. It's really incredible."

"Why?"

"He's brutally honest," Guff said flatly. "Too many lawyers bullshit around, throwing everything at the wall just to see what sticks. Victor barrels forward only with the evidence he has— nothing more, nothing less. If he hasn't proven a point, he admits it immediately; if he has proven something, he doesn't rub your face in it. People are so shocked by the honesty, they fall in love. He may be rough around the edges, but for almost twenty years he's been a master at his game."

"Really that good, huh?"

"Yeah, yeah, yeah, he's the best," Guff said. He opened the door marked ECAB. "Welcome to the Early Case Assessment Bureau," Guff said as they walked through a reception area. Waving hello to the secretary, Guff headed into one of the many offices in the back of the room. He led Sara in, then closed the door behind them.

"So this is where everyone gets their cases?" Sara asked.

"Exactly," Guff said, taking a seat behind the desk. "Although no one's ever heard of it, this is the heart of the entire district attorney's office. Almost every crime in the city—125,000 cases a year—comes through this office. When an arrest is made, the officer fills out a booking sheet explaining why he arrested the defendant. Every day, those sheets are sent here, where the ECAB supervisor—one of the senior ADAs—assigns those cases to you and the rest of the ADAs.

"He doesn't assign them randomly, though. It's done by experience—the more experience you have, the better the cases you get. But if this is your first week on the job, you'll probably get a boring little case no one cares about."

"At least I'll have a case," Sara said. "That's a start."

"But it's not enough," Guff said. "Anyone can get a case. In New York City, there's so much shit going on, finding a crime is like finding a woman: They're on every block in town, but you have to work hard to find one that's worthwhile."

"So how do I get a good case?"

"That's the magic question. And quite honestly, it's one of the best-kept secrets of the office," Guff explained, as Sara listened intently. "To do it, you have to sidestep ECAB and find someone who'll trust you with a case before it gets to this office."

"Who's going to trust a new recruit with a case?" Sara asked.

"Therein lies the problem," Guff admitted. "Sometimes, if the arresting officer really cares about the case—for example, if his partner was injured by the criminal—he'll avoid ECAB and deliver the case personally to the ADA of his choice. Or a judge might see a case he likes and handpick an ADA for it."

"And that's completely legal?"

"It's the office's greatest conspiracy, but it's also the way the system has to operate. Winning the biggest cases is what keeps people's faith in the system. And that faith is the best deterrent to crime."

"That's a stirring speech, but where am I going to find a cop or a judge who'll give me a case?"

"You won't," Guff said. "At your level, the only person who'll help you is the ECAB receptionist— the queen bee herself. She gets all the booking sheets from the precincts. Then she takes each sheet, staples it to the requisite DA's office form, and delivers those to the ECAB supervisor. But, as only a few people know, if you're really nice to her, she may pull out one of the good cases before it goes to the supervisor."

"Is that kosher?" Sara asked.

"I don't know if it's Hebrew National, but that's the way it works."

"So you think that's my best option?"

"Without a doubt. If you can get a case and take it to trial, the higher-ups will know you're not here to play around. And while I'm too low on the totem pole to get a judge or a detective to trust you with a case, I can show you how to get a winner through ECAB. Sweet-talk the receptionist and she'll slip you a case. Then all you have to do is win it."

A slow grin crept up Sara's cheeks.

"Seven hundred thousand dollars?" Jared asked in disbelief. "Where do you come up with a number like that?" Although he had known Hartley was going to ask for a large dollar amount to settle the case, he'd never expected it to be that high. Even if Hartley was overreaching in the hope that the settlement would come out at half that amount, three hundred fifty thousand was still almost double what Jared's client was willing to pay.

"C'mon," Hartley said, brushing his hand over his thin, graying hair. "That number's not completely ridiculous."

"Hartley, if I bring back a number like that, they'll slaughter me. Even you know that's an absurd amount."

"What can I say? We have a strong case here. If our number's so crazy, make me a counteroffer."

Although Jared was authorized to settle the case for two hundred thousand, he was hoping for a far smaller number. And with the right information, he knew he could bring it down to fifty thousand. The only problem was, he still didn't have the information he needed. "I don't know," Jared hedged, hoping to stall. "Maybe we should just go to trial. You and I both know your client completely overreacted."

"So what if she did? You guys still better think long and hard about going to trial. These kinds of cases bring lots of bad press with them."

Jared's eyes narrowed and he shot a cold stare at his opponent. "Y'know, Hartley, you just revealed a whole new side of yourself. You don't think there's a case here—you agreed to represent this nut because you know discrimination cases lead to easy money."

"Don't judge me, son. You have to feed your family; I have to feed mine."

"I'm not your son, and I'm certainly not coming close to seven hundred thousand. So pick another number."

"Do I look nervous?" Sara asked, wiping her hands on her blue pantsuit.

"Nervous isn't the right word," Guff responded. "I'd say 'outwardly calm, but internally terrified' is the best description."

"What do you expect? My job's on the line here."

"Don't think about the job. Now, do you remember our plan?"

"Absolutely. You introduce me; I schmooze; she hands over the case."

"Perfect." Guff opened the office door and stepped into the hallway. "Here we go."

Sitting behind a small oak desk in the reception area, Evelyn Katz was up to her elbows in paperwork. Knowing that the ADAs usually got back from lunch at about two o'clock, she moved as fast as she could—logging in the newest booking sheets and preparing them for distribution.

"Hi, Evelyn," Guff said as he approached her desk. "How's everything today?"

"Do I know you?" Evelyn asked.

"I'm Guff—one of the TPAs from next door. I used to work for Conrad Moore, and I just wanted to introduce you to my new boss." As Sara approached Evelyn's desk, Guff said, "This is Sara Tate. She just started with us today. It's her first time in ECAB."

"I'm happy for both of you," Evelyn said, turning her attention back to the booking sheets on her desk.

Before Guff could say another word, the office door opened and a man wearing an olive-green suit walked in carrying a small stack of booking sheets.

"More?" Evelyn asked.

"The afternoon's just warming up," the man said as he left the office. "See you soon."

When the door closed, Evelyn put the new sheets in her in-box and went on with her work. She continued to ignore Sara and Guff.

Sara shot Guff a look, then addressed the receptionist. "Listen, I'm sorry to bother you. It's just that I'm new here and—"

"Actually, why don't you listen," Evelyn said, putting down her stapler. "I know you're new here, and I know you want a good case, but I don't know you from Adam. So if I let you cut the line, I'm jerking over all the people who I not only like a whole lot more, but who bother me a whole lot less."

Stunned, Sara didn't know what to say. "I didn't mean to be a bother. I'm just trying to save—"

Once again, the door to ECAB flew open. But it wasn't the man in the olive suit. It was Victor Stockwell. Striding across the reception area, Victor looked at Sara. "Still not fired?"

Sara forced a smile. "Can you believe it? I made it through another whole twenty minutes."

"Hiya there, Vic," Guff said. When Victor didn't respond, Guff added, "Love you, too, baby. Kiss ya, hug ya, squeeze ya."

Without another word, Victor headed for the ECAB supervisor's office. Evelyn picked up a stack of booking sheets and followed him.

When she was gone, Sara leaned on Evelyn's desk. "I can't believe this."

"It could be worse," Guff reasoned.

"How? How could it possibly be worse?"

"You could be on fire, or you could have poison ivy. You could even have chicken pox—that would be a whole lot worse."

"Guff, not now," Sara begged.

"I'll tell you what: Let me go beg to Victor. Maybe he'll take some pity on us." Before Sara could object, Guff headed off behind Victor and Evelyn.

Now alone, Sara closed her eyes and started to massage her temples. Once again, the front door opened. It was the man who delivered the booking sheets. "Where's Evelyn?" he asked, holding the newest pile of crimes.

"She's in the back with Victor," Sara explained. As he put the booking sheets in Evelyn's in-box, Sara asked, "Anything good in there?"

"No idea," he said. "But the one in the folder is a request for Victor. You can bet that one won't suck." Sure enough, on the top of the pile was a booking sheet in a plain manila file folder. On a yellow Post-it attached to the folder were the words *Request for Victor Stockwell.*

"That's great for him, but do you have anything for me?" Sara asked.

"Let me guess: You need a good case so you can wow your boss."

"Something like that."

"So hasn't this city taught you anything? If you want something, take it."

"I don't get it," Sara said.

"The case," he said, pointing to the folder. "If you want it, that's your case."

"What do you mean that's my case? It's marked for Victor."

"It's not marked for him—it's a request. That just means the arresting officer, if he had the choice, would like to see Victor on the case." Looking down the hallway, the man checked to see if he could spot Evelyn. He turned back to Sara. "If they request Victor, it's a good case. You should take it."

"Are you crazy?" Sara asked. "I can't take it—it's not my case."

"It's not anybody's case. It hasn't been assigned yet."

"But if it's marked for Victor . . ."

He pulled the yellow Post-it from the folder and crumpled it up. "Not anymore. Now it's marked for no one."

"Wait a minute—"

"Half the cases in this city have requests for Victor. Trust me, he can't do them all. Besides,

Victor's a real asshole. He could use losing a few good ones. If you really need it, just take it."

"I don't know," Sara said nervously.

"Listen, it's your life. I can't tell you what to do," he said as he walked to the door. "But I can tell you that Victor won't miss it. He has dozens of cases." Leaving the office, he added, "Hope it works out for you."

Once again alone in the office, Sara stared at the now-unmarked folder. She couldn't move. It's a guaranteed great case, she told herself. And Victor will never miss it. Unsure of what to do, she could hear Guff and Victor arguing. From the sound of it, Victor wasn't offering his assistance.

"It's not my fault," Victor said from his office. "Welcome to life."

Seconds later, Guff returned to the reception area. "What's wrong with you?" he asked, noting the concern on Sara's face.

Sara pointed to Victor's case. "The delivery guy said that one was an absolute winner."

"Oh, man," Guff said with a smile. "You're thinking of taking it, aren't you?"

Sara didn't say a word.

"Are you sure it's a good case?"

"Yeah, pretty sure," Sara said. "Why? What do you think?"

"Take it. Without a doubt. Believe me, if you want a winner, you're not getting any help from this office."

From up the hallway, Sara could hear Victor and Evelyn wrapping up. Tentatively, she approached Evelyn's in-box. "I shouldn't be doing this."

"But you're going to," Guff said. "Just take it. It's not a big deal."

Sara grabbed the file folder. "This better not get me in trouble."

"It won't," Guff said as they darted to the door.

By the time Evelyn returned to her desk, Guff and Sara were gone. And so was the file marked for Victor Stockwell.

"Have you been listening to anything I've said during the past half hour?" Jared asked. "Four hundred thousand's not even close. If you're going to stick with numbers like that, we'll see you downtown."

"Jared, I'm getting tired of this," Hartley said with a sigh. "You say you want to settle, but you thumb your nose at everything I put out there."

"That's because you're putting out nonsense. There's—" Jared was interrupted by the electronic ring of his phone. He had given Kathleen strict instructions: He should be interrupted only if Barrow called. Lenny Barrow was Jared's best private investigator. While prosecutors had entire precincts of police officers and detectives to dig up dirt on the opposing party, defense attorneys were forced to rely on private investigators for their snooping needs. For the past week, Barrow had been searching for information on Hartley's client. And now, Jared smiled to himself, he would finally have the information to force a reasonable settlement. As always, the research would pay off. Picking up the receiver, Jared wondered if even fifty thousand was too much. Maybe twenty-five and an apology was sufficient. Or just twenty-five. "Jerry, please excuse me for a moment," Jared said, lifting the phone to his ear. "Hello. Jared Lynch."

"J, it's me," Barrow said in his usual calm voice.

"I was wondering when you'd call. Any good news?"

"Actually, I couldn't find a thing. Nothing dirty, nothing juicy, nothing controversial. The woman's a regular yawn convention."

"That's just wonderful," Jared said, trying to look like he was getting good news. "I'll tell him as soon as we hang up."

"You got Hartley in your office?" Barrow asked.

"Oh, yeah," Jared said, smiling. "Right in front of me."

"Then let me add this to your plate. Because I love you, I also did a little extra homework. The guy Hartley filed the claim against—your client?"

"Yeah?"

"He's a real scumbag, J. At the last company he worked for, he had four complaints lodged against him—two of them proven. You just better pray Hartley doesn't have good friends like me, because the way this is going, you're in for some pain."

"No, that's even better," Jared said. "What more can I ask for?"

"Listen, I'm sorry, boss," Barrow said. "Send my love to Hartley. And to Sara."

"I definitely will. And thanks," Jared said as he hung up the phone. Looking across his desk at Hartley, he forced a grin. "Sorry about that—just getting some info on your client. Now let's get back to those numbers."

Sara and Guff raced up the hallway. "Let me see it," Guff said.

"Not here," Sara said, checking over her shoulder. "In the elevator."

"Oh, man, I bet it's a great one. A brutal homicide. No, wait—even better—a double homicide."

"Can you please try to control your blood lust?" Sara asked.

The elevator was empty when Sara and Guff stepped inside. Guff repeatedly pushed the door-close button: "Close, close, close, close, close, close, close," he demanded. As the doors finally shut, Sara opened the file and flipped to the section marked *Description of Crime*. Struggling to decipher the arresting officer's bad handwriting, Sara read the facts of the case. "Oh, no. This can't be happening. Please tell me I'm reading this wrong," she said, handing the file to Guff.

"What? What is it?"

As Guff read the report for himself, Sara said, "I can't even believe it. It's not a double homicide, it's not a single homicide, it's not even an assault. Some guy named Kozlow was caught breaking into someone's house on the Upper East Side. The case that's supposed to secure my future is just an idiotic little burglary. No gun, no knife, no nothing."

"It's definitely a loser," Guff said as the elevator reached the ground floor. "But look at the bright side: At least you have a case."

"I guess," Sara said as they headed out of 100 Centre. "I just hope it's not a whole new headache."

Victor stood in front of Evelyn's desk. "There was a case that was supposed to come in for me. The defendant's name was Kozlow."

"Kozlow, Kozlow, Kozlow," Evelyn repeated,

flipping through the newest set of booking sheets on her desk. "I don't see it here. Sorry."

"What about this pile?" Victor asked indignantly, pointing to Evelyn's in-box.

Evelyn riffled through the new stack in her in-box. Still nothing. "Sorry. Haven't seen it."

"It was a burglary case. Kozlow was the defendant."

"I heard you the first time," Evelyn said. "And I still don't have it. Have you checked with any of the other ADAs?"

"Let me ask you something," Victor said, his eyes narrowing with anger. "Do I answer to you, or do you answer to me? Or to make it even easier, which one of us is the ECAB supervisor?"

"I'm sorry. I didn't mean—"

"I don't care what you meant. All I care about is getting that case. So I want you to go through this office, and I want you to find out who has it. Now."

CHAPTER 3

"So what do we do now?" Sara asked, sitting in her office and staring at the Kozlow booking sheet.

"What do you mean, 'what do we do?'" Guff asked. "What kind of question is that?"

"I mean, this case is garbage, so how can I get rid of it? Can we return it? Can we go back and get another one?"

"You can't return a case once you catch it. It's like buying a pair of pants and having them shortened—once you've messed with them, you can't bring them back."

"But I didn't mess with these pants. I just pulled them off the rack." Waving the Kozlow booking sheet in the air, Sara shouted, "These are perfectly good pants!"

"Well, you still can't return them. No refunds, no exchanges."

"Why?"

"Because if we operated on a return policy, the small crimes, which are the majority of crimes in this city, would never get prosecuted. Everyone would be waiting for the good stuff."

"Guff, I really don't care what the policy is, I need to find a way out of this. Now let's back up. Are you telling me I can't walk right back into ECAB, drop this file on the receptionist's desk, and say, 'Sorry, the delivery guy handed me this by mistake'?"

"I guess you could," Guff hypothesized. "As long as—"

Sara's phone started to ring.

"As long as what?" Sara asked, ignoring the phone.

"As long as the ECAB receptionist doesn't know it's gone. But if she finds out . . ."

"Hold on a second," Sara said to Guff as she picked up her phone. "This is Sara."

"Sara, this is Evelyn from ECAB. Do you have a burglary case for a defendant named Kozlow? If you took it, I need to know. It's important."

"Can you hang on a second?" Sara asked. She put Evelyn on hold and looked up at Guff. "We're in trouble."

"Two hundred and fifty thousand?" Marty Lubetsky asked, his face flushed red with anger. "What the hell kind of settlement is that?"

"Considering the facts of the case, I think we did okay," Jared explained, trying to put a positive spin on his negotiation with Hartley. "He was originally asking for seven hundred."

Marty Lubetsky was the partner at Wayne & Portnoy who supervised the Rose Microsystems account. "I don't give a shit that they were asking for seven hundred thousand—they could've been asking for seven hundred *million* for all I care. Your job is to bring them down to where our client is comfortable. On that endeavor, you failed. Miserably."

Annoyed at himself for trying to explain, Jared knew that Lubetsky didn't like explanations. He liked results. And when he didn't get results, he liked to yell. And when he was yelling, he liked to yell uninterrupted. So for almost ten minutes, Jared stood there silently.

"Dammit, Jared, if you needed some help, why didn't you ask for it? Now I'm left standing here with my thumb up my ass, looking like a schmuck. And that's not even including the fact that you agreed to fifty thousand more than Rose authorized."

"I told them it was contingent on Rose accepting the offer."

"Who cares what you told them? You can't stuff the genie back in the bottle."

Jared again fell silent. "I don't know what you want me to say," he finally replied. "I gave it everything I had. I wouldn't have settled the case if I didn't think it was in Rose's best interest. If you want, I'll be the one to break it to them."

"You better damn well believe you're going to be the one to break it to them. If they have to empty their pockets for this, I want them to know who's responsible."

Unable to face Guff, Sara fidgeted with a pencil on her desk. In front of her was a sketch of a person in the gallows, hanging from a noose. Below the hangman, she made four blank spaces and filled them in with the letters *S-A-R-A*. After she finished the last letter, she stabbed the hanged man with her pencil, breaking its point.

"Are you done beating yourself up yet?" Guff asked.

"That case didn't even belong to me."

"It didn't belong to anyone. And if it makes you feel any better, if she really wanted it, she would've asked for it back."

"The only reason she didn't ask for it back was because they realized it was a bum case."

"Beggars and choosers, boss. Now stop kicking yourself."

"No, you're right. We should focus on what our next step is. Enough with the self-pity."

"Exactly. That's a far better attitu—"

"Let me just say one last thing," Sara interrupted. "You know what the stupidest part of this case is?"

"No, tell me the stupidest part."

"The stupidest part is, *I can't even save my job with it! That's how dumb I am! I stole the one case in this whole damn building that has no real value! And not only is it worthless, it's getting me in trouble!*" Catching her breath, Sara calmly pushed the Kozlow booking sheet to the side of her desk.

"Case—one. Sara—zero," Guff announced.

"It's not funny," she said. "In that one selfish move, I hurt my career and made an incredible enemy."

"Don't worry about Evelyn—she won't stay mad for long."

"Who cares about Evelyn? I'm talking about Victor."

Guff stopped. "Victor knows?"

"I assume so. Evelyn said Victor was the one who asked her about the case. Why? Is that bad?"

"Let's put it this way: On the list of people you want mad at you, Victor's last."

"We have to get some help. Do you think you can find someone who's friendly with Victor? Maybe they can help us make nice."

"Let me make a few phone calls," Guff said, heading for the door.

Guff's departure from the office created a sudden silence. Sara's eyes darted around the mostly bare room, and she was hit with a sense of vertigo. Feeling the walls close in on her, she put her head down on her desk, hoping to shut out reality. For almost a minute, it actually worked. Then the ringing of her phone brought back every one of her problems.

"This is Sara," she answered. "If this is bad news, I don't want to hear it."

"Sounds like we're having similar afternoons," Jared said.

"If it's possible, I think I've actually made things worse." After explaining how she stole the leading ADA's case, Sara added, "And now I'm stuck with this loser case and still can't save my job."

"I don't understand one thing," Jared said. "If it's a nothing, little case, why was it marked for an office hotshot?"

"Some cop obviously wanted him on it."

"Are you sure that's it?"

"What're you saying?" Sara asked, picking her head up.

"Cops aren't that stupid. They know the big guns never take small cases."

Sara replayed the facts in her head. "I never thought about it like that," she said, her voice laced with excitement. "I mean, for all I know, this case is a gold mine."

"Sara, be careful with this. Don't get your hopes up abou—"

"You said it yourself," she interrupted. "There has to be some reason this case was marked for Victor."

"Wait a minute. Victor? As in Victor Stockwell?"

"Yeah. Do you know him?"

"Just by reputation."

"Okay, but now you know what I'm saying—Victor's name was on it for a reason."

"But that doesn't mean the case is a definite winner," Jared pointed out. "If it was, he would've asked for it back."

"Just because it wasn't big enough for Victor doesn't mean it's not big enough for me."

"Now you're reaching," he replied. "Have you asked your assistant about it? Maybe he has some ideas."

"That's the other issue," Sara said, losing steam. "I told Guff I stole the case, but I never told him it was originally marked for Victor."

"Why not?"

"I don't know."

"C'mon, Sara, I can read you like a coloring book."

"It's just that he put his faith in me. I don't want to lose that trust."

"That's fine, but you have to turn it around. Take this case, make the most of it, and bring home a win. As far as I can tell, that's the only way to keep your job."

"No, you're absolutely right. From here on in, I'm taking control."

When she was off the phone, Sara once again felt the silence of the room. But instead of feeling trapped by it, she fought against it. This is it, she told herself. Turn it around or let it beat you down. She stood and walked out to Guff's desk. "Any luck rounding up help?"

"Not yet," Guff said. "How're you holding up?"

"I think I'm finally ready to fight."

"Really? What brought on the sudden change?"

"Nothing more than a little reality. And crazy as it sounds, I'm starting to have a good feeling about this case."

With his fists wrapped tightly around the iron bars of his jail cell, Tony Kozlow had a difficult time keeping his voice to a whisper. "What do you mean she stole the case?"

"Just what I said," Victor said, standing an arm's length away from the cell. "She stole it. The case came in, she had access to it, and she took it. My guess is she must've seen my name on it and assumed it was a high-profile piece. Problem is, she grabbed a bore."

"Don't jerk me around," Kozlow said. With dark hair, a thick black goatee, and a three-quarter-length black leather jacket, Tony Kozlow was what the DA's office called a mutt. Low-class and easily riled, he was visibly annoyed by Victor's tone. "Does Mr. Rafferty know about this?"

Victor stiffened. "Not yet. I haven't been able to reach him. In fact, that's the only reason I'm here—I thought he might be visiting you."

"*Him* visit *me*?" Kozlow squinted at Victor. "Why don't you take some advice and try him again."

Calmly approaching the cell, Victor slid his right arm through the bars and grabbed the back of Kozlow's neck. "Let me tell you something,"

Victor said, holding Kozlow's face against the iron bars of the cell. "Don't tell me what to do. I don't like it."

Enraged, Kozlow shoved his hands through the iron bars, grabbed Victor by the ears, and rammed his face against the bars. "How's this for a threat?" Kozlow shouted. "Touch me again and I'll rip your head off!" Within seconds, a nearby guard ran to the cell and pulled Victor free. With his nightstick, he jabbed Kozlow in the stomach, sending him to his knees.

"Are you okay?" the guard asked Victor.

Without answering, Victor turned away from Kozlow's cell and left the holding area.

"What the hell kind of deal is that?" Joel Rose screamed.

"That's the best we could do," Jared said with his eyes closed, cradling the phone receiver on his shoulder. From the moment he made the call, Jared knew he was going to have to brace himself for the worst. Lubetsky didn't like the final amount of the settlement, but Joel Rose, president and CEO of Rose Microsystems, was the one who was going to have to pay it—which meant he liked the amount even less. Trying his best to sound happy with the result, Jared said, "And considering the alternative, that's not too bad a number."

"Really?" Rose asked. "Say that number again for me, Jared."

"Two hundred and fifty thousand."

"Now listen to me, Jared. That number has eight syllables. And since more syllables usually means more money, eight syllables means a great deal of money. So once again, does that sound like a small number to you?"

"Mr. Rose, I know you didn't want to pay that much, but it really is a fair deal—trust me, it could've come out much worse."

"Trust you?" Rose's voice boomed with fury. "This isn't the damn Boy Scouts, it's a—you know what? Put me on with Lubetsky. I'm sick of dealing with imbeciles."

"Are you sure he'll help us?" Sara asked as she sat down at her desk.

"When Conrad says he's going to do something, he does it," Guff replied.

"What's his story?"

"Conrad Moore is an unbelievable prosecutor—one of the most respected in the office. More important, he's the person I originally worked for when I started here. I asked him if he would give you some advice with the situation, and he said he'd be happy to."

"That's great," she said. "Thank you, Guff."

"Don't thank me yet. Wait until you meet him. He's a bit intense."

"What do you mean, intense?"

"For the past four years running, Conrad has had the largest trial caseload in the entire DA's office. He goes to trial more than anyone."

"Why?"

"It's pretty simple—he never accepts a plea bargain. If you committed a crime, he's going to send you to jail. Period. No negotiating, no pleading to a lower count, no favors. And since he gets great cases, he can afford to do it."

"If he's so busy, where's he finding time to help me?"

"All I know is he just finished mentoring someone else, so when he said yes, I jumped at the opportunity."

"Whatever it is, I'll take it. When do we get started?"

Guff looked down at his watch. "He said he'd call right about—"

Sara's phone started ringing.

"I'd say right about now," Guff said, folding his arms across his chest with a grin.

"This is Sara," she said as she picked up the receiver.

"That's not how you answer the phone," a voice said. "What's your job now?"

"Who's this?" Sara asked.

"This is Conrad Moore. Guff said you needed some help. Now what's your job here?"

"I'm a DA," Sara stammered.

"You're not a DA," Conrad said, his tone stern. "On TV, everyone's a DA. In the movies, everyone's a DA. In real life, though, there's only one DA: Arthur Monaghan. Our boss. And in real life, you're an assistant district attorney. An ADA. So when you answer the phone, you tell whoever's calling who they're dealing with. Understand?"

Sara heard the phone click as Conrad hung up. Five seconds later, her phone rang again. Hesitantly, she picked it up. "Assistant district attorney's office. This is Sara," she answered.

"No!" Conrad shouted. "This is their first impression of you. You want them to think they've reached the receptionist? What's your last name, Sara?"

"Tate."

"Then that's all you give them. In this office, we deal with criminals. And unlike the law firm you used to work at, we don't want more clients—we want less. So we don't need to be nice. We want to be mean. We want people to be scared when they commit a crime. So don't get buddy-buddy with them. From now on, you're ADA Tate. That's all." Again, Conrad hung up.

Five seconds later, Sara's phone rang. Picking it up, she screamed, *"ADA Tate! Now who the fuck is this?"*

"That's good," Conrad said. "That's the intimidation we're looking for."

"I'm glad. Now am I ever going to meet you face-to-face, or are we going to talk on the phone all day?"

"Come over right now," Conrad said, his voice warming up. "I'm at the end of the hall on your right. Room 755."

Hanging up the phone, Sara turned to Guff and took a deep breath. "We're in. Want to come?"

"Are you kidding? I've been waiting all day for this," Guff said. "So what'd you think?"

"He's certainly aggressive," Sara said as she stepped into the hallway. "I just hope he can get us out of this mess."

Victor walked briskly up Centre Street, anxious to get back to the office. The afternoon's events had taken up more time than he would've hoped, and he still hadn't been able to get in touch with Rafferty. But as he was crossing the street in front of the old Federal Courthouse, his cellular phone rang. Unlisted with the DA's office, the number was Victor's private line and was to be used only in emergencies. He flipped open the phone and answered, "Who's this?"

"Who's this?" Kozlow asked, mimicking Victor's deep voice. "How you doing, Vic? Long time, no slam your face in the bars."

Victor stopped a step short of the curb. "How are you calling me?"

"Everyone gets a phone call, asshole. Even I know that. And if Mr. Rafferty makes a quick donation, I get unlimited access—know what I'm saying?"

"Why'd he give you this number?"

"He's not happy with you, Vic. Things aren't going as planned."

Victor looked around at the pedestrians near the courthouse. No one was close enough to hear. "So why doesn't he call me?"

"He doesn't care about speaking to you. He just wants to know what we should do."

"Not 'we,'" Victor said, barely hiding his anger. "I'm done. You guys are on your own."

"That's not how it works."

"Actually, it is. I came in as a favor to our mutual friend, and now I'm stepping out."

"But you can still take the case."

"I told you, I'm done. My things-to-do list is full enough—I don't need to add jeopardizing my career to it. Understand what *I'm* saying, you little psychopath?"

There was a cold silence on the other end of the line. "Just tell me one last thing," Kozlow muttered. "What's our best option now?"

"That's easy," Victor said. "He has to make sure you're found innocent—if you're found guilty, your boss loses. So if I were him, I'd find out all I could about the new ADA who has the case. She's the one you have to beat."

"Her name?"

"Sara," Victor said. "Sara Tate."

CHAPTER 4

Standing outside of Conrad's office, Sara read the two quotations that decorated his closed door: *"Crimine ab uno disce omnes*—From a single crime know the nation"—Virgil; and "Fame is something which must be won; honor is something which must not be lost"—Arthur Schopenhauer.

Sara looked at Guff and raised her eyebrows. "What did you call him? Intense?"

Guff grinned and knocked on the frosted glass. "Come in," a voice growled from behind the door. They entered.

Conrad was standing at his desk, sorting through papers. He was shorter than Sara had imagined, a man of average height, with a compact but powerful build. With jet-black hair and penetrating brown eyes, he looked as intimidating as he sounded. But a warm, gracious smile offset the visual threat.

"Conrad, this is Sara Tate."

Sara reached out to shake his hand. "Good to meet you."

"Please, both of you, have a seat," Conrad said, sinking into his own chair.

"Sara, this is every criminal's recurring nightmare."

"So I hear," Sara said. "Guff tells me you have quite the workload."

"I don't complain about it, and I don't apologize for it," Conrad said, leaning back. "When it comes to the criminal justice system, America may be in love with high-priced defense attorneys, but as far as I'm concerned, only one side isn't going to hell."

"And that's us?" Sara offered.

"Of course it's us. Every time we win a case, we're taking a criminal off the street. It sounds corny, but that means we're personally making things safer for you and for the rest of the people in this city. That's the only reason to do it." Folding his hands behind his head, Conrad added, "So tell me, Sara, why'd you leave law firm life? You must've given up a six-figure salary to come here."

"Who cares about my salary? I thought you were going to help me work on my case."

"I will," Conrad said. "After you answer the question. Now why'd you leave law firm life?"

"Well, let me put it this way: money—great; work—terrible. In my six years there, I participated in only two trials. The rest of my time was spent in the library, doing discovery and drafting motions."

"So you just got sick of it and decided to come on over to the good guys?"

"Not exactly. I wasn't thrilled with firm life, but I was going to be up for partner in the next year or two. And since that meant my investment in misery was about to pay off, I figured I'd stick around. Anyway, to make an immensely pathetic and long story short, I went for my biannual review, and they told me that I wasn't on the partner track. According to them, I didn't have what it took to make it in their firm."

"But you weren't fired for that."

"No. I was fired when . . ." Sara paused. "How did you know I was fired?"

"This is my ninth year in this office," Conrad said pointedly. "I have friends at every firm in this city—including yours."

"You checked up on me?"

"Look, Guff asked me to help you out. For some reason he likes you. But if I'm going to teach someone the ropes, you better believe I want to know what they're made of first."

"Then why'd you ask me a question you knew the answer to?"

"To see if you'd lie," Conrad said flatly. "But I still want to know why you got fired."

"If you know so many people, how come you don't know the answer?" Sara asked.

Conrad smiled. "They said you liked to fight."

"Oh, she likes to fight," Guff said.

"And to answer your question," Conrad added, "maybe I want to hear your side of the story."

"Then how about we save that for another day?" Sara asked. "I've already met my embarrassment quota."

"Fair enough," Conrad said. "Now let's talk about this problem you're having. You're wondering what to do with the case."

"I know what to do with it—I have to prosecute it. I just don't know if Victor's going to let me."

"If Victor and Evelyn both know you have it,

and they still haven't asked for it back, the case is yours. Like it or not, you're stuck with it."

"Do you think Victor's going to take it out on me?"

"He'll be pissed. I wouldn't worry about it, though. All the supervisors are territorial."

"If you say so," Sara said, still wondering why the case had been marked for Victor.

"What about the fact that the case is a loser?" Guff asked. "Do you think it's too small to save her job?"

"It may be a loser, but it's the only thing I've got," Sara said.

"That's exactly right," Conrad agreed. "And if you plan to impress this office, something is always better than nothing." He got up from his seat and walked toward the door. "Now let's get out of here."

"It's time to teach you how to fight crime," Guff said.

"Do I need to bring my cape and utility belt?" Sara asked Conrad.

"Excuse me?" Conrad asked.

"Forget it," Sara replied. As she followed Conrad to the door, she added, "Where are we going?"

"Back to ECAB," Conrad said. Looking down at Sara's hand, he continued, "By the way, let me give you another piece of advice: Lose the wedding ring."

"What?"

"You heard me: Lose the ring. Now that you're a prosecutor, you're going to become enemies with some bad people. The less those people know about you, the better. And believe me, any piece of information you give the other side—no matter how small it is—they'll find some way to use it against you."

* * *

Walking back to his office after grabbing a candy bar in the firm's cafeteria, Jared couldn't wait for the day to end. From Hartley to Lubetsky to Rose, his entire afternoon had been a blur of professional hostility. As he wove his way through the serpentine cherry-paneled hallway, Jared did his best to forget his recent liability and instead thought about his most treasured asset: Sara, the one person who could always help him put things in perspective. He thought about what she would've said to Rose and laughed to himself. She'd never take that kind of abuse. When Rose was done with the attack, she'd rip him apart. He'd regret ever opening his mouth. Indeed, that's what Jared loved about her. She did what *he* couldn't. If Jared satisfied her need for predictability and organization, she satisfied his need for whimsy and spontaneity. Slowly, surely, Jared was able to relax again. That is, until he felt a hand on his shoulder.

"May I speak with you privately for a moment, please?" Thomas Wayne said, motioning to his office. Thomas Wayne was a founding partner of Wayne & Portnoy, and it was a rarity for anyone under the level of partner to have a private word with him. At six foot two, Wayne towered over most of his employees, which had led to the long-running rumor that the firm never hired anyone who was taller than Mr. Wayne himself. Naturally, the rumor was untrue, but Wayne enjoyed the mystique of it and therefore never quashed it. In Wayne's eyes, rumors like that were what legends were made of—and if he'd planned to be anything, Thomas Wayne had always planned to be a legend.

"I hear it's been a rough day," Wayne said as he closed the door to his office.

"It certainly hasn't been my best," Jared responded.

"That may be the case," Wayne said, taking a seat behind his large, but otherwise understated, walnut desk. "But days like this are not what built this firm. You have to understand, Jared, this firm was built with good, hard, roll-up-your-sleeves—"

"I understand what you're saying, sir," Jared interrupted. "But I have to be honest with you— Rose Microsystems may've paid a large sum of money, but I truly believe we saved them from a far worse alternative. No matter how much they kick and scream, I stand behind my work and its result."

"Jared, have you ever heard of Percy Foreman?"

"The name sounds familiar, but I don't know who—"

"Percy Foreman defended James Earl Ray when he killed Martin Luther King, Jr. And regardless of what you think of the moral issues, Percy was one of the greatest defense attorneys of all time. At one point in his career, he was defending a wealthy socialite who was accused of killing her husband. To take the case, Percy charged her five million dollars. *Five million.* Even by today's standards, that's obscene. But the woman paid, and Percy went to work. Throughout the trial, he dodged and slithered and cajoled his way out of every argument. And in the end, he won her a verdict of not guilty. But the press—they couldn't get over the fact that this woman was charged those exorbitant legal fees. So when they got Percy on the courthouse steps, they asked him why he charged five million dollars. And with a straight face, Percy looked out at the crowd and said he charged her that amount because that was *all she had*."

Wayne looked straight at Jared. "That's the kind of attorney we need here. Being smart is fine; being honest is fine; even being aggressive is fine. But to bring in real business, the most important quality you can have is the confidence in your ability to win. Clients want to follow success—if they can smell the confidence *on* you, they'll have confidence *in* you. And if they have that confidence, they'll always trust you, and they'll never argue with your decisions.

"That's the problem you had this afternoon, Jared," Wayne continued. "If Rose had complete confidence in you, he would have written that check with a smile. Instead, he's threatening to leave, taking his three-million-dollar account with him. Now, if you were bringing in new clients, we'd care far less about losing Rose's business. But looking at your records, it appears that client development is hardly your strong suit."

"I know," Jared said. "But I'm trying my best to—"

"Getting new clients requires more than just your best. It requires you to convince people to trust you with their lives. If we don't have that trust, we can't keep old clients, and we certainly can't attract new ones. And if we can't attract new ones, we can't grow as a firm. And if we can't grow as a firm, well, making partner becomes that much more difficult. Do you see what I'm trying to say, Jared?"

"Absolutely, sir," Jared said, struggling to sound enthusiastic. "But you don't have to worry. I know the value of old clients, I know the value of new clients, and without question, I know the value of being a partner in this firm."

"Wonderful," Wayne said. "Then I'm glad we had this talk."

At ECAB, Sara, Conrad, and Guff headed straight to an office in the back of the room. Sara sat down behind the desk.

"Okay," Conrad said. "Ask her the question."

"A man pretending to have occult powers promises a sweet little old lady that he can exorcise the evil spirits affecting her little kitty named Shirley," Guff said. "What can you get him for?"

"Huh?"

"The crime," Guff explained. "What crime can you charge the evil-spirit guy with?"

As Sara looked down at the New York statute book on the desk, Conrad said, "Don't use the book. Use what you know."

"I'm not sure," Sara said. "I guess it would be fraud."

"You guess?" Conrad asked. "You can't just guess. You're an assistant district attorney. When a cop makes an arrest, he comes to you with the paperwork, and you're the one who decides what the crime is. That means you have to know the elements of every crime, as well as the statutes."

"No, you're definitely right," Sara said. "I should've—"

"Don't kick yourself about it. Just keep going— use the book and find the crime."

Opening the book, Sara flipped through its pages. Speed-reading through New York's numerous offenses, she searched for the answer to Guff's hypothetical question. For almost three minutes,

Conrad and Guff stared at her, not saying a word. Finally, she looked up. "Fortune-telling."

"Explain," Conrad said.

Sara read from the book. "In New York, if you pretend to use occult powers to exorcise or affect evil spirits, you can be charged with fortune-telling."

"And the defense is?"

"You can do it if it's for the purpose of entertainment or amusement," she said, wiping her brow.

"Exactly," Conrad said. "Which is why we haven't busted the Great Zamboni and all the rest of them."

"What does this have to do with my burglary case?"

"Are you sure it's burglary?" Conrad countered. "Maybe it's breaking and entering. Maybe it's larceny. And what about robbery? The only way to find out is by looking at the individual facts. Knowing the facts tells you the crime. For example, if you take someone's money and then hit them, it's a robbery. But if you take their money, throw it back at them when they scream, and then hit them to shut them up, it's no longer a robbery because you don't have their property. The key is to get all the details."

"Think of it as a movie," Guff said. "Break it down frame by frame. If you're missing a frame, you still don't have the complete picture."

"Okay," Sara said, refusing to be overwhelmed. "I can do this." She read from the complaint report: "After receiving a radio call reporting a break-in and describing the defendant, the officer picked up the defendant two blocks from the burglary. When they returned to 201 East Eighty-second

Street, the victim identified the defendant as the burglar. After searching defendant's pockets, a diamond Ebel watch, a sterling silver golf ball, and four hundred and seventeen dollars were recovered, all of them belonging to the victim."

"Now," Conrad said, "that gives you about three percent of what actually happened."

"Why?" Sara asked, confused.

"Because of the way arrests work—everyone's trying to make himself look great." Leaning forward, Conrad grabbed the complaint report from Sara's hands. "You can see it right here: The cop uses the word 'burglary.' It's not the cop's job to identify the crime that's supposed to be charged. That's your job. And how do we know the description on the radio matched what Kozlow was wearing? And who reported the burglary? Was it the victim or was it an anonymous tip? If it's anonymous—"

"The judge may exclude the evidence if the source can't be verified," Sara said. "So you're saying I need to talk to the cop."

"Exactly," Conrad answered. He pointed to the tiny video camera on top of the ECAB computer. "Face-to-face on the videophone."

"That's pretty high-tech," Sara said, moving her head close to the camera.

"I actually think it's terrible," Conrad said, "but I won't get into it."

"Well, I think it's fantastic," Guff added. "Things like this bring us one step closer to the Jetsons and their magical animated world of the future."

Ignoring Guff, Sara said, "Okay, so I call the cop up and get all the details. Then when I'm done with that, I write up the official complaint and start all over again."

"What do you mean *start all over again*?"

"I mean, if I'm dead set on keeping this job, I'm going to need more than one measly case, don't you think?"

"I told you she was hungry," Guff said.

"Without question, you should grab every case you can get your hands on," Conrad said to Sara. "But don't forget one thing: As long as Victor's supervising, he's not going to give you anything but throwaways. You're going to be prosecuting every pickpocket in Manhattan."

"Is there any way around that?"

"Considering you already pissed off Evelyn, I doubt it."

"Okay. No big deal. That's why they call it paying your dues," Sara said, trying to sound positive. "Whatever it is, I'm ready to do it."

"Keep up that attitude," Conrad said. "But when you're done catching cases, make sure you go home and rest for a while. The arraignment's going to be at around eleven o'clock tonight."

"Tonight?" Sara asked. "I didn't know arraignments went on that late."

"This is New York City," Conrad said. "Home of sixteen million people, all of whom hate each other. Arraignments here are open around the clock."

"I'll be there." As she picked up the phone and dialed Officer Michael McCabe's telephone number, Conrad got out of his seat. "Where're you going?" Sara asked.

"I have my own work to do. I'll see you in arraignments—it's on the first floor of this building. Get there early to be safe."

"See you later," Sara said as Conrad left the office.

When the officer answered his phone, Sara explained that she was calling about the Kozlow arrest and wanted to speak to him via videophone. She then hung up the phone and waited for the officer to call her back. Two minutes later, her phone rang.

"Pick it up and hit 'Receive,'" Guff said, pointing to an electronic icon on her computer screen.

When she followed Guff's instructions, Officer McCabe's face appeared in full color on her computer screen. "Can you hear me?" Sara asked, leaning toward the tiny video camera.

"Oh, great." The officer rolled his eyes. "A rookie."

"Save your moaning. I know what I'm doing."

"She's got six years of law firm experience," Guff said, sticking his head into the camera's path.

"Who the hell is that?" McCabe asked.

"No one," Sara said, pushing Guff away. "Now why don't we get started. Tell me everything that happened."

With his high-back Moroccan leather chair pulled up to his nineteenth-century French partner's desk, Oscar Rafferty calmly flipped through the pages of the *Cat on a Hot Tin Roof* German rights contract. All it took was a phone call. Actually, that wasn't true. It was a phone call and a quick visit in his office. That's what closed the deal. Since the moment Rafferty entered the world of intellectual property, he'd known the power of making an impression. That was how he had gotten where he was. From the hand-sewn carpets to the Calder mobile in the corner of the room, he always did his best to show the best. And if he needed more proof of the payoff, all he had to do was look at the drying ink on the contract in front of him. It had taken less than forty-five minutes to make that four million dollars. Even by banking industry standards, that was a great hourly rate.

Expanding on a theme, Rafferty always kept three phones on his desk. With current technology, he could easily combine them in one, but the visual effect on his clients was worth the loss of desk space. When the middle phone rang—his personal line—he picked it up on the first ring. "This better be good news."

"I don't know if it's good news, but it is information," the private detective said at the other end of the line. "Her name is Sara Tate. She's thirty-two years old and was born and raised in Manhattan. Six months ago, she was fired from her old law firm, which really brought her down a peg, and she just started at the DA's office. According to some of her old associates at the law firm, she's aggressive, blunt, and as passionate as they come. One guy said she second-guesses herself a lot and that she can be real volatile, but he also agreed she's no fool."

"What else did they say?" Rafferty asked, searching for weaknesses. "How is she in court?"

"Only one of them had seen her do anything firsthand. He said she comes off as a real person, which is a tough feat for most lawyers these days."

"You think she's a threat?"

"Every new prosecutor's a threat. When it's their first case, they're all trying to succeed. What makes Sara dangerous, though, is that it's about more than success—with the cutbacks, she needs this job to survive, and that means she's going to be pulling out every stop to win."

"That's what Victor said."

"The man knows his business."

Rafferty pondered this. "Do we know why she got fired?"

"Not yet, but I can find out. My guess is she crossed someone she shouldn't have. No one would get into it, but I could hear it in their voices. If you push her, she'll push back—hard."

"What about her family?"

"Middle-class background. Dad was a salesman, Mom was a legal secretary. Both of them came from nothing, although you couldn't tell it by looking at Sara. They died years ago in a car wreck, but according to her old colleagues, it's still a rough issue for her."

"Good. That's one way in. Any other relatives?"

"She has a grandfather and a husband."

"Tell me about the husband."

"His name is Jared Lynch. He's from a wealthy suburb in Chicago, but worked hard to get where he is. Dad's a retired stockbroker; Mom still plays housewife. He's got two younger brothers, and they all live in Chicago. Financially, Sara and Jared have a small IRA set aside for them by Jared's family, but in terms of available funds, they're barely scraping it together. When Sara lost her job, the income loss hit them pretty hard. From what I can tell, they cashed in almost all of their savings in the past six months."

"That's what happens when they kick you out of a high-paying job," Rafferty commented. "What does Jared do?"

"For the past six years, he's been doing defense

work at a law firm—big place called Wayne and Portnoy."

"He's a defense attorney?"

"Can you believe it? Two lawyers in one family. Shoot me now or forever hold your peace."

"Actually, that's good news."

"How do you figure?"

"Let's just say I'm starting to see some interesting possibilities."

At their Upper West Side brownstone, a block from the Museum of Natural History, Sara ran up the stairs two at a time and unlocked the front door of their apartment. The living room was dark. "Damn," she said. Jared wasn't home yet. She flipped on the lights and hit the play button on the answering machine. There was one message. "Sara, it's Tiffany. Are you there?" Sara listened to the voice of the young girl she mentored through the Big Sisters program. "Want to hear what it'd sound like if you were a rock star?" Tiffany asked. "Saaaaaara! Saaaaaara!" There was a short pause. "Saaaaaara! Saaaaaara!" There was a longer pause. "You didn't think I'd do it again, did you? Anyway, call me. Don't forget we have plans Thursday night. Hi, Jared. Bye."

Laughing at the message, Sara headed to the kitchen and started dinner. Their division of chores was simple: The first person home did the cooking, the second one home did the cleaning. Given a choice, Sara always preferred to clean and Jared favored cooking. It was something he had picked up from his father, who liked to experiment in the kitchen.

Sara and Jared's one-bedroom apartment

encompassed the second floor of the five-story brownstone. And while it had a separate dining room and a nice-sized bedroom, the largest room in the apartment was the living room. With its overstuffed slipcovered sofa and its wine-colored oversized armchair, it was the best place to relax and unwind.

Decorated in what Sara called a "funky heirloom" style, the apartment was a mixture of Sara's informality and Jared's love of collecting. During law school, Jared had spent his time hunting down lobby cards and rare movie posters. When he graduated, he moved on to actual movie props. And when they had paid back exactly half of Sara's eighty-thousand-dollar law school loans, Jared celebrated by buying his first expensive collectible: one of Kirk Douglas's shields from the film *Spartacus*, which was hung on the wall over the sofa. Since that time, he'd added a bag of corn nuts from *Heathers*, a salt-and-pepper-shaker set from *Diner*, an ornate scroll from *A Man for All Seasons*, and, the prize of his collection, the knife that Roman Polanski used to cut Jack Nicholson in *Chinatown*. Jared saw his collection as a way to preserve pop history, while Sara saw it as a way to keep Jared happy.

Sara, on the other hand, was kept happy by the six framed pictures on the right-hand wall. Over the past six years, on every wedding anniversary, Sara had drawn a portrait of Jared. Although never professionally trained, she had always loved to draw. She didn't like to paint, she never sketched, and when she drew, it was never with pencil—only with ink. She didn't need it to be perfect; what you saw was what you got.

Sara crushed garlic, chopped onions, sliced peppers, and cut up the other ingredients for a home-cooked tomato sauce. In truth, she was just as content eating sauce from a jar, but the hope that she was on the path to saving her job put her in the mood to surprise Jared with the real thing. Fifteen minutes later, Jared walked through the door. He took one look at Sara and smiled.

"Guess your day got a lot better," Jared said.

"It was incredible," Sara said, unable to contain her excitement as she ran to hug him. "I just started working on them, but they're completely my own cases. My own facts, my own defendants, my own everything."

"Wait a minute. There's more than one?"

"I got five. The burglary, plus two shoplifters, a pickpocket, and a drug possession. The burglary's the only one that's really trial-worthy, but it doesn't even matter. It's all finally happening—just like you said."

"You're incredible, y'know that? You really are."

"And how'd everything go with your negotiation? Did it all work out?"

"It was great," Jared said, dropping his briefcase and loosening his tie. "Nothing to really talk about."

Sara watched her husband carefully. She knew that tone in his voice. "You want to try that one again, handsome?"

Jared turned back toward his wife. He wanted to tell her about the negotiation and the scolding. But not today. Not when she was finally feeling good. He wasn't going to ruin it for her. Eventually, he said, "It's really nothing."

"And you think I'm going to believe that?"

"Actually, I was hoping you would."

"Well, I'm not. So why don't you save us some time and tell me the truth."

Jared slumped down on the sofa and rested his head against the oversized cushions. "There's not much to tell. I spent the entire afternoon trying to save them from a risky trial and a ton of bad publicity. Then, to thank me for caving in and screwing up, Lubetsky screamed at me for a half hour, followed by Rose, and topped off by Thomas Wayne, big boss extraordinaire."

"Did you say anything back?"

"They were right. What could I possibly say?"

"How about 'Stop yelling at me, you fat, bloated weasels—I obviously tried my best'?"

"Call me insane, but I don't think that's the best reaction for the situation."

"So, let me guess—instead, you reacted the way you always do. You stood there and—"

"I stood there and let them yell in my face," Jared said as his shoulders sagged. "I thought that was the best way to calm them down."

"Honey, even if they're right, you can't keep letting them talk to you like that. You're still a human being. I know you hate confrontation, but you can't always pick the path of least resistance."

"It's not that I hate confrontation—"

"It's just that you love having things perfect and neat and clean," Sara interrupted. "I know why you do it. And I love the fact that you do it—I wish I could be as self-controlled as you are. But when it comes to your bosses, you can't always avoid fighting with everyone in authority."

"Listen," he said, rubbing his temples. "Can we stop talking about work? I've had enough tension for one day."

"Good," Sara said, "because it's time to open your present."

"You bought me a present?"

"Nothing extravagant—I just wanted to say I love you. Your help this morning meant more than you know."

"You didn't have to . . ."

He trailed off as Sara darted to the bedroom and returned with her leather briefcase. "Here," she said, handing it to Jared as she sat down next to him.

"You're giving me your briefcase?"

"Your present's inside. I didn't have time to wrap it, so I thought I'd pretend the briefcase was a box. Work with me—use your imagination."

"What a wonderful box," Jared said as he admired the briefcase. He quickly opened it and pulled out a red, white, and blue metallic pinwheel.

"I told you it wasn't special," Sara said. "One of the homeless guys was selling them on the subway. You have to read the words on the stick, though—it says 'Welcome to the Puerto Rico.'"

"I love it," Jared said, blowing on his present. As the pinwheel spun, his smile returned to his face. "This is great. I mean it. Go, the Puerto Rico!"

Laughing, Sara took him by the hand and helped him up from the sofa. Dragging him back to the kitchen, she said, "And wait until you see what I made for dinner." When they were standing in front of the stove, she said, "Close your eyes."

"I know what you made. I smelled it the moment I got—"

"Quiet. Close your eyes." When he obliged, she added, "Stick out your tongue." As Jared followed her directions, Sara dipped her finger in the homemade sauce. She then brushed her finger across his tongue. "How's that taste?"

"For the record, that was the most blatant sexual come-on you've ever employed."

"So? Did it work?"

"It always works," Jared said with a grin. Keeping his eyes closed, he felt Sara's hands around his neck. She pulled him close and kissed him. First on the mouth. Then on the tip of his chin. Then down to his neck. Along the way, she loosened his tie and undid the top buttons of his shirt. He did the same thing to the buttons of her blouse. "Do you want to stay here or go into the—"

"Here," Sara said as she pressed him against the counter. "Right here."

CHAPTER 5

W hat'd you think?" Sara asked.

"Are you kidding? It was incredible. That part when you were up on the countertop . . ."

"I'm talking about dinner, dreamboat." Wearing only a T-shirt, Sara sat at the kitchen table across from Jared, who had put on a pair of sweatpants.

"Oh," Jared said. He stared down at his empty plate. "It was great. Everything was great. Especially you."

"Don't give away all the compliments; you deserve half the credit," Sara said, reaching across the table to hold his hand. "By the way, what time is it?"

"Why? You got a date?"

"Yeah. A date with Justice. I have to get back to the courthouse. My arraignment's supposed to come up at around eleven."

"Oh, God—your case," Jared said. "I'm so sorry, I meant to ask you more about it. I've just been so caught up in—"

"Don't worry about it," Sara said. "The case is fine. Well, maybe it's fine. Actually, it probably isn't fine, it's a squeaker. I think it can definitely work out, though. Maybe. If I'm lucky."

"Sounds like you can't lose."

"Don't make fun. You know how I get under pressure: peaks and valleys, peaks and valleys. When I got the case, I was on top of the world; an hour later, I was out of my skin, terrified about my job; an hour after that, I was learning the ropes, obsessed, but somehow confident; and when I got home, I thought it was all going my way."

"And now?"

"Now I'm back in the valley. Not only am I nervous about the case, I'm worried about how I got it. You should've seen me this afternoon. Staring at that stupid little folder, I was in a complete panic. And when that split second came when I had to decide whether I was going to take it—I felt like it was my only chance." Pulling away from her husband, Sara stood up. "Tell me the truth. Was it wrong for me to take the case like that?"

"It doesn't matter what I think," Jared said in his usual diplomatic tone. Deep down, Sara knew he was avoiding the question, but she wasn't in the mood to hear his lecture. It'd be the same as always: When it came to work, her husband kept it on the straight and narrow. "All that matters is how you feel."

"I feel terrible. Now that the adrenaline's gone, I can't stop thinking about it. It's like this gnawing ghost that's floating around in my stomach. And the worst part is, I'm not sure why I'm upset: is it because I know it was wrong to take it, or simply because I got caught with it?"

"Listen, you can't change the past. You saw it,

you grabbed it, and now you have to live with it. Besides, the way you described it, it sounds like no one in the office even cared that you stole it."

"Except for Victor. I haven't seen him yet."

"Speaking of which, have you told your assistant that it was Victor's case in the first place?"

"Not yet. We were running around all afternoon, so there really wasn't time. Besides, I don't think I'm going to tell him just yet—I want to do a bit more digging before I put that relationship at risk."

"You still think there might be something else at play?"

"I'm not sure," Sara said, picking up her blue pantsuit from the floor. "But if this isn't a Victor-level case, I have no idea how it's going to save my job."

When Sara was finished re-dressing for her late-night arraignment, she headed for the door.

"Good luck," Jared called out. "Make 'em suffer."

"You don't have to worry," Sara said. "The defense is in for some serious hurt."

At precisely ten-thirty, Sara entered 100 Centre. At the courtroom that was reserved for arraignments, she was surprised to see Guff leaning against the courtroom door.

"What are you doing here?" Sara asked. "You didn't have to come."

"You're my boss," Guff said. "Where you go, I follow."

"Well, thanks, Guff. I really appreciate the support. Now we just have to wait for—"

"ADA Tate! What are you charging him with?" a voice boomed from down the hallway.

"Burglary in the second degree," Sara barked back while Conrad was still thirty feet away.

When the burly prosecutor reached his two colleagues, he asked, "And why'd you choose that?"

"Because burglary in the first degree requires a weapon, or a dangerous instrument, or a physical injury to a victim, and there's no indication of any of those here."

"Isn't that also required for burglary in the second?" Conrad challenged.

"Not if the building is a dwelling," Sara said, her voice gaining confidence. "And according to the definitions section, 201 East Eighty-second Street is definitely a dwelling. The victim sleeps there every night. I called her myself."

Conrad smiled. "Good for you. Now what about criminal trespass? Why not charge him with that?"

"Because by taking the watch, the golf ball, and the four hundred dollars, the defendant committed a crime, making criminal trespass too light a charge."

"What about robbery?"

"According to the cop, there was no force used. That ruled out robbery."

"And what about breaking and entering?" Conrad asked.

"That's where you were bullshitting me," Sara said. "In New York, there's no such thing as breaking and entering."

"Are you sure?"

Sara stared him down. "Of course I'm sure. It took me an hour to figure that one out. Now can we go inside and get this sucker started?"

"You're the boss," Conrad said, gesturing toward the door.

Because of the late hour, Sara expected to find

the courtroom mostly empty. But as she stepped inside, she was surprised to see it filled with prosecutors, police officers, court employees, defense attorneys, and recently arrested defendants. Prosecutors sat on the right side of the room, defense attorneys on the left. Defendants were held in a waiting room outside the courtroom until their case was about to be called, and in the center of the courtroom, the judge presided over each arraignment, which usually lasted four or five minutes. In that time, the charges were announced and bail was set.

As she stepped into the room, Sara knew whom she was looking for. From a legal perspective, she realized that arraignments were a vital guarantor of freedom and fairness. But from a strategic perspective, she knew that arraignments played a completely different role, not the least of which was allowing the opposing attorneys to get their first look at each other. A strong defense attorney meant a nightmare for a prosecutor, while a weak one might mean an easy victory. Either way, like football coaches who spy on the following week's opponents, the prosecutors of the DA's office loved to know who they'd be facing. Sara was no exception.

"Any idea which one he is?" she asked Conrad as they took a seat in the first row of wooden benches.

Conrad stared at the dozen defense attorneys who were currently sitting, writing, or filing last-minute papers on the left side of the room. "We won't know until they call him."

"Oh, no," Sara said.

"What's wrong?"

Sara pointed to a tall blond man across the

room. He wore a finely tailored suit and carried a black Gucci briefcase. "That's Lawrence Lake, a partner at my old law firm."

"I think he's the one you're going up against," Guff said.

"How do you know?" Conrad asked.

"Are you kidding? I can smell the enemy the moment he enters the room. It's part of my untamed, feral side."

"You're crazy."

"Oh, I'm definitely crazy," Guff said, squinting his eyes to look fierce. "Crazy like a *fox*."

"Or crazy like a psychopath," Conrad said. Turning to Sara, he asked, "Did you find out anything else about Kozlow?"

"Just what's in his file. He's been arrested twice before: once for first-degree assault, the other for first-degree murder. In the assault, he used a switchblade; in the murder, he shoved a screwdriver into someone's throat."

"Jesus," Guff said. "Someone has trouble playing with others."

"Not according to the jurors. He got off both times."

"So he's a good liar," Conrad said. "But if I were you, I'd look at the facts of those cases. Maybe he's got a thing for creative violence."

"I'll check them tomorrow," Sara said.

"Now are you all set on the bail amount?" Sara nodded. "What's your perfect number?" Conrad asked.

"I want it to be at least ten thousand. That's high enough that he shouldn't be able to afford it. But I'm asking for fifteen because I know that judges always lower it a bit."

"I don't think you'll have to worry," Conrad

said. "When the judges rotate into night arraignments, they're usually so pissed off about their jobs, they tend to slap the defendants around just for fun."

"Let's hope so," Sara said, glancing at Lawrence Lake's Gucci briefcase.

Fifteen minutes later, when the court clerk called the case of *State of New York* v. *Anthony Kozlow*, Sara saw Lawrence Lake rise and head toward the defense table.

"Damn," she whispered under her breath.

"Don't cave in," Conrad said.

As Sara walked briskly to the prosecutor's table, Anthony Kozlow was escorted into the courtroom by one of the court officers. He was wearing a ratty black leather jacket and looked like he hadn't shaved in days. Sara couldn't help but wonder how an angry little scrub like him could afford a player like Lake. Approaching the defense table, Kozlow shook Lake's hand as if the two were old friends.

Staring at Kozlow, Sara felt her forehead break out in sweat. This wasn't like her old cases at the firm. She wasn't fighting some faceless corporate entity. She was fighting Tony Kozlow—a man standing only ten feet away. She had never met him, and she didn't know him, but she was going to do everything in her power to keep him in jail.

Without looking up, the judge read from the complaint form that Sara had prepared. He explained that Kozlow was being charged with second-degree burglary, and he checked that an attorney for Kozlow was present. After reading the rest of the complaint to himself, the judge looked up at Sara. "Are you asking for bail?"

"We're asking that bail be set at fifteen thousand

dollars," Sara explained. "The defendant has a long history of violent criminal activity, and—"

"Two arrests are hardly a long history," Lake interrupted.

"I'm sorry," Sara said. "I thought I was in the middle of saying something."

"I understand the prosecutor's point," the judge said. "And I can see Mr. Kozlow's record. Now, Mr. Lake, let's hear the other side."

Lake smiled smugly at Sara. "My client was arrested twice. That's clearly not a long history. To keep it short: Mr. Kozlow has ties to this community, he's lived here almost continuously throughout his entire life, and there isn't a single conviction on his record. There's absolutely no reason why bail needs to be that high."

The judge paused for a moment, then announced, "The 180.80 date is Friday. I'm setting bail at ten thousand."

Relieved, Sara assumed that even if Kozlow could afford Lake, it'd still take at least a few days to raise that kind of money.

Without blinking, however, Lake said, "Your Honor, my client would like to post bail."

"Please see the clerk about that," the judge said. He banged his gavel, and the clerk called the next case. In and out in less than five minutes.

Without saying a word, Sara turned around and walked straight out of the courtroom into the hallway. Guff and Conrad followed. "Okay, so he posted bail," Conrad said. "What's the crisis?"

"The crisis is Lawrence Lake. That guy's not a dial-a-lawyer. It costs about five hundred bucks an hour to talk to him."

"So Kozlow has some money stashed away," Conrad said. "Happens all the time."

"I don't know," Sara said, tempted to tell them about Victor. "I have a bad feeling about this. Kozlow doesn't seem like a kingpin—so where does he get the money and influence to talk to someone like Lake?"

"I have no idea," Conrad said, looking at his watch. "But it's way past my bedtime, and we're not solving this tonight. We'll talk about it tomorrow morning."

Standing in the middle of the hallway, Sara couldn't let it go. "What about—"

"Go home and get it out of your mind," Conrad said. "The workday is done."

Before Sara could argue, Kozlow stepped out of the courtroom and brushed past her. "Sorry, Sara," he whispered. "See you on the streets."

"What'd you say?" Sara asked.

Without answering, Kozlow headed up the hallway.

Unwilling to run in the early morning rain, Jared got to work at eight o'clock and headed straight to the firm's private gymnasium and basketball court, hoping that a good workout would relieve the stress caused by the previous day's events. Located on the seventy-first floor, the private facility had been installed at the request of Thomas Wayne, whose love of basketball outweighed his partners' hopes for an expanded library. Among the lawyers of Wayne & Portnoy, the private facility was affectionately known as "the highest court in the city," and its three plate-glass walls provided a stunning view of downtown Manhattan.

During his half-hour run on the treadmill,

Jared replayed yesterday's conversations in his head. First Lubetsky's, then Rose's, then Wayne's. When the odometer read three miles, he showered and went down to his office.

"Feeling better today?" Kathleen asked as Jared walked past her desk.

"Eh," he shrugged. "Yourself?"

"I'm great. I'm just worried about you." Kathleen pulled a pencil from behind her ear and wagged it at her boss. "But if you want to put yourself in a better mood, why don't you ask me what's going on? It'll be worth it."

Jared crossed his arms. "Fine. What's going on?"

"The usual," she replied. "Lubetsky wants to see you, Rose wants to speak to you, and a brand-new client wants to hire you."

"Someone wants to hire me?"

"He came in about ten minutes ago and asked specifically for you. He's waiting in the conference room."

"Wait a minute," Jared said. "Is this some kind of practical joke to make me feel better?"

"No joke. You wanted new clients, you got 'em. He said you came recommended by a friend. If you'd like, I'll bring him to your office."

"That'd be great," Jared said, his pulse racing. "In fact, that'd be downright fantastic."

Two minutes later, Kathleen returned to Jared's office with a tall, gaunt, dark-haired man in tow. "Jared, this is Mr. Kozlow," she said as she stepped into the room.

"Call me Tony," the man said, extending a hand to Jared.

"Like the cartoon tiger," Jared joked.

"Exactly," Kozlow smiled. "Just like the tiger."

* * *

"You don't think there's anything fishy about Kozlow having such a high-paid attorney?" Sara asked Conrad when she stopped by his office in the early afternoon.

"Not at all," Conrad said. "It happens all the time. These mutts have money stashed in a sock drawer for just this occasion."

"And what about the fact that his lawyer was from my old law firm? I mean, there're thousands of firms in this city. Don't you think it's a little more than a coincidence that they picked mine?"

"Sara, it's time for you to take a breath and calm down. I know you have a lot of emotion invested in this case, but when that happens, you run the risk of losing perspective. Trust me, I know exactly what you're going through: When I started here, I wanted every single one of my cases to be front-page material. But sometimes you have to admit that all you have is a footnote that would barely make the high school newspaper."

"So you think I'm just imagining things?"

"All I'm saying is you should stop worrying about Kozlow's wallet and start worrying about his case. You have a grand jury coming up next Monday."

"Not to mention four other cases to deal with," Sara added.

"Speaking of which, how'd they go this morning?"

"The arraignments? Like last night, but faster. The drug possession and one of the shoplifters were both first-time offenders, so they walked on their own recognizance. Then I got two thousand apiece for the pickpocket and the other shoplifter."

"I take it they had histories?"

"Almost fifty arrests between them. And the pickpocket? If you can believe it, his name is Marion."

"Don't make fun of 'Marion.' That's John Wayne's real name."

Tilting her head slightly, Sara studied Conrad. "Wait a minute," she said. "Did you just make a joke?"

"John Wayne's never a joke, ma'am."

Sara laughed. "Okay, I'll let you have one. That's fair," she said. "But according to his record, John Wayne the Pickpocket has twenty-three prior arrests, and he swears he didn't do any of them—which I guess at least makes him consistent. The shoplifter's not far behind."

"Okay, so it sounds like you can plead out the first two. As far as the others, you're going to have to see what their lawyers say. Don't get too caught up in them, though. Your time's better spent preparing Kozlow's indictment."

"Then can I ask you one last question? What'd the judge mean by a 180.80 day?"

Conrad paused, his brow furrowed. "Didn't they teach you anything in that law firm?"

"All I did was civil work. Now cut me some slack."

"Here's your slack. A 180.80 day is shorthand for the day by which you have to indict the defendant if he's locked up. But since Kozlow posted bail, you only have to worry about the grand jury, where—"

"I know what happens at a grand jury."

"You sure?"

"You don't let up, do you?" Sara asked with a grin. "At the grand jury, I'll have to convince twelve average citizens to indict Kozlow on the burglary charge. If they indict, then the trial can take place. If they don't—"

"If they don't, then you're not going anywhere with this case."

Walking back to her office, Sara thought about Conrad's advice. Maybe he was right. Maybe she was hoping too hard for front-page material. Maybe Kozlow had just stashed away some money. And maybe she was becoming a victim of her own imagination. But no matter how much she tried to downplay the facts, she kept coming back to one key piece of information: Kozlow's case had originally been marked for Victor.

Nearing her office, she noticed that Guff wasn't at his desk. She also noticed that her office door was ajar, even though she knew she had left it closed. She remembered Conrad's advice about ADA offices: Lock everything—confidentiality is paramount, and eyes have a tendency to wander. Through the translucent glass of her door, she could see the fuzzy figure of someone sitting at her desk. She quickly looked over her shoulder to see if anyone was around. Since it was close to lunch, the hallways were relatively empty. Hesitantly, she opened the door. Victor was waiting for her.

"Can I help you?" she asked, unnerved.

"No," Victor said. "Just wanted to see how your case was going."

"How'd you get into my office?"

"It was open. Hope you don't mind."

"Actually, I do."

"I'll be more considerate next time. Now tell me how it's going."

"Why?" she asked defensively. "Is something wrong?"

"Nothing's wrong, Sara."

"Then why're you sneaking in here and trying your best to intimidate me?" She hoped her bluntness would catch him off guard. It didn't.

"That's a pretty impressive imagination. You should be careful it doesn't get the best of you."

"What's that supposed to mean?" Sara asked.

"It means exactly what I said: Be careful. At this rate, you can't afford any more mistakes."

"Is that what you came to tell me?"

"Sara, the only reason I'm here is because you took a case while I was supervising. Now I don't care how desperate you were, or how you got Conrad to kiss your ass, but if you ever do that again, I guarantee one thing: I'll be all over you."

She didn't want to admit it, but of course he was right. "I'm sorry. I—"

"Save the crying. I don't care." Victor got up from his seat and walked to the door. "But if I were you, I'd watch my back. You never know when the ax will fall."

As Victor left, Guff entered Sara's office. "What was that about?" he asked.

"I'm not sure."

"He didn't sound too happy on the way out."

"He was thrilled. I could tell by the way he threatened me. Now, any other bad news before I head out to lunch?"

"Actually, yes," Guff said, waving a two-page fax. "This just came through. It's a notice of attorney. Apparently, Kozlow has retained a new lawyer."

"So?"

"So, look at the new lawyer's name and tell me if it's familiar."

She skimmed the memo, then jumped to the signature at the bottom. When she read her husband's name, she sank into her chair. "I can't believe it. Can he even do this?"

"I don't know," Guff said. "I've certainly never seen it before."

"He has to drop the case," Sara said. She picked up her phone and dialed Jared's number. When Kathleen answered, Sara asked to speak to her husband.

"You just missed him. He said he was meeting you for lunch. Is everything all right?"

"It's fine." Sara hung up the phone and bolted out of the office.

Guff tailed behind, following her down the hall. "What do you want me to do while you're gone?"

"Find out if this kind of thing is even allowed. The last person I want to face in this case is my husband."

Twenty minutes later, Jared's cab dropped him off in front of Forlini's, which was not only the closest Italian restaurant to the courthouse, but also the most popular. He stuffed a ten-dollar bill in the driver's hand and strode into the restaurant. "Hey, beautiful," he said to Sara, excited to share the good news with his wife.

"Where the hell have you been?" Sara asked.

"Stuck in traffic." Jared sat down at the table. "Is everything okay?"

"No, everything's not okay."

Jared touched Sara's arm. "Tell me what's—"

"I just don't understand why you agreed to take the case—especially when you know my job is riding on it. I mean, you're the one with the big firm job, and all I have is this—"

"Whoa, whoa, whoa," Jared interrupted. "Slow down a second. What case are you talking about?"

"My burglary case. Why'd you agree to take the other side?"

"Take the other side? I don't know what you're—"

"The Kozlow case. I just got your counsel notice."

"Wait a minute," Jared said. "That's *your* case? You have Tony Kozlow's case?"

"I told you that last night."

"You never told me his name. You just said it was a burglary."

"Well, didn't you think it was odd when you got your own burglary today?"

"He didn't say it was a burglary—all he said was it was a minor felony. And that they'd send me the file later."

"What about the notice-of-counsel memo?"

"All we had was the docket number of the case. Kathleen typed up the memo and faxed it over to the DA's office. They match up the number and forward it to the prosecutor. I swear, honey, I'd never do that to you on purpose."

"So you'll drop the case."

"What?" Jared asked.

"I'm serious. Are you going to drop the case?"

"Why should I drop it?" Jared moaned. "This is a new client. It's a big deal for me."

"Jared, for you, it's a client. For me—"

"No—you're right. This is your job. You were there first. I'll step down."

"You will?" Sara asked.

He paused. "Of course I will." Growing more confident, he added, "For you."

Sara put her hand on one of his. "You're a good man, Charlie Brown. I know how much—"

"Sara, you don't have to say anything."

"Yes, I do. And I want you to know that I'm sorry for putting you in this position. It's just that this whole new job thing is reminding me of the—"

"The law firm was an isolated incident, and you shouldn't judge yourself by it. No one's supposed to make partner in a New York firm. It's not expected."

"Then what are you doing?"

"I'm trying my best to beat the odds. And to cheer up my wife."

"Well, you're doing a pretty good job," Sara said. Circling the top of her water glass with a finger, she added, "Let me ask you this: If we did have to face off against each other, who do you think would win?"

"You would," Jared said with a smug smile.

Sara laughed. "You're so full of yourself, y'know that?"

"What'd I say?"

"You don't have to say anything. I can read you like a—"

"Like a coloring book?"

"Don't play games, Lynch. I'm warning you."

"Then what do you want me to say? You asked me who would win. Do you want the truth or do you want to be lied to? I'll do whatever makes you feel better."

Sara laughed again. "Do you even realize how conceited you are sometimes?"

"Wait a minute. Are you calling me conceited?"

"No, I'm calling you deaf." Raising her voice, she announced, "You are so conceited!"

Jared tried to avoid the stares of the restaurant customers. "You know I hate it when you do that."

"That's why you wouldn't stand a chance. You've got too many buttons to push."

"So that's what you'd do? You'd bring the jury to a restaurant and yell like a maniac?"

"Whatever it takes. That's my motto."

"It's a great motto, but it's not going to get you far in court. Don't forget, you've never even handled a criminal trial."

"Sure, if you want to be formalistic. But we're not talking about who knows more about the law. We're talking about who would win the case. And if you've been paying attention, you'd know you wouldn't have a chance against me."

"Oh, I wouldn't?"

"No, you wouldn't."

"And why's that?"

"Because while you may be Mr. Book-Smart Sophisticate, you have no idea how to fight."

"And you do?"

"Boy, I've been whipping your ass for the past six years."

Jared laughed out loud. "Is that another come-on?"

"I'm serious," Sara said. "To win a fight, you have to know your opponent's weaknesses. And I know all of yours."

"Name one."

"You hate it when people say that everything's been handed to you in life."

Jared paused a moment. "Name another."

"Oh, you're so predictable."

"Don't pat yourself on the back so hard," Jared said. "Now name another."

"You don't like seeing me hurt—which means you wouldn't be effective in a fight against me."

"Trust me, if I needed to, the kid gloves would come off."

"You can't stand it when everything isn't perfect."

"And *you're* terrified of failure," Jared countered. "Now let's hear a real weakness."

"You're afraid of cats."

"I'm not afraid of them. I just think they're plotting against me."

"When you were little, you read through an entire volume of encyclopedias."

"Just the volumes *J* and *Li to Lz*. My initials."

"You have a favorite columnist."

"Most people do."

Leaning into the table, Sara held up her pinkie and whispered, "Your penis—it's teeny."

"That is *not* funny," Jared said, laughing. "Take it back."

"Fine, fine, I take it back. But don't tell me I don't know how to push your buttons."

"You definitely know how to push my buttons. But I can push yours just as well."

"That's why I don't want to face you in court," Sara said. "It'd be a bloodbath."

"Well, lucky for both of us it's not coming to that. I'm dropping the case as soon as I get back."

"Glad to hear it," Sara said. She reached across the table and took both of Jared's hands in her own. "I just want you to know, I appreciate you looking out for me."

"Sara, you don't need me to look out for you. I

only do it because I love the view." He pulled her hands close and lightly kissed them. "I'd never do anything to hurt you," he said. "Now let's stop stressing about the case. For once, we've got the problem solved."

When lunch was finished, Jared and Sara got up and stepped outside. The day was still pale gray and the clouds were again starting to hover. "More rain," Sara said.

Jared nodded. "Do you want me to drop you off?"

"No, that's the opposite direction for you. I can walk from here."

He gave his wife a kiss good-bye and watched her head up the block. Sara had a slight bounce in her walk, and even though Jared loved to tease her about it, he also loved to watch her in motion. When she turned the corner, he stepped toward the cab that was stopped in front of the restaurant. As soon as he opened the door, he realized someone was already in the backseat. It was Kozlow.

"How're you doing there, doc?" Kozlow asked. "Come on in."

Jared hesitated a moment.

"Don't worry," Kozlow said. "It's safe."

Cautiously getting into the cab, Jared sat next to Kozlow. "What's going on?" Jared asked. "What're you doing here?"

"You'll see."

"What're you talking about?" Jared asked as the driver pulled into traffic. "What do you—"

"Shut up already. We'll be there soon enough."

The cab pulled up to a landmark town house on East Fifty-eighth Street whose polished brass doorknobs and handrails sparkled even in the absence of sunlight. A uniformed attendant opened the door for Jared, who slowly stepped out of the cab. Kozlow didn't follow. "You're not coming?" Jared asked.

"Not my kind of place," Kozlow said. "You're on your own." He slammed the door shut and the cab sped away.

"Mr. Lynch," the attendant said. "This way, please."

Jared hesitantly followed.

The attendant ushered Jared through a paneled hall with a magnificent antique mirror along one wall and down a broad, curving, carpeted stairway. Jared nervously ran his hand against the grain of his two o'clock shadow. Craning his neck in every direction, he tried his best to scout ahead. There were no other people in sight, but he was clearly in a club. At the foot of the stairs, a beautifully appointed bar stretched off to the left. Straight ahead was a large lounge decorated in an unusual mix of French antiques and African artifacts. Dark and intimidating, the room had wooden hand-painted tribal masks along the walls and clusters of wing chairs and Louis XV end tables. African music played softly from hidden speakers.

The uniformed man led Jared to an unmarked door in the back, which opened into a private room. Inside, centered around a marble fireplace, were a sofa and two antique chairs. In one of the chairs sat a tall, elegant man with an angular face, wearing a hand-tailored black blazer. His slightly graying blond hair was brushed back from his forehead, and although it was impossible to tell by looking at him, one of his legs was imperceptibly shorter than the other. The disproportion was caused by an old football injury that he wore as a badge of honor. Indeed, for him it wasn't just a football injury. It was a *Princeton* football injury. And in his mind, that made all the difference.

Hearing them approach, he stood and extended a well-manicured hand. "So nice to finally meet you, Mr. Lynch," he said.

"Do you mind telling me what this is about?" Jared asked.

The man ignored him. "My name is Oscar Rafferty. Won't you please sit down?" He gestured to the sofa, then turned to the attendant. "That'll be it, George, thank you." The smooth graciousness of Rafferty's voice suggested that he was a man who was accustomed to having things go his way.

Jared assumed the same when he noticed the signature gold B on the black buttons of Rafferty's Brioni blazer. Even Thomas Wayne didn't wear two-thousand-dollar Brioni jackets. So for Jared, Rafferty's buttons meant one thing: This wasn't going to be a typical client meeting.

Cautiously taking a seat on the sofa, Jared picked up a matchbook from a bowl on the coffee table between them.

"I understand you're from Highland Park," Rafferty said in an engaging tone. "Do you know the Pritchard family, Judge Henry Pritchard? Both his sons are clients of mine. One's a playwright, the other's a producer—which means he does much of nothing."

Confused by Rafferty's attempt to find common ground, Jared said, "I don't mean to be rude, but is there something I can help you with, Mr. Rafferty?"

Suddenly, Rafferty's expression changed. He didn't like being cut short. "Actually, there is, Jared. And since I'm the one who'll be paying

Tony Kozlow's legal fees, I thought we should get together. There are a few pieces of information you're still missing."

"Well, if it's about the case, I want you to know that, regrettably, I have to withdraw as counsel. I just found out my wife is the prosecutor on the other side."

"That's all right. We don't mind."

"But I do," Jared said. "That's why I'm stepping down. If you want, though, I'm happy to recommend someone else at the firm to take over the case."

Rafferty's eyes grew dark as he looked disapprovingly at Jared. "I don't think you understand," he said. "You're not stepping down. You're our lawyer on this."

"Oh, I am?"

"Yes. You are," Rafferty said coldly. "Like it or not, Jared, we have to win this case. And while you're obviously impressed with your own over-inflated, career-climbing résumé, you really have only one thing to offer us—you're married to the prosecutor. You therefore know how she thinks, how she approaches a problem, and most important, how to exploit her weaknesses. To be blunt, you know how to beat her."

"But I'm not taking the case," Jared insisted.

"Jared, I don't think you understand what I'm saying. Our friend Anthony Kozlow cannot be found guilty. And if you're hoping to continue with your sexual exploits on the kitchen counter, you'll make sure he's not."

"How do you know we—"

"Pay close attention," Rafferty said calmly. "We'll all be happier if you win the case."

"*All be happier?* What the hell does that mean?"

Without answering, Rafferty handed Jared a large manila envelope. When Jared opened it, he saw a stack of two dozen black-and-white photographs. All of them of Sara.

"That's Sara on her way to the office," Rafferty said as Jared looked at a clear outdoor shot. "And that's her coming home." The photos showed most of the places that Sara had been in the past twenty-four hours. When Jared got to a shot of Sara waiting near the edge of the subway platform, Rafferty added, "That's when she was coming home late after last night's arraignment. I guess she was anxious to get home, because she kept sticking her head over the edge, looking to see if the train was coming. That's not a safe thing to do, Jared. One little push is all it takes."

Staring straight down at the pictures, Jared felt nauseated. The drumbeats of the African music seemed to be blaring from all directions. The photos of Sara blurred in a rush of dizziness. Closing his eyes, he struggled to pull himself together. Eventually he looked up at Rafferty. "What do you want?" he asked.

"I want you to win," Rafferty said. "That's all."

"And if I don't?" Jared asked.

Without saying a word, Rafferty picked up the photographs and put them back in the envelope.

"Answer me," Jared insisted. "What if I don't?"

Rafferty resealed the envelope. "Jared, I think you know the answer to that." He let his words sink in. "Now listen to what I'm about to say, because I know what you're thinking. If you go to the police, or any other law enforcement body, I promise you, you'll be haunted by that decision for the rest of your life. Silence is golden—if you tell anyone, including your wife, we'll kill her.

The moment you open your mouth, she's dead. I'll have Kozlow standing on her throat faster than you can put down the telephone," Rafferty warned. "Naturally, I know it won't come to that—you're an intelligent lawyer, Jared. For the next few weeks, all we ask is that you do your job. Prepare for trial, be the good defense attorney, and deliver a win. That's what it has to be—no settlements allowed. Make it disappear or get me a win. You do that, and we're out of your life. No headache, no trouble. Am I making myself clear?"

Slowly, Jared nodded, his eyes locked on the crimson tapestry that covered the floor.

"I'll take that awkward silence as a yes," Rafferty said. "Which means Kozlow will be at your office first thing tomorrow morning. Enjoy what's left of your day."

Rafferty stood up and escorted Jared to the front entrance of the club. Outside, a private car was waiting for him. As Jared got in the car, Rafferty said, "Good-bye, Jared." Jared barely registered the remark. It wasn't until the door slammed shut that the full weight of the moment hit him. Sitting alone in the back of the car, Jared replayed the scene in his head. He pictured Rafferty and the photo of Sara standing on the edge of the subway platform. And then he pictured Kozlow. Oh, God, Jared thought, undoing his tie and gasping for air. What the hell have I gotten us into?

CHAPTER 6

"Hello, I'm looking for Claire Doniger," Sara said, reading the name off her legal pad.

"This is she," Doniger sang in a voice that was eager to please from years of cocktail parties and hoarse from years of cigarette smoking.

"Hi, Ms. Doniger, this is Sara Tate from the district attorney's office. I spoke to you yesterday about your burglary."

"Yes, of course," Doniger said. "How are you?"

"Everything is fine here. We're moving forward on your case, and I was just wondering if we could go through the story one more time."

"Well, I just don't know what there is to tell. I was dead asleep, and at about three-thirty in the morning, I heard my doorbell ring. So I got up to answer it. When I looked through the peephole, I saw a police officer. And when I opened the door, he was standing there with a young man who he said just robbed my house. I was naturally shaken, and I said there must be a mistake. Then he held out my watch and my sterling golf ball and asked me if they were mine."

"And were they yours?" Sara asked, writing notes on a legal pad.

"Without question. I recognized them that instant. The watch was a 1956 Ebel that my father bought as a twenty-fifth-anniversary gift for my mother—they stopped making the platinum version that same year. And the golf ball was a thank-you gift from my breast cancer organization—I did some fund-raising work for their celebrity golf tournament. My name is etched into the bottom of it. Apparently, the young man had just stolen them, and the officer caught him as he was walking up our block."

Remembering Conrad's advice to ignore the complaint report and to always ask broad, open-ended questions, Sara asked, "How did the officer know to pick up Mr. Kozlow?"

"That's his name? Kozlow?" Doniger asked.

"That's him—our favorite criminal," Sara joked, hoping to keep Doniger upbeat and talkative. "Now how did the officer know to pick him up?"

"Well, from what the officer told me, he received a radio message that someone had seen a prowler leave my house."

"Do you know who made that initial call to the police?"

"My neighbor from across the street. Patty Harrison. Her brownstone faces mine. She told me she couldn't sleep, so she was up having a late-night snack. Or so she says."

"Do you have any reason to doubt her?"

"She's a little busybody. Knows everyone's business. I wouldn't be surprised if she was staring out her window just to see who on the block was coming home late. Anyway, she apparently saw the man leave my house. She thought he looked suspicious, so she called the police and gave them a description. Luckily, the officer was walking up Madison, so he just turned the corner and picked him up. Incredible, if you ask me."

"It definitely was," Sara agreed. Looking over her notes, she tried to picture all of the events, frame by frame. Slowly, her mind played through each individual fact, searching for any detail she might have missed. Eventually she asked, "Ms. Doniger, does your house have an alarm system?"

"Pardon?"

"Your house. Does it have an alarm system?"

"Yes, it does. But I must've forgotten to turn it on that night, because it didn't go off."

"And were there any other visible signs of entry? Any broken windows? Any other entrances he could've gotten through besides the front door?"

"Not that I can think of. No," Doniger said. "And I don't mean to be rude, but I'm late for a meeting with some friends. Can we finish this another time?"

"Actually, I think that about covers it," Sara said. "Hopefully, we can go over this one more time before the grand jury meets on Monday."

"Yes. Certainly," Doniger said. "We can talk about it later."

When Sara hung up the phone, she made a few more notes to herself on the legal pad.

"I wouldn't do that," Guff warned as he walked into the office.

"Do what?"

"Take notes like that. You're never supposed to take notes."

"Why's that?"

"Because in New York, any prior recorded information from someone that you intend to call as a witness must be turned over to the defense before the trial. So you're better off not writing anything down."

"Are you telling me that if my witness changes her story between now and the trial, the defense can use these notes to make us look like fools in court?"

"That's the law," Guff said. He tossed a file folder on Sara's desk. "By the way, I got the information you wanted about the other new ADAs." As Sara opened the folder, Guff explained, "There were eighteen other ADAs who started the same day as you. So far, every single one of them has managed to get themselves at least a couple of cases. I split them up by category."

Reading through the list, Sara saw that everyone had a minimum of three misdemeanor cases. In addition, nine of her colleagues had felony cases, and two were assisting on homicides. "Damn," Sara said. "Why is everyone in New York so competitive?"

"Nature of the game, baby. In this city, the moment you think about doing something, there are already five hundred people waiting in line for it." Guff waved his arms through the air in a wide circular motion. "This may look stupid, but right now, there are at least a dozen other people in this town doing the exact same thing. Original thoughts don't exist in New York. That's the beauty of the ambitious beast."

"And it's about to take a bite out of my butt."

"I don't know why you're so surprised. When the cutbacks were announced, every slacker in this office started looking productive."

"Then maybe I should turn it up even more. Maybe I can get some more cases."

"It's not how many you have, it's how many you win," Guff said. "And considering you already have five, I wouldn't take any more."

"But I'm going to plead out two of those. . . ."

"Sara, what do you think's more impressive: handling a dozen cases and being overwhelmed, or handling five cases professionally and by the book?"

"In this city? I'll go with the twelve."

"C'mon, you know that's not true."

"I know, it's just—"

"You're tempted to grab more cases. I understand. But trust me, the more balls you try and juggle, the more likely you're going to drop them all. Plead out the losers, stick with your good cases, and win whatever you keep. That's the way to get noticed."

"So if it looks like we have a chance, we go for the win, and if it looks like we're in trouble, we cop the plea."

"That's the Colonel's secret recipe," Guff said. "Follow that and you'll never lose."

As a staff member in the DA's public-information office, Lenore Lasner spent most of her time talking to reporters and private citizens about the inner workings of the office. They asked her about the outcomes of certain cases. They asked her about the qualifications of certain judges. And every once in a while, they asked her about a particular assistant district attorney.

"Sara Tate, Sara Tate," Lenore said as she scrolled through the directory. "I don't think I have her here."

"She just started on Monday," the man said as he leaned against the counter and stared at Lenore's long, manicured fingernails. He had a deep voice that weighed heavily in the air and sunken cheeks that made him look sickly.

"Why didn't you say so?" Lenore asked. She turned to the back of the directory, where a single sheet of paper was stapled to the inside back cover. "Tate, Tate, Tate," she said as her fingernail ran down the list. "Here she is."

"Very pretty nails," the man said.

"Thank you," Lenore said with a slight blush. "Now, what do you need to know about ADA Tate?"

"I just want to know where her office is."

"We're actually not supposed to give out that information. I can give you her phone number, though."

"That'd be great. And if I could bother you for some paper and a pen to write with . . ."

"I have that right here." As Lenore turned around to get a notepad from her desk, the man looked down at the directory. Next to Sara's name was her phone number, and next to that were her address and room number: 80 Centre Street. Room 727.

"Y'know what? I just remembered I have her phone number," the man said. "I'll give her a call later."

"Are you sure?" Lenore asked as she returned to the counter.

"Positive," the man said. "I know exactly where it is."

"Are you okay?" Kathleen asked the moment Jared returned to the office. He looked terrible, his complexion ashen.

"I'm fine," he answered. "My lunch didn't agree with me." After entering his office, Jared closed the door behind him, collapsed in his chair, hit the do-not-disturb button on his phone, and put his head down on his desk. Who could he call? He wanted to tell the police. Or the feds. His brother knew someone in the FBI. But he couldn't get Rafferty's warning out of his head. And more than anything else, he couldn't stop thinking about Sara. No matter the threat, no matter the moral consequences, he knew he'd do anything— anything at all—to protect his wife. For Sara's own safety, he had to tell her. As he picked up the phone, though, he realized how impossible it'd be to keep Sara quiet. The moment she found out, she'd go right to her friends in the DA's office. And if she confronted Rafferty, it would only make things worse. For both of them. More important, Rafferty might already be listening. That's impossible, Jared argued with himself—it's too soon. With the right equipment, however, they could do it without ever entering the office. Putting down the receiver, Jared was frozen. He couldn't win.

Then he grabbed the phone, and before he could talk himself out of it, dialed Sara's number. He had to tell her.

"ADA Tate's office," Guff answered. "Can I help you?"

"This is Jared—Sara's husband. Is she around?"

"Hey, Jared. Sorry, she's out of the office. Can I take a message?"

"Can you please tell her to call me as soon as she gets in? It's an emergency."

"Is everything okay?"

"Yeah. Just tell her that I want to talk to her. It's important." As Jared hung up the phone, there was a loud knock on his door. Before he could say "I'm busy," the door opened and Marty Lubetsky walked in.

"Where've you been all day?" Lubetsky asked. "I've been leaving messages since this morning."

"Sorry about that. I've been swamped."

"So I hear. I just got a call from Oscar Rafferty."

"You know him?" Jared asked.

"As much as you can know someone in a three-minute phone conversation. He called and told me that he's retained you for an acquaintance of his."

"Why'd he call you?"

"To make sure you'd have enough time to work on the case. To be honest, I thought you put him up to it. He knew I was your supervisor and said the only reason he came to us was because of your good reputation. He said that if things work out with this case, he might throw all of his business our way. And it sounds like he has a good deal of potential business."

"Wouldn't that be great?"

"You bet it would," Lubetsky said. "Anyway, I just wanted to say congrats. I'm sorry about yesterday, but it looks like you're turning things around. Keep at it."

"I'll try," Jared said as Lubetsky left the office. Jared reached into his pocket and pulled out the matchbook from the club. Gold letters spelled out TWO ROOMS. He hit the intercom button on his phone.

"What's up?" Kathleen asked.

"I need a quick favor. There's a club called Two Rooms on East Fifty-eighth Street. Can you ask Barrow to run a quick search on it and tell me what comes up?"

"No problem," Kathleen said. "Who should I bill it to?"

"No one. I'm paying for this myself."

"What'd you find?" Jared asked as he anxiously leaned toward his speakerphone twenty minutes later.

"Did you get the fax?" Barrow said from the phone.

Before Jared could answer, Kathleen entered his office holding a small pile of papers. "Here you go," she said, dropping them on his desk.

Jared flipped through the stack of press clippings and real-estate records.

"You're welcome," Kathleen said. He still didn't respond. She was tempted to say something, but she knew now wasn't the time. Instead, she left the office, closing the door behind her.

"As you can see, it's just the usual high-society nonsense," Barrow explained. "There's no sign out front, but it's somehow still known by all the right people. And it used to be called Le Club, until someone finally had the good sense to change the name. Otherwise, the only things I can find are society column mentions and a few restaurant reviews. It's a serious place, J—superexclusive.

Apparently, it's impossible to get in, which means the Ladies Who Lunch casually stalk the place on a regular basis."

"Is it private membership only?"

"Don't know—they weren't answering the phone. If you want, the number's on the top sheet."

"Thanks," Jared said, still distracted.

"Also, I looked up your friend Kozlow. Have you seen his file yet?"

"We're still waiting for it to come over from his old attorneys. Anything interesting?"

"I don't know if I'd call it interesting, but I'll tell you one thing: The guy is one sick bastard. Anyone who uses a screwdriver to—"

"I'll read it myself," Jared interrupted.

"You have to hear this, though. He took a screwdriver and—"

"Lenny, please, I really don't want to talk about it right now."

There was a short pause on the other line. Finally, Barrow asked, "Does this have anything to do with what got you so upset at lunch?"

"How do you know I was upset at lunch?"

"Kathleen. She said you came back a mess."

"That's not even true. I just have a lot on my mind."

"J, we've been at this a long time. You don't have to lie."

"I'm not," Jared insisted. "And even if I was, I'd never do it to you. Now how much do I owe you for the research?"

"You think I'd take money from you? If I did that, Sara would starve," Barrow said with a deep laugh. "If it's important and it's personal, it's free. Just make sure you get the next dinner check."

"Thanks, Lenny."

"No big deal. Let me know if you need anything else."

Jared hung up the phone and dialed the number for Two Rooms.

"Two Rooms. Can I help you?"

Jared recognized the voice of the uniformed attendant. "Hi, I wanted to get some information on your club. Is it private, or is it open to the public?"

"We're open to the public, sir."

"So that room downstairs—anyone can rent that for lunch?"

"Sorry, we're not open for lunch. Just for dinner."

Confused, Jared said, "I was just there an hour ago. I had a meeting with Oscar Rafferty."

There was a short pause on the other line. Then the attendant said, "There haven't been any meetings today."

"Sure there were," Jared insisted. "I even recognize your voice—you're the guy who walked me downstairs."

"Sir, I don't know what you're talking about. Believe me, there was no meeting." A moment later, Jared heard a click. The attendant had hung up.

What the hell is going on? Jared wondered.

As he walked home from the subway, Jared felt exhausted. Throughout the entire commute home, he had looked over his shoulder at least thirty times, trying to see if someone was following him. On the subway, he had cut through three different cars, and just before the doors slammed shut, he had gotten off at the Seventy-second Street stop rather than his usual Seventy-ninth. As he headed up Broadway, he checked his reflection in every storefront window he passed to see if anyone was nearby. He then spontaneously started running. Not jogging. Full-speed running. Moving as fast as he could, he made an abrupt right on Seventy-eighth and ducked into the first doorway he came to—a narrow service entrance for the corner grocery store. But from what he could tell, no one was in pursuit. Maybe Rafferty was bluffing, Jared thought as he approached his home. Maybe it was just a threat to keep him in line.

Jared walked into his building and pulled out his keys to check the mail. At his feet, he heard a quiet crunching. Looking down, he noticed shards of broken glass scattered around the small alcove. He used his foot as a makeshift broom and swept the glass into one corner. On his way upstairs, he stepped over more shards of glass. He saw the source of the broken glass at the top of the stairs: The large framed picture of sunflowers on the landing was smashed to pieces. Then he noticed that the front door to his apartment was ajar. A cold chill ran down his back as he stepped forward cautiously. Ignoring the crushed glass beneath his feet, he looked up and down the short hallway and checked the next flight of stairs to make sure he was alone. There was no one in sight. Slowly, Jared opened the door and peeked inside.

The first thing he noticed was the overturned oak bookshelves that he and Sara had spent so much time putting together. Then the country pine chairs that had been thrown in the corner. Then the matching table that was flipped over. Then the ransacked kitchen.

He headed for the living room, stepping over

the hundreds of books that covered most of the floor. His Bogart poster was pulled from the wall, the cushions had been ripped from the armchair, the sofa was turned on its side, the halogen lamps were knocked over, the glass coffee table was shattered, the TV was facedown on the floor, the videotapes were scattered everywhere, and the plants were tipped over, their soil spilling onto the carpet. Although all six of Sara's portraits of Jared were still hanging on the wall, their glass frames had been shattered. Oh, my God, Jared thought as he looked around the room. Not a single item had gone untouched.

As he searched for the phone to call the police, Jared heard a blunt thud from the bedroom. Someone was still in the house. Jared scrambled to the corner of the living room and ducked behind the overturned sofa. From there, he heard the intruder leave the bedroom and walk toward the kitchen. Heavy footsteps pounded against the hardwood floor. He heard the stranger picking through the kitchen drawers. In the center of the room, Jared spotted a silver letter opener. It wasn't far. He had to get it. Slowly, Jared crawled forward, carefully avoiding the compact discs that were scattered everywhere. Praying that he wouldn't hit a creaking floorboard, he picked up the letter opener. As silently as he could, he climbed to his feet. He still had the element of surprise on his side. But as Jared readied his makeshift weapon, he heard the stranger return to the bedroom.

Peeking out from the corner of the living room, Jared confirmed he was alone. He darted for the kitchen. Once there, he saw that every drawer had been shuffled through, and every cabinet had been searched and emptied. Holding tight to the letter opener, Jared leaned against the refrigerator and caught his breath. He was a sweaty mess. Hold it together, he told himself. Deep breaths.

Ten seconds later, he left the kitchen. Quietly, he walked toward the closed door of his bedroom. As he got closer, he could hear the muffled sounds of frantic rummaging. From what he could tell, they were picking through the contents of the large dresser on the right side of the room. As anxiety gave way to anger, Jared arched the letter opener over his head and put a hand on the door-knob. He was shaking. On the count of three, he said to himself. One . . . two . . . Throwing the door open, Jared ran full speed into the bedroom. But as soon as he cleared the doorway, he felt something hit him in the shins. Someone had tripped him up. They were waiting for him. As he crashed to the floor, he let go of the letter opener. And before he could grab it, he heard a familiar voice say, "Are you nuts?"

Sara stood over him with a kitchen knife in her hands. "I thought you were the burglar," she said as she dropped the knife. "I could've killed you."

"I'm sorry," Jared said, climbing to his feet. He anxiously embraced his wife. "As long as you're safe. Thank God you're safe."

"It's okay. I'm fine," Sara said.

"When did you get home?"

"About ten minutes ago," Sara explained. "When I walked in, I almost fell over. I called the police, then came in here to see if they got my mom's jewelry."

"And?"

"Luckily, they missed it. From what I can tell, they took the cash from the top drawer of my dresser, the gold pocket watch Pop gave you, and some of our silver frames, but they never found the jewelry." Walking into the living room, Sara took her second look at the devastated mess that was their apartment. While she turned the potted plants upright, Jared noticed that his *Chinatown* knife was pristinely placed on top of one of the sofa cushions.

He picked up the protective case that held his most prized collectible and noticed a small note taped to the bottom. His stomach dropped as he read the note's three words: *Shut your mouth*.

"They must've thought it was a regular knife," Sara said.

"Huh?"

"Your knife. If they'd known what it was, I'm sure they would've taken it."

"Yeah, definitely," Jared said as he pulled off the note and crumpled it in his hand.

Picking up the phone, Sara said, "I still can't believe this. I start working for the good guys, and some lowlife decides to rip us off. I'm going to call Conrad to make sure—"

"No!" Jared said, cutting Sara off. Seeing the surprised look on his wife's face, he added, "The police'll be here soon enough. Then we can see what else is missing and figure it all out."

"Yeah, I guess," Sara agreed as she picked up a pile of books from the living-room floor. "But let me tell you something: If we catch the bastards who did this, you better believe I'm going to prosecute them personally. You touch my junk and cause me heartache—you're asking to be kicked in the head."

"Yeah," Jared said without emotion.

"Hey, are you okay?"

"Yeah. Yeah, I'm fine."

"Are you sure? You look terrible."

"What can I say? Our apartment just got broken into and our stuff's all over the floor. Should I be thrilled with that?"

"Of course not. But look at the bright side—they were gone by the time we got here, no one was hurt, and in all likelihood, we'll never hear from them again."

"Yeah," Jared said, all too aware that Rafferty wasn't going away. "We sure are lucky."

"Meanwhile, tell me why you called this afternoon. What was so important?"

Jared's fist tightened around the note in his hand. "It was nothing."

"Guff said it sounded urgent."

"It was nothing," Jared insisted. "Just an imagined crisis."

By midnight, the police had come and gone, the apartment was dusted for fingerprints, and Jared and Sara had cleaned up most of their belongings.

"The cops seemed really thorough," Sara said, lying down on the sofa.

"They'd better be." Jared sat in his favorite chair. "You're one of *them* now." He was trying his best to act unaffected, but he couldn't take his eyes off his wife. If he did, something could happen. Something *would* happen. And it'd be his fault. It was in his hands. Searching for a smooth segue, he added, "By the way, now that we're done with this whole mess, let me bring up another. I can't step down from the Kozlow case."

Sara shot up in her seat. "What do you mean

'can't'? You're a grown man—you can do anything you want."

"I'm serious. I can't."

"Why not? Does someone have a gun to your head?"

"No," he said bluntly. "I just need to be on the case."

"Don't tell me that, Jared. You promised you'd—"

"I know what I said, but it's not happening."

"Listen, the only reason Kozlow picked you is because you're my husband. He's obviously toying with us."

"Thanks for the compliment."

"You know what I mean."

"Well, regardless of why I was picked, Lubetsky found out that the guy who's paying the bill has deep pockets. He figures if I take the case, we can get his other business as well."

"So let Lubetsky take the case. I'd love to smack his seven double chins across the courtroom."

"Kozlow wants me. And Lubetsky said he's not letting me off the case. I tried, honey. I really did try."

"You didn't try hard enough," Sara said, raising her voice. "If you stay on this case, you're messing with my career. And if I take a loss to my husband, I'm going to ruin my one pathetic chance to actually keep this job."

"Just calm down a second."

"Don't tell me to calm down. You try spending six months sending out résumés to every firm in this city. You try getting two hundred and twenty-five rejection letters. In the legal market, I'm used goods. And since my self-esteem has already taken enough of a beating, I don't need another one."

"Hold on a second," Jared said as he sat down next to his wife. "Do you really think I'm doing this to jeopardize your career? Sara, you're the most important thing in the world to me. I'd never do anything to hurt you. I just . . ." Jared's voice trailed off.

"You just what?"

"Nothing, I . . ."

"What?" Sara demanded. "Say it already."

Jared paused a moment. Finally, he said, "Lubetsky told me that if I don't take the case and bring this guy in as a client, I won't make partner. I'll be fired on the spot."

Sara was stunned. "Are you kidding? He said that to you?"

"After what happened yesterday, this is his line in the sand. They're voting on me in the next six months. In my six and a half years at the firm, I haven't brought in a single client."

"But you've handled some of their biggest—"

"Those were other people's cases. Now I have to have my own cases. And the bottom line in a law firm is the bottom line. It may be a group of lawyers, but it's still a business. If I can't make that business grow, I'll be in the same position you were six months ago."

Sara was silent.

Hoping to exploit his opening, Jared continued to hammer away. "I don't know what else to do. With all your loans, we can't afford to—"

"They're really going to fire you?"

"That's what he said," Jared replied. "I know it might hurt you if you lose, but by then, your office will realize what a thorough prosecutor you are. They're not going to get rid of you just because you lost your first case."

"Who said I'm going to lose?" Sara asked with a strained smile.

Jared breathed a sigh of relief. "Thank you, honey. I really appreciate what you're doing."

"I'm not doing anything. If you're on the opposite side, I'm still going to come at you with guns blazing."

"I wouldn't expect any less."

Sara got up from the sofa and followed her husband out of the room. As they walked toward the bedroom, Sara asked, "So if Kozlow's not paying his own bill, who's signing the check?"

"I can't tell you that," Jared said defensively as he entered the bedroom. "You're the enemy."

"Uh-oh, here we go," Sara said. "Now the real battle begins."

Leaning back in his seat and staring at the small black receiver on his desk, Rafferty smiled. "Well?"

"Sounds like round one goes to our boy," the other man said as he took off his headphones. "He really knows how to pull her strings."

"That's why we picked him," Rafferty said. "Now we just have to hope he can do the same thing in court."

"And if he can't?"

"I'm not entertaining that thought."

"But Kozlow said—"

"Don't even bring him up. I should put him through a wall for what he did."

"And I'm sure you would—except for the small fact that he'd rip your head off first."

Rafferty ignored the comment. "Don't let him intimidate you. He was smart to go with the burglary idea, but that doesn't solve our problems. Until Kozlow wins, we're all in trouble. So regardless of what I have to do, he's going to win."

At a quarter to two in the morning, Jared was lying awake in bed. In the past hour, he had dozed off four times. But each time, just as he was about to lose consciousness, just as he was about to forget it all, he was jolted awake. And in that single moment, it all came back again. Each time, he instinctively turned to his wife. He watched the rise and fall of her chest to make sure she was breathing. That was all he cared about. As long as she was safe, he could handle the rest.

By seven o'clock Wednesday morning, Jared was standing on the subway platform, waiting for the train. Avoiding the edge of the platform, he spent most of his time checking over his shoulder and scanning the crowd. The man wearing the blue shirt and red tie looked unusually suspicious. So did the man wearing the olive suit. So did the woman reading the newspaper and the younger man with the headphones. Backing away from the crowd of strangers, Jared tried not to let his fears get the best of him. But as new commuters filled the platform, he found himself jumping at every random glance. Finally, he turned around, left the station, and hailed a cab.

By the time he arrived at the office, it was almost seven-thirty. Between the break-in, the bad night's sleep, and the morning commute, he was mentally and physically drained. His eyes were tired, his shoulders sagged, and his stomach was still churning from lying to Sara. Without a doubt, he was in no shape to get an early start on the day. But if he was going to protect his wife, he knew he had a great deal of work ahead of him. Facing someone like Sara meant that every detail had to be accounted for. As he had learned from his very first appearance in court, a good attorney could take even the smallest opening and turn it into a victory.

Heading up the hallway, though, Jared wasn't thinking about trial strategies or witness preparation or jury selection. Instead, he was still trying to recall every possible circumstance that required a lawyer to recuse himself from a case. When he reached Kathleen's desk, he forced a smile.

"Good morning," Kathleen said. "Starting early today?"

"Yeah," Jared said. "Clear my calendar for the rest of the month. This Kozlow case just became top priority."

"Why? It's just a burglary."

"That doesn't mean it's not important," he snapped.

"Take it easy. I'm only asking a question."

Jared leaned on Kathleen's desk and lowered his voice. "I don't want anyone to know this, but the prosecutor on the case is Sara."

"You're facing your wife?" Kathleen blurted. Jared scowled.

"Believe me, I'd love to get off the case. That's why I need your help. As far as I can figure, having a husband and wife against each other has to present some sort of conflict-of-interest problem. Ethically, it seems to be a minefield for everyone involved, especially the client. So I want you to get a legal assistant to go through the rules of professional conduct and double-check whether this sort of arrangement is prohibited."

"Why not just take her on? We'll bury her."

"Don't you dare say that," Jared warned.

Kathleen stopped writing and looked up at her boss. "Take it easy, it's a joke. I'll let you know what they find."

Turning toward his office, Jared took a deep breath. Maybe this will actually work out. As he opened the door, he heard someone say, "Hiya, boss. What's on the agenda today?"

Kozlow was stretched out on the chair in the corner of Jared's office. His feet were propped up on the wastebasket.

"How'd you get in here?" Jared asked, annoyed.

"Ancient Chinese secret," Kozlow said. "I wouldn't mention it to Kathleen, though. She strikes me as the type who hates surprises."

Walking over to the chair, Jared stared down at his new client. "Let me tell you one thing," he said as he pushed Kozlow's feet from the wastebasket. "I know you were the ones who broke into my house."

"Your house got broken into?" Kozlow asked innocently.

"Don't be a smart-ass," Jared warned.

Kozlow shot up out of his seat, grabbed Jared by his tie, and dragged him forward. "Then don't use that tone with me," Kozlow shot back. He held on to Jared's tie with a tight grip. "Do you understand?"

Jared nodded, shocked by the outburst.

"You have a job to do, and we want to make sure you do it. Don't take it personally."

* * *

"Here's what I want," Sara said, sitting at her desk as Guff took notes. "First, I want you to find out if a husband and wife can even face each other in court. That stinks more than a truckload of manure, so if you can find anything that says one of us has to recuse ourselves, maybe Jared will drop the case. Second, I want—"

"You're scared of facing him, aren't you?" Guff asked.

"Who, Jared? Not a chance. Why? Do I look scared?"

"Forget I even asked. Now, what else did you want?"

"I may be a little nervous, but I don't think I'm scared."

"Okay, I got it. You're not scared."

"I'm serious. It won't affect me," Sara insisted. When Guff didn't reply, she added, "What do you expect me to say? Of course I'm scared."

"Why? Just because he's your husband?"

"There's that but there's also the fact that things have a way of working out for Jared. They just fall into place for him."

"I don't understand."

"Let me put it to you this way: During our third year of law school, we took a class on the legal aspects of the American presidency. On the first day of class, the professor asked everyone in the lecture hall to stand up. Then, when everyone in this huge room was standing, he said, 'Anyone who's female, sit down. Anyone who was not born in the United States, sit down. Anyone who's five-eleven or shorter, sit down.' And one by one, the whole room started sitting down. When he was done with his list of questions, the only person still standing was Jared. And then the professor said, 'This is the only person in this group who, except for the age requirement, is qualified to be president.'"

"So big deal. All it means is Jared's squeaky clean and six feet tall."

"That's not just it, though. No matter how smart you are, or sneaky you are, or aggressive you are, Jared will always have an uncanny knack for making things work to his own advantage. That's how he put himself through law school, and that's why, despite the fact that he's having trouble bringing in clients, he's still close to making partner. It's hard to explain, but he's one of those guys who, even though he has to work hard at it, makes everything look easy."

"I hate those guys," Guff said.

"And I married one of those guys. Which means we'll have to work even harder to win," Sara said. "Anyway, back to business. I still want to get Doniger's neighbor on the phone . . ."

"Patty Harrison," Guff said.

". . . get her on the phone so we can do an initial interview. She's by far the best witness we have for the grand jury—she's the only one who actually saw Kozlow leave the house. Third, I want to speak to Doniger again. We should make sure she's fully prepped before we walk into the grand jury. And fourth . . . what was fourth?"

"You want to interview Officer McCabe again. He's waiting out in the hallway."

"What? He's out there now?"

"As we speak," Guff said. "You were busy running around yesterday, so I called him up and asked him when he could come in. He works late on Friday and through the weekend, so he asked if he could do it today."

"Great," Sara said. "Let him in."

A minute later, Officer Michael McCabe walked into Sara's office. He had sharp eyes and a tired, almost droopy mouth, and he was thinner than Sara had remembered from their encounter on the videophone. Removing his police cap to reveal a head of thick black hair, McCabe took a seat in front of Sara's desk. "So how's the office treating you?" he asked in a heavy Brooklyn accent.

"Everyone's been terrific," Sara said as she flipped to a page of questions on her legal pad. "Now let's go over your testimony for the grand jury. Tell me again what happened that night."

"It was actually pretty simple. I cover the East Side, from Eightieth Street to Ninetieth, and from Lexington to Madison. So at about three-thirty in the morning, I get a call on my radio that some-one just reported a burglary at 201 East Eighty-second. They describe the defendant, so I take off for Eighty-second Street."

"You ran there?"

"Of course I ran there. I walk beat, remember?"

"Of course," Sara said, trying her best to sound knowledgeable. "You walk beat."

"Anyway, about two blocks from the crime scene, I spot someone who meets the defendant's description, so I pick him up."

"And what was that description?"

"Black jeans, long black leather jacket, goatee. He fit the description."

"Was he doing anything else suspicious? Was he running? Did he resist arrest? Anything at all that made him look guilty?"

"At three-thirty in the morning, on an empty street, two blocks from the crime scene, he matched the physical description of the burglar perfectly," McCabe said dryly. "What else do you want?"

"So you searched him right there?"

"Yeah. Found the watch, the golf ball, and the money."

"Let's do that again," Sara said. "When I have you in the grand jury, they're going to want more information than that." Handing McCabe a copy of the complaint report, Sara started over. "Okay, Officer McCabe, now tell us what you found on the defendant."

Reading from the sheet, McCabe answered, "A platinum Ebel watch, a sterling silver golf ball, and four hundred and seventeen dollars."

"Perfect," Sara said. "Just like that. Now, when you brought Kozlow back to 201 East Eighty-second Street, you woke up Ms. Doniger."

"Yep. She didn't even know she was robbed."

"But she identified the items as her own?"

"Oh, yeah. She paused a second, but then she did. Her mother's name was on the watch and her own name was on the golf ball."

"Was anything else taken besides that and the money?"

"That's all I could find, and that's all Doniger said was missing. The way I figure it, Kozlow was grabbing stuff, and then for whatever reason, he got scared and ran."

"And did you talk to Doniger's neighbor, Ms. Harrison?"

"No," McCabe said. "I didn't know she was the one who called in the tip."

"Wait a minute," Sara said, looking up. "You never got a positive ID on the night of the crime?"

"I didn't know the neighbor called it in."

"Okay. That's okay," Sara said. "But you did get Doniger's place fingerprinted?"

McCabe shook his head no. "I already had the suspect—I didn't think I needed his prints."

"Are you kidding me?" Sara asked. "Of course you need his prints. That's probably the best way to prove he was in the house."

"Hey, don't get mad at me. I'm not a detective. I just round 'em up and bring 'em in. Besides, we're on a budget. We don't fingerprint every place there's a crime. Unless there's a body, or it's a big case, Crime Scene stays at home and we follow up as best we can."

"Well, that's real helpful," Sara said. "Remind me to thank the budget cutters when I lose the case." Scanning her notes, she added, "Okay, just a few more questions. How long have you been friends with Victor Stockwell?"

"What kind of question is that?"

"An important one," Sara insisted.

"I know who he is, but we've never met."

Confused, Sara asked, "Then why'd you request him on the case?"

"What're you talking about?"

"When I first picked up this case from ECAB, the booking sheet was marked for Victor. If you barely knew him, why'd you request him?"

"I didn't request anyone," McCabe said. "Victor asked me if he could have the case."

Sara paused. "Really? Victor approached you?"

"Yeah, he called me a few hours after the arrest—while I was doing the paperwork. He said he wanted the Kozlow case and asked me to put his name on the file. I figured he had some personal interest in it, so I wrote him in." When he saw the puzzled look on Sara's face, he asked, "Is something wrong with that?"

"I don't know," Sara said. "That's what I'll have to find out."

When McCabe left Sara's office, she shut the door behind him and returned to her desk. There had to be an explanation for why one of the office's best prosecutors wanted such a low-profile assignment. Struggling to come up with a list of possible reasons, she picked up a nearby paper clip, unbent it, and started wrapping it around her index finger. Maybe Victor thought the case was interesting. Maybe he wanted to lighten his workload. Maybe he knew one of the parties involved. Maybe he knew Claire Doniger, and he was doing her a favor. Or maybe he knew Kozlow. As she continued to twist the paper clip, she thought about all the reasons why she should keep her suspicions to herself. But as her finger turned a light purple, she realized she had no idea what her next step was. The office was still uncharted territory, and without question, she needed help.

Pulling off the paper clip, she looked for the intercom button on her phone. There wasn't one—and this wasn't her old firm. Leaning forward on her desk, she shouted, "Guff, can you come in here a second?"

When Guff arrived, Sara asked him to close the door.

"Uh-oh, what happened now?" he asked.

"There's something I have to tell you."

"Let me guess: You want to see my secret list."

"Your what?"

"My secret list of funny words. I know people're talking about it. I put a couple on E-mail last week, and now everyone's clamoring for the rest. I'm not giving them out, though. You'll have to be satisfied with what you have: salami, wicker, Nipsey Russell—"

"Guff, please listen for a second. Remember when we were in ECAB the day I took the case?" Guff nodded. "When the cases were delivered, you were talking to Evelyn and Victor. So what you never saw was that Kozlow's case was originally marked for someone else—that's why I decided to take it."

"So what's the big deal? Cops request good ADAs all the time."

"That's exactly what I thought. But I just found out that it wasn't the cop who requested this particular ADA—it was the *ADA* who requested the case."

"Which ADA?"

Sara was silent.

"Tell me whose case it was, Sara. This isn't funny. It can really be—"

"Victor's," she finally said. "It was Victor's case."

"Oh, no. Why'd you have to go do something stupid like that? That's like teasing a rabid dog."

"The delivery guy pulled off the Post-it. He said it was just a request—I didn't know any better."

"Obviously not."

"Guff, I know it was a stupid move, but I can really use your help with this. There's no one else I trust."

"I don't know. I think this one is out of my league. If I were you, I'd go to Conrad."

"Conrad'll bite my head off if he finds out I stole a case from another ADA."

"Listen, it's your decision. But if I was choosing between the two, I'd take Conrad over Victor any day."

"How'd it go?" Conrad asked when Sara walked into his office.

"How'd what go?"

"Your talk with McCabe. Wasn't that this morning?"

"Yeah," Sara said, trying not to rush into anything. "It was pretty good. Not great." As she took a seat on Conrad's olive-green vinyl sofa, she asked, "Where'd you get this sofa?"

"Have Guff call down to purchasing. You'll get one by next year," Conrad said. "Now tell me about the interview."

"What's to tell? The cop seems like a nice guy, but he made some stupid mistakes. Never got fingerprints; never got an ID."

"So typical—eighty percenter."

"Huh?" Sara asked.

"In the DA's office, twenty percent of the ADAs do eighty percent of the work," Conrad explained. "The same thing applies to the judges in the courthouse and the cops and detectives on the street. To eighty percent of the people, this is just a nine-to-five bureaucracy."

"It's not a bureaucracy," Sara said. "The people here—"

"Sara, do you know how many open warrants there are in Manhattan? Five hundred thousand. That means there are half a million criminals *that we know about* running loose on the streets—and then there are all the ones we still haven't found. For the most part, we're an assembly line. Eighty percent of the people just want their paycheck. They don't want to risk their life and family to stop some scumbag criminal, and they don't want to do what it actually takes to stop crime. It doesn't make them bad people; it just makes them bad public servants."

"And for some reason, you think I'm part of the twenty percent?" Sara asked.

"Actually, I do. You're thirty-two years old, which means you know what you're getting into. And at that age, like it or not, this is your career. You may be unpolished, and you may be new, but you speak your mind, and Guff trusts you, which, believe it or not, says more than you think. If you can get this indictment and take it to trial, Monaghan will know you're not here to play around. And since I'm always looking for someone to stand on the twenty percent side of the scale, I'll do everything in my power to keep you aboard. So tell me what else happened with the cop and I'll tell you how to fix it."

"Well, as I said, he never got an ID."

"No big deal," Conrad said. "Set up a lineup so the neighbor can come in and pick Kozlow out. If there's no time, have her do it in the grand jury. Then the jurors can see it for themselves."

"What about the fingerprints?"

"You're screwed on that one."

"Lousy eighty percenter," Sara growled.

Conrad smiled. "Any other problems?"

Sara's eyes fell to the floor. "Just one," she said hesitantly. "There's something I haven't been completely honest about: When the case originally came into ECAB, there was a note on it that said, 'Request for Victor Stockwell.'"

A suspicious crease formed between Conrad's eyebrows. "What happened to the note?"

"The delivery guy took it off, and I let him throw it away," Sara said. Before Conrad could interrupt, she added, "I know it was wrong, but I figured Victor gets so many requests, he wouldn't miss one more. When I interviewed McCabe, though, I found out he didn't mark the case for Victor—Victor requested the case from him." As she finished the story, the room was silent. She could barely look Conrad in the eye.

Finally, Conrad leaned forward in his chair. "You really love to make it hard on yourself, don't you?"

"That's what I'm good at." Looking up, she noticed that the crease between Conrad's eyebrows was gone. "You're not mad?" she asked.

"Sara, if you knew Victor wanted the case, would you have stolen it from him?"

"Not a chance. I only—"

"Then that's that. I'd never fault you for trying to race to the front of the pack. If anything, that's what we need more of."

Conrad's reaction wasn't at all what she expected. Still processing it, she gave him an appreciative nod.

"You don't have to worry," he continued. "I'm on your side."

The way he said it, Sara knew he wasn't lying. "So what do I do about Victor?"

"Has he said anything to you about the case?"

"I know he's pissed off, but he hasn't asked for it back."

"Then what's the problem?"

"Don't you think it's a little weird? I mean, why would Victor even want this junky little case in the first place?"

"How should I know? People request cases all the time—most often because they want to get another shot at a repeat offender or because they know someone involved in the case. Maybe Victor's the one who first prosecuted Kozlow and he's still pissed that Kozlow walked. Maybe he's a friend of Doniger and he wanted to do her a favor."

"Or maybe this case is about more than just a burglary."

Conrad shook his head. "You're still not giving up on the front page, are you?"

"I can't," Sara said despairingly. "It's all I've got. Besides, this isn't just my active imagination."

"You sure about that?"

"I think I'm sure. I mean, we have a burglary where, of all the expensive things that can be taken, only two small items are missing; then there's the low-life burglar who somehow has access to the city's best lawyers; then there's the fact that of the two firms he hires, one is my old one and the other is my husband's. And if that weren't enough, we've got the world's best prosecutor begging for the case *and* lurking in my office. What else do you need? A big neon sign that says 'Suspicions "R" Us'?"

"I still think you're overreacting—there's a logical explanation for every single one of those."

"Really? Then how about this one: If everything's so normal, why didn't Victor ask for the case back?"

"Wait a minute, what are you accusing Victor of?"

"I'm not accusing anyone of anything. I just think you have to admit it's worth a look around."

"I'm reserving judgment," Conrad said. "But

since you're dead set on investigating, what do you plan to do next?"

"I'm not sure. I figured I'd start with Victor, but I didn't know where to look."

"If you want, you can check out AJIS—that's the information system that'll tell you who Kozlow's old prosecutors were. You can also check it to see if Victor had another case with Ms. Doniger. But I'm going to warn you again: There are a dozen good reasons for Victor to want that case. So if I were you, I'd skip the delusions of grandeur. All they do is get your hopes up."

"Don't worry," Sara said, her voice racing with nervous excitement. "I've got it all in perspective."

Watching as Sara furiously scribbled notes to herself, Conrad shook his head.

"What?" Sara asked, looking up. "What'd I do?"

"Nothing," Conrad said. "Is there anything else?"

"One last thing: How do I catch the bastards who broke into my house?"

"Yeah, Guff told me about that. While you were interviewing McCabe, we placed a call to the Twentieth Precinct. They're on it, but they don't have a clue. Chalk it up to bad luck and forget it."

"What're you talking about? What about your speech? About doing everything you can to stop crime?"

"That was just for show," Conrad joked. "Although you may get lucky when they get the fingerprint results."

As Conrad finished, Guff entered the office. "Shame, shame, shame," Guff said. "Now you're sounding like a real eighty percenter."

"Do you eavesdrop on every conversation?" Conrad asked him.

"Just the good ones," Guff said. Turning to Sara, he added, "Got you some news on the trial front. First, Doniger's neighbor, Patty Harrison, said she's happy to testify. You can call her today to set up a time. Second, I looked up the conflict-of-interest issues. According to the rules, husband against wife is a definite conflict. The bad news is you can get around it as long as you get written consent from the client after a full disclosure of the conflict."

"Damn," Sara said. "So all Jared has to do is—"

"Hold on a second," Conrad interrupted. "Your husband's the defense attorney?"

"I told you it's not my imagination," Sara said. "Got any advice for this one?"

"Tell him to get off the case or you'll divorce his ass," Conrad said. "I saw this once before—you're looking at an ugly situation."

"So it's allowed?" Sara asked nervously.

"Only under certain circumstances," Guff said. "The firm has to do some legal maneuverings, and at the very least, Jared has to get written consent from Kozlow. Also, Jared must be able to conclude that despite your involvement, he can adequately represent the interests of the client. That's how they deal with the conflict-of-interest problems."

"And you better get all of that in writing," Conrad said. "The last thing you want is to win and then have your victory taken away when Kozlow appeals and cries that he was given an unfair trial."

"So as long as Jared gets consent, he can stay on the case?" Sara asked, not looking forward to the answer.

"Sorry, I wish it were better news," Guff said.

Conrad pointed a finger at Sara. "Be careful with this one. I know you're dying for the victory, but don't let the case take over your entire life."

"Too late," Sara said.

Ignoring hunger pains and a pile of pink message sheets, Jared worked straight through lunch. He reread the burglary statute, made a list of possible defenses, and started searching for every criminal case in the past ten years that had similar facts.

Even Jared's office showed off his current obsession. The Woody Allen poster that had hung on the wall behind his desk was now replaced by a large piece of poster board containing a professionally enlarged image of the crime scene—from Doniger's and Harrison's houses, to Officer McCabe's location when he received the call on his radio, to the exact spot where Kozlow was stopped. Every morning, Jared planned to start his day the same way: He'd come in and stare intently at the poster, silently accounting for every second of the incident. Each day, he'd run through all the details, constantly searching for another debatable point he could use to his advantage. At trial, all he needed was the tiniest of mistakes— one slip-up, one misidentification, one moment unaccounted for. That was all it took to win on the facts; that was all he needed to protect his wife.

At the same time, if he couldn't win on the facts, he could try to win on the client. As he had seen in countless trials, some defendants were so believable—indeed, so likable—that the jury couldn't help but vote not guilty. But as Jared watched Kozlow bite his nails and spit the remnants into a coffee cup, he realized Kozlow wasn't one of them.

Kathleen walked into the room. "Ready for a pick-me-up?" she asked. "I've got Brownie on the phone."

Jonathan Brown was one of Manhattan's least prominent and most unlikely antiques dealers. Specializing in entertainment memorabilia, he was also Jared's one-stop-shopping source for the hardest-to-find collectibles. They had met at an antiques show when Jared was in law school, but it wasn't until Jared bought the *Chinatown* knife that Brownie realized he had a client for life. A salesman first and a collector last, Brownie always said that Jared got the exclusive first look at his newest inventory. And since he liked Brownie, Jared, for the most part, believed him.

"Ready to deal?" Brownie said as Jared picked up the phone.

"Listen, Brownie, now's really not the—"

"Uh-oh, here he goes—he's taking out his violin. *Ohhhh, Brownie, we're still paying off loans. Lower the price a little bit and I'll think about it.* Well, that gig's not working today, baby. Because I just found me the veritable goose that lays the golden eggs."

"I'm serious—"

"Before you say it, let me finish. Remember that wish list you gave me? The one with the words 'If You See These, Buy Them for Me' in big letters? Well, I found the number three item on your list. For a price to be negotiated, you can soon be the owner of your very own—get a load of this, Mr. Movies—your very own scuba mask from *The*

Graduate! I'm talking authenticity here. From the famous pool scene. Good as old and almost sol—"

"Brownie, I don't have time for this now." Jared hung up the phone. "You almost done with that paperwork?" he asked Kathleen.

"Here you go," Kathleen said, handing a small pile of papers to Jared.

After quickly reading each page, Jared walked to Kozlow and placed them on his lap. Handing Kozlow a pen, he said, "Read these, and if you agree with what they say, sign them."

"What are they?" Kozlow asked.

"They're consent forms to let me be your attorney. And more important, by acknowledging that the prosecutor is my wife, they also show that you've had full disclosure about the situation and that I've obtained adequate consent. That way, if we lose, you can't go tell the appellate court that you need a new trial because you didn't know we were husband and wife."

"So if I don't sign these, I can still get that appeal."

"Sure you can. But if you don't sign them, Sara won't bring the case. She's too smart to not require this paperwork."

As Kozlow leaned over to sign his name, Jared said to Kathleen, "Have you been able to get in touch with Doniger's neighbor or the officer yet?"

"Why so early?" Kathleen asked. "We usually wait until after the grand jury. At this point, we don't even know if they'll indict."

"I don't care. I want you to call them," Jared said, refusing to take his eyes off Kozlow. "When it comes to this case, we have to pretend the worst has already happened."

* * *

At four o'clock that afternoon, Sara picked up her phone and dialed Jared's number. Kathleen put her through.

"What do you want?" Jared answered.

"Nice greeting," Sara said. "Very warm."

"Sorry, I don't have time right now. Are you okay?"

"I'm fine."

"Are you sure?"

"Of course I'm sure. Why wouldn't I be?"

"No reason," Jared said. "So what do you want?"

Surprised by her husband's tone, she asked, "What's wrong with you?"

"I'm just busy with the case. Now what's up?"

"I wanted to make sure you know about the consent forms so we can—"

"I already had them drawn up and sent out. They'll be there first thing in the morning."

"Good," Sara said. "Now are we still on for dinner tonight?"

"Dinner? Oh, crap, I forgot. I'm sorry. I'll never make it in time; I'm completely swamped."

"Jared, don't give me that. You promised Pop you'd be there."

"I know, but—"

"But what? You have too much work? Kozlow hasn't even been indicted yet."

"Don't start with me," Jared said. "If you do your job, I need to be prepared for the results."

"Fine, pull an all-nighter. It won't do you any good—I'm still going to kill you in court."

Jared didn't respond to the jab.

"Hello?" Sara said. "Is anyone there? Someone who can take a joke, perhaps?"

"Listen, I have to go," Jared said. "I'll see you at home."

Sara heard a click and her husband was gone.

"Everything okay?" Guff asked, looking through the case files on Sara's desk.

"I don't think so. He's working awfully hard, considering there's no indictment."

"Maybe he's just trying to get ahead on things."

"Maybe," Sara said. "But I can tell when my husband's nervous, and right now, something's got him crazy. From here on in, the honeymoon's over."

CHAPTER 7

At seven that evening, Sara and Guff stood outside the Second Avenue Deli, where the smell of kosher pickles and fried knishes drifted through the air. As a stream of East Siders followed their noses into the land of giant pastrami sandwiches and insulting waiters, Sara noticed the chilly air. "Winter's on her way," she said.

"You think?" Guff asked, blowing into his cupped hands and jogging in place to stay warm. "Now tell me again why your grandfather wants us standing out here when it's nice and warm inside?"

"Guff, I told you ten times already—don't call him my grandfather. He's Pop. He likes being called Pop. That's what we call him. And if we want to eat with him, we have to meet him outside. Otherwise, he thinks we're not meeting him, and he'll go home. Trust me, it sounds ridiculous, but it's no joke. I've been stood up enough times to know."

"He's a real character, huh?"

"That's why I invited you. He may be my closest surviving relative, but he's a little overwhelming one-on-one. If you have two people against him, he's easier on the senses."

"Why didn't Jared come?"

"Jared said he was busy, but I think it's also because he and Pop don't always see eye-to-eye."

"Why?"

"When Jared and I first started going out, Pop said that Jared wasn't the right type for me."

"So?"

"So, he said it to Jared's face—the night they first met."

"I assume you disagreed."

"Of course. Regardless of what my Pop says, Jared's always been *the one*."

"How'd you know?"

"What do you mean how'd I know? There's no one reason. You just sort of . . . know."

"Don't give me that sentimental claptrap. There must be something you can point to—one incident that gave you some kind of sign."

Thinking for a moment, Sara said, "Actually, there was this one thing. When I was little, around nine or ten, my dad started going on a ton of business trips—he was a salesman for a women's clothing company. At the same time, I started having this recurring nightmare about being deaf. It was terrifying. Everyone would be talking, but I couldn't hear anything. And then, even if I was screaming at the top of my lungs, no one could hear me. This went on for almost two years."

"Because you missed your father."

"Exactly. When my mom took me to a psychologist, he told her that the nightmare was based on my fear of being alone. Since I was an only child, and my parents were away from home a lot, it was a natural occurrence. With some help, I eventually got over my little prepubescent fears and moved on with my life. Then, twelve years later, my parents died. And the nightmare came back. The same terrible, haunting dream: I'm ten again, I'm deaf, and even though I'm screaming like a maniac, I can't hear myself, and no one can hear me. This time, though, no matter how hard I tried, no matter how many psychobabble techniques I used, I couldn't shake it. It was torturing me. But when I started going out with Jared, the dream suddenly disappeared. I haven't had it since. And that's at least one of the reasons I knew he was the one. Naturally, Pop disagrees, but that's just his nature."

"I don't understand—how can one person be that bad?"

"You'll see," Sara warned with a smile. "And let me give you one last hint: When you're stuck for something to say, don't ask him about the garment industry."

Expecting a crotchety old man, Guff was surprised when Pop finally turned the corner. With soft, alert eyes and a mild smile, the old man was far more sympathetic looking than Guff had imagined. As he got closer, Guff also realized how big he was. A former beat cop in Brooklyn, Pop was no longer a mass of muscle, but in his determined, lumbering strides, Guff could see hints of the man he used to be.

After giving Sara a kiss hello, Pop stared at Guff. After a moment he asked, "What's wrong with your hair? Is it fake?"

"It's real," Guff said. "And I'm Guff. Nice to meet you, Pop."

"Call me Pop," Pop said as he shook Guff's hand.

"And I'm just kidding about the hair part. Just good fun and all that." Guff shot a look at Sara as they followed Pop into the restaurant. "Where's that suck-up husband of yours?"

"He's working on a case," Sara explained. "He said to send you his best."

"Don't lie to me, sister. I've been stood up by better than him."

"I'm sure you have," Sara said.

The hostess seated Guff, Sara, and Pop in a booth in the back of the restaurant. "So is this place any good?" Guff asked.

"Good?" Pop said. "This is the Second Avenue Deli! They've been putting out pastrami since Eisenhower first scratched his giant-sized forehead in the White House."

"Eisenhower had a big forehead?" Guff asked.

"Oh, yeah," Pop said. "Ike had a huge melon. So did Jack Kennedy. Only difference was, Kennedy had hair. Look at the pictures—it's true."

"I never knew that," Guff said, fighting back a smile. "Who else had a big head?"

"My gosh, back then, everyone did. That's why we all wore hats. Goldwater, Nixon, Milton Berle, even that fella de Gaulle from France—he had a giant one. It was like a secret code."

"Secret code?"

"Oh, sure. Wearing a hat meant something. It's like the letters in a deck of cards. Add them together and you get—"

"The number fifty-two!" Guff said, now excited. "I know that code!"

As Sara started laughing, so did Pop.

"What's so funny?" Guff asked. The two struggled to catch their breath. "Wait a minute—you told him about my deck of cards thing, didn't you?"

"And you fell for it!" Pop said.

"I'm sorry," Sara added, "but when you got so excited, I couldn't help myself."

"That's beautiful," Guff said, picking up a menu and putting it in front of his face. "Just pick on the new guy. If it makes the Tate family feel good to be bully for the day, be my guest."

Outside the deli, the man with the sunken cheeks leaned on a silver parked car. He was in his early thirties, but his stark features made his age hard to guess. From his vantage point he had a clear view of Sara, Guff, and Pop. For five minutes he stared at them, lingering over Pop's features. There's another chink in her armor, the man thought as he crossed his arms.

"So how are you enjoying your new job?" Pop asked as he picked up his pastrami and corned beef sandwich. "Fun or dreck?"

"Fun," Sara said.

"And about to get even funner," Guff said. "Tell him about the case."

"What case?" Pop asked.

"Nothing . . ."

"Tell me," Pop insisted. "Listen to your friend."

"It's not that big a deal," Sara said. "In my first case, Jared and I are going up against each other."

"So that's it," Pop said. "No wonder he's not here. You're at each other's throats?"

"No, not yet," Sara said, picking at a potato pancake. "He's just been working hard, which makes me—"

"It makes you nervous, doesn't it?" Pop asked.

Sara put down her fork and pushed away her plate. "Not only is he a great lawyer, but he knows me better than anyone."

"Well, you have nothing to worry about. When it comes to convincing a jury, you're much more believable than he is—no matter how much preparation he does. He's had it easy his entire life, and people notice those things."

"Pop, please don't say that. He's worked very hard to get where he is—he hasn't had it easy."

"He *has*. He had it easy when I first met him, with his hotshot Yale cuff links, and he has it easy today. I love him like a son, but he doesn't know what it's like to struggle. He has no sense of appreciation." Turning to Guff, Pop added, "First day I met him, we came right here, to my favorite deli, and he tries to pick up the check. Then he eats only half his sandwich, and I tell him to have it wrapped up so he can take it home. He says, 'Why don't you have it? It'll just go to waste if I take it.' Can you believe the gall?"

"I'm surprised you let him marry Sara at all," Guff said.

"Guff, don't encourage him," Sara begged. "And Pop, please drop it."

"Fine, fine, consider it dropped. But believe me, a jury won't buy what he's selling. They'll be more impressed with you—you're real people. Real, hardworking American people."

"That's great, Pop. Now if you could only tell that to my boss."

At half past ten, Sara finally arrived at home. She hung up her coat in the closet and walked into the kitchen. Opening the refrigerator, she stared inside, looking for nothing in particular. Suddenly, she heard footsteps behind her and felt a hand on her shoulder. She grabbed the neck of a bottle of wine. Spinning around, she swung it through the air, but stopped herself short. It was Jared.

"Don't do that!" Sara said as she lowered the bottle. "You scared me!"

"Sorry, I didn't mean to," Jared said, embracing his wife.

"What? Now you're suddenly being nice to me?"

"I missed you. I was worried about you."

"Then why were you such a jerk on the phone before?"

"I was just really busy," Jared said. "You know how I get when I'm working." As he continued to hug his wife, he added, "Do you know how much I love you?"

"Of course."

"No, really," Jared said, looking intently in Sara's eyes. "Do you know how much I care about you? And how much I worry about you? Do you know I'd do anything for you?"

"Absolutely," Sara said, wondering what had brought on this rush of emotion. "Jared, are you sure everything's okay at work?"

"It's fine. Everything's fine."

"Good. That's what I like to hear." She gave him a kiss. "I just don't want to see this case come between us."

"It won't," Jared said, holding his wife tight. Over her shoulder, he caught a glimpse of the six portraits that Sara had done of him. The broken glass was long swept away, but the pictures were now unprotected. Staring at the vulnerable images of himself, Jared pulled her closer. "Nothing'll happen," he whispered. "I promise."

"Can you get Barrow on the line for me?" Jared asked Kathleen the moment he walked into the office the following morning. "It's important."

"He really has you scared, doesn't he?" Kathleen asked.

"What're you talking about?"

"Kozlow. That's what you want from Barrow, isn't it? You want him to take a deeper look at Kozlow?"

As always, Kathleen was on the mark. But that didn't mean he was going to tell her the rest. That would only put her at risk. "Why would I want to investigate my own client?" he asked.

"C'mon, Jared, don't treat me like an imbecile. You can't hide the bags under your eyes—you haven't slept well in days. Since the day you met him, you've been running yourself ragged. And you're getting to work so early, you're almost catching up with me. Besides, it doesn't take a genius to figure out the guy is bad news."

Jared looked around the office. No one would hear. "What makes you think that?"

"Haven't you read his old file yet?"

"I know he's got two arrests, but I haven't had a chance to get through the rest of it. I've been busy with everything else."

"Or maybe you've been putting it off because you're afraid of what you'll find."

His jaw shifted. "Just tell me what it says."

Checking the hallway herself, Kathleen leaned

forward on her elbows. "If I were you, I'd be careful with him. The guy's a walking time bomb.
Two years ago, he had a run-in with a Brooklyn
lowlife named Joey Gluck. According to the file,
Joey comes home from a night of heavy drinking,
arm in arm with a local prostitute. They quickly
get undressed, but what they don't know is that
Kozlow, the little maniac, is hiding under the bed.
As Joey is about to jump in the sack, Kozlow
takes a switchblade and nails Joey's bare foot to
the floor. Then he crawls out and pushes Joey backwards, just to make it hurt a bit more. The scary
thing is that when the case goes to trial, Joey un-
expectedly decides to change his testimony. Says
he suddenly can't remember anything."

"What about the prostitute?"

"They found her body the night after the attack. Heroin overdose, if you believe the autopsy."

"You think Kozlow killed her?"

"You tell me. Here's case number two: A con-
struction worker named Roger Hacker comes
home after a long day of work, heads straight for
the bathroom, and takes a seat on the toilet. Suddenly, Roger thinks he hears a noise in the shower.
Before the poor guy can even stand up, the shower
curtain flies open and Kozlow jumps out. From
what they could piece together, Kozlow punches
Roger in the Adam's apple and sends him to the
floor. Kozlow kicks him in the face, and the head,
and then one final one right in Roger's shoulder.
Collarbone shattered. For Kozlow, the message has
been sent. Then our boy Roger does something
stupid. He climbs to his feet, grabs a screwdriver
from his nearby tool belt, and lunges at Kozlow as
he's leaving the apartment. Poor Roger never knew
what hit him. The next-door neighbor, who of

course wound up changing his testimony at the trial, said it sounded like someone was torturing a cat. And when the police finally arrived, they found the screwdriver jammed straight into Roger's throat, while his eyes—"

"I don't want to hear any more," Jared interrupted.

"Let me just finish the last part: When they did the autopsy on Roger, they found at least a dozen wounds that they identified as postmortem blows—which means that even after Roger was dead, Kozlow kept tearing him apart just for fun."

"I said I don't want to hear it."

"Jared, I know it's not the best news, but you're dealing with a killer. You have to—"

"Please don't tell me what I have to do. Just call Barrow and let him know I want two people checked out. The first one's Kozlow; the second one's Oscar Rafferty."

"Who's Oscar Rafferty?"

"That's what I want to find out."

"Then that's what we're doing," Kathleen replied. "I'll make sure we get everything: backgrounds, bank accounts, wives, club memberships, anything that's revealing."

"And tell him to keep it close to his chest. I don't want Rafferty getting wind of it."

She wasn't used to seeing Jared so paranoid. "This really isn't safe, is it?"

"Not if they find out."

"Want to talk about it?"

Jared paused. "No. Not now."

Kathleen stared at her boss. In the four years she'd known Jared, she had learned to tell the difference between when he was serious and when he wanted her to pry further. Today wasn't a day to pry. "Whenever you're ready, I'm here," she said. Down the hallway, Kathleen noticed Kozlow walking toward them, led by one of the firm's receptionists. She motioned to Jared, and then, in a loud voice, announced, ". . . and after that, I'll have them pull all the cases that deal with burglaries. You'll have it by lunch."

"Thanks," Jared said, eyeing Kozlow.

Dressed in his standard three-quarter-length leather jacket, Kozlow strolled into Jared's office. A small metal chain dangled from the front pocket of his faded jeans. "So what are we doing today? More legal stuff?"

"Yeah, more legal stuff." Jared followed Kozlow into his office as Kathleen thanked the receptionist. "Now get in here so we can get started. Today, we work on your testimony."

"I'm testifying? At the grand jury?"

"Without a doubt," Jared said, taking a seat at his desk. "If we can get your story into a more believable form, we might be able to convince the grand jury not to indict. And if by some miracle they like you, chances are, they won't vote against you."

"Everyone likes me," Kozlow insisted as he took a seat across from Jared's desk. "Now what do I have to do?"

"First, I want you to get a good suit."

"I have a good suit."

"I'm sure you do, but I want you to have a business suit. Like mine."

Kozlow looked at Jared's pin-striped navy-blue suit. "Why would I want to dress like you?"

"There's a good reason," Jared said. He hit the intercom button on his phone. "Kathleen, can you come in here one second?" When Kathleen entered the room, Jared continued, "At about ten o'clock, I'd like you to take Mr. Kozlow shopping. He'll need a conservative business suit, a nice understated tie, some loafers, and some wire-framed glasses. He needs to look believable."

"I'm impressed—I haven't been dressed that nice since the service," Kozlow said.

"You were in the military?"

"Yeah, army for a bit. Now tell me who's paying for all this."

"It's billed to Rafferty as an expense," Jared said. "Nothing we do here is free. But if you want to convince people you're innocent, the first step is looking the part."

When Kathleen left, Jared pulled a legal pad from his briefcase. He was trying his best to treat this as if it were any other case, but he could feel his impatience growing. "Let's go over your story. Tell me your version of it."

"I was walking down the street, minding my own business, and some cop grabs me and tells me I'm under arrest," Kozlow explained, his hands waving to accentuate his point. "Then he takes me to this woman's house and says to her, 'This is the guy that robbed your house, isn't it?'"

"Is that the way he asked the question?" Jared asked as he made some notes. "Was it leading like that?"

"Oh, yeah. She couldn't say anything but yes."

That'll work, Jared thought. "Now, where did you get the Ebel watch?"

"I found that on the street as I was walking."

"And what about the silver golf ball?"

"I found that in the garbage. I thought it was my lucky night."

Jared stared angrily at Kozlow. "You're going to

have to come up with some better answers than
that. The grand jury isn't that stupid."

"How about this: He planted them both on me."

"If the cop has a sketchy background, that may
work. Now what about the four hundred and
seventeen dollars?"

"That was my money," Kozlow insisted. "It was
even in my money clip when the cop pulled it
from my pocket. Ask him—he'll tell you."

"Fine, I'll ask him," Jared said impatiently. "Now
what about this: If you live in Brooklyn, what were
you doing on the Upper East Side at three in the
morning?"

Kozlow stopped. "That's a pretty good question. I hadn't thought of that before."

Jared threw his pad on the desk. "Well, think
now! We need a good answer. Without that, we're
going to get eaten alive in there."

"Why? Rafferty said there's no cross-
examination in a grand jury. If that's how it
goes, then ask me all the softball questions."

"There's no cross-examination because only
one lawyer is allowed to talk in a grand jury. And
that lawyer is the assistant district attorney. Sara
can ask you whatever she wants, and I can only sit
there."

"Then maybe I shouldn't testify."

Jared leapt from his seat and strode around the
desk. "Listen carefully to what I'm saying. I'm the
lawyer here. Not you. Now if you were any other
client, I wouldn't give a damn if you lost this case.
But I'm going to do everything I can to win it,
and I'm not letting some dumb monkey wreck it
for me. So if you're not serious about this, tell me
and I'll—"

Kozlow jumped up and shoved Jared, sending

him crashing into the wall. Grabbing him by the lapels, Kozlow pressed his elbows into Jared's rib cage. "What'd I tell you yesterday? I'm not an idiot, so stop treating me like one."

As the adrenaline wore off, Jared knew he was in trouble. "I'm sorry, I didn't mean—"

"I know exactly what you meant," Kozlow said, letting go of Jared. While Jared readjusted his shirt and tie, Kozlow silently stared out the window, pressing his head against the glass. He lightly tapped the window with his forehead. "If I testify, do we really have a better chance of winning?"

"If you testify and you're *believable*, we can start learning the victory dance tonight. Misidentification cases are some of the easiest cases to confuse a jury on. Come up with a rational reason for why you were there, and the rest is easy. You know how many New Yorkers are running around in dark jeans and a dark leather coat?"

"Half a million?"

"At least," Jared said. "Now let's start over so we can get your story straight."

"So Victor has never prosecuted Kozlow before?" Sara asked, leaning over Guff's shoulder and staring at the computer screen.

"That's what it says," Guff replied. "Both of Kozlow's cases were done by ADAs who no longer work here. But that doesn't mean Victor and Kozlow don't know each other. For all we know, Victor might've used Kozlow as a witness, or an informant, or for any other reason."

"Can we check that through here?"

"Not really. AJIS is mostly an abridged database—just the main facts. There's a section for witness lists, but most of them aren't filled in. If we want to see every person involved, we have to go through the files manually."

"Fine. Let's do it."

"Sara, Victor's been in this office for almost fifteen years. We're talking close to a thousand case files—each of them six inches thick. Just to pull the files will take at least a week."

"I don't care. I want those files."

"But—"

"Guff, if there's a connection between Victor and Kozlow, I'm going to find it. And I don't care how long it takes me or how many pages I have to read."

"It's your eyesight."

"Actually, it's yours, too," Sara pointed out. "Now we've got until one o'clock, when Doniger gets here. If you can get the most recent files, we can start now and work our way backwards."

"So I shouldn't get them all at once?"

"No—I don't want Victor finding out about this. If he realizes what we're doing, we're dead. Order fifty of his cases, fifty of Conrad's and fifty of some other hotshot's. If anyone asks, tell them we're studying how the best ADAs win in court."

Guff smiled wide. "You're really getting into this, aren't you?"

"Damn right I am. For the first time since this started, I know exactly what I'm doing."

"What the hell am I doing?" Sara groaned four and a half hours later, her desk and most of her office submerged under piles of case folders and storage boxes. "This is absolutely hopeless."

"I warned you," Guff said. "But did you listen? No. Did you trust me? No. Did you go off on your own, and act all cocky, and think you were going to save the day with one simple idea? Yes, yes, and yes. And what do we have to show for it? Dust. Dust on our hands, dust on my tie, dust in my lap. I'm serious, missy, I'm not happy about this. Not happy one bit."

"Guff, did anyone see you put in the request for these?"

"I don't think so."

"And is there any way to tell if someone else checked them out before us?"

"There should be, why?"

"I'm just trying to figure out if Victor knows what's going on. I mean, maybe he already went in and altered some of the files."

"Now you're being neurotic. The sad truth is that there's no mention of anyone. Not Kozlow, not Doniger, not Doniger's neighbor, nobody."

"Speaking of which, where is Doniger?" Sara asked, looking at her watch. "She was supposed to be here at one."

"She's only a half hour late," Guff said. "Give it time. She'll be here."

"I don't know," Sara said, leafing through the file on her lap. "I have a bad feeling about this. This is just another thing that stinks."

"Why? Just because your prime witness is late for her interview? Big deal. We can't find the witness in the pickpocket case either."

"Guff, you know it's different."

"Listen, we're hunting through every file in this building. That'll tell us if Victor has any other ties to Kozlow or Doniger. But until that happens, you can't keep thinking everyone's a boogeyman."

"But what if everyone *is* a boogeyman?"

"Forget about the imaginary monsters and focus

on the real ones. You still have four other misdemeanor cases to deal with, as well as this felony and its big bad grand jury. And since the misdemeanor courts are backlogged beyond capacity, this may be the only one where you're going to get a chance to strut your stuff. So if you don't get the grand jury to indict, you're not getting to trial. And if you don't get to trial, it doesn't matter how suspicious everyone is acting."

"I know, I know—you're right—if I mess up this trial, there's no way I'm saving my—" Sara's thought was interrupted when her phone started ringing. "ADA Tate," she answered.

"Sara, this is Claire Doniger."

"Of course, Ms. Doniger," Sara said. "Where are you? Is everything okay?"

"I'm fine, dear. I just wanted to have a word with you about this burglary case. I was thinking about it last night, and I realized that I really can't spare the time that you require. For that reason, I've decided that I don't want to press charges. Considering that I got all my belongings back, I'm willing to turn the other cheek."

"Turn the other cheek?" Sara asked, stunned. "That doesn't make any—"

"I know it's short notice, but that's how I feel," Doniger interrupted. "So you can just call the case off."

"Actually, it doesn't work like that. Once we arrest someone, we're the only ones who can decide to drop a case. And that's our decision to make, not yours."

"Well, then I guess you know exactly what you're doing," Doniger said, sounding insulted. "Hopefully, though, you'll stop interfering with my life."

"Ma'am, I never meant—"

"We don't need to get into it. I'm busy enough as it is. Good-bye."

As Sara hung up the phone, Guff asked, "What's going on? She wants you to drop the case?"

"So she says."

"Do you think she'll still testify?"

"I'm not sure," Sara said, reaching for the phone. "But just in case she doesn't . . ."

"Who're you calling?"

"Doniger's next-door neighbor. If we can't get the victim, I want to make sure we still have Patty Harrison. And truthfully, she's our best witness— she's the only person who saw Kozlow actually leaving Doniger's house." Sara quickly dialed Harrison's number.

"Hello?" a voice answered.

"Ms. Harrison, this is Sara Tate from the district attorney's office. I know we were supposed to meet this afternoon, but I was wondering if we could move your appointment to some time earlier today."

"Oh, no. I'm sorry, Ms. Tate, but I can't give that testimony anymore."

"Excuse me?"

"I can't do it," Harrison stuttered. "I'm far too busy—you'll have to find someone else. I'm very sorry. Have a nice day." With that, Harrison hung up.

Sara looked up at Guff. "What the hell is going on?" she asked.

"Don't tell me she's out, too."

"If she is, we're in serious trouble," Sara said as she redialed Harrison's number. The phone rang five times before Harrison picked up.

"Hello?" Harrison said, her voice soft and anxious.

"Ms. Harrison, this is Sara Tate calling again."

"I'm sorry, but—"

"Listen to me, Ms. Harrison," Sara interrupted. "I'm not sure who threatened you, but I want you to know that if you give us their names, you'll never hear from them again."

"No one threatened me," Harrison shot back. "No one at all. Now please leave me alone."

"Ms. Harrison, yesterday you said you'd be happy to testify. Today, I can't keep you on the phone for thirty seconds. Now, I understand you're scared, but if you don't testify, you're only encouraging this kind of behavior. If you truly want to feel safe, tell me who approached you, and I'll have our officers pick them up within the hour. There's no reason for you to be afraid."

"I'm not afraid."

"How about if I come over there right now? That way we can talk and—"

"No!" Harrison insisted. "You can't come over here. Now, I appreciate what you're trying to do, but I've made up my mind. Good-bye."

As Sara put down the receiver, Guff said, "I can't believe you just confronted her like that."

"Oh, c'mon," Sara said. "There's no reason to tiptoe around. Kozlow's done this two times before—there's no way he's not responsible now." Hearing a knock on the door, she shouted, "Who is it?"

Victor opened the door and stepped inside. Sara and Guff simultaneously closed the folders they were holding and fell silent.

"Can I help you?" Sara asked, straightening a pile of files and trying her best to block Victor's view of her desk.

"Just came to see how things were going,"

Victor said. He looked around the office. "What's with the old cases?"

"Extra research," Sara stammered. "Trying to be as thorough as possible."

"Whatever makes you feel secure. Just be sure you don't lose track of the real problem."

"Thanks for the advice. Now is there anything else? I'm incredibly swamped."

"I think that's it," Victor said, tapping his knuckle against one of the file boxes. "Be careful, though. I know it's a hard idea to swallow, but you're not as smart as you think." When Victor left the room, Sara waited until the door slammed behind him.

"What was that about?" Guff asked.

"He knows," Sara said, collapsing in her seat.

"Knows what?"

"That we have his old files. That's why he came in here—to tell us that he's watching. He knows about the files, he knows about the case, and even though he'd deny it, he knows what happened to our witnesses."

"What do you mean they're not testifying?" Jared asked.

"Just what I said," Rafferty answered, his voice sounding grainy as it came through the telephone. "They're not testifying. For some reason, they've both had second thoughts."

Looking up at Kozlow, who was riffling through a magazine in the back of the office, Jared felt suddenly light-headed. "Can you hold on a second?" he asked Rafferty. Before Rafferty could reply, Jared put down the phone and went out to Kathleen's desk. "What time were you done shopping with Kozlow this morning?"

"About a quarter to twelve, why?"

"And then what'd you do?"

"He said he had some errands to run, so I went to pick out some ties," Kathleen said hesitantly. "We met up about an hour later. Why? What's wrong?"

"So he was alone for at least an hour?" Jared asked.

"He came back late, so it was actually almost an hour and fifteen min—"

"Jesus," Jared said. He rushed back into his office and picked up the phone. "You shouldn't have threatened them," he said to Rafferty.

"Threaten them? I did no such thing," Rafferty said. "That would be against the law."

"That's not funny."

"Just be happy and enjoy the good news. It should make your case that much easier."

As Rafferty hung up, there was a knock on Jared's door. "Come in," Jared said.

Sticking her head into the room, Kathleen said, "I'm really sorry. I didn't—"

"Don't worry—you couldn't have known." Noticing the pink message sheet in her hand, he added, "Did someone call?"

"Lubetsky wants to know if you're finished with the AmeriTex motions."

"Oh, shit," Jared said, shuffling through the pile of papers that covered his desk. "Tell him he'll have them first thing in the morning."

"He said to remind you that it has to be filed by five o'clock this afternoon."

Startled, Jared looked up at Kathleen. "You're kidding, right?"

"Not a chance."

"Okay," Jared said as he glanced at his watch.

"That gives me three and a half hours." Turning on his computer, he opened the AmeriTex file. "I'm going to need two paralegals to do some research and a third- or fourth-year associate for the procedural issue. Have them meet me in a conference room in a half hour."

"Any associates in particular?" Kathleen asked.

"Anyone who's good," Jared said as Kathleen shut the door.

"I'm impressed," Kozlow said. "But what makes you so sure everyone else is going to drop what they're doing?"

"This is a big law firm," Jared said. "With 168 partners, 346 associates, and a hundred-something paralegals, we can always find someone. That's what you pay the big money for."

"Is that why you do it? The big money?"

"That's part of it."

"And what's the other part?"

Surprised by the interest in Kozlow's voice, Jared took a second to respond. This was his chance to break through, he thought. If anger hadn't worked this morning, maybe honesty would work now. "You want to know the real reason I keep doing defense work? It's because I think there's enough justice to go around," Jared explained. "All I'm doing is distributing it to the side that sometimes gets shut out."

"You sound like a Boy Scout."

"That's what Sara says," Jared replied. Hoping to stay on topic, he added, "Speaking of which, why don't you tell me what happened with Doniger and Harrison?"

Kozlow fell silent and shut his magazine. His eyes narrowed in anger. "Don't ever do that again."

"What?" Jared asked, taken aback.

"Don't play fuckin' stupid, Jared—I'm not going to be your little friend."

"I just thought we were—"

"Shut the hell up!" Kozlow shouted, his voice
booming through the office. "Shut up and do your
job."

"You must be kidding me," Conrad said, leaning forward on the front of Sara's desk.

"Not a bit," Sara said. "He walked in right as
I hung up with Harrison. The files were everywhere."

"I knew I should've stopped you on this. There's
no reason for you to be investigating someone like
Victor."

"I'm not going after Victor—I'm just trying to
figure out why he wanted the case."

"Either way, you better be careful. He's not
someone you mess with. If he finds out what you're
doing—"

"I know. I've been thinking about that all afternoon. And even if I can handle Victor, I still don't
know what to do with Doniger and Harrison. Both
of them said they won't testify."

"They'll testify," Conrad insisted, pushing himself away from the desk. "They just don't know
it yet."

"Uh-oh—here he goes," Guff said. "Make way
for the testosterone parade."

"I'm serious," Conrad said. "They can cry and
whine all they want, but they'll be there Monday
morning. Guff, have you prepared a travel kit for
Sara?"

"Had it ready the day she got here," Guff said
proudly. He left the office, then returned with a

brown accordion file that he placed in front of Sara.

"Open it," Conrad said to Sara.

The file was divided by alphabetical tabs. "It's under *S*," Guff said.

She reached into the *S* section of the file and pulled out the small stack of papers.

"Know what those are?" Conrad asked.

"Blank subpoenas," Sara answered.

"You got it, Clarence. When you completed your paperwork on your first day here, you gained the power of the pen, also known as subpoena power. Sign two of those, serve them on our witnesses, and by the order of the law of the state of New York, they'll have to have their asses sitting in that grand jury on Monday. Terrified or not."

"I don't know," Sara said. "Doniger was a bit rude, but Harrison really seemed scared. I wouldn't want anything to happen to—"

"Don't ever do that again," Conrad interrupted, raising his voice.

"Do what?" Sara asked.

"Go on the defensive like that. You're an assistant district attorney—you don't back down to threats. Bringing them in is part of the job. I'd never want you to put a witness at risk, but giving up isn't the solution."

"Then what is?"

"You tell me. Solve the problem."

"Conrad, enough with the lecturing-lawyer shtick."

"Then you'd better come up with a real solution. Solve the problem."

"You want me to solve it? Then this is what I'm doing: Instead of hitting her with the subpoena tonight, I'll have a couple of officers serve it on her early Monday morning. That way, if there's any trouble, the officers are there to protect her. And they'll also be there to make sure she comes in."

Conrad was silent for a moment. Finally, he said, "Good. That's a nice start."

"Then let's discuss how this happened in the first place. I assume we all agree it was Kozlow?"

"Hey, boss," Guff interrupted. "It's two-thirty."

"Are you serious?" Sara asked, looking at her watch. She stood up. "I'm sorry, but I really have to run. I have an appointment I can't miss."

"What about preparing for the grand jury?" Conrad asked. "You've barely scratched the surface."

"Trust me, that's my top priority," Sara said, grabbing her jacket from the coatrack. "Grand jury means *indictment*, which means *trial*, which means *win*, which means *happily ever after*. There's no way I'm losing in the first round—especially when there's still so much to dig up."

"That's a wonderful use of the transitive property, but when are you actually going to prepare for this miraculous event?"

"We have tomorrow, and Guff said we could all meet this weekend."

"Really?" Conrad asked, looking at Guff.

"What's the big fuss?" Guff said. "You're here every weekend."

"I'm busy tomorrow, but I can do Saturday," Conrad said. "Let's not forget I have my own cases to deal with."

"I know—and I really appreciate the help," Sara said, dashing for the door. "I'll see you both tomorrow."

"Hold on," Conrad said. "Don't run out just yet.

What's so important that you have to leave right now?"

"I have a meeting with my little sister."

"You have a sister?"

"Not a real sister," Sara said. "I volunteer as a mentor through the Big Sisters program."

"Really?" Conrad asked. "What do you do on the weekends? Donate blood or feed the homeless?"

"That's original," Sara said sarcastically.

"How long have you been doing it?"

"Since about a month after I got fired from my law firm. That was about how long it took for me to get sick of sitting around waiting for the phone to ring. I figured this was better for my psyche than paying for that extra session at the therapist—not to mention far more fun."

"Well, I think it's nice," Guff said. "Good for you."

"Thanks for the approval," Sara said. "And while I'd love to recruit you both to the cause, I've really got to go. I'm late."

"One last thing," Conrad said. "When you get home tonight, talk to your husband about your witnesses. Tomorrow morning, we have to figure out what the hell is going on."

"Consider it done," Sara said as she ran to the door.

At twenty after three, Sara crossed 116th Street and ran up Amsterdam Avenue. On her right were the modern, state-of-the-art facilities of her alma mater, Columbia Law School, and on her left were the timeworn, regal buildings of Columbia University. As she headed north, however, the buildings became far less majestic, and in the span of one block, marble statues, Gothic architecture, and sculpted archways gave way to run-down storefronts, beat-up automobiles, and the worst of the city's potholed streets. At 121st Street, Columbia University officially ended. And as Sara had learned during her first year at the law school, there was a clear line between the Ivy League and Harlem, New York.

When Sara reached Ralph Bunche Elementary School, the front entrance of the battered brick building was humming with hundreds of kids glad to be done with the school day. As she turned the corner and made her way through the crowd of students, Sara heard a voice yell, "You're late." Sitting on the trunk of a white car was Tiffany Hamilton, Sara's little sister. Sara knew that Tiffany was tall for a seventh-grader, but her recent decision to start wearing lipstick made her look far older than thirteen. She had wide eyes, dark brown skin, and a long, immaculate braid that ran down her back. She also had an attitude that hit like a truck.

"I said, you're late," Tiffany repeated.

"I heard what you said," Sara said as she reached the car. "I just chose not to respond."

"Where were you?"

"At my job."

"Oh, that's right," Tiffany said, hopping off the car. Her pink lipstick was shining in the afternoon sun. "I forgot you started. Can you arrest people yet? Do they give you a badge?"

"No, we don't get a badge," Sara said, laughing. "We just get a bucketful of lipstick. These days, that can be quite a weapon—blinding our opponents and all that."

"Very funny," Tiffany said, squeezing her lips

together self-consciously. "So tell me more about work. Do you like it?"

"Of course I like it. This case I'm working on is driving me a little bit crazy, though."

"Really? Is it a murder? A shooting?"

"It's a burglary. And guess who the defense attorney is?"

"Perry Mason."

"How do you know who Perry Mason is?"

"I got a TV."

"Well, you're still wrong. Guess again."

"Is he fatter or thinner than Perry Mason?"

"What makes you think it's a man? Women can be lawyers."

"Okay, fatter or thinner?"

"Thinner."

"Uglier or better looking?"

"Better looking."

"Taller or shorter?"

"I don't know. Let's say the same."

"Now I know it's a guy. More or less hair?"

"Less," Sara laughed. "Especially in that one spot right on the back of his—"

"Jared?"

"The one and only."

"Oh, my God! You're going to wipe the floor with him! Can I come and watch?"

"We'll see," Sara said.

"What's it like going up against him? Is it weird? Is he scared?"

"I don't think he's too scared," Sara said as she thought about her two witnesses.

"That means he's beating you, doesn't it? How bad is it? Are you about to lose?"

"He's not beating me," Sara said. Hoping to

change the subject, she added, "Now tell me about school. How're you doing?"

"Great," Tiffany said as they passed Columbia Law School. "So where're we going today?"

"That depends. How'd you do on your math test?"

"Eighty-nine percent."

"I don't know—that's still not an A."

"C'mon, Sara, you said if I got it up to ninety—"

"I know what I said—and last I checked, eighty-nine is still lower than ninety."

"Sara, please. I worked all last week to get that grade. And I'm only one tiny point away. One teeny, tiny point."

"Fine, fine, fine. You're breaking my heart. Name your poison."

"Can we go back to the Metropolitan Museum of Art?"

"That's great with me, but answer this: Do you actually want to go to the Met, or do you just want to sit on the stairs and play Count the Tortured Artists?"

"I want to play Count the Tortured Artists. With fifty extra points for black berets."

"That's what I thought," Sara said. "Pick another poison."

"How about we go bowling and then eat dinner at Sylvia's?"

"I can't do dinner tonight," Sara said. "I have to prepare for—Hey!" Sara had the wind knocked out of her when someone walking in the opposite direction crashed into her. She lost her balance and fell back on the concrete. Caught up in the momentum, he stumbled over her.

Looking up, Sara saw a dark-haired man.

"I'm sorry," he said. "That was completely my fault."

"Don't worry about it." As Sara picked up her briefcase, she couldn't help but notice how his sunken cheeks punctuated the edges of his face.

"I guess I was thinking about something else," the man explained, taking a close look at Tiffany.

"Don't worry about it."

"Are you sure?"

"I'm positive," Sara said. "No harm done."

As she and Tiffany continued their walk toward the main part of campus, Tiffany said, "Freaky-looking guy, huh?"

"He was kind of weird," Sara admitted. When she readjusted her purse on her shoulder, she realized something felt wrong. She looked down in her purse. "Son of a bitch!" she shouted, spinning around.

"What?" Tiffany asked.

"That guy just lifted my wallet." Sara ran as fast as she could up Amsterdam Avenue and turned the corner on 117th Street. The stranger was gone.

CHAPTER
8

Climbing the stairs to his apartment, Jared noticed that the broken glass was completely cleaned up and the picture of the sunflowers had been reset in a new frame. The night of the break-in was now a two-day-old memory, but to Jared, the sound of crunching glass was still a raw wound. At the top of the stairs, he wondered why anyone would ever smash the hallway picture in the first place. It makes no sense, he thought. There's no benefit—except for the joy of mindless violence. And then it all became clear. To Kozlow, it's just a game.

Unable to shake the image of Kozlow smashing the original frame, Jared heard the entryway door on the first floor slam shut. Someone else was in the building. Was it Sara? No, the footsteps were too heavy. Refusing to look over the railing, Jared raced to find the key to his apartment. He dropped his briefcase to make it easier. Behind him, he could hear someone lumbering up the stairs. As he opened the top lock, his hands were shaking. Bottom lock, bottom lock, bottom lock, he thought, fishing for the key. When he finally put it in, he turned it toward the left. It was stuck. Damn it, not now! Open up, you prewar piece of—Suddenly, the lock clicked, the door flew open, and Jared stumbled inside. He slammed the door shut and looked through the peephole. The man on the stairs was Chris Guttman, their neighbor from the third floor.

Annoyed at his own paranoia, Jared headed for the bedroom. "Sara? You here?" There was no reply. He threw his briefcase down next to his nightstand and took a seat on the bed.

Take a breath, Jared told himself. Don't let him have this one. He went into the bathroom and splashed cold water on his face. Out of the corner of his eye, he thought he saw something move in the shower. He quickly pulled open the curtain. It was nothing. Empty. He ran back to the bedroom and checked under the bed. Then his closet. Then Sara's. Then the linen closet. Nothing in any of them. Empty. Empty. Empty. Without a doubt, there was no one else in the apartment. It didn't make Jared feel any safer.

By eight-thirty, Jared was sitting in the living room, fighting with the *New York Times* crossword and anxiously awaiting the return of his wife. She's fine, he told himself, glancing at his watch and then checking the clock on the VCR. It's a long commute—that's why she's late. In the past half hour, he'd called Sara's office three times. No answer. Determined to distract himself, Jared started wondering how she was going to react to two of her witnesses canceling on her. He imagined she'd first blame him, then start fishing for information. His analysis complete, he looked back at his watch. And the VCR clock. She's fine, he repeated. Please, let her be fine.

Ten minutes later, Sara finally arrived home. The moment Jared heard her key in the door, he pulled the paper back onto his lap. "How was your day?" he called out.

"It was wonderful," Sara said sarcastically. "First your client threatens two of my witnesses, then someone smashes into me and steals my wallet."

Putting down the paper, he first thought of Kozlow. "Are you all right?" he asked. "Where did it happen?"

Sara entered the living room and quickly relayed the story. "The son of a bitch got everything— credit cards, my license . . ."

"I hate to say it, but I told you you should get a purse with a better clasp," Jared said. Was it him? "Now tell me how my client threatened your witnesses."

"C'mon, Jared, you know what hap—"

"I honestly have no idea what you're talking about."

Sara approached Jared, leaned over, and stared straight into his eyes. "Say that again."

"I have no idea what you're talking about," Jared repeated, carefully pronouncing every syllable. Don't blink, he thought as he held his breath. Don't blink or she'll know.

Sara scrutinized her husband. If he was lying, he was getting better at it. Finally, she said, "I talked to both Ms. Doniger and Ms. Harrison after lunch and they both told me they didn't want to testify. Harrison was so scared, I could hear her sniffling on the other end of the phone."

"So you think Kozlow said something to them?"

"Who else?"

"There's no one else," Jared said firmly. "But I can tell you that Kozlow was with me all morning."

"What about the rest of the afternoon?"

"I was working on a motion for Lubetsky all afternoon. We had to crank it out by five. Anyway, I thought you said you heard from them right after lunch."

"I did," Sara said. "I was just checking."

"Well, you can stop with the accusations. I don't know what you're talking about," Jared said. Realizing that the longer he stayed on the topic, the more likely she was going to find him out, Jared switched subjects. "Let's get back to your wallet. How much money did we lose?"

"I don't know and I don't want to think about it," Sara said, flopping on the sofa. "I'm exhausted."

"Are you going in this weekend?" Jared asked anxiously.

"Yep. You?"

"Of course," he said. "So what do you want to do tonight?"

"Honestly, I just want to sit here and veg for a few hours."

"You in the mood to give a haircut?"

"Sure. Get the stuff." Sara had first cut Jared's hair during their second year of law school. When Jared came home butchered by the Columbia Barber Shop, Sara challenged that even she could do better. A month later, Jared gave her the chance. Since that day, he had never paid for another haircut.

After washing his hair in the shower, Jared entered the kitchen with a towel wrapped around his waist and took a seat at the table. Combing through his hair, Sara said, "It's getting mighty thin up here, my man."

"No doubt about that. When I'm outside, I can feel a cold breeze like never before. But if I'm meant to be bald, I'll be bald."

"Judging from the view, it's already been decided."

"That's great," he said. "Now, can I ask you another question about the case?"

"Fire away," Sara said, holding a clump of hair between two fingers.

"How would you feel about a dismiss and seal?"

"A what?" Sara asked as she started clipping.

"Dismiss and seal," Jared repeated, feeling the cut hair run down his shoulders. "It's a settlement. You agree to wipe out and seal Kozlow's file. There's no record of it and Kozlow is out of your hair—no pun intended—forever."

Sara stopped cutting, her brow furrowed. "And I benefit from this *how*?"

"To put it bluntly, you don't look like a fool. Instead of failing in the grand jury on Monday, or taking a loss at trial, you get to walk away before anything's counted against you. That way you don't start with a losing average."

With an angry snip, Sara chopped a large clump of hair in half.

"What's wrong with you?" Jared asked as he saw the remains fall to the floor.

"What makes you think I'm such a loser?"

"This isn't about you; it's about your case. You said it yourself—two of your witnesses canceled on you. You owe it to the city to not waste its resources. If they canceled, you shouldn't prosecute just for job stability's sake."

"First, I still have the cop. Second, of the two

that canceled, one came back. Doniger agreed to come in."

"She did?" Jared asked.

"Actually, no," Sara said as she resumed her cutting. "I made that up to see your reaction."

"You what?" Jared asked, pulling away.

That was all she needed. "You knew all along that they both dropped out, didn't you?"

Jared stood up to face his wife. She was closing in. "Sara, I—"

"Who told you?" Sara asked, pointing the scissors. "Was it someone in my office, or did Kozlow tell you himself?"

"I didn't—"

"It was Kozlow, wasn't it? Man, I'm going to charge him with tampering and intimidation first thing tomorrow."

"Sara, I really don't think it was him." Jared fought to maintain eye contact with his wife. That was the only way it worked. "Honestly. I swear."

"Then how'd you find out that Doniger and Harrison canceled?"

"They told me themselves. I called them to get their side of the story. There. Now you know." It wasn't a complete lie, Jared told himself, searching for confidence. After speaking to Rafferty, he did call them both to back up his story.

"And why'd you pretend not to know when I first walked in?"

He felt a flash of inspiration. "The same reason you lied about Doniger testifying—I wanted to see what you knew."

As she stared at her husband, a smile broke across her face.

"What?" Jared asked, forcing a smile of his own.

"Look at us. I mean, can we be more psychotic?"

Jared stared at his wedding ring. "Actually, we probably could."

"I'm sure we could. But that doesn't mean we have to play mind games."

"No, you're right," Jared said. He still had to push her a little farther. "It's just that this case—"

"I know it's important, but you really have to calm down about it," Sara said as she resumed her cutting. "Stop being so obsessed."

"Then start reading between the lines. I'm not doing this just for myself—I'm doing it for you."

"What're you talking about?"

Jared got up from his chair and faced his wife. "You should take another look at what you're working with. I know you're suspicious about what's going on, but you don't have the evidence to prove it. Your cop's unhelpful; your witnesses are hostile. If you take the dismiss and seal, at least you won't lose your first case. Then you can go in and pick up a better one. All I'm trying to do is help you, honey. And you and I both know that's the best way to show everyone that you're an asset to the office—let them see that you can move things along."

"I don't know."

"Sara, if you take these facts to trial, you're going to lose. And if you lose, in the blink of an eye, you're back on the unemployment line."

Sara didn't move. The way her lips were pressed together, Jared could tell she was upset. "How about pleading out for a reduced sentence?" she stuttered.

"No settlements," Jared said. He wanted to let up, but he couldn't. "So if you're happy going back on unemploy—"

"Stop saying that!" Sara shouted.

"Don't get mad at me—I didn't create the problem. I'm just trying to help you out of it. Now what do you say?"

Stepping away from her husband, Sara gazed aimlessly around the room. Jared knew he had her. The lying left a hole in his stomach, but it was about to pay off.

"Do you really think I'm going to lose?" Sara asked.

"Yes," he said without pause. "I really do."

"I'm serious. Don't lie about this one."

He took a deep breath. All he wanted to do was protect his wife. "I'm not lying to you, Sara."

"Then let me sleep on it. We can talk about it tomorrow."

Sara left the room and Jared closed his eyes. He was almost there.

Arched over the kitchen sink, Jared cleaned the remaining dishes from the Thai dinner they had ordered in. Although he knew he had to keep applying pressure, he felt, for the first time, that things were finally looking up. When the phone rang, he called out to Sara, "Hon, can you get that?"

Soon after, he heard Sara shout back, "It's for you."

Jared shut off the water, dried his hands with a nearby dish towel, and picked up the phone. "Hello?"

"Hi, Mr. Lynch, it's Bari Axelrod with American Health Insurance. I just wanted to get back to you with that address for Dr. Kuttler. A colleague just told me I could access it from your file."

"I'm sorry, but I have no idea what you're talking about."

There was an awkward pause on the other line. "I'm sorry, is this Jared Lynch?"

"Yes, it is."

"Mr. Lynch, can you give me your date of birth and social security number?"

"I don't think so. Now who'd you say you were again?"

"My name is Bari Axelrod and I'm with American Health Insurance, your insurance provider."

"Why do you need that information?" Jared asked suspiciously. "Don't you already have it?"

"Sir, I just spent a half hour on the phone with someone who said his name was Jared Lynch. If that wasn't you, I have to figure out who I'm speaking to. If it makes you feel any better, I know the last three claims you filed were for Doctors Koller, Wickett, and Hoffman, in that order. Believe me, I already have your information. Now, can you please give me your date of birth and social security number?"

Hesitantly, Jared obliged. "What did he want?"

"And for verification purposes, can you tell me which knee Dr. Koller treated you for?"

"My left. Now tell me what he said."

"He asked me to go through all of his expenses so he could get a better idea of what he spent."

"And you just gave him my confidential medical information?"

"I thought he was you. He gave me your birthdate and social security number. Said he was trying to put together a budget."

Wiping his forehead with the dish towel, Jared started pacing across the kitchen. "What exactly did you tell him?"

"I went through Dr. Hoffman's dental bills, Dr. Wickett's annual checkups, and the visit to Dr. Koller for your knee, including the charge for making the brace. And then when I got through those, he started asking about your wife."

"What'd you tell him?" Jared asked, his voice shaking.

"Sir, I had no idea—"

"Please just tell me what you told him."

"I just went over expenses. That's all we have here. Her prescriptions for birth-control pills, Seldane for allergies, and the four-month prescription for antidepressants from her psychiatrist. That's when he asked me for Dr. Kuttler's address or phone number. He said he wanted to check her rates. I didn't realize we had them here, so I asked him if he wanted to hold. He said it was no big deal, that he could look it up himself. And then when I found out that I could access them, I called you back and realized that—"

"I don't believe this," Jared said.

"I'm truly sorry, sir. He had your policy number, so I—"

"How would someone get that?"

"I have no idea. It's printed on your health insurance card. Have you lost your wallet recently?"

"Is everything okay?" Sara asked as she entered the kitchen.

Jared nodded to his wife and turned his attention back to the phone. "Ms. Axelrod, I'll have to call you back later. I don't have those papers in front of me."

"But—"

Jared hung up the phone. "What's wrong?" Sara asked, assessing his expression.

"More problems with our insurance company,"

Jared said as he again wiped his forehead. "Nothing to worry about."

"Are you sure, because—"

"I'm sure," Jared insisted. "They just messed up one of our claims. I can take care of it."

Wandering up and down the narrow aisles of the neighborhood grocery store, Jared spent the early part of Saturday morning doing some not-so-necessary shopping. Over the past four days, he hadn't once slept straight through the night. Regardless of how exhausted he was, he found himself waking up at three, four, and five o'clock in the morning. Always for the same reason— always to check on Sara. He was hoping that Saturday was going to be the day when he'd be able to sleep late and catch up on the lost hours. But when Sara's alarm went off at eight o'clock, Jared was forced to face the day. He did everything in his power to lie in bed and keep his eyes shut, but again, it was no use. He couldn't get the question out of his head: Are they going to take her? That was what he asked himself every morning, and that was all he cared about.

Unwilling to face the answer, Jared crawled out of bed. While Sara showered, he decided to run to the market. Fifteen minutes later, he headed home carrying two bags of groceries and half a dozen bagels. Walking past dozens of other New Yorkers who were carrying similar packages, Jared still couldn't take his mind off his wife. She'll be safe, he told himself. Otherwise, he'd have to—

His thoughts were interrupted by the shrill siren of an oncoming ambulance. With the traffic lights on its side, it flew down Broadway. When

Jared first looked up, the ambulance was four blocks away. Seconds later, the ambulance was about to reach Eightieth Street—the block Jared and Sara lived on.

Don't turn, don't turn, please don't turn, Jared whispered to himself as he stood on the corner of Seventy-ninth. All around him, people covered their ears to block out the deafening scream of the siren, but Jared didn't notice. He was too focused on the ambulance. Especially when it turned down Eightieth Street.

The first thing he did was run. That was instinct. Clutching his bags, Jared darted up Broadway at the fastest sprint he could manage. Not Sara, he begged. Don't let it be her. He was moving quickly, but for him, not fast enough. Without hesitation, he let go of the groceries and took off. He could hear the wail of the siren echo down the narrow street. When he turned the corner, he saw that the ambulance had stopped halfway down the next block, right in front of their apartment. "Sara!" he shouted. But as he took his first few steps down Eightieth Street, he saw the ambulance move farther down the block. It had stopped to inch its way past a double-parked car. And as it maneuvered past the obstacle and turned onto Columbus Avenue, Jared finally stopped running. It's all right, he thought, standing there with his hands shaking. Sara was all right. She had to be.

With a confident stride and a commanding look in her eyes, Sara strolled across the grand jury room. "Ladies and gentlemen of the jury, you are here today to do one job—and that job is justice."

" 'That job is *justice*'?" Conrad interrupted as he sat in the front row of the jury box. "This isn't a congressional hearing—we want these jurors to take you seriously."

"I can't help it," Sara said, throwing her legal pad on the table in the front of the room. "Every time I get nervous, I start spouting clichés. All those years of bad movies are finally catching up with me."

"Didn't they teach you about juries in your old law firm?" Guff asked, seated next to Conrad.

"I told you, I did two trials in six years. We settled everything else."

"Ah, the paralysis of passive resistance," Guff said. "How I long for that stagnant touch."

"Make another joke, and I'll ram my stagnant touch straight up your stagnant—"

"Leave the boy alone," Conrad interrupted. "Let's get back to juries." He stood up and moved next to Sara in the front of the room. "Whether you're in a grand jury or a regular trial, juries are always about trust. If they trust you, they'll take your side. If not, you lose. But there's a difference between having a jury like you and having a jury convict for you. If you want a jury to vote against the accused, you need more than a few warm smiles and some smooth hand gestures."

"So what's the trick?"

"The trick is language," Conrad said. "There'll be anywhere from sixteen to twenty-three people on the grand jury. All you have to do is convince twelve of them that the facts justify a felony charge. They're not voting to convict him; they don't have to put him in jail. All they have to do is find reasonable cause to believe that Kozlow committed the crime. That's a pretty low threshold, but it's easy to get tripped up."

"What do you mean by language? What do you have? Magic words?"

"You bet your stagnant ass we have magic words," Conrad said. "Rule one: Never use the defendant's name. Never call him Kozlow, or Anthony, or Tony. That humanizes him and makes it harder for the jurors to vote against him. Call him 'the defendant,' or 'the accused.' Rule two: Always use the victim's name, the cop's name, and the witnesses' names. Ms. Doniger, Officer McCabe, Ms. Harrison. That makes them seem more human and believable. Rule three: Never use the actual words of the crime you're charging the defendant with. In other words, don't say, 'He committed a *burglary*,' or 'He committed *murder*.' Those words sound scary to people, not to mention the fact that the jurors will start asking about all the elements of the crime before they'll vote. To make it easier, say, 'If you believe the accused *stole from* Ms. Doniger . . .'"

"And this really works?" Sara asked skeptically.

"In my nine years here, I've never lost in a grand jury," Conrad said. "I may not win at trial, but I always get there. And I get there because I was taught to focus on the details."

"And who granted you these pearls of wisdom?"

"The United States government," Conrad said proudly.

"You were in the military?" Guff asked sarcastically. "No way. You're so laid-back."

"I gave them a three-year commitment, they put me through law school. But after three years, they force you out of the criminal side. When they told me I had to do boring civil stuff like wills and taxes and divorce work, I made the jump over here."

"Love that combat zone, don't you?"

"Can't live without it," Conrad said. "Now let's get back to the point. Do you know what your game plan is?"

"I'm calling people in order of involvement. I'll start with the cop, then Doniger, and then Harrison. Kozlow goes on last."

"So Kozlow's decided to testify?"

"He filed notice," Sara explained. "I guess Jared figures he'll make a likable witness. I'm hoping if he goes on last, the jury will have already made up their minds." Pausing for a moment, Sara thought about the rest of her witnesses. Harrison was easily the best, since she was the only one who had seen Kozlow leave the house. But if she refused to testify, or even worse, denied that she had seen anything, Sara knew that Jared was right: The entire case was in trouble. Looking at Conrad, she continued, "One last thing—I know you won't like this option, but if everything starts falling apart tomorrow, I have to think about dismissing it."

"I'd never argue that with you," Conrad said. "This is your case. And believe it or not, I appreciate the consequences." Noticing the distant look in Sara's eyes, he added, "I'm serious about that. It's okay to be realistic."

"Says the man who never settles."

"Sara, not every case is a winner. Think about what you've faced: shaky witnesses, a shifty defendant, even your own husband. When it comes to emotional baggage, you've got more than a small piece of carry-on luggage here."

"But *this* case—"

"I know you wanted this to be your break-through case, but you can't make something from nothing. Well, sometimes you can, but now isn't the time. When you get in there tomorrow, you'll make your decision. And no matter what happens, you'll live with the outcome."

"It's not the outcome that scares me, it's the motivation behind it. You should've heard Jared last night—he did a guilt dance on my head that would've made my mother proud. And trust me, that's saying something."

"I believe it. Between the lack of witnesses and Victor breathing down your neck, you've got a ten-ton argument for washing your hands. You may not like dismissing it, but in this situation, it's far better than losing."

"I guess," Sara said despondently. "Though it's hard to see the difference."

Rafferty reached across his sculptural leather sofa and answered the ringing phone.

"You said you wanted me to check in," Kozlow said on the other end of the line.

"Have you forgotten how to say hello, or is that just a Neanderthal greeting?" Rafferty asked.

"Hello. How are you?" Kozlow growled. "Are we set for tomorrow?"

"We should be. Sara's planning to subpoena both Claire and Patty at the crack of dawn."

"Really? Are they going to be there to receive them?"

"Without a doubt," Rafferty said. "Then when they give up nothing at the grand jury, we're done with this nonsense."

"Are you sure that's the best way to do it?"

Rafferty refused to answer the question. "Where are you calling from?"

"Don't worry," Kozlow said. "It's a pay phone. What do you think I am, stupid?"

"I'm not sure. Was it stupid to grab that diamond watch and the sterling silver golf ball?"

"Why do you have to keep bringing that up? I was—"

"I don't want to hear it, you greedy little leech. If you'd never done that, we wouldn't be in this situation."

"What'd you call me?" Kozlow asked. "You think *I'm* greedy? Let me tell you something, you Kennedy-complex wanna-be, you were the one who—"

"Good-bye," Rafferty interrupted. With a flick of his wrist, Kozlow was gone.

CHAPTER 9

Early Monday morning, Sara paced up and down the dark, tiled hallways on the ninth floor of One Hogan Place, trying her best to look calm. Outside the grand jury room, a small line of assistant district attorneys was forming, all of them waiting for a chance to present their cases. Since the waiting room couldn't accommodate everyone, the hallway was also filled with dozens of witnesses, family members, and defense attorneys. Sara stared intently at the ever-growing group, hoping to take her mind off her anxieties.

Lawyers in the crowd were easy to identify, with their navy-blue or gray single-breasted suits and stark white shirts. Anyone who wasn't wearing the uniform was, by default, a witness, a victim, a defendant, or a family member there for moral support. To separate the ADAs from the defense attorneys, Sara needed only to read body language. The defense attorneys were relaxed and at ease. Since they were not allowed to participate in grand jury proceedings, they had nothing to lose. By comparison, the ADAs were usually younger, with a slight but noticeable tinge of nervousness in their eyes. A hand anxiously arched on a hip, bitten fingernails, a few too many glances at a watch—that was all it took to identify the prosecutors. That and their unmistakable attempts to look as calm as possible. The moment she realized the pattern, Sara stopped pacing.

Behind her, a man in a gray suit said, "I was hoping we'd be first, but I hear we're seventh and eighth."

Turning around, Sara recognized the man from her first day's orientation. "Seventh and eighth?"

"To appear in front of the grand jury," the man said. "Of the seventeen other ADAs who started with us, six have already done it. All got indictments but one. That guy Andrew from Brooklyn tanked it something fierce. My bet is he'll be the first one to go. And rumor says layoff decisions are being made today."

Sara raised an eyebrow at the news. "I'm sorry, what's your name again?" she asked.

"Charles, but people call me Chuck."

"Charles, Chuck, the both of you—do me one small favor? Don't talk to me right now."

The grand jury was selected once a month in a manner Guff called "the criminal justice version of bingo." But unlike a traditional jury, which made a guilt determination in only one case, the grand jury usually heard dozens of cases each day and decided only whether there were reasonable grounds for the DA's office to prosecute the case. Since the jurors served for a full month, the first Monday of the term usually meant a new grand jury—and the worst day to present a case. In the beginning of the term, the jurors were cautious novices, trying carefully not to indict the wrong man. By the end, they were jaded veterans, realizing that an indictment was only the first step of the process. In the beginning, they were nice people trying to do the right thing. By the end, they were average New Yorkers, ready to believe the worst about anyone.

Another twenty minutes went by before Sara heard Guff's voice from down the hallway say, "Look who I found." Turning around, she saw Guff wheeling a small metal cart that contained all of her files on the case—she was determined to be prepared for everything. Behind him came Officer McCabe, Claire Doniger, and Patty Harrison. McCabe looked calm, Doniger looked annoyed, and Harrison looked terrified. As she approached her witnesses, Sara said, "I hope you understand why we had to—"

"Don't treat me like a child," Doniger blurted, her tinted salon-styled hair bouncing with a life of its own. With her Adolfo suit, bottled tan, obvious face-lift, and tiny purse, the fifty-four-year-old Doniger looked exactly as Sara had imagined. When Doniger walked right past her, Sara realized their conversation was over.

Turning toward Harrison, Sara lightly touched her shoulder. "Are you all right?"

"Yeah," Harrison said unconvincingly.

"Do you want to tell me who threatened you?"

"Nobody threatened me," Harrison insisted. Her jet-black hair was pulled back and clipped with a black velvet bow, and her ice-blue eyes danced as she spoke. "But I'm telling you one thing: I will not become a leper in my own neighborhood."

"Who's making you feel like a leper? Ms. Doniger? Kozlow?"

"I don't even know who that man Kozlow is. I saw him that one night leaving Claire's house. He looked shady, so I made a phone call. That's all I know."

"And that's all I need you to say. Just tell the story."

Harrison turned away. "No. I'm not doing it."

"It's your duty to do it."

"I don't have a duty to anyone except myself. My husband left me eight years ago for his big-haired personal assistant; my daughter moved out to San Francisco and I never hear from her, and the highlight of my week is flirting with the meat guy at the deli counter in the supermarket. It may be pathetic, but it's my life, and I enjoy it. And I'm not giving it up for some mythical sense of duty." When Harrison noticed some of the other people in the hallway staring at her, she turned to them and yelled, "Mind your own damn business, you nosy twits."

Giving Harrison a moment to calm down, Sara waited silently. Finally, she said, "You're right. It's your neck on the line, not mine. But when your daughter is strolling around in that fresh California air one night and someone bashes her head in, I hope the person who sees that crime has more backbone than you do."

Harrison stared straight at Sara. "Are you done?" she asked.

"I've said my piece," Sara said, and walked away.

As she headed back down the hallway, Sara saw Jared arrive with Kozlow, who looked impressive in a pinstriped suit and stylish-but-sensible glasses. Typical Jared move, she thought. From her husband's hand motions, it looked like he was telling Kozlow to wait at the other end of the hallway, away from Sara's witnesses. Kozlow stayed behind and Jared came walking toward his wife.

"Is everything okay?" he asked, reading Sara's body language.

"I'm fine," she said. She took a deep breath.

"Are you sure?" Jared asked. He reached over to rub her arm.

Sara quickly pulled away. "Not here. Not now."

"I'm sorry—I didn't mean—"

"It's not the time."

"I understand," Jared said, getting back to the point. "Have you thought about the dismiss and seal?"

"Of course I've thought about—"

"Sara!" Guff yelled down the hallway. "You're on!"

"So?" Jared asked, looking into his wife's eyes. "Do we have a deal?"

Sara paused and stared down at the floor.

"I have the paperwork right here," Jared added. He had her. He could feel it.

She knew what this meant to him. And hurting him meant hurting herself. Looking up, Sara gave her answer. "I'm sorry. It's not right."

"But—"

"Please don't ask me any more," Sara said, walking toward the jury room. "You're already hitting below the belt."

Jared clenched his jaw and turned away.

Holding the door open for Sara, Guff said, "Good luck, boss."

"Aren't you coming?" she asked.

"No can do. If I'm not a witness or a member of the New York bar, I can't come in. Lucky for me, I'm neither. Now go kick some heinie."

As Sara stepped into the room, she could feel all eyes turn toward her. Sitting in two rows of benches were the twenty-three men and women of her first grand jury. They were a typical New York jury: mostly retired men and women, a few older mothers, a waiter, a manager of a retail store, a young editor, a mechanic, a graduate student, and so on.

Kozlow was being seated on the right side of the room, while Officer McCabe, Claire Doniger, and Patty Harrison were all waiting in the nearby witness room. As Sara surveyed her surroundings, Jared walked in and sat down next to his client. He looked at Sara with dismay and fought to get her attention.

Refusing to make eye contact with her husband, Sara knew she shouldn't have agreed to let him in the room. She walked toward the empty table in front, put down her briefcase, and faced the grand jury. "How's everybody doing today?"

No one said a word.

"Okay. Great," Sara said, opening her briefcase. As a slight blush took her face, she looked up. "Excuse me for a moment." She walked to the door, opened it, and stuck her head into the hallway.

"What's wrong?" Guff asked, leaning against the wall.

"The files?"

"Oops," Guff said, pushing the rolling cart toward Sara.

Rolling it into the room, Sara once again smiled at the jury. "Here we go. Are we ready to get started?"

* * *

When Officer McCabe finished testifying, Sara was feeling somewhat hopeful. He was hardly the world's best witness, but he kept to the story and told it well.

"Does anyone have any questions?" Sara said, still refusing to make eye contact with Jared. Unlike regular "petit" jurors who heard and decided full cases without interacting with the parties involved, grand jurors were permitted to ask their own questions of each witness, which allowed them to flesh out the story for themselves. In Sara's view, as long as they didn't ask about why McCabe hadn't fingerprinted the house or gotten a proper ID of the defendant, she was home free.

A juror in the second row raised his hand first.

"Hold on, let me get there," Sara said as she approached the juror. She leaned over and the juror whispered his question in her ear. It was the ADA's job to screen each question and make sure it was appropriate. If it was, the ADA had to pose the question to the witness. Hearing the juror's question, Sara reacted exactly as Conrad had taught her. No change of expression whatsoever. She turned to McCabe. "The first question is, 'Did you check to see if the defendant's fingerprints were in the house?'"

"We don't have the budget to do that," McCabe replied.

The juror whispered another question to Sara.

"But isn't that the best way to see if the defendant was there?" Sara repeated.

"Probably," McCabe said indignantly. "But it can't always be perfect."

Sara turned her back to McCabe. It went downhill from there.

* * *

By the end of Doniger's testimony, Sara was a wreck. Sitting at the witness table with an angry look on her face, Doniger was hostile and uncooperative—hardly the sympathetic victim Sara hoped for. Trying to turn things around, Sara opened the floor to questions.

Immediately, a female juror in the first row raised her hand and whispered a question. "So you never saw Mr. Kozlow in your house?" Sara said, passing it along.

"No, I didn't," Doniger said.

A follow-up question was whispered. "Then you really don't know if he's the thief," Sara announced.

"I definitely don't."

As the questions continued, Sara eventually couldn't help herself. Hesitantly, she glanced over at Jared. From the look in his eyes, she knew what he was thinking—it didn't take a genius to see that Sara was drowning. Then Jared pushed a piece of paper to the corner of the defense table, signaling for Sara to read it. Casually, Sara strolled toward the table and leaned on the corner of it as Doniger answered the latest question. When she looked down, Sara read Jared's message: "Ready for the dismiss and seal? You could use it."

Looking back up at her husband, Sara was tempted to accept—to shut Doniger up and end it right there. Even if she got the indictment, what was she proving? With witnesses like Doniger and Harrison, the trial would be an even bigger disaster. Even Conrad agreed that dismissing it was better than losing. More important, Sara couldn't stand facing off against Jared. Playing a few harmless mind games was one thing, but watching him get hurt by her actions was ripping her apart. Maybe he's right, she thought as she walked back to the prosecution table.

When Doniger was done testifying, Sara knew it was time to make her decision. She could dismiss the case with Jared or barrel forward with Harrison. The question was difficult, but the answer, for Sara, was obvious.

"If you can bear with us for another second, I have one last witness," Sara said, turning away from her husband. Responsibility had to come first. "I'd like to call Patricia Harrison."

At twelve-thirty, Guff and Sara walked into Conrad's office. "Victor, let me call you back," Conrad said into his phone. "They're just walking in now." He hung up the phone and looked at his two expressionless colleagues. "Well? Did you get the indictment?" he asked.

"What do you think?" Guff shot back.

"I think you got it, and I think you're playing it extra cool because you have some vain hope that you can actually surprise me."

"We are!" Guff screamed. "We nuked those commie bastards back to the Stone Age!"

"All right!" Conrad said. He jumped up to give Sara a big hug, then quickly pulled away. She smiled weakly.

"You should've seen her," Guff said, crouching into a fighting stance. "There she was, defenseless, with nothing but her wits and three bad witnesses to protect her. She eyed the jury and shot them a sneer—they knew she meant business. Then, just when they thought she was going to zig, she zagged. And when they expected a zag, she zigged. Zig! Zag! Zig! Zag! It was like my parents at an all-you-can-eat buffet—food was flying faster than the human eye could follow."

"What're you talking about?" Conrad asked.

"I'm using food as a metaphor for intense legal issues," Guff said.

"So the intense legal issues were flying faster than the human eye could follow?"

"Exactly. And then, when she was on the ropes, her spirit almost gone, she rose, like a gleaming, legal-studying, precedent-setting phoenix, from the ashes of the grand jury room."

"And you saw all this even though you weren't in the room?" Conrad asked.

"Believe me, I had my ear to the door," Guff said. "And if I were going to brag about any of my physical qualities, I would have to go with the excellence of my auditory abilities."

"So if we take out the useless exaggerations, the true story is what?" Conrad asked.

"The true story is Patty Harrison saved the day," Sara said, finally, putting her briefcase on the floor.

"The scared woman came through, huh?"

"She certainly did," Sara said. "When she took the stand, I asked her one question: 'Who was the person you saw coming out of Ms. Doniger's house that night?' There was this long pause. It felt like an eternity. Conrad, it was so quiet, I swear I could hear the earth rotating. And finally, she raised her hand, pointed right at Kozlow, and said, 'It was him.'"

"Jared must've died."

"He wasn't happy. And Kozlow didn't look too pleased either."

"Did you see Doniger's reaction?"

"I meant to look, but I forgot," Sara said, her tone growing serious. "I was too busy staring at Jared."

Conrad gave her a long look that was difficult to read. "He really got to you, didn't he?"

"You can't imagine what it's like. He knows exactly where to hit."

"Then you better prepare yourself. From this point on, it's only getting worse," Conrad said. "Now tell me more about Doniger. Any idea what her story is?"

"To be honest, at first I thought she was just pissed because I ruined her schedule—one less day that she'd be able to shop for the perfect hand towels. But she was purposely terrible up there. For whatever reason, she was taking a high-platform dive."

"Well, now that you have the indictment, you can figure the rest of it out. That's what your trial preparation should be about—filling in all the missing pieces. If I were you, I'd take the rest of the day to catch my breath and then get started on the case."

"What about Victor?" Sara asked.

"What about him?"

"Why were you talking to him when we walked in?"

"He just called to see if you got the indictment."

"Did he ask anything else?" Sara asked. "Did he ask about his files?"

Conrad pointed a warning finger at Sara. "I still don't think you have any business accusing—"

"I'm not saying a word," Sara interrupted. "At least not until we finish going through the files."

"Then get on it," Conrad said. "Your only goal now is to prepare for trial, dig for those answers . . ."

"And kick what's left of your hubby's scrawny behind," Guff added.

"Speaking of which," Conrad said, "did he say anything to you after the grand jury?"

"He didn't say a word. He picked up his brief-case, walked to the door, and left. Trust me, though, I'll hear all about it tonight. The Tate-Lynch match-up just hit round two."

When Jared got back to the office, he threw his briefcase on his desk and loosened his tie. Instinctively, he looked up at the poster board map of the crime scene. Nothing new popped out. All he saw was how close Kozlow was to Doniger's house when the officer found him. So close, he thought. So close, he was nearly there. "Damn!" he shouted, ripping the poster from the wall.

The instant he collapsed in his chair, Kathleen's voice came through the intercom.

"I have Oscar Rafferty on the line," she said.

"Don't—"

Jared's phone rang. Then it rang again. And again.

Sticking her head in the doorway, Kathleen said, "Did you hear me? That's Mr. Rafferty calling for you."

The phone continued to ring, but Jared still didn't pick it up.

"Jared . . ."

"I can't talk to him now," Jared said, slumped in his seat.

Kathleen left the room and the phone stopped ringing. From his desk, Jared could hear Kathleen's voice. "I'm sorry, but he must've stepped out. I'll have him call you as soon as he gets back." Returning to Jared's office, Kathleen said, "What happened?"

"You know what happened—I lost. Sara got the indictment, and now we have to go to trial."

"So why can't you tell Rafferty that?"

"Because I can't," Jared snapped. "How many times do you need to hear that? I can't do it right now."

Surprised by the outburst, Kathleen moved toward Jared's desk and took a seat. "Now do you want to tell me what's really going on?"

Jared's gaze dropped to the floor.

"C'mon, Jared, you can tell me. What's happening with Rafferty?"

"It's nothing," Jared said, refusing to look up at his assistant.

"Don't give me that." She knew she was overstepping her bounds, but this was important. "What'd he do? Did he say something to Lubetsky? Did he say something about Sara?"

"Please drop it!" Jared insisted.

"What'd he say to Sara? Was it to her face or to you?"

"That's enough, Kathleen."

"Is he bothering her? Is he harassing her? Is he threatening her?" Jared was silent. "That's it, isn't it? That's why he hired you: He wants you to beat Sara. And if you don't he's going to—"

"Don't let your imagination get the best of you," Jared said dismissively. "You couldn't be further from the truth."

Kathleen crossed her arms and stared at her boss. "Do I look that dumb to you? I mean, do I look so stupid that I would actually believe that?"

When Jared didn't respond, Kathleen said, "Just tell me I'm right, so we can move on to the next step. There's no reason that you have to keep this all to yourself. We can go to the authorities, or to Barrow, or to—"

"Kathleen, please—don't do this."

"Okay, that's it. That's all I need to hear." She stood up and headed for the door. "I'm sorry, but it's time to get some help. I'm going to call Lubetsky and explain—"

"Wait!" Jared said. She turned. He realized he had no choice. "If I tell anyone, they'll kill her."

Kathleen froze. "Pardon me?"

"You heard me. If I tell anyone, they'll kill Sara."

"Is that what he said?"

Again, Jared didn't respond. He had promised himself that he'd keep the secret, but he had to admit it felt good to open up. Rafferty's threat was starting to take its toll and, as long as Jared could keep things quiet, he could use another brain working on a solution. He took a long look at Kathleen. After all his years at the firm, there was no one else he trusted more. Finally, he said, "Here's what happened." After explaining the entire story, from the meeting at the club to the break-in at their apartment to the constant threats, Jared turned away from his assistant.

Kathleen let the information sink in. "So that's why he was asking me all those questions about you and Sara this morning."

"He asked you questions about us?"

"Tons of them. He called while you were in the grand jury—wanted to know everything. Your reputations, temperaments, work habits. Of course

I didn't give him anything, but he was trying to figure out how you tick and how you work."

"Maybe."

"Definitely." She stood from her seat and added, "We have to do something about this."

"I put Barrow on the case," Jared said in a panic.

"That's not enough—that just tells us if Rafferty's a heavy hitter. Why don't you tell Sara? She has a right to know."

"I can't tell her, Kathleen. You know how she'll react. She'll be after Rafferty before I can even finish the story."

"That's because she's smart."

"No, it's because she's a hothead. And in this case, confrontation isn't the best solution."

"But don't you think—"

"Kathleen, I've thought of everything. This is my wife we're talking about. My whole world. For the past week all I can think about is losing her. Do you know what that's like?" Jared asked. "I go to sleep every night wondering if they're going to take her away from me. And that's the first question I ask myself every morning. Throughout the day, she's all I can think about. Last night, I dreamt about what I would say at her funeral. Do you know how terrifying that is? She's my life, Kathleen."

Kathleen put her hand on Jared's shoulder. "I'm sorry," she said.

Jared wiped his eyes. "All week, I've been searching for the best solution. Should I go to the police, or should I stay quiet? Should I tell Sara, or is she safer not knowing? I'm dying to tell her. How can I *not* tell her? But I believe Rafferty when he says he's watching my every move. I believe him when he says that if I tell anyone, he'll go after her."

"Then why'd you tell me?"

"You figured it out. Once you got that far, I knew the only way to keep you quiet was to fill you in on the consequences."

"But—"

"There is no 'but.' If I tell Sara, she'll flip. She'll start hunting everyone involved, which'll only make things worse. The best way to protect her is to make sure she never finds out. And since it's my problem, that's how I'm choosing to deal with it. If you disagree, you can call personnel and have them assign you to a new lawyer. Otherwise, I'm asking you to please do things my way. Regardless of what you think, I could really use the support."

"So you're just going to do what they say?"

"I'm *supposed* to do what they say—winning the case is my job, remember?"

"What if you don't win?"

"Believe me, I'll win," Jared said. "No matter what I have to do, I'm winning this case. Now what do you say?"

Kathleen gave him a warm smile. "You already know the answer. If I didn't like spending time in your trenches, I would've walked away years ago."

"Thank you, Kathleen," Jared said. "I pray you don't regret it."

Sara skipped lunch and spent the next hour at her desk catching up on her other cases. The first shoplifter and the drug possession both agreed to community service, so those were two out of the way. But the second shoplifter and the pickpocket were doing their best to stall. Experienced at manipulating the system, they knew it'd take months to schedule them for trial, and once Sara checked the impossibly long wait lists of the misdemeanor courts, she knew that they were right.

Frustrated, she turned her attention back to Kozlow's burglary and continued her search through Victor's old files. She couldn't find a single link between Victor and Kozlow or Doniger. Kozlow had never been a witness for Victor or an informant for him. Neither had Doniger. Hoping for a breakthrough, Sara closed the last of the yellowing folders and pulled out a brand-new legal pad. Staring at the blank page, she asked herself: Why would Victor want this case? Silently brainstorming, she made a mental list of possible answers: because he knows Kozlow, because he hates Kozlow, because he wants to punish Kozlow, because he wants to help Kozlow, because he thinks it's a good case. A knock on the door interrupted her thoughts. "Come in," she said, still staring down at the legal pad.

Absently, she heard the door open and someone step inside. It was Guff, she thought. He closed the door softly. Then she heard the metallic thunk of the lock falling into place.

She looked up. There he was right in front of her—that face, those sunken cheeks—the man who had knocked her over and stolen her wallet. "What do you think you're doing?" Sara asked as she stood from her seat.

"Giving us some privacy," the man said. He wore an inexpensive gray suit and his voice was low, with a hint of ridicule in it.

"You have about one second to open that door before I—"

"I can open the door, but I didn't think you'd want everyone hearing us talk about the Kozlow case."

Sara took another good look at her visitor. "Please. Sit." As the stranger obliged, Sara added, "I'm sorry, I didn't catch your name."

"I didn't throw it. I'm just a friend of the victim."

"So you know Doniger?"

"I said the victim," he replied. "And by the way, I heard about your performance in the grand jury today. I'm extremely disappointed in you."

"Stop right there. Let me guess: Kozlow sent you to threaten me. He doesn't want me to go forward with the case."

"Actually, you have it backwards. I not only want you to go forward with the case, I want you to win the case. But after what happened this morning with your husband—well, in my opinion, you almost blew it today."

"What're you talking about?" Sara said. As she asked the question, she pulled her legal pad onto her lap.

"What're you doing?" the man asked.

"Taking some notes," Sara said. She kept the pad out of view as she discreetly sketched a picture of her visitor. "Now tell me how I almost blew it today. What's the story there?"

"The story is about your husband and the way he tried to manipulate you." Dropping his voice to a deeper tone, he said, " 'C'mon, Sara, do it for us. It'll be great for both our careers. Dump this case, pick up a better one, and bring home a real victory.' "

Sara stopped sketching. "Where'd you hear that?"

"It's amazing what you can hear in a crowded hallway. Let's just make sure it doesn't happen again."

Now Sara was annoyed. "Let me tell you something: You keep using that tone with me, and I'll charge you with menacing, coercion, and obstructing governmental administration."

Showing no fear, the man replied, "I'm impressed. You finally know your statutes."

Sara didn't move.

"Sara, tell me if you recognize this story. There's this little girl who's afraid of nothing. Suddenly, she gets fired from her job, and that loss not only forces her to seek psychological help, but also reignites feelings about the death of her parents. Then, things get so bad, she has to start taking medication to deal with the depression. The crazy thing is, she's so desperate to get a job, she never reports the medication on her employment application. And since it's a government position, that omission is now a potential legal problem for her."

"That application was submitted before I ever got the prescription."

"But it's your job to keep the application up to date. Even if you didn't do it on purpose, seems like they'd be pissed about that."

Slowly, Sara's expression turned from hostile to distressed.

"Isn't it frustrating when everyone knows your business?"

"What do you want?" Sara asked, in a slow, deliberate monotone.

"Not much. You see, I know you stole this case

from Victor. So all I want is for you to live up to that responsibility. More importantly, I want you to know that if you truly love your husband, you'll do everything you can to win this case."

"What do you mean?" When the man didn't reply, Sara said, "Answer me."

"Don't play stupid, Sara. You know exactly what I'm saying. He's not hard to get ahold of. So keep your head down, keep an eye on your husband, and do your job."

Before Sara could say a word, her phone started ringing. She didn't pick it up.

"I wouldn't ignore that," he warned. "It could be an important call."

The phone rang again. Sara stared coldly at her visitor.

"I'm serious," he said.

As Sara reached across the desk to pick up the phone, the stranger grabbed the legal pad from her free hand. She tried to pull it back, but it was no use. He was too fast and his grip was too strong. Wresting it away from her, he ripped off the top sheet, which contained Sara's sketch. "Nice picture," he said, admiring the likeness. Then he crumpled it into a ball.

"ADA Tate," Sara said into the phone. The man pulled out a lighter. With a quick flick, he set the ball of paper on fire and threw the small burning mass on Sara's desk. Jumping from her seat, Sara grabbed her statute book and slammed it down on top of the paper, smothering the fire.

"Ms. Tate, are you there?" a voice squawked from the phone. "This is Arthur Monaghan."

As soon as Sara heard the name of New York's district attorney, her heart sank. Oh, God, she thought. Not now. "Hello, sir," she stuttered. "How can I help you?" As she watched the stranger walk toward the door, she covered the mouthpiece on the phone and yelled, "Don't go anywhere!"

"Are you talking to me?" Monaghan asked.

"No, not you, sir," Sara said, turning back to the phone. Without a word, her visitor left the office. "I was just talking to my assistant. Now what can I do for you?"

"I have some personnel matters I'd like to discuss with you. I want you to come over to my office."

"Right now, sir? Because I—"

"Yes," Monaghan said. "Now."

"Yes, sir," Sara said. "I'll be there right away." Throwing down the phone, Sara ran into the hallway, hoping to catch the stranger. But he was gone. On her left, at the far end of the hallway, she saw Guff. "Have you seen an ugly-looking guy in a gray suit run by?" she called out.

"No. Why?" Guff asked.

Without giving an answer, Sara looked to her right and ran up the hallway. Maybe he went the long way around, she thought as she flew past Conrad's office. "Has anyone seen a guy in a gray suit run by?" she yelled. Of the dozens of ADAs, police officers, and assistants scattered throughout the hallway, no one answered in the affirmative. By the time she reached the elevators at the end of the corridor, Sara realized he had disappeared. "Damn," she said, catching her breath.

When Sara got back to her office, Guff was waiting. "What's going on?" he asked, sniffing the air. "Smells like a campfire."

"Come in, but don't touch the doorknob," Sara said as she stepped inside. After throwing away the charred remains of her sketch, she pulled her accordion file from her bookshelf and opened it to the letter *G*. Pulling out a pair of latex gloves, she added, "I assume these were put in here to handle evidence?"

"Yeah," Guff said as Sara put on the gloves. "But what're you . . ."

Sara gingerly took hold of both doorknobs and twisted them in opposite directions. Eventually the rusty knobs gave way and she was able to unscrew them from the door. "Give me the evidence bag from the travel kit," she said to Guff.

Guff pulled out a plastic bag and opened it. Sara dumped the knobs in the bag and took off her gloves. "Take those over to Crime Scene. I want them dusted for fingerprints."

"You think someone was in your office?"

"I know someone was in here. Now I want to know who it was."

Five minutes later, Sara arrived on the eighth floor at One Hogan Place, the office of District Attorney Arthur Monaghan. After passing through security, she walked up the long hallway until she reached a visitor's waiting area. Two other new ADAs from her orientation class were already there. As Sara remembered, the woman with the oval glasses had just graduated from NYU, while the blond man with pale freckles was a fellow Columbia grad. Both of them looked uncomfortable. When Sara got closer to her coworkers, she shot them a weak smile. "I take it we're in trouble," she said.

"I'd rather not talk about it," the woman from NYU said. "This city is the worst-run organi—"

"Are you Sara Tate?" a woman's voice asked from the far right side of the waiting area.

Turning, Sara saw the DA's secretary, a thin woman with an outdated feathered hairstyle.

"Yes, I am."

"Go right in," the secretary said. "He'll explain."

"Good luck," the man from Columbia called out.

Unnerved both by the ease of her entry and the looks on her colleagues' faces, Sara slowly walked past the secretary. In her stomach, the butterflies were again swarming. As she stuck her head in the doorway of Monaghan's office, she saw that the long room was centered on an enormous mahogany conference table. And although the rest of the office furniture was hardly top of the line, she also noticed it was clearly nicer than the government-issue wares of the ADAs: a shiny oak desk instead of an ugly metal one, a leather chair instead of a squeaky vinyl one, and new filing cabinets instead of the standard rusty ones.

"What took so long? All you had to do was cross the street," Monaghan said, inviting her into the office. With a bright smile and an obvious toupee, District Attorney Monaghan looked like he was trying to please. But as office rumors suggested, he rarely achieved his goal.

"So how are you doing today, sir?" Sara asked as she took a seat in front of Monaghan's desk.

"Every day's a bear. Now let's talk about these budget cuts. Got an opinion?"

"Looks like an election ploy to me," she answered, forcing confidence into her voice even as she shifted uncomfortably in her seat.

"Of course they're a ploy—but they work. And that's exactly why the mayor loves them. These days, everyone loves gritty budget-cutting reality. Fuck moderation, let's get back to the raw, real basics. The more it hurts, the more people think it's good for them. We've become a city of masochists. Destroy welfare, lose the entitlements, cut it all. People see it as tough love. If something good is taken away, it must be because it wasn't good for us—otherwise, the politicians wouldn't be taking such risky stands. It's the ultimate reverse psychology: We keep the things we don't want and slash the things we love."

"I guess, sir. Although I think—"

"Y'know what, though? None of that matters." Laying his hands flat on his desk, he said, "Let's talk about your future in this office."

Sara's hands filled with sweat. Without thinking, she blurted, "I have five cases, and I just got an indictment. I pled out two of them, but if you want, I can do extra work, or take another case—"

"Don't take any more cases," Monaghan interrupted. "If you leave, that's another trial we'll have to replace you on. Just stick with the ones you have and do your best work on them. In the next thirty days, you're going to be judged against your peers, so if you can prove you're worth having around, we might be able to keep you on board."

"Does that mean I'm safe for the next month?"

"*Safe* is a nonsense word. But if I were you, and I were playing the odds, I'd start looking at other job options."

"Really?"

"Really."

Sara walked back to her office in a daze, her mind still reeling from the afternoon's one-two punch. The moment Guff saw her, he said, "You got fired, didn't you?"

"Not yet," Sara said. "But never fear. It's coming soon to a theater near you." Rather than sitting behind her desk, Sara sank to the floor and leaned against the wall. "Think Purchasing will deliver my new sofa within the next month?"

"Tell me what happened," Guff said. "Are you okay?"

"I think so," she said unconvincingly.

After Sara had relayed Monaghan's news, Guff said, "Well, at least you weren't fired. Now what's the story with the doorknob guy? What'd he do?"

"Ah, yes, Sunken Cheeks. First and foremost, he threatened me. Besides that, he really freaked me out. He had all this information about me, and he said if I don't win my case, he's going after Jared."

"Do you think he's serious?"

"I don't know what to think. I was hoping that when his fingerprints came back, we'd know if he was dangerous or not."

"Well, Crime Scene said they'd have them first thing tomorrow morning. They said if you can give them some more information—hair color, physical features, anything like that—it will speed up the ID."

"Actually, can you hand me my legal pad and a pencil?" Sara asked. "I started sketching him, but he stole the sheet when I reached for the phone. That's what he lit on fire."

"Then what do you need this for?" Guff asked, handing her both items.

"You'll see." Lightly brushing the side of the pencil lead against the top sheet of the legal pad, Sara revealed the outlines of her original sketch.

"Holmes, you're a genius," Guff said.

"You have to pick your moments."

"Did he say anything else?"

"Not really. I just wish I knew who he was. Then I'd know if I was dealing with a blowhard or a real lunatic." When Sara's phone started ringing, Guff picked it up. After a few seconds, his face went white.

"What is it?" Sara asked.

"It's Pop," Guff said. "There's been an accident."

Running through the emergency entrance at New York Hospital, Sara raced toward the information desk, followed by Guff. "I'm looking for my grandfather," she said to the nurse as panic flooded her voice. "Maxwell Tate. He was admitted here about an hour ago."

Checking her clipboard, the nurse said, "He's currently undergoing surgery."

"Is he going to be okay?" Sara asked.

"He's in the O.R. Should be out pretty soon."

Wiping her forehead, Sara closed her eyes. "Please, God, don't take him from me."

An hour later, Sara and Guff were sitting in the sparsely decorated hospital waiting area. While Guff flipped through year-old magazines, Sara sat motionless, staring at the starkness of the light blue wall.

Eventually, Guff put his hand on Sara's shoulder. "He'll pull through. You'll see."

"It always happens with a phone call," Sara said.

"What're you talking about?"

"Everyone thinks that death comes when you're in a hospital, surrounded by loved ones. But death is far more random and chaotic than that. It doesn't ease in during a moment of silence. It leaps in— exactly at the moment you're not ready for it."

"Is that how you found out about your parents? On the telephone?"

"I should've been so lucky. In my case, the wonderful hospital administrators decided to leave the news on my answering machine. Can you imagine that? You play your messages and that's what you get: 'Sorry. Your parents are dead. Sleep tight.'"

"You just walked in and played it?"

"I had just gotten home from studying for finals," Sara explained. "As long as I live, I'll be able to picture that little blinking light. I can still do the message by heart: 'Hi, this is Faye Donoghue. I'm the patient advocate for Norwalk Hospital in Connecticut, and we need to speak with a family member for a Mr. Robert Tate and a Mrs. Victoria Tate. It *is* an emergency.' She had a slight tinge of a Massachusetts accent but otherwise, there was no emotion in her voice."

"That was all she said? She didn't say they died?"

"She didn't have to. I knew the moment I heard it. You get that feeling. I hit the play button right as I walked in the house, and since my feet were cold, I headed to the kitchen to warm up some cider. I heard a message from a classmate who wanted to study for torts; a message from Jared, who, even though he barely knew me, still wanted my outline for civil procedure; and then the message from Faye Donoghue—'It *is* an emergency.' That's what I kept hearing: It *is* an emergency, it *is*, it *is*. I played it back three times to make sure I heard it correctly."

Afraid to say the wrong thing, Guff remained silent. Finally, he offered, "I'm really sorry."

"It's not your fault. It just taught me that there's no such thing as a romantic death—and to always prepare for the worst. That's the real lesson. As long as I do that, I'll never be surprised when it actually happens."

"That's no way to live your life."

"It's not like I have a choice, Guff—that's just the way my life works. Whenever I let my guard down, I get smacked in the face. As soon as I got excited about this job, I found out about the layoffs. The second I got excited about the case, I found out my husband was on the other side. When I got excited about chasing Victor, I found out he was the one chasing me. Then today, the moment I finally started feeling good about the grand jury, they called me about Pop. And since it happened right after that guy came into my office—"

"Sara, I know what you're thinking, but this probably has nothing to do with that guy in your office."

Sara stared skeptically at Guff.

"I'm not saying it definitely doesn't. Just don't let your fears get the best of you. When Pop gets out of surgery, we'll hear the story."

Ten minutes passed before a doctor entered the waiting room. "Are you Ms. Tate?"

"That's me," Sara asked, jumping up. "How is he?"

"He took a bad fall down a flight of stairs," the doctor explained. "He has a fractured pelvis, which is why he needed surgery, and he has a Colle's fracture."

"A what?" Sara asked.

"It's a break in the distal radius," the doctor said. "His forearm. Probably happened while he was trying to break his fall. He also has a contusion on his forehead, which is nothing more than a bump."

"Will he be okay?"

"Considering his age, he's holding up pretty well. He'll be out of commission for a while, but he made it through the surgery without incident."

"When can we see him?" Sara asked.

"He's in recovery right now. Why don't you go find out where his room is. They'll be bringing him up there within the hour."

Twenty minutes later, Sara waited impatiently in her grandfather's semiprivate hospital room, fluffing his pillows, rearranging the flowers she had brought, and making sure the TV worked. Finally, the door to the room opened and two orderlies wheeled Pop in on a gurney. He looked awful: His features were pallid, his arm was in a cast, and a gauze bandage covered the right side of his forehead. The moment Sara saw him, tears flooded her eyes.

"Pop, are you okay?" she stuttered.

"Alice?" he asked, his eyes still closed, his voice creaky.

"Pop, it's me. It's Sara."

"Sara?" Confused, Pop slowly blinked his way to recognition. "Sara. Sara, you're here. How're you doing?"

"Terrific," she said, wiping her eyes and laughing. "How're you?"

"I don't know. I can't feel anything."

"That's normal, Pop. Don't be scared. Just tell me what happened. Were you attacked?"

He shook his head as the orderlies lifted him off the gurney and moved him onto the bed. "I lost my footing."

"No one pushed you?" Sara asked.

"Pushed me?" Pop's breathing was heavy, but he fought to speak. "I was . . . the subway stairs after lunch . . . I hear the train coming . . . then swarmed by a crowd of people . . . all trying to make it. I get bumped pretty hard . . . hit the concrete. Always . . . everything's a fight in New York."

Sara looked over at Guff, trying to gauge his reaction to the story.

"Did you get a look at the guy who bumped into you?" Guff asked.

Again, Pop shook his head. "I barely knew . . . what was happening."

At that moment, the door opened and Jared rushed in. "How is he?" Jared asked, heading directly for Sara.

Sara enveloped her husband in a tight hug as the tears again filled her eyes. "He's okay," she said. Thinking about what the stranger said in her office, she held Jared even tighter. "He's going to be fine."

"I'm so sorry, Pop," Jared said. "I just got the message."

Pop reached out for Jared's hand and grabbed it tight as soon as he approached. With a reassuring nod, Jared tried his best to look unaffected. But all he could think was that this was a warning from Rafferty.

"Don't worry, we're here," Sara said, unnerved by the scared look that was still on Pop's face.

"We'll make sure you—" Her sentence was interrupted by the ringing of the phone on the nightstand.

"That's probably the head of the Transit Authority calling to apologize," Guff said as Sara picked up the phone.

"Hello," Sara said.

"Hi, Sara. I was just calling to see how your grandfather was doing."

"Who is this?" Sara managed.

"You forget me so soon? We just met a few hours ago. Now why don't you take my advice: Stop investigating me and start working on your case."

"I know it was you," Sara said.

"Me?" he asked glibly. "It's a crowded subway. That's no place for an old man wearing a navy-blue jacket and a pair of wrinkled khakis. Anything can happen if you're not ready for it."

"Tell me wh—" Before Sara could make the demand, she heard a click. He was gone. Pretending to continue her conversation, she added, "Great. Great. No problem. And thanks for all your help, Doctor." Hanging up the phone, she saw that everyone in the room was staring at her. "That was Pop's doctor," she explained.

Jared's eyes narrowed at his wife's tone. "Is everything all right?" he asked.

"No, yeah, it should be," Sara said. "The doctor just wanted to warn me that it may get worse before it gets better."

At eleven o'clock that evening, Sara and Jared returned home. After hanging her coat in the closet, Sara headed straight for the bedroom. Jared followed.

"Considering he just went through surgery, I think he looks pretty good," Jared said as Sara unbuttoned her blouse.

"Yeah," she answered.

Noticing his wife's blank expression, Jared said, "What's wrong? You've been quiet all night."

"It's nothing," she said, unhooking her bra and pulling off her skirt. When she was done getting undressed, Sara put on an old Columbia T-shirt and climbed into bed. "Do you think he'll—"

"Pop's a fighter," Jared said, joining her under the covers. "He didn't live this long by being fragile."

Jared carefully considered Pop's accident. It could've happened to anyone, he told himself. There's no reason to think it was a message from Rafferty. Over a dozen times, Jared repeated the logic to himself. Not once did he actually believe it. Hoping to take his mind off the subject, Jared curled up next to his wife. "Please, don't," Sara said as she pushed him away.

Surprised, Jared took a careful look at her. Lying on her back, Sara was staring at the ceiling and holding on to the covers with a tight fist. Her eyes jumped with an anxiousness Jared hadn't seen for some time. After what happened with Pop, she was clearly afraid.

Jared moved in closer and gave her a tiny kiss on her cheek. "He'll be okay," he said.

"That's only part of it."

"What's the other part? Your parents?"

"No," Sara said. C'mon, she thought to herself, ask one more time.

"Then what is it?"

"It's the case," she said. "I want you to drop the case."

"What? Why would the case—"

"I don't want to go up against my family, Jared. Life's too short for that." As she let her statement sink in, she watched his eyes for a reaction. When he looked away, she knew she had hit home. Hoping to close, she added, "I mean, you and Pop are the only—"

"Sara, I appreciate that you're worried about Pop, but how many times do we have to go through this?"

"You don't underst—"

"I do—I know what today did to you. And I love him as if he were my own family. I just . . ."

"You just what?"

"I just . . ." Jared wavered for a moment. With Pop hurt, she needed him. He didn't want to turn away. Then, as always, he came back to Rafferty. That was all it took. Regardless of what else was happening, he wasn't going to risk her life. "I know Pop's injury is opening old wounds, but there's nothing I can do. I'm sorry."

Sara knew he was right. It wasn't just Pop, though. It was Jared. Turning away from her husband, she once again mentally replayed her conversation with the stranger in her office. That was where it originally unraveled. It started with him. Then the threat about Jared. Then Monaghan. Then the pain in Pop's eyes when he was wheeled into the hospital room. Then the stranger's phone call. Then the loss of her own parents. For Sara, it always seemed to come back to that. Shutting her eyes tightly, she fought against the fit of emotion that she could feel working its way up from her stomach. She gritted her teeth and breathed slowly. Gradually, she regained her calm. Wiping her eyes to show no sign of tears, Sara turned over and looked at the curve of Jared's back. Without question, he was the most important thing in her life, and she'd do anything she could to keep him safe. Tapping him on the shoulder, Sara said, "I just want you to know, I'm only doing this because I love you."

"I know," Jared whispered. "I love you, too."

"I think he was about to tell her," Rafferty's guest said, pulling off the headphones.

"No, he wasn't," Rafferty said.

"You weren't even listening."

"Believe me, he wasn't," Rafferty insisted. "He's too smart to do that."

"If you're so confident about him being quiet, why am I still listening to their conversations?"

"Because after a day like today, anyone would be tempted to tell their spouse. Sara's grandfather's in bad shape—that really sent them at each other. But if Jared didn't say anything tonight, you can believe he's going to keep his mouth shut in the future." Standing up, Rafferty adjusted his tie. "Now what do you think about her grandfather's accident? Think anything's fishy there?"

"Sounds like he just lost his footing on some stairs. Happens all the time. Why?"

"I'm not sure," Rafferty said. "I'm just nervous that someone else may've put another piece on the board."

CHAPTER
11

"How's your grandfather?" Conrad asked when Sara and Guff entered his office.

"He's okay. The nurse said he slept through the night, which is a good sign."

"That's good to hear," Conrad said. "And on the bad side, Victor told me about your conversation with Monaghan."

"He did?" Sara asked, confused.

"I don't understand this guy," Guff said. "Last week, he wanted to tear you a new one, and this week he's your BFF." Realizing that no one knew what he was talking about, Guff added, "BFF—best friend forever. Didn't you ever have that in junior high?"

Ignoring the joke, Conrad studied Sara's face. "You still think Victor's wrapped up in this, don't you?"

"I'd be a fool if I didn't. No matter what I do, he always knows what I'm up to. And that means one thing: Victor Stockwell's either really concerned, or, much as it offends you, really dirty."

"Don't say another word." Conrad checked the hallway, then closed the door. When he returned to his seat, he explained, "This isn't something to be flip about. Victor's been here for almost fifteen years. He's got a lot of friends wandering these halls, and he's not the type of person you want as an enemy."

"That's fine," Sara said. "But where does that leave me?"

"Accusing a veteran with no proof," Conrad said. "Now did you finish going through his old files?"

"Most of them, but I think it's time to move past the cobweb stuff. We have to get back to the original question: If you were one of the best prosecutors in the office, why would you request this petty burglary in the first place?" Sara asked. "I was thinking about this on the train this morning. Besides prosecuting a case, what else can an ADA do with it?"

"We can decline prosecution, or we can downgrade it to a misdemeanor," Conrad answered.

"Besides that," Sara said. "And think about the other party in this case. From hiring my old firm to hiring Jared, someone is obviously looking out for Kozlow. He's clearly connected to someone. Now assume Victor is also connected to those people. If you were a dirty ADA, what else could you do?"

"You could bury the case," Guff said.

"Exactly," Sara said, pointing at her assistant. "That's exactly what I was thinking. Victor promises some hotshot that he'll bury a case. But when the case comes in, some eager new ADA grabs it before it hits his desk. When Victor hears the news, he goes nuts and has the ECAB secretary call every ADA in the building until they find out who has it."

"But if that's all true, why didn't Victor just take the case back?" Guff asked.

"He couldn't at that point. I had already brought it into the open. It was too late to—"

"Are you both out of your heads?" Conrad asked. "You think Victor Stockwell is burying cases?"

"It's a possibility."

"There's a difference between something being possible and something being provable," Conrad said. "And if I were you, if you can't prove it, I wouldn't say it. Besides, you've got no business going after someone like that in the first place."

"If you really mean that, why do you keep encouraging me?"

"Excuse me?"

"You heard what I said. From the very start, you've been warning me away from Victor, but every time I need help going through his background, you're more than happy to point me in the right direction. So what's the truth?"

Conrad showed the tiniest of smirks.

"I'm right, aren't I?" Sara asked. "You think he's dirty, too."

"I'm reserving judgment. But the truth is, I trust your instincts. There're too many unexplained coincidences in this case, and if there's one thing I know, it's that I don't believe in coincidences. Now if you want to keep looking, I'll help you look, but once again, I'm not going to let you put Victor's career at risk unless you have proof."

"I'm not bringing him up on charges. I'm just trying to figure out what's going on."

"Whatever you're doing, I still think you're missing part of the picture," Conrad said. "Even if you did bring the case out in the open, if Victor really wanted to bury it, he could've taken it back and declined prosecution."

"Are you kidding? Once I saw the facts, Victor couldn't just decline prosecution. It may've been small, but it was still a good case."

"Maybe," Conrad said. "Although he still could've pled it out. All he had to do was give Kozlow a reduced sentence or downgrade it to a misdemeanor."

"Unless, for some reason, the person pulling the strings didn't want any record of the burglary at all."

"I'd believe that," Guff said, shrugging his shoulders.

"You also believe all vegetarians are evil," Sara said.

"Don't laugh," Guff said. "Hitler was one."

"There's still one flaw in your theory," Conrad said to Sara.

"Which is?"

"You have no explanation for why this minor burglary was supposed to be hidden."

"I know," Sara said. "That's where I get stuck every time."

"How about this?" Guff asked. "Maybe Kozlow is related to someone and they're trying to keep his record clean."

"Or maybe Kozlow's on parole in another state, and any record here would get him crucified there," Conrad added.

"I checked that the first day," Sara said. "Kozlow's been arrested twice, but he's never been convicted."

"Maybe he's up for a job where he can't have

any sort of criminal background on his record," Conrad said.

"Now that's interesting," Sara said.

"Wait, I got it," Guff said. "Maybe Kozlow made a bet with some really bad-ass tough guy. And the bet was that Kozlow wouldn't get arrested for a whole month. Then, he pulled the burglary and got arrested. So now, he has to hide the arrest, or he'll lose the bet."

"Yeah, that could be it," Conrad said sarcastically. "The way I hear it, betting on your own likelihood of being arrested is all the rage these days. It's sweeping Vegas like an electric broom."

"C'mon, stay with me," Sara said. "Any other ideas?"

"I think the first step is finding out more about Kozlow and who's footing his legal bills," Conrad said. "When you get that, you'll at least know the parties involved. Then we can try to put together the motive."

"And then we can figure out how they're related to the doorknob guy from yesterday," Guff said.

"The doorknob who?" Conrad asked.

Sara shot Guff a look. "He means Kozlow," she said abruptly. "If we can link him with his money-man, we'll have a much better idea of what's going on."

"Did you do it?" Jared asked the moment Kozlow entered his office.

"Do what?" Kozlow asked, strolling to his usual chair in the corner.

Jared shot out of his seat and slammed his door

shut. "You know exactly what I'm talking about," he said. "Sara's grandfather fell down a flight of stairs last night and—"

"Calm yourself. I heard what happened."

"How'd you hear?"

"Like I said, I heard . . . but I had nothing to do with it."

"You expect me to believe that?"

"Believe what you want, but I'm telling you the truth. If we did do it, we'd make sure you knew about it. Otherwise, what's the point?"

Jared thought about the logic of Kozlow's argument. "So it wasn't you?"

Kozlow smiled. "For once, boss, we're innocent. The old man just took a fall down some stairs."

Sitting alone in her office, Sara picked up the phone and dialed the general number for Jared's law firm. "Wayne and Portnoy," the receptionist answered. "How can I help you?"

"Can you please transfer me to Accounts Receivable?" Sara asked.

After a short pause, a female voice answered, "Hello, this is Roberta."

"Hi, Roberta," Sara said in her most congenial tone. "This is Kathleen calling from Jared Lynch's office. I was just wondering if you could help me find some information on a client who—"

"Who the hell is this?" Roberta asked.

Panicking, Sara said, "It's Kathleen."

"Kathleen who?"

"Kathleen Clark," Sara said, remembering Kathleen's last name from last year's holiday card list.

"Well, that's real funny, because Kathleen Clark

was just down here two minutes ago buying some stamps," Roberta explained. "Now do you want to start over, or do you want me to call the cops?"

Without saying another word, Sara hung up.

A minute later, Guff walked in without knocking. Taking one look at Sara, he asked, "Who sunk your battleship?"

"No one," Sara said. "I just tried calling Jared's law firm, and—"

"They busted you, didn't they?" Guff asked, shaking his head. "I told you not to do that. It's unethical and you know it."

"Oh, and suddenly you're Mr. Ethics?"

"Sara, I know who I am. I know my faults. I over-generalize, I'm generally pessimistic, I don't like kids, I don't floss, I don't believe in spontaneous combustion, I think most people are fad-following sheep waiting for their televisions to show them the next great logo to plaster on their chests, and I think guys with goatees are fundamentally stupid. But I also know my days are numbered. And I understand, deep down in my black heart, that when my time has come, my reckoning will have paid attendance. Just to torture me, they'll televise it. But I can live with that because I understand myself. I know my lot in life."

"And I don't?"

"No. You don't," Guff said. "You're an ADA now. Don't do anything you'll regret."

"Guff, have you forgotten what happened yesterday? That guy threatened Jared and put my Pop in the hospital."

"You don't know—"

"I *do* know," Sara insisted. "I saw him with my

own eyes and heard him with my own ears. It doesn't take a genius to put the rest together. We're talking about the two most important people in my life. If I lost either of them, and it was my fault, I . . ." She paused. "That's when it's over for me. So when the consequence is my family's safety, calling my husband's firm is hardly the sin of the century."

"All it takes is one snowflake to start the avalanche."

"Guff, please—I'm having a hard enough time with this as it is."

"I know you are, and I know how much they mean to you. I'm just trying to watch your back."

"Thank you. I appreciate that," Sara said.

"Meanwhile, as long as we're on the topic of lying, why didn't you tell Conrad about the doorknob guy?"

"Because I knew what his reaction would be. If he found out this guy threatened me, he'd be all over the case, lecturing me on how ADAs can't be intimidated. And you and I both know that the fewer people I tell, the more I protect Jared. Besides, I'm not so sure I want him knowing. He's been a bit big in the mouth lately."

"Hold on. Are you saying you don't trust Conrad?"

"I trust him, but he has been yakking too much to Victor."

"C'mon, he's not revealing anything that's private."

"My personal life isn't private? My success on this case isn't private?"

"Sara, he's just shooting the shit and you know it. Office gossip rules our world."

"But don't you think Victor is—"

"You know I think Victor's being uncomfortably nosy. But that has nothing to do with Conrad."

"Fine, I get your point," Sara said. "But I still don't want to tell him. Now did you get the information from Crime Scene?"

"At your service," Guff said, handing Sara the manila folder he was holding. "One fingerprint test coming up."

"What'd it say?" Sara asked, opening the folder.

"The doorknob had a clear print, but it didn't make any sense," Guff said. "They matched it perfectly, and it led to a guy named Sol Broder."

"Who's Sol Broder?"

"That's the thing. His picture didn't look like your sketch, but when they ran his name through BCI, Sol came up with a rap sheet that reads like a Scorsese script."

"That's great. So what's the problem?"

"Well, I don't know how else to say this, but . . . Sol Broder died three years ago."

Sara dropped the folder on her desk. "You're telling me the guy I spoke to, the guy who pushed Pop down the stairs, is a dead man?"

"Either that, or a really good magician."

Sitting in the back of his town car, Rafferty was annoyed. Born and raised in Hoboken, New Jersey, only three houses away from where Frank Sinatra was born, Rafferty had spent most of his young-adult life trying to avoid not only the multiple Italian boyfriends of his Irish mother, but also the lower-middle-class legacy of his hometown. The first in his family to go to college, he had escaped early and never looked back. He won a local scholarship to Brooklyn College, but after one year transferred to Princeton. Always bigger, always better.

At Princeton, Rafferty's roommate was a loud-mouthed little screamer who also happened to be the heir to a well-established magazine publishing company. From him, Rafferty learned how to speak, how to eat, and how to dress. All of it meant to impress. During winter break of that same year, Rafferty was invited to his roommate's getaway house in Greens Farms, Connecticut. There he met his roommate's father, who offered Rafferty his first job in the publishing industry: a summer internship in the subscriptions department. For Rafferty, the old-boy network was no longer just a rumor; it was within reach.

The only negative aspect of the job was that the low pay forced Rafferty to live at home with his mother. After a winter in Greens Farms, a spring trip to Martha's Vineyard, and a year at Princeton, the return to Hoboken was crushing. In Rafferty's mind, it wasn't where he belonged. After that summer, he never spent another night in his hometown. Always bigger, always better. So as his car wove its way through Hoboken's narrow streets, Rafferty had a hard time concealing his anger.

From Manhattan, Hoboken was only a ten-minute drive through the Lincoln Tunnel, and Rafferty stared out the window the entire time. When the car reached its destination, he realized much had changed. From the newspapers, he knew that Hoboken was now populated by two polar-opposite communities: the deep-rooted Italians who claimed favorite son Sinatra as their hero, and the up-and-coming urban professionals who believed living in Hoboken was the best way to avoid paying New York City taxes. Riding through the streets he grew up on, Rafferty could see the results of gentrification—the main streets were now filled with yuppie cafés, the side streets still had the mom-and-pop bakeries, and the back streets, as always, had the local neighborhood kids, talking about the ways they were going to break free.

As the car approached 527 Willow Avenue, Rafferty said, "This is it. Double-park near the funeral home." The driver followed Rafferty's instructions and pulled up in front of the funeral home on the end of the block.

"When was the last time you saw him?" Kozlow asked as the car came to a stop.

Rafferty didn't answer. He opened the door and stepped outside.

Following Rafferty toward the four-story brick brownstone, Kozlow asked, "Did you tell him we're coming?"

Rafferty pushed the buzzer for apartment eight. "I'd rather catch him unprepared."

Through the intercom, a grainy voice asked, "Who is it?"

"It's me," Rafferty said. "Buzz us in."

"Who's 'me'?"

"It's Oscar," Rafferty barked.

"Oscar who?" the voice said.

Pounding the intercom with his fist, Rafferty shouted, "Open the damn door or I'll break your f—".

A rasping buzzer sounded, granting them access to the building. Rafferty pulled down on his lapels and straightened his jacket. There was no reason to be upset, he told himself. By the time they had climbed the four flights of stairs, both Rafferty and Kozlow were out of breath. As they approached apartment eight, the door flew open. It was the man with the sunken cheeks. "Hello, boys."

Walking into the spartan one-bedroom apartment, Rafferty wanted to shove him in the chest. Just enough to scare him. Old instincts were returning, but he restrained himself. There was no reason to regress. "Elliott, I thought you were going to clean this place up." Rafferty flicked a chip of paint from the wall.

"Give me some money and I'll be happy to oblige," Elliott said. "What's up, Tony?"

"Same old same old," Kozlow said.

"I've already given you money," Rafferty interrupted, following Elliott into the beat-up living room.

"I mean real money. The big bucks."

"You know where we are with that," Rafferty said as he approached a metal folding chair in the corner of the room. He brushed off the seat with his hand before sitting down on it.

"So you didn't come by to give me good news?" Elliott asked.

"Actually, I came by to ask you a question," Rafferty said. "Monday afternoon, Sara Tate's grandfather fell down a flight of stairs in the subway. Fractured his pelvis in a nasty spill. I want to make sure you didn't know anything about that."

"And Sara Tate's the DA who has Kozlow's case?" Elliott asked.

"That's correct," Rafferty said, looking for a hint of deceit on Elliott's lean features.

"Sorry, I don't know anything about that."

"So you've never approached Sara? Never spoken with her?"

"Hey, I don't even know what she looks like," Elliott said with a twisted grin. His tone was taunting, like a man without a care. Or someone who was enjoying a rare moment of control. "The woman's a complete stranger to me."

"Elliott, can I steal some soda?" Kozlow called from the kitchen.

"It's what you do best," Elliott called back, not taking his eyes off Rafferty.

"Don't fuck with me," Rafferty warned.

"Would I be stupid enough to dick you around? You're like a father to me."

"Sure I am," Rafferty said.

"You are. Besides, what're you so worried about? I thought you had it all taken care of."

"I do," Rafferty said. "Unless someone starts changing the plans."

"Well, you can stop suspecting me," Elliott teased. "I already got what I wanted. Besides, I want you to succeed. If I didn't, I never would've let you meet Tony."

"And that worked out so well, didn't it?" Rafferty replied.

"Hey . . ." Kozlow said from the kitchen.

"So is there anything else I should know?" Elliott asked.

"Not yet," Rafferty said as he headed to the door. "But don't worry. I'll be in touch."

Rafferty and Kozlow were both silent until they had left the building. Stepping into the crisp September air, Kozlow finally asked, "Do you believe him?"

"You know him better than I do. What do you think?"

"I trust him. He may be vindictive, but I don't think he'd do that to us. Sara's grandfather took a fall on his own."

"Let's hope you're right," Rafferty said as he got into the car. "For all our sakes."

"All right, then. That's fine," Jared said coldly into his phone. "If you want to see him, put your request in writing."

"Are you kidding me?" Sara asked. "All I want to do is interview Kozlow. Why make me put it in writing when you can agree to it right now on the phone?"

"Sara, don't take it personally, but that's what I do with every client. If you want him, you have to go through the proper channels."

"Fine, I'll send it over," Sara said, sounding angry. "I'll talk to you later."

"Don't forget we have the prom tonight," Jared added.

"Do I really have to—"

"Yes, you have to be there. It's important to me, and it'd look terrible if you weren't, so I'll see you there at nine."

As Jared hung up the phone, Kathleen walked in the room. "She wants to see Kozlow?"

"Of course. But she's crazy if she thinks I'm going to make it easy for her."

Before Kathleen could respond, there was a heavy knock on the door. "Anyone here?" Barrow asked as he entered the room. He was carrying a small brown bag that clearly contained a bottle of wine.

"Where've you been? Drinking?" Jared asked the moment he saw his favorite private detective.

"On the job? You know me better than that," Barrow said, his salt-and-pepper beard looking more salt than pepper. "This bottle is purely about fingerprints. Snotty client of mine has me spying on her rich husband." Jared and Barrow had known each other since Jared first started at the firm. In the past six and a half years, they had become close friends and enjoyed more than their fair share of laughs and good times, including the night Barrow spied on Sara so that Jared would know exactly what time she would be home for her surprise thirtieth birthday party.

On a professional level, Barrow had unearthed information that had single-handedly won at least four of Jared's cases. But from the look on Barrow's face, Jared knew this wasn't going to be one of them. "So what's the bad news?" Jared asked. "Who're we dealing with?"

Sitting in one of the chairs in front of Jared's desk, Barrow said, "To be honest, I'm not sure myself. I ran Rafferty's name through every information network I have access to, but I came up with almost nothing. He was born in Hoboken, which means he's probably not from money. By some miracle, and a textile-workers-union scholarship, he clawed his way to Princeton—big surprise. He lives in some fancy building on the Upper East Side—again, big surprise. He owns a partnership interest in a fifty-million-dollar theatrical property company called Echo Enterprises, and the only thing I can conclude is this: If I were you, I'd stay away from this guy."

"What makes you say that?"

"I can tell he's bad news, J. People don't hide themselves unless they have something to hide. And the more I dig, the less I find. Oscar Rafferty is in control of his life, and he's structured it to keep us out."

"What about Kozlow? What's his story?"

"Tony Kozlow is a handful if ever there was one. When I asked around about him, the two most common descriptions were 'violent' and 'unstable.' Apparently, he doesn't follow orders well—he was kicked out of the army for insubordination. The thing is, he's never the one in the driver's seat. Both times he was arrested, he was following someone else's lead: knifing someone for a loan shark in Brooklyn, then making a payback call for some small-time drug dealer. On that alone, I'd say he and Rafferty have an employer-employee relationship."

Jared was silent as he mentally tested Barrow's hypothesis. Eventually, he said, "Could they be Mafia?"

"Not a chance," Barrow said. "Mob connections leave obvious tracks. Trust me, though, these guys are just as dangerous."

"What makes you say that?"

"Because they already approached me," Barrow said definitively.

"What?"

"Believe it. Somehow, they knew you hired me to check them out. So on my way over here, they approached me with a better offer. Rafferty said he'd pay me double if I fed you some bullshit info."

"What'd you say?"

"I told them I'd do it. Cash is cash."

"But all that stuff—"

"You think I'd ever feed you bullshit?" Barrow asked. "It'll take a lot more than a few grand to buy my integrity and make me turn on a friend.

But that doesn't mean I won't take their money with a smile."

"So they think you're telling me——"

"They think I'm telling you that I couldn't find a thing on either of them. That I never heard of Tony Kozlow, or his loan shark, or Echo Enterprises, or Rafferty's slick Upper East Side address, or his dying-to-be-upper-crust background. Fuck them if they want to be stupid."

"You really think that's going to fool them?"

"You got any better ideas?" Barrow asked, his voice growing serious. When Jared didn't answer, he added, "These guys aren't playing around. The fact that they knew you'd turn to me means they're looking into your background and sniffing in all the right places. And after spending a total of five minutes with them, it's clear they're serious about this staying quiet. Whatever it is, they have some big secrets to hide."

"What do you think I should do?"

"What else?" Barrow asked slyly. "Let me keep digging in their direction. They can't screw with you and not expect repercussions."

"I don't know. I don't think it's smart to pick a fight."

"Come on!" Barrow said, standing from his seat. "You're not picking a fight. You're just trying to find information. If Rafferty ever confronts you, just say that I couldn't find anything. He'll never know the difference."

"I'm not sure that's the best—"

"Good. It's decided," Barrow said. "Now we're back in business." Before he left the office, Barrow reached into the brown paper bag he was carrying, pulled out an empty champagne bottle, and slapped it on Jared's desk.

"What's that?"

"That, my friend, is an actual champagne bottle from the New Year's Eve scene in *Godfather, Part Two*. And that is also how I spent the first couple hundred dollars of their money. I figured it would really piss 'em off. Happy early birthday."

Jared was unusually quiet. He didn't even reach for the bottle. "You shouldn't have done that, Lenny."

"Listen, there's no reason to get concerned. You'll be thanking me later."

"I'm sure I will," Jared said dispassionately. "I just want you to be careful."

"Worry about yourself," Barrow said as he walked to the door. "You're the one they're watching."

At a quarter past seven that evening, Sara sat on one of the many park benches that lined the esplanade of Battery Park City, overlooking the Hudson River. Located at the southernmost tip of Manhattan, Battery Park City was, for Sara, a spot where she could truly escape New York. Unlike Central Park, which was packed with tourists and locals vying for jogging, Rollerblading, and relaxing space, the riverside jogging path of Battery Park City was used primarily by local residents and a few commuters who worked in the nearby financial district. And its tree-lined, twisting walkway made it the perfect place for a quiet, secluded meeting.

Checking her watch and wondering what was taking so long, Sara heard a voice behind her shout, "Don't worry, I'm not standing you up." As Sara turned, she saw Barrow walking toward her, a wide smile across his face. She didn't return the smile. "Why the long face?" he asked as he sat next to her on the park bench.

"I was just worried you weren't coming."

"So I see," Barrow replied, looking down at her chewed-apart cuticles. "Now how about telling me the real story? What's the big to-do that you had to bring me all the way out here?"

"I need to ask you a favor. And it's not an easy one, so I thought it'd be better to ask you in person."

"Sara, if you're hunting information about Jared, the answer is no."

"Please just hear me out," Sara begged. "I know it's an uncomfortable position for you, but I'm in real trouble."

"C'mon, Sara. He and I—"

"I know you go back a long way. And I know you'd never do anything to hurt him. But I really need your help with this. Believe me, do you even think I'd ask you if it wasn't life-or-death important?"

Barrow looked out toward the Hudson River. "It's really that important?"

"I swear to God, Lenny. I wouldn't be here if it wasn't."

Still refusing to look at Sara, Barrow kept his eyes focused on the giant Colgate clock that floated in the Hudson River. "Tick tock, tick tock," he whispered. Eventually, he turned back to his friend. "I'm sorry, hon. I can't do that to him."

"You don't understand," Sara pleaded. "This is—"

"Sara, don't put me in this one. It's hard enough as it is. When I asked Jared if it was okay to meet with you, he told me to feed you phony info. I wouldn't do that to you, and I can't do anything against him. That's the only way to make sure I keep you both as friends."

"So you're not going to help me at all?"

"I'm sorry," Barrow said. "For this case, you're on your own."

Walking down the stairs that led to the lower level of Rockefeller Center, Sara was a wreck. Her meeting with Barrow had gone far worse than she'd expected, only adding to her fear that Jared's safety was slowly slipping out of her grasp. So when she finally reached the ground-level entrance to Wayne & Portnoy's annual fall formal, affectionately known as the prom, she took a deep breath and tried to ignore the day's events. Even if her calm was only superficial, she didn't want Jared to see her upset.

After checking for Sara's name on the twenty-two-page, over-one-thousand-person invitation list, the hostess pointed to the enormous tent that was covering what was usually Rockefeller Center's ice-skating rink. "As you can see, we've tented the rink for a bit more privacy. You'll find the dance floor in there, with music by your DJ, Sir Jazzy Eli. For food and a more formal atmosphere, you can head over there." The hostess pointed to the indoor concourse of shops that ran along the perimeter of the ice rink.

"Are the restaurants open?"

"Not tonight," the hostess said proudly. "We rented out the restaurants and the café. The whole place is yours."

Sara rolled her eyes at the exaggerated presentation. Heading for the coat check, Sara took off

her jacket, revealing a dramatic black dress. En-
crusted with thousands of tiny black beads, the
dress clung to the outlines of her body. Once inside the enormous tent, she saw a makeshift dance
floor crammed with young couples, all of them
bouncing in sync to the thundering beat. They
looked so young, she thought. Probably right out
of law school. She remembered when Jared took
her to his first prom. It was at the Carlyle then.
Jared had just started at the firm, and he and Sara
had only been married a month. Bowled over by
the extravagance of the event, they had spent the
entire first hour of the party counting and tasting
every single one of the fifteen hors d'oeuvres,
from the sushi to the grilled tomatoes to the lamb
chops. Then, after a few minutes of schmoozing
with Lubetsky and some of the other partners,
they hit the dance floor. Every year since then,
whether it was Jared's prom at Wayne & Portnoy
or Sara's equivalent event at Winick & Trudeau,
Jared and Sara danced less and schmoozed more.
So much simpler, Sara thought as she turned away
from the tent.

Entering the indoor concourse that surrounded
the rink, Sara saw that the only thing that had
changed since the Carlyle was the location. The
regular restaurants were now replaced by the
standard Wayne & Portnoy party configuration.
Hors d'oeuvre stations were scattered throughout the rooms, drinks were being served at six
different bars, and the same old lawyers in their
same old tuxedos were having the same old conversations.

"Sara! Over here!" someone shouted from across
the room. She recognized Jared's voice and craned
her neck to find him. As he waved her over, she

saw that he was standing with an older man who was graying at the temples. "Fred, I want you to meet my wife," Jared said as Sara approached them. "Sara, this is Fred Joseph—maybe the best defense man in the whole firm."

Putting on her best party smile, Sara politely shook Fred's hand. "So nice to finally meet you," she said.

"Isn't it, though," Fred replied. Only Jared laughed at the joke. Undeterred, Fred added, "Jared tells me you two are on opposite sides. Must be tough trying to talk to each other."

"Yeah," she said. She couldn't even force a laugh. "Listen, Fred, would you mind excusing us a moment? I haven't seen him all day and—"

"No need to explain," Fred said. "Jared, we'll talk later."

"That'd be great," Jared said with a full smile. But as soon as Fred was out of sight, the smile was gone. "What the hell is wrong with you?" he barked at Sara. "He's a partner."

"I don't care if he's your mother," Sara shot back. "I'm not in the mood."

A few people were starting to stare. Refusing to make a scene, Jared took her by the hand and calmly walked to the corner of the restaurant. Still finding no privacy, he headed toward the swinging doors of the kitchen. Inside, there were waiters with silver platters running in every direction. All Jared cared about, though, was that there were no lawyers.

But before Jared could say a word, a waiter approached the couple. "I'm sorry, sir, but I can't have you standing here. We've got hot plates—"

"This is an emergency," Jared insisted. "Just give me a minute."

"But, sir . . ."

Jared pulled Sara to the far wall of the kitchen, next to an ever-growing stack of dirty dishes. "We're out of the way. Now give me a minute." The annoyed waiter left, and Jared looked back at his wife. "Don't ever embarrass me like that again," he said to Sara. "This is my life."

"You knew I didn't want to come tonight."

"But you said you would."

"I don't care what I said—I don't want to be here."

"And you think I do? I'm up to my ears in work. This case is killing me."

"You always have it the worst, don't you?"

"Actually, I do," Jared said, raising his voice. "So the least you can do is make it easier for me."

"Why? You're not making it easier for me to see Kozlow. Instead, I have to put it all in writing."

"So that's what this is about. You're mad because I'm sticking to protocol. Well, sorry, hon, but if you didn't want to play hardball—"

"Don't give me your macho clichés. This isn't hardball and it's certainly not protocol—it's just you being a pompous ass."

"Oh, it is?"

"It definitely is. Why else would you make me jump through your paper-shuffling hoops?"

"Why would you call my law firm's billing department pretending to be Kathleen?" Jared shot back.

Sara froze. "What're you talking about?"

"Sara, I know you were the one who called. What'd you think, they weren't going to tell me that someone was trying to get Kozlow's billing information? The moment I heard it, I knew it was you."

Sara didn't say a word.

"And you think *I* was playing unfair?" Jared continued. "What you did not only violated a half dozen ethics rules—it also violated our trust. You know my career is at stake, and you still played dirty behind my back. I'd never do that to you."

"You wouldn't?"

"No, I wouldn't," Jared insisted.

"Then why'd you tell Barrow to feed me bogus information about the case?"

Jared stared angrily at his wife.

"Oh, no, you'd never do anything behind my back," Sara said sarcastically. "You're all perfect and proper with your superstar firm, and its big parties, and its never-lose attitude. Well, let me tell you something: When all is said and done, you're just as ruthless as I am. The only difference is I don't pretend that I'm pitching my tent on the moral high ground."

"I don't need the lecture," Jared interrupted. "I know what I did, and I take full responsibility for it. So if you want to talk about this case, let's talk. Otherwise, I don't need to spend every night fighting about our individual trial strategies."

Sara leaned against one of the industrial refrigerators and took a deep breath. "I agree. Now what else is there to talk about?"

"How about the realistic conclusion of this case?" Jared asked. "The way I see it, we should get this wrapped up as soon as possible. The longer we keep it going, the less time we have for Pop, who I'm sure would—"

"You son of a bitch."

"What'd I—"

"Don't you dare use him against me!" Sara

shouted. "He's not a bargaining chip! He's my family! Do you understand?"

"Sara, I swear I didn't mean anything by that. I was just—"

"I know exactly what you meant. Now if you want to talk, that's fine, but leave Pop out of it. I don't even want to hear his name mentioned."

"Fine, then let me get straight to the point. As far as I can tell, you have nothing to work with. You won a weak indictment based on the testimony of an incompetent cop and an unreliable witness—both of whom you know I'll rip apart at trial. When you take them out, this is nothing more than a simple mistaken-identity case. So to make it easy on you, I'm giving you one last offer: Take the dismiss and seal now, or take the loss at trial. It's your choice."

"That's a nice speech," Sara said. "But there's no way you're avoiding a trial."

Jared's fists tightened and his face flushed with blood. "Dammit, Sara, why do you have to be so stubborn?"

"That's funny," Sara said coldly as she walked out of the kitchen. "I was just going to ask you the same question." Pushing her way through the doors, she added, "Enjoy the rest of your party."

"You look terrible," the elevator operator told Sara a week later.

"You should've seen me when I woke up," Sara said. Bags under her eyes darkened her fair complexion. "It took me a full hour to make myself look this good."

"It always happens that way—you start losing your case, you start losing your sleep."

"Who said I'm losing my case?" Sara asked as the elevator doors shut.

"Don't get mad at me, I'm just telling you what I hear. Word on this ride is that you're facing off against your husband. Honey, if you wanted to hurt yourself, there are less painful ways to do it." When Sara didn't show a hint of a smile, he added, "It's getting down and dirty, isn't it?"

Sara nodded. "When he first got on the case, I was torn up by the idea that I might potentially hurt him. But now . . . now it's starting to get personal. Every day, we're finding new ways to stab each other in the back."

"Of course you are—the best way to hide fear is with anger. It's the next logical step. You shouldn't be surprised."

"I'm not surprised, I'm just disappointed. I thought we were stronger than that."

"It's got nothing to do with strength. The longer it goes, the uglier it gets. And honey, you're going to see a whole lot more of ugly."

"Darnell," Sara said, leaning against the back of the elevator, "you give a real shitty pep talk."

"Then how's this?" he asked as the elevator approached the seventh floor. Doing his best Ethel Merman impression, he sang, "You'll be swell, you'll be great—gonna have the whole world on your plate. Starting here, starting now . . ."

"Everything's coming up roses . . ." they both sang as Sara plodded out of the elevator. "Thanks, Darnell," she added through the closing elevator doors.

Heading up the hallway, Sara saw Officer McCabe leaning on the corner of Guff's desk, waiting for her to arrive. She glanced over her shoulder at the attendance board. The small magnet next to

Victor's name was in the "Out" column. He hadn't arrived yet. Relieved, Sara rushed toward McCabe and pulled him into her office.

"Is something wrong?" he asked.

"Not at all," she said, shutting the door behind him. "I just had a quick question that I was hoping you could help me with."

"Ask away," McCabe said.

"After an arrest, do you follow up on all your cases?"

"That depends on the case. If it was one where my partner got shot, or a buddy or relative was hurt, I'd definitely follow up on it. But if it's something small, there's no time to follow it up—especially since most cases get plea-bargained."

"Is this case considered a small one?"

"An unarmed burglary? It might as well be jaywalking. I have a few of those every week. I don't have the time to check up on all of them."

"So if I—or someone else who got the case—had sat on it forever, you would've never known about it."

"I'd know if I followed up on it, but the odds say I probably wouldn't bother. I just have to get Kozlow off the street—you guys take care of the rest."

"I guess we do," Sara said. "Especially when we think no one's looking."

Leaving Sara's office, McCabe noticed two fellow officers from his precinct in the hallway. After a quick discussion of their cases and a recap of office news, McCabe headed for the elevators. When he turned the corner at the security guard's table, someone was blocking his exit through the turnstile. It was Victor.

"Are you Michael McCabe?" Victor asked with a cold stare.

"That depends," McCabe said. "Are you going to serve me with a subpoena?"

Forcing a strained smile, Victor said, "Nothing like that. I just wanted to introduce myself." He extended his hand. "I'm Victor Stockwell."

"So you're the famous Victor," McCabe said, shaking his hand. "What can I do for you?"

"Well," Victor said, putting a hand on McCabe's shoulder, "I just wanted to ask you a few questions."

"Will it take long? Because I have to get back—"

"Don't worry," Victor said. "It'll only take a second."

A half hour later, Sara called Patty Harrison. There was no answer. She hung up and dialed Claire Doniger's number.

"Hello," Doniger answered.

"Hi, Ms. Doniger. This is Sara Tate calling. I'm sorry to bother you, but I wanted to—"

"What is it?" Doniger asked.

Trying to keep her voice soothing, Sara said, "I wonder if you could set aside some time for us to come up to see your house. As we put together the case, it'd be helpful if we could get the exact layout of your home so that the jury can see—"

"I'm sorry, but as I told you last week, I've been quite busy lately. Now, I don't mean to be rude, but I must get going. Good-bye, Miss Tate." The line went dead.

Sara stormed over to Conrad's office. "Can you help me get a detective?"

"Why do you want a detective?" Conrad asked.

"Because if I'm going to figure out what the hell is going on with Claire Doniger, I'm going to need some professional help. I'm not Miss Marple—I can't do this alone."

"Calm down," Conrad said. "Now start over. What'd Doniger do?"

"She hasn't *done* anything. She's just completely unhelpful. She doesn't want to talk about the case, she doesn't want to testify, she doesn't want to let us into her house. You'd think we're the enemy."

"Don't let her do that to you," Conrad said, pointing at Sara. "I told you before: You're the one who's in control and it's your job to make her cooperate. If she doesn't want to make time for you to come over, tell her she has a choice: She can let you take a half-hour tour of the house, or you can show up with an order to examine the scene and six of your closest police pals, a photographer, and a reporter, all of whom would love to take the new and improved eight-hour tour of her house while tearing through her stuff. Who knows what you'll turn up. And if she doesn't respond to that, you grab her by the shoulders and shake her until you knock some sense into her brain." To illustrate, Conrad shook an imaginary person in front of his desk. "Screw her if she doesn't want to toe the company line."

Smiling at Conrad's solution, Sara said, "Y'know, you're pretty cute when you're angry."

"Thank you," he replied, straightening his tie. "It's the shaking back and forth part that got you excited, isn't it?"

"Whoa, whoa, whoa," Sara laughed, surprised by Conrad's reaction. "Who said I was excited?"

"Not me. I didn't say a word."

"Good, because I wasn't even close to excited. At best, I was mildly amused."

"That's fine. Back away from it all you want. I don't want to put words in your mouth. Now is there anything else?"

"I told you," Sara said, regaining control of the conversation. "I need a detective who'll help me investigate."

Twenty minutes later, Guff walked into Conrad's office. "What's going on?" he asked.

Sara held her hand up and whispered, "Conrad's trying to get us a detective."

"No, I understand," Conrad said. "I appreciate the help." He put down the phone and turned to Sara. "Forget it. You're on your own."

"He said no, too?" Sara asked.

"I can't believe it," Conrad said. "Between the precinct and the squad, no one would assign a detective. I've never seen anything like it."

"Why're they being so tightfisted?"

"First and foremost, they're understaffed. Besides that, it's the budget cuts. Everyone's so worried about their jobs, they're not willing to take a minor case."

"Or maybe there's more to it than that," Sara said. "For all we know, Victor might've—"

"Sara, you have to stop," Conrad interrupted. "Even Victor doesn't know every detective we're calling."

"But he may know all the precinct sergeants

who're in charge of assigning those detectives," Sara pointed out.

"Big deal," Guff said from the sofa. "I say we go down there tomorrow and have a look around ourselves. We don't need some overrated detective to do the work for us."

"I don't know," Conrad said. "I know this may sound strange coming from me, but maybe you should just plead out the case and be done with it. Considering what Monaghan said, it's far more important that you don't lose your first case at trial. And based on your witness list, it doesn't sound like you have much to work with."

Biting her lip, Sara couldn't help but agree. But ever since Pop's accident, she knew it wasn't about her job. The stakes had been raised. The fight was for Jared. "No," she insisted. "I can't plead out."

"But if you get rid of this, you can take your other cases and—"

"I'm taking care of the other cases."

"Are you?" Conrad asked.

"I'm taking care of them," she repeated. "If I can't get a detective on this one, then I'll go up there myself. Tomorrow morning, we'll visit Claire Doniger and see what we can find."

At one-thirty, Jared headed to "Chez Wayne," the firm's private dining room, for lunch. Every day, over three hundred employees swapped stories, shared gossip, and stuffed their faces in Chez Wayne's enormous dining area.

Sitting alone in the back of the room, Jared ignored the conversations of his fellow employees. He dug into his minestrone soup, his mind focused on the case. Although he didn't want to jinx himself with overconfidence, he was feeling good about his position. Sara still had almost nothing in terms of information, and her witnesses were becoming even more difficult to work with. Things were finally looking good for the defense, and best of all, his wife would be safe. So when he saw Marty Lubetsky enter the room, Jared waved his hand to get his boss's attention.

Approaching Jared's table with a tray of food, Lubetsky asked, "What's got you so happy?"

"Nothing," Jared said. "I was just thinking about the AmeriTex case from last week."

"Jared, don't fish for compliments."

"I wasn't."

"Sure you weren't," Lubetsky said as he set his tray down and took a seat. "Don't worry, though. I got copies of the motions. It was nice work."

"Thanks," Jared said.

"Now tell me about the Kozlow case. How do things look?"

"Good. Very good. I'm still hoping for a dismiss and seal, but I don't think Sara's going to go for it."

"How's her case?"

"It's starting to crumble. By the end of the week, I think she'll realize she's stuck with a loser. And as she starts getting desperate, I've got a few more tricks."

Resting against the doors of the subway car, Sara knew she was in trouble. From the moment she had taken the case, things had been sliding downhill. And no matter how hard she tried to climb back up, she could feel everything collapsing around her. As the train headed uptown, swarms of commuters packed in and Sara was pushed to the center of the car. With her back and shoulders pressed against strangers, she started to feel claustrophobic. She opened her coat to cool herself off, but the subway's dry, chalky air caused her to break into an uncomfortable sweat. Closing her eyes, she tried to forget her fellow passengers. She tried to forget about Jared and Kozlow and Sunken Cheeks. And she tried not to think about her parents and her family and what would happen if she lost the case. But regardless of how hard she tried, and how many other things she could shut out, she couldn't stop thinking about Pop. She'd never forget the fear in his eyes when he was wheeled into the hospital room. She had almost lost him, and he knew it. They had broken Pop. That was what she couldn't shake, and unless she could prevent it, that was what they were going to do to her husband. Hold it together, she told herself, clutching the handle of her briefcase. It'll be fine.

When the train reached Seventy-ninth Street, Sara shoved her way out of the car, desperate to get a breath of fresh air. As quickly as she could, she climbed up to the street and finally breathed a sigh of relief. On the walk home, she did her best to convince herself that everything would be okay—that she just needed to calm down and stay focused. But as she turned down her block, she heard someone behind her say, "Hey, Sara. What's going on?"

Whirling around, Sara was relieved to see that it was just her upstairs neighbor, Joel Westman. "Sorry, Joel. I thought you were someone else."

"Didn't mean to scare you," Joel said as he caught up to Sara. "Are you okay? You look sick."

"I'm fine," Sara said as they approached their

building. "I think I'm just coming down with a cold. It's been a rough week."

"I know what you mean. Work can really get in the way of life," Joel said. "Meanwhile, what happened to your briefcase?"

Looking down, Sara saw that someone had scratched the word *Win* into the side of her leather briefcase. Her heart skipped a beat. The threat was closer than she had known—indeed, so close it had been standing right next to her on the subway.

CHAPTER 12

On Thursday morning, Sara stood in front of 201 East Eighty-second Street, anxiously waiting for Conrad and Guff to arrive. It had been over a week since she had spoken to Patty Harrison, and Sara knew that if she didn't turn up something soon, she was going to have a hard time at trial. Staring at the old but pristine brownstone with potted plants on the doorstep and elegant tall windows, she couldn't help but compare Claire Doniger's home with her own. If Sara and Jared's brownstone had Upper West Side character, Doniger's had Upper East Side polish.

A cab pulled up and Guff and Conrad got out. "So this is where Kozlow picked the original fight?" Guff asked, staring up at the house.

"Take a good look at it," Conrad said. "Try to imagine all the events as you know them and make sure they physically could work in this location." Following Conrad's instructions, the three coworkers stared at the building, trying to imagine Officer McCabe dragging Kozlow to Doniger's door and Patty Harrison peering through her peephole.

"Okay, I'm done," Guff said within thirty seconds. "Can we go inside now?"

"Shut up," Conrad and Sara said simultaneously.

When they were done looking at the facade of the building, Conrad and Guff climbed the steps. "Hold on a second," Sara said. "I want to talk to Harrison first. I haven't been able to reach her since the grand jury." She walked across the street to Harrison's brownstone. Conrad and Guff followed.

As Sara rang Patty Harrison's doorbell, Conrad put his finger over the peephole in the door.

"Why're you doing that?" Sara asked.

"If she sees us and doesn't want to speak to us, she'll pretend she's not home," he whispered. "This way, she has to ask—"

"Who's there?" a voice called out from behind the door. Conrad smiled.

"Ms. Harrison, it's Sara Tate," Sara said. "I just wanted to ask you a few questions."

"No," Harrison shot back. "Go away."

"It'll only take a minute," Sara said. "I promise."

"I said go away. I'm through talking to you."

Confused, Sara looked at Conrad. "Ms. Harrison, is everything okay?" she asked.

There was no answer.

Banging on the door, Conrad said, "Ms. Harrison, this is Assistant District Attorney Conrad Moore. I'm giving you two options: You can open the door now, or we can come back with a search warrant, a carload of cops, and a battering ram. Either way we're coming inside."

"You don't have probable cause for a search warrant," Sara whispered.

"She doesn't know that," Conrad said under his breath. Then, raising his voice, he yelled, "Ms. Harrison, you have three seconds to make up your mind. After that, we'll make sure the whole neighborhood knows you're refusing to cooperate with the authorities. *One . . . two . . .*"

The dead bolts clicked and the door opened.

As Sara walked inside the cluttered house, Harrison had her back turned, with her head in her left hand. "Is everything okay?" Sara asked, touching her shoulder.

When Harrison turned around, Sara saw a deep purple bruise under her swollen left eye. The right side of her bottom lip was gashed and another bruise marked her right cheek. Harrison's right arm, in a fiberglass cast, hung from a sling around her neck. As soon as Sara saw her, she felt nauseous. Harrison was no longer just a witness. She was now a victim.

"Who did this to you?" Sara asked.

"Please, leave . . ." Harrison begged as the tears filled her eyes.

"Tell us who did this," Sara said. "Was it Kozlow?"

"We can protect you," Conrad added as Harrison sat on the sofa in her living room.

"She said she could protect me, and look where that got me," Harrison said, pointing at Sara.

"But this time—"

"He broke my wrist with his hands!" Harrison shouted, the tears streaming down her cheeks. "With his bare hands!"

"Tell us who he is," Sara said, putting her arm around Harrison.

"Get off me," Harrison said, pulling away. "Get out of my house. Just by coming here, you've put me at risk. If you want to bother someone, go bother the Donigers. They're the ones who started this."

"Please, Ms. Harrison, let us help you."

"I don't want your help! I want you out of my house!" Harrison screamed, her face flushed. "Now get out! *Get out of my house!*"

Searching for words, Sara headed for the door.

"I was just trying to be a good citizen!" Harrison shouted after her. "That's it—a good citizen!"

"We know that," Conrad said as he followed Sara. "That's why we—" The door slammed shut.

Guff looked over at Sara. "Oh, my God," he said. "Can you believe that?"

"He used his bare hands," Sara said. "He snapped her wrist with his bare hands. What kind of animals are we dealing with?"

"I'm not sure," Conrad said. "But I have a few questions for Claire Doniger." Conrad walked across the street and banged on Doniger's door. Putting his finger over her peephole, he waited for an answer.

There was none. Conrad rang the doorbell and banged one more time.

"She probably heard you shouting," Sara said.

"Or maybe she's just not home," Guff added.

"That's bullshit," Conrad said. "I know she's in there." Banging his fist against the door, he shouted, "Open up, Ms. Doniger! We know you're in there!"

"Forget it," Guff said, heading for the front steps. "We'll find her later."

When there was still no response, Conrad followed Guff down to the sidewalk. "Are you coming?" Conrad asked. Sara was still standing in front of Doniger's door. Moments later, she walked down the steps and joined Conrad and Guff. "What was that about?" Conrad asked.

"Ms. Harrison said that we should talk to the Donigers, as if there were more than one. I checked the mailbox, and it said 'Mr. and Mrs. Arnold Doniger.' Apparently, Claire Doniger is married."

"Then how come we've never heard of this Mr. Doniger?" Guff asked.

"You got me," Sara said. "But it shouldn't be too hard to find out."

In her office, Sara called Claire Doniger. "Hello, this is Claire," Doniger said when she answered the phone.

"Hi, Mrs. Doniger. This is Sara Tate calling. I was wondering if I could ask you a quick favor."

"Please, we went through this yesterday," Doniger said. "I—"

"Actually, I'd just like to speak to your husband."

There was a short pause on the other line. Then Doniger said, "My husband is dead."

Startled, Sara said, "I'm sorry to hear that. When did he die?"

Again, there was a short pause. "This past Friday."

"Really?" Sara asked, trying not to sound suspicious. She mentally counted the days. "I hope your testifying didn't interfere with the funeral. When was it?"

"Saturday." Before Sara could ask another question, Doniger added, "To be honest, this last week has been terribly hard. He was sick for a bit—the diabetes got the best of him in the end. That's why I really didn't want to get involved with this whole burglary thing. It seemed so pointless compared to everything else I've been going through."

"No, I understand perfectly. I'm sorry I've been pressing so hard."

"It's okay," Doniger said. "And I'm sorry I've been so short with you. It's still a new adjustment."

"Of course," Sara said. "You have my deepest sympathies. I'm sorry to have bothered you." The moment Sara hung up the phone, she looked up at Conrad and Guff.

"He's dead?" Guff asked.

"She says he died this past Friday," Sara explained. "Apparently he was a diabetic. Says he was sick for a while."

"You don't believe that for a second, do you?" Conrad asked.

"Are you kidding? We've spent the past two weeks in close contact with this woman and she fails to mention that her husband died? We saw her on Monday, and she never said a word. At that point, she'd barely been a widow for seventy-two hours."

"What are you going to do?" Guff asked.

"You tell me," Sara said. "What does it take to get a body exhumed?"

At eight-thirty, Jared was alone in his office. Kozlow had left almost two hours earlier, and Kathleen had just gone home to be with her husband. Relishing the quiet, but unable to relax, Jared sat on the edge of his chair and planned his upcoming conversation with Sara. First, he'd tell her that he'd spoken with Pop at lunchtime. That would get her guard down. Then he'd ask her how work was going. Although that would probably get her guard up, he knew he had to hit the issues quickly. Over the past few nights, no matter the subject, he'd seen Sara's patience shrinking, and a prolonged discussion about work wasn't going to make talking to her any easier.

Jared looked at his watch. He couldn't wait any longer. He'd been tempted to make the call since lunch, but it was smart to hold off until late in the day. By this time, Sara would be tired and frustrated, the long workday taking its usual toll. As his corporations professor in law school used to say, "The wearier the prey, the quicker the kill." It was the professor's corniest line, but at this moment, as Jared picked up the phone, he couldn't have agreed more with its accuracy.

Dialing Sara's number, he eventually heard her answer, "ADA Tate."

"Sara, it's me."

"What do you want?"

Jared kept his voice warm and sincere. "I just wanted to see how you were doing. Is that okay?"

"That's fine. What else is going on?"

"I spoke to Pop today. He sounds like he's doing well."

"I know. I went by to see him during lunch," Sara said. "Thanks for checking in on him."

"Not at all." They paused.

"Okay, Jared, what's the real point of this call?"

Jared shook his head. His wife knew him too well. "I wanted to make you one last offer."

"Jared!"

"Just listen a second. I'm not going to badger you about what's good for my job or your job. We're talking about something bigger than careers. You said it yourself—we're talking about our marriage and our lives. As long as this case goes on, all of that's at risk. You've seen what's happened in the last week and a half. Every day's spent grating against each other; every night's spent ignoring what's really important. Sara, if we use the dismiss and seal, we can end that right now. Then we can get back to our lives, and our marriage, and Pop, and everything else we've been trying so hard to juggle."

"And that's your final offer? The famous dismiss and seal?"

"That's it. After today, I'm starting to prepare the evidentiary motions. And once that starts, even though I'm trying to protect you, we're going to find ourselves at trial. Now c'mon, honey, what do you say?"

"No matter how you couch it, Jared, it's pure manipulation. You don't think I see that?" Sara laughed. "Besides, I'm not making a move until I hear from the medical examiner."

"What does the medical examiner have to do with this burglary?"

"Well, if we can get him to dig up Arnold Doniger's body, he'll tell us if we have to also charge your client with murder."

Jared leaned forward in his seat. "Who's Arnold Doniger?" Without getting an answer, Jared heard a click. His wife had hung up.

"What'd he say?" Conrad asked.

"I think he wet his pants right there," Sara said.

"I can't believe you hung up on him like that."

"He deserves it on this one. He calls me up, acting like he's Joe Law, expecting me to grovel at his feet just because he pulls a couple heartstrings.

I hate it when he uses Pop and my career against me—he knows it makes me crazy."

"Those're your Achilles' heels. Any good opponent would exploit them."

"Well, I don't want an opponent. I want a husband."

"If you love him so much, how come you're not willing to give, Sara?"

Sara looked up at Conrad. She was tempted to tell him about Sunken Cheeks. And that she was only fighting this hard to protect her husband. But instead, she lied, "Because he's the man on the other side. Giving him a hard time is my goal."

Conrad watched her carefully. "Do you want to try that one again?" he asked.

Fidgeting with some paper clips, Sara didn't reply.

"Have it your way," he said. "I'm done asking."

Ten minutes later, Guff returned to the office and handed Sara a few pieces of paper. "Here's the copy of your order to exhume. Judge Cohen signed it, and they're digging him up tonight. The autopsy's scheduled first thing tomorrow morning."

"That's great," Sara said as she put the papers in her briefcase. "And thanks again for getting the signature."

"Don't thank me. Conrad was the one who knew the judge."

"Then thank you," Sara said, nodding her head to Conrad.

"For you, my friend, the world."

At ten P.M., Jared grabbed his suit jacket from behind the door and stepped into the hallway. Although there were dozens of young associates still working throughout the firm, almost all of the support staff had gone home. As a result, the hallways were deserted. Walking toward the elevators, Jared was still digesting Sara's news. When he'd gotten off the phone with her, he searched Lexis's computer databases for information about Arnold Doniger. All he could find was a *New York Times* announcement of his engagement to Claire Binder, a Radcliffe grad and antiques expert twelve years his junior, and a short obituary from the previous Saturday. Why didn't Rafferty tell him?

While he was waiting for the elevator to arrive, Jared thought about the newfound confidence in Sara's voice and what that meant for the case. His palms abruptly filled with sweat, causing him to drop his briefcase. As he bent over to pick it up, the elevator arrived. Inside were Rafferty and Kozlow.

Forcing a smile, Jared said, "What are you . . ."

Before Jared could finish his sentence, he felt Kozlow's fist rip into his stomach, sending him crashing to the ground. As Jared gasped for air, Kozlow dragged him into the elevator. When the doors shut, Rafferty pressed the emergency stop button. The blaring emergency alarm screamed. Not giving Jared a chance to breathe, Kozlow kicked him two more times in the stomach. He then picked up Jared's briefcase and opened it, dumping all the papers on Jared's now-heaving body.

As the paper littered the elevator floor and the alarm continued to wail, Kozlow kicked him again. He then put his foot on the back of Jared's head and forced Jared's face into the floor. "Oh, we're having fun now, aren't we?" Kozlow asked. Trying to pick his head up, Jared didn't answer. He started to spit blood. "I asked you a question!" Kozlow shouted. "Are we having fun, or not?" With a quick push, he once again pressed Jared's face into the floor. Jared felt like he was going to black out. "Answer me!" Kozlow shouted. "Answer me or I'll kick your head in!"

"Enough, Tony," Rafferty said, pulling Kozlow away from Jared.

"Don't touch me!" Kozlow yelled at Rafferty. "I know what I'm doing."

"I'm sure you do," Rafferty said. "But I need to talk to him. Now catch your breath and calm down." As Kozlow stepped back, Rafferty leaned down toward Jared's face. "You told me not to worry," he whispered. "Isn't that what you've been telling me?"

"I'm sorry," Jared moaned, saliva running down his chin. "I didn't know she had—"

"Don't feed me any more bullshit. I'm full. We need to find out what Sara knows. Get her notes, read her mind, do whatever you want, but find out what the hell is going on. This cannot turn into a murder trial."

Rafferty stood up and shut off the emergency alarm. In a few moments, the elevator arrived at the first floor of the building. Jared remained on the floor as Rafferty climbed over him and left the elevator. When Kozlow followed, he ground his boot into Jared's right hand. "Pick yourself up," Kozlow warned, pressing his heel against Jared's fingers.

"I mean it," Rafferty added as the doors slid shut. "Tomorrow morning I want some answers."

Jared arrived home at a quarter to eleven. He waited impatiently on the sofa until Sara walked in at eleven-thirty. The moment the door slammed shut, Jared was out of his seat, approaching his wife.

"Tell me what happened," he said before she had even unbuttoned her coat.

"I can't," Sara said. "Now drop it or change the subject."

"What's the story with Arnold Doniger? Why is he—"

"Jared, are you listening to what I'm saying?" Sara asked, glaring. "Please stop asking me about it."

"Just tell me if you're going to do an autopsy, so I'll know what I'm doing tomorrow."

Sara walked into the bedroom and started to undress.

"Please," Jared said. "I have to know."

She understood what he was doing, but she wasn't going to budge. Pretending not to listen, she hung her suit jacket and skirt in her closet. After taking a T-shirt from her dresser, she made her way to the bathroom. Jared followed her, standing in the doorway as she washed her face.

"Sara, don't ignore me like this. I need your help. I don't know what else to do."

He was begging now, and the tone caught her off guard. Not just because of the way it tugged at her emotions, but because she could tell it was true. Jared was drowning. He needed her help. And with a few pieces of information, she could take his pain away. No, she told herself. Don't let him do that to you. Keeping her eyes shut, she rinsed off the soap. Then, in one quick movement, she buried her face in a towel. Don't look at him, she told herself. It's the only way he can get to you.

"Please, Sara. You're my wife." As Jared said the words, Sara heard the smallest of cracks in his voice. He wasn't just begging anymore. He was crying. She lifted her face from the towel; she couldn't help herself. As she looked up, she saw pain in his eyes. No, not just pain. Fear. "Please," he repeated.

Sara felt her mouth go dry. Her heart sank. She never wanted to do this to him. But she had to. "I'm sorry, Jared. I can't." Dropping her gaze to the floor, she tried to squeeze past him, but Jared put his arms around her.

"Sara . . ."

She pulled away. "Please . . . it's hard enough."

Jared stood in the doorway of the bathroom, watching his wife get into bed. As she shut off the light on her nightstand, he didn't move. Finally, from the dark, she spoke. "Good night."

For two and a half hours, Jared lay motionless in bed, pretending to be asleep. Lying with his back to Sara, his eyes long adjusted to the dark, he stared at the pale beige radiator in the corner of the room. He thought about the day they had moved into the apartment and the day he had suggested repainting the radiator to match their wine-and-beige-colored comforter. Sara had told him that no one in New York would be caught dead color-coordinating a radiator and had refused to participate in such a "useless" project. But Jared pressed on and painted it, his sense of order outweighing his wife's commitment to her city's constant chaos. And now, as he tried to keep himself awake, he once again stared at the radiator and wondered why they had spent so much time fighting over something so inconsequential.

When the electronic numbers on his digital alarm clock read 2:30, Jared slowly turned toward his wife and whispered, "Sara."

No answer.

"Sara, are you awake?"

Still no answer.

As quietly as he could manage, Jared raised the covers and slid out of bed. Silently, he tiptoed around the bed. On the way, he hit a loose floorboard that let out a tiny shriek. In response, Sara turned over on her side, facing the nightstand that Jared was aiming for. He stopped in his tracks. "Sara?" he whispered.

No response.

Jared crept forward and crouched next to his wife's briefcase, which was leaning against the nightstand. But as he reached for it, he paused. My God, what am I doing? Pulling away, he wondered why he had ever thought he could go through with it. Then he caught sight of Sara, and the answer again became perfectly clear: Her life was worth the risk. Steeling himself against the churning in his stomach, Jared held his breath and gently lifted Sara's bag.

His hands were shaking as he opened the single clasp and raised the leather flap. Feverishly fingering through the folders inside, he pulled out the one marked KOZLOW. As he was about to open it, he looked again at his slumbering wife. She looked beautiful. Transfixed, Jared continued to stare at her. He didn't want to betray her, but he needed to know what she knew. And before he could talk himself out of it, he opened the folder and started reading.

"What the hell do you think you're doing?"

Jared quickly stood up. Sara was wide awake.

"Sara, before you say anything, let me——"

"Get out."

"It's not what——"

"Get out! I want you out of this house! *Now!*" she shouted. Hopping out of bed, she pulled the folder from Jared's hands. "How dare you do this to me! How dare you! Do you really have that little respect for me?"

"Of course not, I just——"

"You just what? You were looking for gum? You needed a pen to write down your dream? You wanted to break every ethics rule in the book? What's the lame excuse of the week?"

"Trust me, I know it doesn't look good, but I can explain."

"Trust you? You want me to trust you?" She dropped the folder and smacked Jared. First in the chest, then in the shoulder. "This is our trust, Jared! This is our trust, and you just ripped it apart!"

He tried to block her as best he could. "Sara, just let me explain!"

"No, no, of course. Go ahead—explain. I'm dying to hear this one."

Jared took a deep breath. He was shaking. Nowhere to turn. "I know you're not going to believe this, but this has nothing to do with you. It's only about the case. Like I said from the beginning, you have to realize how much it all means to me. I wasn't looking for a free ride; I just wanted to know what I was going to be facing tomorrow."

"And did you do the same thing before I went in front of the grand jury? Did you raid my files then? And are you going to take another peek before the actual trial?" As Sara rattled off the questions, she stepped closer to Jared. She pushed her finger into his chest with each accusation.

Instinctively, he backed up, moving farther away from Sara's side of the bed. "Don't use that tone with me," he said. "I barely even saw anything."

"That's because I woke up and stopped you!"

"Listen, I'm sorry we had to get into this, but if the situations were reversed, you'd have done the same thing to me," he said, his back pressed against Sara's dresser. "Now if you want me to move out, I'll be happy to oblige, but you better think very carefully before you do anything you'll regret."

Sara turned around, reached into the top drawer of her nightstand, pulled out a set of keys, and threw them at Jared. "These'll get you into Pop's apartment. Take your stuff and get out of my face."

"Are you kidding me?" Jared asked, stunned.

"That's my decision," Sara said. "Now leave."

"Are you sure you—"

"Get out. Now."

He shook his head with confused rage. "You're going to regret this one."

"We'll see."

He stormed to his closet with his jaw clenched. Wait until she's alone, he thought. Then she'll see she overreacted. In a blur of hostility, he pounded from room to room until he was done collecting suits, toiletries, and enough clothes to get him through the weekend. But it wasn't until he was finally ready to leave that Jared realized what was happening.

As he carried his black hanging bag to the door, he saw Sara sitting in the dark of the living room.

Her briefcase was leaning against the couch. Instantly, rage gave way to reality. "I'm going," he said in a soft voice.

She didn't respond.

"Sara, I'm—"

"I heard you."

Jared put his hand on the doorknob. "I just want you to know I'm sorry."

"You should be."

"I am. I really am," he said. He didn't want to leave now, but he had no idea what to say. Searching for the perfect words, he came up empty. Finally, he blurted, "Are you sure you want me to go?"

Again, Sara didn't respond. She watched him carefully. He looked so vulnerable as he stood there, his hanging bag sagging from his shoulder. An awkward silence filled the room. Jared tried to read his wife's blank expression. Slowly, he lowered his bag to the floor.

"Don't do that," Sara said.

"But you—"

"I'm not changing my mind, Jared. I want you out."

That was it. She wasn't going to take it back. Turning away, Jared opened the door. Without another word, he was gone.

The first thing that hit him was the silence. He was unfazed by the photographs of Sara and her parents that decorated the long walls of the entryway. He barely registered the familiar stale smell that was reminiscent of his own grandparents' house. But as he entered Pop's modest apartment on East Seventy-sixth Street, the one thing Jared couldn't ignore was the piercing silence.

"Hello?" he called out just to make some noise. "Anybody here?" No one answered.

With his hanging bag still slumping from his shoulder, Jared dragged himself inside and dropped his belongings. He headed quickly to Pop's bedroom, and just as quickly decided that he didn't want to sleep in Pop's bed. It didn't feel right. After hunting around for the linen closet, Jared pulled out some sheets and a blanket, opened the sleeper sofa, and made his new bed. All he had to do was lie in it.

It's only until the case is over, he told himself. That's all she meant, isn't it? Unwilling to face the answer, he walked back up the entryway and double-checked the lock on the front door. Unlike the door in his own apartment, which had two different dead bolts as well as a chain, Pop's front door had only a single lock—the same one that had originally been in the door when Pop moved in, almost twenty years ago. For Pop, the single lock was more than enough to make him feel safe. For Jared, it was an entirely different story. Jared wasn't worried about a lock. He wasn't even worried about himself. He was worried about his wife. And the longer he was gone, the less Sara was protected.

Returning to the living room, Jared picked up the phone from the coffee table and dialed his home number. C'mon, honey, pick up. The phone rang again. C'mon, Sara, I know you're there. And again. Are you there? And again. Where are you? And again. Sara, now you're scaring me. Are you—

"Hello," she finally answered, her voice groggy and hoarse.

"Sorry to wake you. I just wanted to let you know I got in okay and that—"

Sara hung up.

Jared quietly put down the phone. She was safe. For now.

She hadn't been able to sleep since his phone call. She was fine when he left the apartment, and she was fine when she didn't know where he was, but from the moment he called to say he was okay, she couldn't relax. Maybe it was the sound of his voice, or maybe it was her conscience. Either way, it was finally starting to sink in. She'd have to do this one alone.

At four-thirty in the morning, Sara was still wide awake. First she tried a cup of hot tea with some warm milk. Then she tried listening to classical music. Then she wondered if there was something else she was missing. In her experience, she knew that if she couldn't fall asleep, it was either because she was still reliving the previous day, or because she was afraid of facing the coming one. In this case, Sara realized that both statements were true. And as she instinctively curled up to the pillows on Jared's side of the bed, she knew it wasn't going to be an easy night.

"What'd he die of?" Walter Fawcett asked bluntly the following morning. A heavy, rough-spoken man with a thick mustache and even thicker glasses, Fawcett was one of the ten medical examiners assigned to perform autopsies in Manhattan. Standing outside the autopsy room, in the basement of the office of the chief medical examiner, Fawcett and Sara went over the details of Arnold Doniger's death.

"According to his wife and his death certificate, he went into a coma brought on by his diabetes," Sara explained, rubbing her bloodshot eyes. "Apparently, his blood sugar was too low."

"Earlier, you said the paramedics brought him in. Was there anything significant in their report?"

Handing Fawcett a copy of the report, she explained, "According to this, Arnold was acting a bit cranky throughout the night of his death. His wife said he regularly had fits of anger caused by his diabetes, so she just assumed his blood sugar was low and gave him some apple juice and a granola bar. A few hours later, right before he went to bed, she saw him give himself a shot. When she wakes up the next morning, he's lying dead next to her. She freaks out and calls an ambulance. End of story."

"That's never the end," Fawcett said. "We'll find more." When he was done looking at the report, he handed it back to Sara. "You staying for the autopsy?" Lost in her own world, Sara didn't reply. Fawcett snapped his fingers in front of her face. "You with us here?" he asked.

"Huh?" Sara asked, jolted back to reality. "I'm sorry. What'd you say?"

"One, I asked if you're staying for the autopsy. Two, I'm asking what's got you so preoccupied?"

"Nothing really—just another part of the case," Sara explained. "And as far as the autopsy goes, I have to be in court by noon, but I was hoping I'd be able to watch. Everyone in the office said it'd be helpful to see how one's done."

"They don't know what they're talking about," Fawcett said as he headed toward the autopsy room. "But if you think it's critical, go put on some scrubs."

"They're doing an autopsy?" Rafferty asked as he took a seat in front of Jared's desk.

"According to the one file I did see, they dug the body up last night, and they're dissecting him this morning," Jared said.

"And that's when she caught you?" Kozlow asked from his usual chair in the back of the office. "Oh, man, you must've—"

"That's enough," Jared interrupted. "I don't want to hear it."

"Lame move, buddy."

"I'll take care of it," Jared said. "I only took about three days' worth of clothes with me, so I still have an excuse to go back there. Besides, it's not like she changed the locks."

"Not yet," Kozlow said.

"Is there anything we can do to stop the autopsy?" Rafferty demanded.

"We can try to block it, but personally, I think that'll do more harm than good. The last thing we want is to appear more suspicious."

"Then what do we do?"

"We schedule our own autopsy, which'll hopefully contradict the findings of their pathologist. Conflicting reports always confuse a jury. Besides that, the best thing we can do is wait. I know that makes you crazy, but there's no reason to get excited until we know what they find."

"What if they find something suspicious?" Kozlow asked.

"That depends," Jared said. "If it's a debatable issue, the pathologist we hire might be able to downplay it. But if they can link it directly to you, they may charge you with mur—"

"I told you, I don't want this turning into a murder trial," Rafferty interrupted.

"Well, sorry to disappoint you, but that's out of my control at this point."

When Sara and Fawcett were done scrubbing up, Fawcett handed her a piece of spearmint gum. "Chew this," he said.

"Huh?" Sara said, taking the gum.

"You're not supposed to bring in food or drink, but it'll keep you from getting nauseous. The smell can turn stomachs."

"I'll be fine," Sara said as she pocketed the gum and pulled her surgical mask in place. "I've been inside a mortuary before."

Shrugging, Fawcett walked toward the autopsy room. The enormous, immaculately clean room was sectioned into eight individual working areas and contained eight autopsy tables. The metal tables had hundreds of small holes to drain internal fluids away from the body. At the moment, three other autopsies were taking place. When Fawcett opened the door to the room, the stench of decomposing bodies hit Sara like a freight train. As she frantically reached for the gum, she caught sight of Arnold Doniger's unearthed remains. She saw the greenish hue that now colored his complexion. And the decomposition that had just started to eat away at his shoulders and the outside of his thighs. And the slippage of skin that made his face seem almost liquefied. Before she could even get the gum out of her pocket, Sara lurched forward and vomited into her surgical mask, causing a stream of discharge to run down the front of her hospital gown.

Fawcett immediately pulled Sara out of the room to avoid contaminating the area. Watching her clean up in a metal sink next to the autopsy room, he asked, "Would you like that piece of gum now?"

"I think so," Sara said as she spit out the remainder of her breakfast. After rinsing her mouth and splashing some water on her face, she looked up at Fawcett.

"Ready to try again?" he asked, handing her a new surgical gown.

"Ready as I'll ever be."

Fawcett took a quick scan of Doniger's body, then stepped on the foot pedal that started his hands-free recorder. His voice became careful and meticulously measured. "There are embalming incisions in the left and right femoral triangle, as well as the left side of the neck. The embalmed body is a well-developed, well-nourished sixty-six-year-old white male measuring sixty-eight inches, and weighing one hundred and seventy-four pounds. He has brown hair and no discernible exterior injuries." Opening Doniger's eyes, Fawcett pulled out two plastic disks that looked like opaque contact lenses.

"What're those?" Sara asked.

"Eye caps," Fawcett said. "Mortician's favorite trick. They're lenses with ridged teeth on them—that's what keeps your eyes closed. Permanently."

"Nasty," Sara said.

"But they work," Fawcett replied. "I just hate having them in there. Personal taste." He put the eye caps aside and picked up a scalpel. With a quick flourish, he sliced a large Y into Doniger's chest. The incisions ran down from each shoulder, met at the center of his chest, then went down to the pelvis. "Chew," Fawcett said when he noticed that Sara's mouth wasn't moving. "This is the worst of it."

Following his directions, Sara frantically chomped on her gum. It still didn't prepare her. Fawcett reached into the center of the Y and peeled Doniger's skin away from his body, revealing darkened ribs and most of his internal organs. That's when the sweet, alcoholic smell of the embalming fluid hit.

"You still there?" Fawcett asked.

"I . . . I think so," Sara muttered. All she tried to think of was the freshness of her spearmint gum.

"Good—because I was lying. This is the worst part." He put down his scalpel and picked up four-foot-long stainless steel cutting shears. "For a gardener, it cuts heavy branches; for me, it's just as good on old bones." He then went to work on Doniger's ribs, cutting through the lowest ribs and working his way up. Each crack was like a wooden bat against a baseball. To clean it up, he drew the breastbone away from the heart, then pulled away five ribs that were lodged in the diaphragm.

"Spearmint gum, spearmint gum, spearmint gum," Sara whispered to herself.

When the ribs were gone, Fawcett took a survey of the now easy-to-reach organs. "Nice," he said, seeming pleased. "They didn't trocar him much.

Most of it's intact." Turning to Sara, he added, "What'd you say she fed him the night he died?"

"Apple juice and a granola bar. Why?"

Fawcett leaned into the open body, took his scalpel, and sliced around Doniger's stomach. Satisfied with his cuts, he slid his hands under the organ, lifted the stomach, and put it into a nearby metal pan. He then looked back at Sara. "Because we're going to peek inside and see for ourselves."

Three and a half hours later, on the last piece of her second pack of gum, Sara left the autopsy room. She watched through the door as Fawcett pulled a sheet over the body, then made some final statements into his recorder. When Fawcett joined her, she could barely contain her excitement. "What'd you think?" she asked eagerly. "Is it a murder?"

"I can only give you facts—you draw your own conclusions."

"That's great, but I've spent the last three and a half hours listening to you talk about anterior chambers and aqueous equilibration. I need you to put it in plain English. Did Arnold Doniger die in a coma caused by his diabetes?"

"As near as I can tell, yes," Fawcett said as they took off their gowns. Well accustomed to Conrad's black-and-white approach to answering questions, Sara was frustrated by Fawcett's conditional responses. "The relevant question now is: Was the death natural or was it caused by a third party?"

"I don't understand," she said as they headed back to his office.

"There's enough information to support both—you just have to decide which scenario is more logical. According to the decedent's wife, her husband was cranky, so she gave him some apple juice and a granola bar. When you're a diabetic, the crankiness is caused by low blood sugar. To raise your blood sugar, you commonly have some form of caloric intake—an apple, a cookie, something like that. And if the food makes your blood sugar too high, you ordinarily take an insulin shot to lower it. At least, that's generally the case."

"So food brings your blood sugar up, and an insulin shot brings it down."

"Correct," Fawcett said as he stepped into his cluttered office and headed directly for the overcrowded bookshelf on the far wall. As he looked for a particular book, he continued, "And if you give yourself a shot when your blood sugar is low, the shot will bring it down even further and you'll fall into a coma or have a stroke. Essentially, we know his blood sugar was low at the time of the shot, because it caused him to go into the coma. The trick is finding out what his blood-sugar level was hours before the shot."

"How do we do that?"

"As I said, that's the trick. Remember the Claus von Bülow case? Detecting blood sugar levels to prove a murder is a difficult game. It's an almost undetectable crime."

"What do you mean 'almost'?" she asked, trying to drag concrete answers out of him.

"Ah, here we go." Fawcett pulled a small white textbook from the shelf. As he scanned a few pages, he rubbed his right earlobe between two fingers. Eventually, he explained, "According to traditional practice, a few hours after someone dies, you can't tell their blood-sugar level. It's undiscernible in most of their body. But if you subscribe to some of the superior medical journals—which were recently sliced from our budget—you'd know that it's still detectable in one place: the anterior chamber of the eye."

"Are you telling me that when you were dissecting Arnold's eyes, you were actually measuring his blood-sugar level?"

"Science can only give you the facts if you know where to look," Fawcett replied. "Equilibration in the eye is very slow, so the fluids of the eye don't match the fluids of the rest of the body. As a result, while the fluids in your body may dissipate, the fluids in your eye linger and leave a mark that's as clear as a fingerprint—which allows us to track the body's blood-sugar levels."

"And what did Arnold Doniger's eyes say?" she asked anxiously.

"They said his blood sugar was normal, but you have to remember that the eyes are always a little bit behind the rest of the body. Which means that if he died of low blood sugar, which is strongly suggested by the autopsy results, his blood sugar dropped precipitously in the end."

"But doesn't that support Claire's story that his blood sugar was low and that that's why she gave him the juice and the granola bar?"

"Don't lose sight of the facts. You saw what was in his stomach—there were no signs of food. He hadn't eaten for several hours."

"So they starved him, and then when his blood sugar was low enough, they gave him a shot of insulin and finished him off?"

"Or they gave him an overdose of insulin. That's if a third party caused the death. Either way, it's a wonderful way to kill someone. As a pathologist, even if I'm diligent enough to check the eyes, it's still difficult to reach a solid conclusion. Whoever did this, you have to admire their ingenuity."

Sara nodded. "What about pinpointing the time of death? According to my theory, he died about four days earlier than his wife says. Any way to prove that?"

"That'd be simpler if he was a fresh kill, but he's been in the ground for almost a week. Were there any odd smells reported by the paramedics when they came to get the body?"

"I don't think so, but I'll ask," Sara said. "Anything else suspicious?"

"Actually, there was some tearing in the lining of the brain, which is sometimes the result of intense cold or freezing temperatures. But since the brain is now mostly a mass of decomposed mush, I'm not convinced that's what caused it. It did strike me as odd, though."

As she processed the information, Sara glimpsed Fawcett's clock; it was almost eleven forty-five. "I'm late," she blurted, leaping out of her seat. As she rushed to the door, she added, "Let me ask you one last question: Do you think your findings are convincing enough to prove that Arnold Doniger was murdered?"

"You're the one who draws the conclusions— were you convinced?"

Sara opened the door and smiled wide. "Thoroughly. Now all we have to do is convince the jury."

Running up the steps of 100 Centre Street, Sara glanced at her watch and cursed the New York City traffic that had held her taxi hostage for the past half hour. It was now almost quarter past twelve, which meant she was already fifteen minutes late for Kozlow's arraignment. Hoping that Kozlow still hadn't entered his plea, she darted into the building, through the metal detector, and took the elevator to the eleventh floor. She read room numbers as she ran and headed up the hallway until she reached room 1127. Pausing in front of the courtroom, Sara took a moment to catch her breath. The much-needed minibreak made one thing clear: If she didn't go to the bathroom soon, she was going to explode.

Looking through the glass window in the door of the courtroom, she saw that Kozlow was seated on the left side of the room. He still hadn't been called, which meant the proceedings were running late. She raced for the bathroom. Inside, she headed straight for the first of the four bathroom stalls. Moments later, she heard someone else enter the bathroom and turn on the water at one of the sinks. Curious, Sara peeked through a crack in the door. But by the time she got a good look at the sinks, the person was gone. Sara was startled by a loud knock on the door of her stall.

"Who is it?" she asked nervously.

"It's me. Rise and shine." The familiar voice sent a chill through Sara's chest, and there, peering over the top of the stall, was the man with the sunken cheeks.

She jumped to her feet, readjusted her clothes, and barreled out of the stall.

Sunken Cheeks was leaning against one of the sinks, waiting for her. "Caught you with your pants down, huh?" he asked as she charged toward him.

"What the hell are you doing here?"

"Just checking up on my inves—"

Before Elliott could finish his sentence, Sara swung her briefcase through the air, attempting to hit him in the face. Raising his hand to block her attack, he caught her briefcase in midair. "Nice briefcase," he said. He threw it to the floor. "I see you rubbed my message out."

"Stay away from me."

"You're not the one I care about, Sara—although I'm glad you kicked your hubby out."

"Don't you dare touch him."

Elliott grabbed Sara by her lapels. "Don't tell me what to do." He shoved her backwards, sending her crashing into the stall. Tripping over the toilet, she banged her head on the back wall. As Elliott left the bathroom, he added, "By the way, check out Doniger's basement. You'll like what you find."

Picking herself up as fast as possible, Sara raced after Elliott. But by the time she reached the hallway, he was gone. "Damn," she said, vigorously rubbing the bump on the back of her head. Her heart was drumming as she peered through the window in the door of the courtroom. To her surprise, Jared and Kozlow were standing at the defense table, addressing the judge. With a sharp tug, she pulled open the door.

When she walked into the room, she heard the clerk of the court ask Jared, "How does your client plead, sir, guilty or not guilty?" Wondering how the arraignment was proceeding without her, Sara headed briskly to the front of the room. Maybe she should shout an objection, she thought, her mind scrambling for a solution. But as she was about to open her mouth, she noticed that Conrad was sitting at the prosecutor's table. Nodding, she offered a silent thank-you to her mentor.

"Not guilty," Jared said, standing next to Kozlow at the defense table.

In response, Conrad approached the bench and handed a bundle of papers to the judge.

Without saying a word, Sara sat at the prosecutor's table. Glancing to her left, she locked eyes with Jared. He looked haggard, with heavy bags under his eyes. He clearly had had a rough night. Purposely turning away, Sara waited for Conrad to return to the table. When he sat down next to her, she whispered, "Thank you. The autopsy ran longer than I thought and traffic was—"

"Don't sweat it," Conrad interrupted. "You're just lucky Guff had copies of your files. He's the one who really saved your ass."

Turning around, Sara saw Guff in the front row of the spectator section. He winked at her.

"The motion day is set for two weeks from today," the judge announced from the bench. "Report to Part Thirty-one on October third. The case will be heard by Judge Bogdanos."

When the judge banged his gavel, Jared approached his wife. "Nice to see you. I was starting to get worried."

"I had some extra work to do," Sara said.

"You mean the autopsy," Jared said definitively.

"Exactly."

"So what'd they find?"

"I don't think she has to answer that," Conrad interrupted, standing from his seat.

Annoyed, Jared said, "You must be Conrad."

"And you must be Jared."

"That's right. Her husband. And last I checked, Sara was able to answer questions for herself."

"Well, last I checked, defense attorneys knew

that they shouldn't expect shortcuts. So stop begging for autopsy results you're not entitled to yet."

"I didn't realize this was your case," Jared said.

"It's not," Sara said, stepping between the two men. "Conrad, back off. Jared, we'll discuss this later."

"Whatever you want," Jared said, still staring at Conrad. "Give me a call when you're ready." Motioning to Conrad, he added, "Nice to meet you."

"You, too," Conrad said coldly.

As Jared and Kozlow walked out of the courtroom, Sara looked at Conrad. "What was that about?"

"I just didn't want to see him walk all over you," Conrad said, packing up his briefcase.

"I appreciate the concern, but I can handle my husband just fine."

"I'm sure you can, but—"

"There is no but," Sara interrupted. "I may be new, and I may still be learning, but I'm not a lightweight. The only reason I let him broach the subject of the autopsy was because I wanted to see how much he knew. Jared's got a great information network and I want to know where it starts. So stop thinking you can swing in on a vine and save me from the bad guys."

"Sara, just so you know: Not once, ever, have I thought you were a lightweight."

Caught off guard by the compliment, Sara took a second to respond. "What's that supposed to mean?"

"It doesn't mean anything. That's just how I feel."

"Then don't treat me like a novice. I finally know what I'm doing with this one."

"So I guess you didn't need me to stand in for you today? You had the whole thing covered yourself, right?"

Sara had to grin. "C'mon, don't go mucking up my impassioned arguments with some lame logical flaw," she joked. "I know I needed you to stand in for me. I just—"

"I get the picture—he's your husband, so you're the only one who can pick on him. Now can we get out of here? You have a trial to prepare for."

"Yeah, yeah, yeah—we all can't wait for the trial," Guff said as they walked out of the courtroom. "Now tell us about the autopsy. Did you puke all over yourself, or were you able to hold it together?"

Looking over Guff's shoulder, Sara saw that Jared and Kozlow were still lingering in the hallway. "Not here," she said. "Wait until we get back to the office."

After returning to 80 Centre, Sara spent the next forty-five minutes relaying the findings of the medical examiner's autopsy. She told them about the fluid in Arnold Doniger's eye and the lack of food in his stomach. She told them that he could've been killed by a forced injection by a third party, or he might have accidentally given the injection to himself. Slowly and methodically, Sara explained all the details, trying her best not to sway her colleagues' opinions. If they were going to be convinced it was murder, she wanted them to reach that conclusion themselves.

When she was done explaining, Conrad said, "So his stomach was completely empty?"

Sara nodded.

"Then she couldn't have given him anything to eat," Conrad continued. "Even if everything else can be logically explained, Claire lied to our faces."

"That's what did it for me," Sara added. "You can't ignore that fact."

"And if it's a murder, that also tells us why almost nothing was taken during the burglary," Guff said.

"It all fits," she said. "Every single piece of it." Looking at Conrad, she added, "So be honest: What do you think?"

At first, Conrad was silent. Eventually, he said, "Sounds to me like you might be able to upgrade this case to a homicide. Nice going."

"Yeah?" Sara asked, her voice rising. Unable to hide her excitement, she beamed with delight. For the first time since Pop went into the hospital, she saw the path for saving Jared.

"Between Claire and Kozlow, we've got too many fishy actions in too short a time span," Conrad said.

"Oh, man, I can't believe it," Sara said, pounding her desk. "I knew this case had something to it. Now who do we charge with murder? Both of them or just one?"

"You tell me. Who do you think is the killer?"

"I think Claire is full of crap, but I don't think she's the one who did the deed. My guess is she hired Kozlow to give the injection."

"And maybe the so-called stolen watch and golf ball were payment for the kill," Guff added. "If we check Claire's bank accounts, we'll be able to see if she was out of cash or not."

"Great. Perfect. Let's get those as soon as possible," Sara said. "I don't want to waste any time with this." Turning to Conrad, she asked, "What else can we do?"

"If I were you, before I filed new charges, I'd do some more research. You have the *how*, but to make a good murder case, you need to know the *why*. Look into Claire Doniger's cash flow, check out Arnold Doniger's will, find anything you can that would suggest a motive. And when you have that, file new charges with a new complaint and rearrest the party you want to charge. You have a lot of work ahead of you, but you're well on your way." Conrad stood and walked to the door. "Meanwhile, I hate to run, but I really have to get back to my work for a change. Keep me informed about what you find."

"You can count on that," Sara said. "And thanks again for filling in for me today—you have no idea how much that meant to me. Really. Thank you. For everything."

"Anytime," Conrad said.

As Conrad left, Guff watched his boss. She was already feverishly writing up a to-do list. "Don't worry," Guff said. "We're going to be able to save him."

"Only if we're organized. That's the only way to beat him." Seeing that Conrad was gone, Sara carefully picked up her briefcase and set it down on her desk in front of Guff. "Can you take this down and have it fingerprinted for me?"

"Why?" Guff asked.

"Because when I was rushing to get to court on time, I was lucky enough to once again meet up with Sunken Cheeks."

"He was in the courthouse?"

"Spying on me," Sara said. "And since we still don't know who he is, I did the only thing I could think of—I swung my briefcase at him, hoping he would catch it."

"So now you have the fingerprints on this bad boy?" Guff asked. When Sara nodded, he added, "You're one sneaky son of a bitch, y'know that?"

"I try," she said, leaning back in her seat. "And you, Mr. Guff—thanks again for saving my butt."

"It was nothing. To be honest, Conrad was dying to fill in. And watching him confront Jared was well worth the price of admission."

"I still don't understand why he did that."

"What's to understand? He's got the hots for you."

"Oh, please. Conrad's got no hots."

"Sara, through poor planning and bad timing, you almost missed today's arraignment. You didn't call to make sure you were covered, you didn't have anyone to back you up, you just plain missed it. And what was Conrad's reaction? Did he ream you? No. Did he make the big vein appear on his forehead? No. Instead, he said, 'Oh, I'll cover for her—no big deal.' Anyone else he would've slaughtered. But you, he covers."

"Maybe he's just calming down as he gets older."

"Conrad'll never calm down. We're talking about a man who, even when he stays in a hotel, makes his own bed. That's the person you think is calming down? The only reason he got in Jared's face is because he's got the hots for you."

"I wouldn't read too much into it," Sara said. "He was just doing me a favor."

Later that evening, Jared took a cab across town to the Upper East Side. Amid the designer boutiques and stylish storefront cafés that lined

Madison Avenue was the home office of Lenny Barrow. Located on Madison and East Sixty-fifth Street, above a boutique that sold overpriced children's clothes, was a sign that read SURE YOU KNOW WHERE HE IS? LEONARD BARROW—PRIVATE INVESTIGATOR. Entering through a narrow doorway next to the clothing store, Jared walked upstairs and knocked on Barrow's door.

Barrow greeted him wearing a sport coat and a tie. "What're you so dressed up for?" Jared asked.

"You know how it is in this neighborhood," Barrow said as he pulled off his jacket and loosened his tie. "Everyone's got to make an impression." He walked back to his desk and slouched down in his beat-up leather chair. The office was cramped and tiny, but Barrow knew the location guaranteed a clientele who'd pay their bills on time. "Now what's so important that you had to come all the way over here?" he asked.

"To be honest, I'm scared of even talking in my office anymore," Jared explained. "The walls have ears."

"All walls have ears. The important question is, who's listening?"

"I know who's listening. That's why I want to know what else you found."

"Well, if it makes you feel any better, I did some digging into corporate records and found out that Rafferty's company, Echo Enterprises, is co-owned by our dearly departed chum, Arnold Doniger."

"What?" Jared asked.

"They've been partners for years—built it into a real gold mine."

"You've got to be kidding me. So Rafferty had Arnold killed to get control of the business?"

"Depends who gets the business," Barrow said. "Time will tell."

"What about the tap on Rafferty's phone? Is that set up yet?"

"I meant to put it in yesterday, but I didn't have time. I checked his phone bills, though."

"And?"

"And nothing. Local calls aren't itemized, so I can't see who he's calling. Sara can get them, though. The DA's office can have them itemize everything."

"I don't care about the DA's office. In fact, don't mention them anymore—they're not going to help us. I need information that's accessible now. Understand?"

Tapping his thumbs on his desk, Barrow stared at his friend. "I take it there's still a problem in the bridal suite."

"I'm sorry, that wasn't directed at you. Sara and I are just hitting a few speed bumps."

"I think having you move out is a little worse than a speed bump."

"How'd you know I moved out?"

"It's my business to know."

"Okay, so Kathleen told you."

"Of course Kathleen told me. What do you expect? She's worried about you. Says you're starting to get obsessive—even refusing another piece of movie memorabilia."

"That has nothing to do with me moving out. I just want to win the case."

"And Sara's given you a few too many reasons to think that's not possible anymore?"

"It's hard to explain. It's just that two days ago, she was down for the count, and now she's hitting like Muhammad Ali. Everything's been going her way lately."

Watching Jared fidget with the tip of his tie, Barrow asked, "You really don't like losing, do you?"

"I hate it," Jared said, looking up.

"And the fact that your wife's the one who's beating you is making you even crazier."

"I don't know. There's more at stake than that."

"More than your marriage? What's bigger than that?"

"Nothing I can really talk about," Jared said despairingly. "Please just drop it."

An awkward silence took the room. "You're really in trouble, aren't you, J?"

Jared didn't move.

Leaning forward, Barrow opened his bottom drawer and pulled out a .38-caliber handgun. "Here," he said. "In case."

Jared took the handgun from Barrow and stared at it. "I don't know. I don't think I'm the gun-toting type."

"If you're in as much trouble as I think you are, you should have a gun," Barrow said. He rolled up the leg of his slacks, revealing an even smaller pistol in a leather ankle holster. Unfastening the holster, he handed it to Jared. "If you don't like the big one, take this instead. It's small, compact, and easy to hide." When Jared didn't reach for it, Barrow added, "Just in case."

Reluctantly taking the gun, Jared rolled up his own pants and put on the holster.

"You barely even notice it's there, do you?"

"I guess," Jared agreed. "Let's just hope I don't have to use it."

* * *

Sitting in the driver's seat of his plain white rental car, Kozlow stared at the inconspicuous entryway to Barrow's office and wondered what was taking so long. Give it time, he told himself. It's just like Rafferty said: "They have a lot to discuss. Jared's getting nervous, and as that happens, he'll start looking for a way out."

As usual, Rafferty was right. Jared was in the office for almost a full hour. When he did finally leave, Kozlow watched him disappear up the block. He seemed even more tense than when he had walked in.

Looking up at Barrow's private-detective sign, Kozlow knew it wouldn't be long. Twenty minutes later, Barrow left his office and headed across Sixty-fifth Street. Here we go, Kozlow thought. Time to return that favor.

With a semihot cup of coffee in hand, Sara arrived at work early Saturday morning. Between the newest developments with Kozlow, the maintenance and negotiations of her other two cases, and the paperwork from the two cases she pled out, Sara was finally starting to understand the temptation of keeping a change of clothes in her office.

Putting the coffee down on her desk, Sara picked up the phone and checked her voice mail. The only message was from Tiffany, who wanted to know why Sara hadn't picked her up from school yesterday. "Oh, no," Sara said as she listened to the message. Replacing the receiver, she tried to think of a way to make it up to her.

Sara then flopped in her chair and kicked her feet up on her desk. This is going to be a great day, she thought, putting Tiffany out of her mind. Pop was feeling better; her mundane burglary was now a cut-your-teeth homicide; and while she missed her husband, she felt confident she could keep him safe. For the first time in months, Sara was flushed with confidence. It was all going to work out.

Ten minutes later, Guff stuck his head into Sara's office. He took one look at her and asked, "What flavor canary did you eat last night?"

"Can't I just be in a good mood for once?"

"Actually, I was going to ask you the same thing," Guff said with a mischievous smile, "because *today's your lucky day*!" Darting out to the hall, Guff shouted, "Bring it in, boys!" He high-stepped back into Sara's office, followed by two delivery men carrying a brand-new olive-green vinyl sofa.

"You actually got one!" Sara said in disbelief. "How'd you pull this one off?"

As the men put the sofa down on the right-hand side of the room, Guff explained, "Let's just say we owe the cute little redhead in Purchasing a favor."

"What'd you do? Go out with her?"

"Exactly the opposite. I promised her I wouldn't call her for six weeks. She tried to make it a full two months, but I held my ground."

"You sure did," Sara said. She sat on the sofa and patted its cushions. "Ohhhhh, genuine American vinyl."

"Nothing but the shiniest for my boss," Guff said as the delivery men left the office. "And that's not even the best part." Guff reached behind his back and pulled something from his back pocket. "Guess what I'm holding in my hand right now?"

Sara thought for a moment. "A giraffe?"

"Smaller."

"A canoe."

"Smaller."

"A shrunken head."

"Uhhh, smaller—depending on how shrunken it is."

"A magic lasso that makes you tell the truth."

"Oh, you're never going to get it," Guff said. "The paperwork came in during your first week, and although you're supposed to pick it up yourself, I fudged the rules and picked it up for you. You were so busy, I figured—"

"Just give it to me already," Sara demanded.

"Okay, close your eyes," Guff said as Sara obliged. "On three. One . . . two . . . three."

When Sara opened her eyes, she saw what Guff was holding: an official gold badge with the words *Sara Tate, DA,* and *New York County* engraved into it. Sara's badge seemed to sparkle in the morning light.

"Congrats," Guff said, handing her the badge in its black leather case. "You're officially an assistant district attorney."

Mesmerized, Sara couldn't take her eyes off of her newest form of ID. "Incredible," she finally said. "I feel like a cop."

"And now you can do all those cool cop things, like walk onto a crime scene and get good seats at the movie theaters. Most important, you can whip it out and scream, 'Sara Tate! ADA!'" Guff yelled as he pulled out his own imaginary badge.

"This is terrific. Thank you, Guff. I really mean it. You didn't have to do all this."

"Just do me one favor in return. Let me see you flash the badge."

Sara got up from her new sofa and crouched into position. She then brandished the badge and yelled, "*Sara Tate! ADA! Stop or I'll blow your ass away!*"

"You can't yell a rhyme," Guff said, laughing. "No one'll take you seriously."

Before Sara could make another attempt, Conrad stormed into the office. He didn't look happy.

"Check it out," Sara said, holding out her badge. "Real solid-metal authority." When she didn't get a response, she added, "Put on a smile—we're having a good time here."

"You don't even know, do you?" Conrad asked.

"Know what?"

A dire tone blanketed Conrad's voice. "Sara, I think you may want to sit down."

"What happened?"

"Just take a seat."

"Is it Jared? Is he okay? What—"

"Jared's fine."

She was frantic now. "It's Pop! Oh, God, it's Pop! What happened? Is he—"

"Your family's fine," Conrad interrupted. "It's your private-eye friend, Lenny Barrow. They found him murdered last night."

"Lenny's dead?" Sara asked, stunned. "When did it happen? How?"

"A hit-and-run driver plowed into him a block away from his office," Conrad explained. "Crushed his skull on impact."

Sara sank to the sofa. "I can't believe it. We've known Lenny for years. He took me to the hospital when I had my appendix out—carried me from the cab."

"If you want, I can get you the homicide report on it," Conrad offered. "It may have some more information."

"I can't believe he's dead," Sara said.

"Are you okay?" Guff asked, sitting down next to her.

"Hand me the phone," Sara said to Conrad. "I have to tell Jared."

"Dead?" Jared asked, his voice cracking.

"Sara called about a half hour ago. He was found

dead last night," Kathleen explained. "I'm really sorry, Jared. I know you two were close."

"I don't believe this," Jared said. As he undid his tie and the first button of his shirt, his hands were shaking. "Have you heard from Rafferty or Kozlow?"

"Not yet. I don't think they're coming in today." Seeing the sweat form on her boss's forehead, Kathleen asked, "Are you okay? Do you want me to get you some water?"

Jared stood up and walked to the door, perspiration running down his back. "I'm fine. I just need to get some fresh air." Lurching down the hallway, Jared had trouble catching his breath. He staggered into the men's room and over to one of the three marble sinks. Leaning forward, he felt as if he was going to throw up. For two minutes, he fought his nausea and struggled to slow his breathing. He then turned on the cold water and splashed it against his face.

Eventually, he looked up, staring at himself in the mirror. It's my fault, he thought I never should've gotten him involved. Looking away, he wished there were some way he could undo the past weeks' events. That he could get rid of the case, protect his wife, and, most important, bring back his friend. As he replayed the events in his mind, he kicked himself for going to Barrow's office last night. He should have known better than that—Rafferty had said he'd always be watching. Still unable to look in the mirror, Jared closed his eyes and tightened his fists. In the span of a heartbeat, painful remorse turned to tormenting anger.

He opened his eyes. *"You dumb son of a bitch! How could you do that to your friend?"* he screamed.

Then, without thinking, Jared pulled back and thrust his fist into the mirror, shattering the glass into the sink. Blood ran down to his elbow, but he stood motionless. The senseless act of rage didn't make him feel any better. It didn't take away his pain, and it didn't allay his fears, but it did remove the mirror. And for a short but fulfilling moment, Jared Lynch didn't have to face himself.

At five o'clock that evening, Jared arrived home from work exhausted and devastated. For the past seven hours, he had been sitting at his desk, accomplishing nothing. So when Kathleen finally told him to go home, for once he didn't argue. And when she said the word *home*, Jared knew she didn't mean Pop's house. She meant home—his home, Sara's home, their home—the only place he wanted to be. As he opened the door and stepped inside, he expected to find an empty apartment. Instead, he was surprised to see his wife.

"Jared, I'm so sorry," she said, approaching her husband. She opened her arms and took him in.

As he buried his head against her shoulder, he began to cry.

"I'm here," Sara said, softly running her hands across his back.

The couple stood there, locked together. For a minute, their problems were gone. Then Sara noticed the white gauze bandage on Jared's hand. "What happened to your hand?" she asked.

"It's fine. I'm okay," he said as he pulled away.

"But how'd you—"

Sidestepping his wife, Jared went into the kitchen. "I cut myself with a letter opener. It's nothing." He poured himself a glass of red wine, then headed for the bedroom. Sara followed.

Entering the bedroom, Sara noticed that her briefcase was sitting open on the bed. As casually as possible, she closed the front flap and moved it to the floor.

"You really don't trust me, do you?" Jared asked as the tears welled up inside him. "Sara, I'd never do that again. I know there's no reason to believe that, but I swear to you, it really is the truth. You caught me off guard with the murder charge, so I guess I got desperate."

"Jared—"

"I know you don't want to go through this right now, but I didn't know where else to go. I just . . . I don't know . . . I really . . . I love you, Sara."

"I love you, too," she said. "And I understand."

"Then with Lenny . . ."

"Really. You don't have to explain. I know what you're trying to say."

"You do?" he said. "So you don't mind if I come back to—"

"Jared, our friend was just killed—I don't want you to be alone at Pop's."

He reached to embrace her.

As they hugged, Sara added, "Do you really think I'm so heartless that I wouldn't let you stay here tonight?"

Jared pulled away. "What do you mean 'tonight'?"

"I don't know, I just thought that since the trial's coming up . . ."

He was already grinding his teeth. Without saying a word, he stormed out of the bedroom. As he passed the kitchen, he threw his wineglass in the sink. The glass shattered in every direction, and red wine went flying.

"Damn," Sara whispered. She just wanted to protect him. Without him there, it'd be one less thing for Sunken Cheeks to harass her about. Chasing after him, she called, "Jared, I'm sorry. I shouldn't have said that. If you want to stay, you can."

"No way. Not a chance," he said as he headed for the front door.

"Please—I really want you to stay." When he didn't respond, she added, "Honey, I swear to you, I want you to stay. I mean it."

Jared stopped and turned around. "If you wanted me to stay, you never would've said that in the first place."

"That's not true. I still—"

"He's dead!" Jared shouted. "Lenny's dead and you're still worried about your files! Do you understand how twisted that is?"

"Jared, please . . ."

"I don't want to hear it," he said. "I'll be at Pop's." He pulled open the door, his back to his wife. "And if you care, Lenny's sister called. The funeral's tomorrow, so if you're not too absorbed in your own damn world, you should be there."

"Of course I'll be there."

"Great. I'll see you then." Without looking back, Jared walked out, slamming the door behind him.

"Enough of this," Kozlow said as he listened to the end of Jared and Sara's conversation. "She's kicking our asses all over the mat. Let's kill her and be done with it."

"Are you that much of a moron?" Rafferty asked, sitting at the desk in his study. "Sara's the best bargaining chip I have. Without her, I have nothing over Jared."

"Who cares about Jared? If he's not in the house, he's useless. I say we go back to Victor and tell him to—"

"Enough with Victor. I told you a dozen times, he won't touch the case. So I don't want to hear any more about it."

"All I'm saying is Jared hasn't done anything lately to—"

"Are you listening?!" Rafferty shouted. "I said I don't want to hear it!"

In one quick movement, Kozlow reached across the desk and grabbed Rafferty's left ear. Pulling him forward, he whispered, "How many times do I have to tell you—don't yell at me. I don't like it."

"Let go of me," Rafferty demanded. When Kozlow obliged, he asked, "What the hell is wrong with you?"

"Nothing," Kozlow said. "I just don't like being talked to like that."

"You've made your point." Running his hand over his hair, Rafferty slowly regained his composure. When this was done, he'd deal with Kozlow.

"So you think if we want to win, our best bet is still with Jared?" Kozlow asked.

"That's it," Rafferty said. "Now you know everything."

Sitting in her empty apartment, Sara tried to picture his face. She had been friends with Lenny for half a dozen years, but as she knew from personal experience, the simplest things are usually the easiest to forget. In a few weeks' time, her vivid memories of his physical presence would begin to fade. She'd always remember who he was as a person, and what he was like as a detective, but the artist in Sara wanted something more visual. Sure, she could always look at old photographs, but that wasn't the same. She wanted to recall how he moved across a room, and how he gestured with his short, fat fingers, and how his shoulders bobbed when he laughed. That was what she needed to remember, and that was what she spent the next two hours trying to do.

Drained by the effort, Sara reheated some leftover pasta and, standing at the kitchen counter, ate it from the container. Then, hoping to focus on something less stressful, she emptied the hamper into her purple laundry bag and headed for the laundry room in the basement of the building. Dragging her bag down the stairs, she walked out the front entrance of the brownstone, pulled out her keys, and opened the black metal gate that led to the basement door. Closing the gate behind her, she entered the laundry room and slowly separated her clothes into colors and whites.

The laundry room itself was typical for New York: quiet, musty, and difficult to access. Set off from the room was a small area for residential storage and another area that contained a poorly lit labyrinth of pipes and circuit breakers. Since the day they moved in, Sara had found the room creepy—the concrete walls made it feel like a tomb. When she was finished loading the washers, she took out her key, opened the gate, and returned to her apartment.

A half hour later, she returned to the basement. Once again, she opened the metal gate to reach the laundry room. Still regretting what she'd said to Jared, she moved her clothes from the washers to the dryers. I should call him, she thought. Tonight's not a night to be alone. In the midst of the transfer, she heard a clanging noise from the back of the basement. Those loud pipes that keep us up all winter, she thought. But when she heard the noise get closer, she peered over her shoulder. Out of the corner of her eye, she saw something move. Startled, she dropped the pile of clothes in her hands. Just a mouse, she realized, watching it scurry behind one of the washers. Although she was somewhat relieved, something still felt wrong. When she was done loading the dryers, she stepped outside to the black gate and realized that she had left her keys in the laundry room. She turned around and headed back. But when she checked the tops of the washers and dryers, the keys weren't there.

Sara pulled open the door of one of the dryers and rifled through her wet clothes. Nothing. Leaning into the second dryer, she pulled out one piece at a time, carefully searching for her missing keys. Suddenly, she heard another noise behind her. She turned around expecting to see the mouse. But then, suddenly, the lights went out.

Sara was enveloped by darkness. Her first thought was that someone else was in the room. Don't move, she told herself. That's how he'll find you. Holding her breath, she listened carefully. But all she heard was the monotonous churning of the spinning dryer. Over and over, the sound filled the air—it was maddening. Maybe it's just a blown fuse, she thought. There's no reason to panic. Then she felt a hand cover her mouth. Someone was behind her. He gripped her jaw tightly.

"Hiya, Sara," he whispered in her ear. She knew that voice anywhere. It was Sunken Cheeks.

She thrust her elbow into his stomach. It was just enough to make him let go. Sara darted in the direction of the door. Elliott was right behind her. She still couldn't see, but running her hands along the cold wall she found the door and tore it open. When she reached the black metal gate, she grabbed the bars and screamed, *"Police! Hel—!"*

Before she could even finish the word, she again felt his hand over her mouth. Elliott punched her fingers until she let go of the gate and dragged her back into the laundry room. The door closed and darkness returned. She thrashed in every direction, trying to pull herself free. Holding both of Sara's wrists in one hand, he threw her up against the wall. She was still struggling against his grip. Elliott backhanded her across the face. She stopped fighting. He leaned in and clutched her throat. She could smell the stale remnants of alcohol on his breath. "Keep him out of this house. Do you understand me? I don't want him fishing through your stuff."

Sara nodded vigorously.

Still holding her by the wrists, he threw her to the ground. In the pitch dark, she had no idea where he was—behind her, in front of her—he could have been anywhere. She lay completely still on the floor. Again, she listened carefully. And again, all she heard was the churning of the spinning dryer. Stay still, she told herself. He's at just as much of a disadvantage. Then, above the sound of the dryer, Elliott's deep voice cut through the room.

"Nothing's sacred," he warned. "Not even you."

Before Sara could react, she caught a crack of

light by the door. Then she heard the black metal gate swing open and slam shut. He was outside. She ran out the laundry room door and saw Elliott on the other side of the gate.

"Police! Someone! Help!" she screamed.

"Not in this city," Elliott said. He took Sara's keys and put them on the farthest step from the basement. "Someone'll be along soon." As he walked up the block, he added, "See you in court."

Monday morning, Sara arrived at work hoping for a relaxing day. The combination of Lenny's funeral and seeing Jared there had left her completely exhausted. So as she headed up the hallway, the last thing she expected to see was two workmen packing up boxes in her office. "What do you guys think you're doing?" she asked.

"Moving files," one of the workers said.

"I can see that. Who gave you permission to come in here?"

"Conrad Moore. He said we had to get all the Kozlow files, since they were removing the ADA."

As Sara's mouth dropped open, Guff entered the room. "What's going on?"

"I'm fired," Sara said, rushing out the door.

"Excuse me?" Guff asked. Chasing after Sara, he followed her to Conrad's office.

"Why the hell didn't you tell me?" Sara asked as she barged inside.

"Calm down a second," Conrad said. "I can explain."

"How can you possibly explain? You found out I got fired and you didn't even have the decency to tell me!"

"What're you talking about? You're not fired."

"I'm not?" Sara asked.

"No," Conrad said. "You're just off the case."

"What?"

"That's what Monaghan told me. He says he can't have a novice handling a first-class homicide. It's too complex and there's too much on the line. You're supposed to turn over all your files to me."

As Conrad's words slowly registered, Sara turned to Guff.

"It'll be okay," Guff said. "We'll figure out a way to—"

"No," Sara blurted. "I have to stay on this case. This is my case."

"I'm sorry," Conrad said. "I know you're upset, but I have to do what he says."

"This has nothing to do with me being upset," Sara said, her voice deadly serious. "I have to stay on this case."

Conrad glanced over at Guff, then looked back at Sara. "What aren't you two telling me? There's obviously something important you're leaving out."

"There's nothing," Sara insisted. "I just need to be on the case."

When Conrad stared at Guff, Guff said, "Stop looking at me—I didn't do anything."

"Sara, something is obviously going on."

Her glance dropped to the floor, but she didn't say a word.

"If you tell me, I can help you with it. Otherwise, you're on your own and off the case."

Still, Sara was silent.

"Fine, have it your way," Conrad said, walking to the door. "I can get the rest of the files myself."

As Conrad was about to leave, Sara looked over at Guff, who nodded back at her. Sara spoke up.

"If I tell you, you have to give me your word that you'll do things my way."

Conrad closed the door and turned around. "Go on."

"First, give me your word. Promise me that you'll do things my way."

"I'm not promising anything. Now tell me what the hell is going on."

"Forget it," Sara said.

Shaking his head, Conrad said, "Give me one good reason why I should take orders from you."

"Because if you don't, you'll be putting my life and my family's life in jeopardy."

Sara let her statement sink in. Eventually, Conrad said, "I promise you, I'll never do anything that will put you or your family in danger."

"And I have your word on that?"

"You have my word."

Taking a deep breath, Sara explained how she had been approached by Sunken Cheeks, and how he told her she had to win the case. From the threat he made about Jared to what he did to Pop, she told Conrad everything. Conrad didn't interrupt once. Then, the moment Sara was finished, he said, "Are you telling me an outside party threatened you and you never reported it to anyone? What did I tell you about that? The system is set up to protect you when—"

"Conrad, no offense, but I don't want to hear your lectures on the system right now. The system didn't protect Pop, and it certainly can't protect my husband. This psycho, whoever he is, has the fingerprints of a dead man, knows everything about me, approached me on a subway without me even knowing, and somehow got into my basement without a key. The truth is, he scares the hell out of me. Every time I walk into my house, I check the closets to see if he's there. In the bedroom, I look behind the door to see if he's waiting for me. He's not your basic criminal, and until we know who he is, I see no reason to piss him off. He's just asking me to do my job."

"He's not asking you to do your job. He's threatening Jared's life."

"He wants me to win," Sara shot back. "That's all he wants. And you and I both know that I can give it to him. You may be a better prosecutor, but no one knows my husband better than I do. I know how he thinks, and how he fights, and who he talks to."

"Like Lenny Barrow," Conrad interjected.

"Exactly. Like Lenny Barrow," Sara said. "Believe me, I don't plan on letting this guy off the hook, but I can't let you shut me out of this. It's my family, my problem, and my case."

"I don't know . . ."

"Conrad, since the day we first met, I've followed your rules. If you said it, I did it. And I'll always be grateful for that. Just this once, though, I'm asking you to see things my way. Help me stay on this case. That's all I'm asking."

For the next minute, no one said a word. "Let me think about it," Conrad finally said. "We'll talk again first thing tomorrow."

"As long as you think carefully," Sara said, heading for the door. "That's all I ask."

The following morning, Sara and Guff sat in Sara's office, waiting impatiently for Conrad to arrive. "Do you think he's going to go for it?" Guff asked.

"I have no idea," Sara said. "Sometimes he seems so predictable, other times I can't figure him out."

"Predictable? Conrad's never predictable. He may love to follow the rules and preach morality, but the moment he thinks it's necessary, he's prepared to drop that shtick and do what's right. Don't forget, he's both a New York resident and a government employee. By definition, that makes him a realist."

"I pray you're right," Sara said.

Ten minutes later, Conrad walked into Sara's office. He shut the door and stood directly in front of her desk. "Here's my offer," he said. "First, I'm not dropping this case."

"Then you can—"

"Hear me out," he interrupted. "I'm not dropping this case, because Monaghan won't let you do it alone. But I will agree to colawyer it with you. To everyone else, it'll look like I'm in charge, but between us, we'll be equal partners on it."

"So I still get to run it and manage it as I see fit?"

"As *we* see fit," Conrad corrected. "You have a lot riding on this case, but I won't let you do anything illegal or stupid just to make a point. In my experience, emotion always wrecks rational thought. So if you step out of line, I'm going to yank your ass back."

"But you'll help me win?"

"Make no mistake, Sara, we're going to win. No matter what your husband does, no matter how many motions he files, no matter how many designer-suit-wearing, expensive-tie-buying, Saab-driving, salon-styling, manicure-getting, mahogany-loving, conspicuous-consuming, over-billing, prestige-sucking, rich-ass lawyers he can find in that overhyped law firm, they're going to shine our industrial-carpeted floors by the time we're done with them. And whoever this fucker is that hurt your Pop—when this is all over, we're going to do our end-zone dance on his mysterious but guaranteed to be kicked-in face."

Sara grinned broadly.

"I knew he was going to say that," Guff said. "So damn predictable!"

"Now, do we have a deal?" Conrad asked, offering a handshake.

"As long as you don't tell Monaghan about the guy who threatened me."

"Monaghan won't hear a word. The only thing I've told him is how aggressive you are as a prosecutor and how late you love to work. You know he loves to hear that. Now, are you sure you're ready to continue hunting for this guy?"

"I wouldn't have it any other way," Sara said, shaking Conrad's hand.

"Good," Conrad said as he sat next to Guff on the couch. "Because that's where I want to start right now."

"Wait, before we do that, tell me something," Sara said. "What convinced you to keep me on the case?"

"All I had to do was put myself in your shoes. The moment I did that, I realized I'd want someone to step up for me. Now does that answer your question, or do you need me to feed you some psychological bullshit about how I needed to do this to exorcise my own personal ghosts?"

"Nope. That's enough," Sara said. "But if you keep doing nice things for me, I'm going to start telling people what a big softy you really are."

"They'd never believe it," Conrad said. He opened his briefcase and pulled out a sealed interoffice-mail folder. "Anyway, getting back to personal ghosts, this just arrived from Crime Scene. It looks like the fingerprint results you requested."

"The ones from my briefcase? What'd they say?"

"I didn't want to open it without my co-counsel," Conrad said. He threw the envelope to Sara. "You do the honors."

Sara ripped open the envelope and flipped through the report. "I don't believe this," she said.

"What?" Guff asked. "The prints belong to that same dead guy?"

"No, it's not the same dead guy. It's a new dead guy. According to the report, the prints on my briefcase belong to Warren Eastham, a petty criminal who was murdered last year."

"I don't understand it," Guff said. "How the hell does a man have two sets of fingerprints?"

"Maybe he works in Crime Scene and he's sabotaging all the searches we run," Conrad suggested.

"Or maybe Crime Scene is blowing the searches on its own," Guff added.

"I don't care how he does it," Sara said. "I just want to know who he is."

Dressed in tight black biker shorts and an oversized, faded Michigan sweatshirt, Elliott walked straight into the lobby of the medical examiner's building. "Messenger," he announced to the security guard, flashing the bright yellow nylon backpack that hung off his shoulder. "I'm looking for a Dr. Fawcett."

"Take the elevator to the basement," the guard said. "Room B-22."

When Elliott reached the basement, he quickly found room B-22. Opening the door, he saw Fawcett sitting behind his desk. "How're you doing?" Elliott asked with a smile. "I'm here to pick up the final autopsy report on Arnold Doniger."

"Are you from the DA's office?" Fawcett asked suspiciously.

"Oh, yeah," Elliott said, pulling a clipboard from his backpack. "Let's see here—I'm supposed to deliver it to Assistant District Attorney Sara Tate at 80 Centre Street ASAP. She apparently wants it yesterday."

"They always do," Fawcett joked. He handed Elliott the sealed envelope.

"Thanks, doc," Elliott said, putting the envelope in his backpack. "Say hi to the stiffs for me. Tell them they're really stinking up the place."

"Will do," Fawcett said as Elliott left the office.

Two and a half weeks later, a sharp October wind signaled the early arrival of winter. Although wool overcoats began to decorate the urban landscape, there was no other sign that anything was different in the city that never noticed. Sirens were still blaring, traffic was still overwhelming, Chinese food was still being delivered at all hours of the night, and Sara, Conrad, and Guff were still struggling to put together the pieces of the case.

"I got it," Guff said, waving a stack of papers in his hand as he entered Sara's office.

"Got what?" Conrad asked, leaning against Sara's filing cabinet.

"Oh, my good man, do you not know what you thus miss? I have acquired that most honored of all items—the tome of worldly bequests."

"The what?" Conrad asked.

"His will," Sara explained, sitting at her desk. "The surrogate court finally agreed to turn over Arnold Doniger's will."

"Agreed?" Conrad asked. "You should've subpoenaed it from them."

"You subpoena, I ask," Sara said. "The result's the same." Turning to Guff, she asked, "So what's it say?"

"You were right about one thing—Arnold Doniger wasn't lacking in the rich department. If you total all the monetary gifts in his will, he was worth at least seven million dollars. And that doesn't include his New York City house, his weekend home in Connecticut, or his interest in Echo Enterprises, which I'm assuming is his business."

"Big deal," Conrad said. "Half the East Side can go dollar-for-dollar. The real question is, who benefits?"

"That's the crazy part," Guff said, handing Sara the will. "We've been assuming Claire Doniger hired Kozlow to cash in on her husband, but according to the will, Claire doesn't get a single cent. When they were married ten months ago, she signed the prenup to end all prenups."

"But can't she still take her elective share?" Conrad asked. "From what I remember from law school, spouses can always get a guaranteed percentage, even when they're left out."

"Not in this case," Sara said. "Claire waived her elective share and everything else in her prenup. She doesn't even get the house they lived in."

"So you're telling me Claire doesn't have a motive to kill her husband?" Conrad asked.

"Not if that motive was an inheritance in the will. Based on this, she doesn't get a thing."

"Then who does?"

"Again, there's no one in particular. The monetary gifts are designated for a dozen or so different charities, the house in Connecticut goes to the local historical society, and the proceeds from selling the New York house are earmarked for Princeton, his alma mater."

"He doesn't have any other family?"

"No kids and no siblings. He's got a few cousins and an aunt in Florida, but all they get is a few thousand. Nothing worth killing anyone for."

"What about the business?" Conrad asked. "Who gets that?"

"Echo Enterprises is given to the other partners of the firm. My guess is he didn't want to mix family and business."

"I don't believe this," Sara said, standing up. "How can Claire not be the one who hired Kozlow? It made such perfect sense."

"Sure it did," Conrad said. "Except for the small fact that she doesn't have a motive."

"That's not necessarily true," Guff said. "Maybe she had him killed precisely because she didn't take anything under the will."

"I don't know," Conrad said. "That seems a little shortsighted. Once her husband dies, she loses her home, her security, her entire livelihood. If I were Claire, and I was pissed about being left out of the will, I'd keep my hubby alive and sock away all the money I could."

"Maybe she simply hated her husband," Sara suggested. "That's possible."

"Now you're projecting."

"I'm serious," Sara said. "Why do we need her to take money under the will? Tons of people kill their spouses for lesser reasons than that."

"That's true," Conrad said. "But when a not-so-wealthy fifty-year-old woman kills her sixty-six-year-old, recently married millionaire husband, there's got to be a good reason for it. And in all of my years working here, it's almost always got to do with money."

"Which is the one thing Claire doesn't get."

"Maybe that's the point," Guff said. "Maybe Claire isn't involved with this at all."

"No way," Sara said. "Claire is definitely involved with this. She's acted way too weird to not have some connection."

"Then we need to figure out what that connection is," Conrad added. "Otherwise, we're going to have a hard time making this case."

"So we have the victim, and the cause of death, and the will, and the possible triggerman, but we still don't have the motive," Guff said.

"And without the motive, we're stuck."

"They know," Claire Doniger said, fidgeting with her wedding band as her daily juice and jasmine tea sat untouched in front of her. "They definitely know."

"Don't get hysterical," he said. "If they knew, you'd already be indicted as an accomplice. They can't prove a thing."

"But how long is that going to last? They keep asking me when they can look through the house. What if they find something that—"

"I told you, I'm taking care of everything. Jared is working right now to make sure that visit never happens."

Claire stood and nervously started to clear the

table. "You've been saying that all along. But what if he can't stop them? What if—"

Grabbing Claire's wrists, he forced her to set down the teacup and saucer she was holding. He then pulled her toward his chair and onto his lap. "I want you to take a deep breath for me and listen to what I'm about to say: If it were only about the money, I would've walked away weeks ago. Do you understand? I don't like being alone. So no matter what it takes, no matter what I have to do, I'm not letting them take my best prize away from me. You're the reason I got into this, and no matter the consequences, we're going to come out of it together." Holding both of Claire's hands in his own, he added, "Now tell me who loves you."

Forcing a weak smile, Claire said, "You do."

"You're damn right I do," Rafferty said. "Damn right."

Massaging his temples and doing his best to ignore his throbbing headache, Jared stared at his computer screen. For the past two weeks, he'd sought out the firm's best criminal-defense attorneys. From each one, he tried to learn one more trick, one more hint, one more maneuver to win the case and save his wife.

Even the poster board was getting more attention than usual. Every day, he stared adamantly at the layout of the crime scene. Arriving no later than seven in the morning, he spent the first fifteen minutes of each day playing it through his head. Leaving no earlier than eleven at night, he always took one final look. He catalogued every moment. He indexed every minute. He did everything in his power to visualize every nuance of the crime.

Finally, to pick up where Barrow left off, Jared hired a well-recommended private detective, who scoured every inch of every block between Doniger's house and the spot where McCabe picked up Kozlow. Under Jared's instructions, the detective spoke to the garbagemen who did the early morning pickup, questioned the late-shift doormen from nearby buildings, and even called local taxi companies to see which drivers were in the neighborhood on the night in question. No matter how tenuous, how unlikely, or how outrageous the lead was, Jared and his staff searched for anyone who might be able to put Kozlow at a spot that was different from the one where McCabe said he was. But, in the end, after all the examining and exhaustive research, they couldn't find a single new witness.

"There must be someone we're forgetting," Jared said, staring at the poster on his wall.

"Are you kidding?" Kathleen asked. "We've thought of everyone."

"Did you ever find out about the paperboys?"

"Which ones? The *New York Times, New York Post, Daily News,* or *Newsday*? I spoke to all of them and none of them started delivering before five-thirty that morning."

"What about—"

"There's no one else," Kathleen interjected. "We've been through everyone. The local bakeries that start kneading dough at sunrise, the corner groceries that are open all night, even the high-end escort services that frequent the area. I think the only person we haven't spoken to is Arnold Doniger, and that's only because he's dead."

"I know," Jared said. "I just don't want to miss anything."

"Jared, killing yourself isn't going to bring Lenny back. And it's certainly not going to save your wife. When we find out about your motions, we'll know a lot more about the shape of the case. But until that happens, you can't keep running yourself like this."

"I'm fine," Jared said, turning toward his computer screen.

"Jared, you're not—"

"I said I'm fine," he insisted, raising his voice. "Now let's move on to the next subject."

"How much farther is this place?" Guff asked, sitting between Sara and Conrad in the backseat of the taxi.

"Stop asking already," Conrad said as the cab pulled out of the Holland Tunnel. "We'll be there soon enough."

"I can't help it," Guff said. "I get anxious during field trips. It makes me feel like I'm back in junior high."

"Junior high, huh?" Conrad asked. "Then how's this? Shut up until we get there, or I'll stuff you into a gym locker."

"Ahhhh, childhood," Guff said with a smile. "How I miss those now-gone days."

Ten minutes later, the cab pulled up to the front entrance of the Hudson County Pistol Range. As the three coworkers got out of the car, Conrad announced, "Here it is—the best firing range in the tristate area."

"You mean besides Manhattan itself?" Sara asked.

Within twenty minutes, Conrad, Sara, and Guff were armed, outfitted, and ready to begin their shooting practice. Following Conrad through the long, understated brick building, Sara and Guff were led to an enormous room that held eight private shooting booths. At the far end of each booth was its respective target. Some booths had standard bull's-eyes, others had outlines of animals such as deer and lions, and still others had outlines of human beings. The booths were organized into beginner, intermediate, and advanced areas, with the target located twenty feet away for the beginners and thirty yards away for the advanced. Without pause, Conrad walked straight to an advanced booth.

"I guess we're beginners," Sara said to Guff.

"No way," Conrad said. "Stay here with me."

"But I've never shot a gun in my life."

"Doesn't matter," Conrad said. "Best way to teach someone to swim is to throw them in the deep end."

"What if I don't want to learn how to swim?" Sara asked.

Conrad pointed to the booth next to his. "Everybody swims. Now get in."

When all three of them were in their booths, Conrad put on his protective goggles and headset. "Can everyone hear me?" he asked through the headset's small chin microphone.

"I read you loud and clear, Bandit," Guff said through his own headset. "Now how 'bout helping me with these here smokeys on my tail."

Ignoring Guff and getting a thumbs-up from Sara, Conrad picked up the .38-caliber handgun he had rented. With six quick shots, Conrad ripped

apart the paper target of the human being thirty
yards away.

"Not bad, Slim, but check this out," Guff said,
aiming his own gun. He fired six shots, then lowered the gun and looked at the target. He hadn't hit
a thing. "My gun's broken," he said.

"Your turn, Sara," Conrad said.

"Before I go, I have to once again ask my little
question: What the hell are we doing here?"

"I already told you, we weren't getting anywhere sitting in the office, so I thought we could
use a change of scenery. And whenever I hit a logic
wall, this is always the best place to calm down
and reevaluate."

"This is how you calm down? Wearing yellow
glasses and an oversized headset while shooting
giant holes through paper people?"

"Some people like classical music; others prefer
a more aggressive aesthetic," Conrad explained.
"Either way, we all needed our heads cleared. Now
stop complaining and start shooting."

"Whatever you say, colonel," Sara said. "But I
still don't understand how this helps us with the
case." Holding up her gun, Sara carefully aimed
at the target. She fired one shot. Then aimed again.
Then fired another shot. Then aimed again. Then
fired another shot. After six shots, she hadn't hit
the target once.

"You're trying too hard," Conrad said when Sara
was done. "Shooting a gun is an instinctive act.
The gun's an extension of you. It's like throwing a
baseball—you can't wait around and aim it—you
just have to throw it."

"Ohhhh, another physical-fitness analogy," Sara
said. "And this time a Zen one."

"I'm serious," Conrad said. "Try again, but this time just point and shoot."

After reloading, Sara once again faced the target. "Here we go," she said. "Be the bullet." She then raised her gun and fired off another six shots. This time, two of them hit the very top of the target.

"Not bad," Conrad said, stepping into her booth. "I think the only problem is your stance. Your center of gravity is off, so the kick of the gun is forcing you back and making you shoot high." After reloading Sara's gun, Conrad said, "Don't keep your feet together. Put one in front of the other and let your back leg be your anchor." When Sara rearranged her feet, Conrad stood directly behind her and positioned her hips.

"Easy there, cowboy. Now you're getting a little personal."

"That's the point," Conrad said. With a grin, he held on to her waist. "Now center your weight there. Your back leg's your anchor, but your weight's balanced there."

"I'm anchored," Sara said. Then, in a quick blur, she pulled her gun and got off six shots. Four of them hit the paper human target. One of them plowed through his face.

"Oh, my, where'd you learn to shoot?" Conrad asked.

Sara looked over her shoulder. She winked and lowered her voice to a growl. "Chinatown, Jake."

"Oh, my God," Guff said. "That's totally it."

"What's it?" Sara asked. "Chinatown?"

"No, no," Guff said. "Doniger's motive."

"Doniger's motive is Chinatown?"

"It's not what you said, it's what you did," Guff explained. "This whole time we've been going for the obvious motives. We went through greed, jealousy, hatred. But we never considered lust. I didn't even think about it until I saw the two of you together in the booth."

"What happened in the booth?" Sara asked.

"Yeah," Conrad added.

"No offense to either of you—since I hold you close to my heart—but are you really that blind?"

"Me?" Sara asked. "I wasn't—"

"Forget about how he got there; focus on the result," Conrad interrupted. He stepped out of the booth and approached Guff. "So if the motive is lust, where does that leave us?"

"I have no idea," Guff said. "It's only been a minute. That's as far as I've gotten."

"Maybe Arnold was sick and she killed him to put him out of his misery," Conrad suggested. "That's a killing out of love."

"No way," Sara said. "She's not that nice."

"Maybe she was in love with someone else, and she killed her husband so she could be with her true love," Guff suggested.

"Too romantic," Conrad said. "Besides, even New Yorkers are civilized enough to file for divorce."

"Not when there's something to be gained by the death," Sara countered.

"What do you mean?" Conrad asked.

"What if the person Claire loves is one of the people who takes in the will?"

"I see where you're going," Guff said. "So *both* of them hired Kozlow to kill her husband. She grants them easy access to the house, her lover foots the bill."

"There's only one problem," Conrad said. "According to the will, all the assets go to charities and other organizations."

"Except for one item," Sara said. "Echo Enterprises. That goes to the company's other partners."

"So you think one of Arnold's partners was sleeping with Claire, and when they realized that his death would not only allow them to be together but would also make them both rich, they hired Kozlow and bumped him off?" Conrad asked.

"It works for me," Guff said.

"Me, too," Sara added. "Although I want you both to know there was nothing going on in the booth."

"Oh, c'mon now," Guff said. "Does the sun set in the east? Do New Yorkers love to wear black? Was Elvis buried in a white suit, powder-blue shirt, and cashmere tie? Yes, yes, and yes. We're all simple creatures. So do I know flirting when I see it? Absolutely."

"The sun doesn't set in the east," Conrad pointed out. "It sets in the west."

Guff looked over at Sara, then back at Conrad. "That doesn't change the facts!" Guff shouted over Sara's laughter. "Flirting went on in that booth!"

CHAPTER 14

Sitting behind his antique desk in his office at Echo Enterprises, Rafferty wasn't happy. His breakfast with Claire had been stressful, his business lunch at CBS had been an ordeal, and as he stared across his desk, he realized the worst part of the day was right in front of him—Kozlow was in his office. "You better speak to Elliott. We have some serious problems."

"You don't have to tell me," Kozlow said, sitting in one of the two chairs opposite Rafferty's desk. "You're the one who's—" The ringing of Rafferty's intercom interrupted his thought.

"What is it, Beverley?" Rafferty asked.

"Sir, I have someone named Sara Tate out here who says she wants to see you," his secretary said.

"She's out there right now?" Rafferty asked, his fist tightening around the receiver.

"Yes, sir. Says she's from the district attorney's office and asked if she can take a minute of your time."

Rafferty paused and thought about the situation. Finally, he said, "Beverley, I want you to listen very carefully to what I'm about to say. No matter what Ms. Tate says, don't let her know who's with me in my office. If she asks, you have no idea who Tony Kozlow is, and you've never heard of him. I want you to give us five minutes, then I'll buzz you and you can show her in."

The moment Rafferty put down the phone, Kozlow said, "Sara Tate called here?"

"Worse than that. Sara Tate *is* here. Right outside as we speak."

Kozlow jumped out of his chair. "Now? She's here?"

"Calm down," Rafferty said. "Let's get you hidden, and then we'll deal with her." He walked to the corner of his office, pulled open a swinging panel, and revealed the entrance to his private bathroom. "Get in," Rafferty said.

"In the bathroom?" Kozlow asked. "Don't you have another entrance or something?"

"Get in!" Rafferty barked. "She'll be here in a minute."

Kozlow stepped inside. "See you soon," Kozlow added as Rafferty closed the paneling.

Two minutes later, Sara, Guff, and Conrad walked into Rafferty's office and found him sitting behind his desk, signing letters.

"Hi, Mr. Rafferty, I'm Sara Tate," Sara said, extending her hand. "These are my colleagues, Conrad Moore and Alexander Guff."

"Nice to meet you, Ms. Tate," Rafferty said as he shook her hand. "Please, take a seat." As Sara and Conrad sat down, Guff pulled up a chair from the far corner of the room. "Now what can I do for you?"

"Well, sir, we're following up on the murder of Arnold Doniger, and—"

"What?" Rafferty interrupted. "You think he was murdered? I can't believe it."

"That's the theory we're investigating," Sara said. "We actually came by to subpoena some of Echo's corporate records, but we thought it might be helpful to talk to some of the firm's partners."

"No, of course," Rafferty said. "Anything I can do to help, just let me know."

"Can you tell us a little bit about Echo?"

"Absolutely," Rafferty said. "Of course. Yes." Forcing a stutter, he explained, "Echo is an ownership company that deals in intellectual property. In layperson's terms, we own and are responsible for the copyrights for various theatrical properties."

"Anything we've heard of?" Sara asked, trying to gauge the value of the business.

Rafferty's answer was quick. "*A Chorus Line, Inherit the Wind, Cat on a Hot Tin Roof, A Streetcar Named Desire*—there are a few others. If someone wants to produce the play, be it a high school or a fifty-million-dollar production company, they come to us first. In exchange for our approval, we usually work out some sort of percentage agreement."

"So you get a percent of the take," Conrad said. "I imagine that's quite a cash cow."

"It pays the bills," Rafferty said.

"It may do more than that," Conrad said accusingly.

"I'm sorry, are you insinuating something?" Rafferty asked, trying to keep the conversation friendly.

"Not at all," Sara said as she glared at Conrad.

"We're just trying to determine if there's anything we've overlooked. Now, let me ask you: How many other partners are there in the business?"

"There are over forty employees, but the only two partners are Arnold and myself."

"Really?" Sara asked. "Then does that mean you have full ownership of the business now that Mr. Doniger is dead?"

"That depends on Arnie's will. When we first set up Echo, we decided that specific bequests would take precedence over our partnership agreement. So if Arnie gave his share to someone else, I'm now a partner with them. To be honest, though, knowing Arnie, I'm pretty sure he donated his share to charity. He was a true philanthropist."

"Actually, he left his share of the business to the partners of Echo," Sara explained. "Which I guess means you."

"What?" Rafferty asked, sounding shocked. "That can't be. There must be some sort of mistake."

"There isn't," Conrad said suspiciously. "Mr. Rafferty, how close are you to Claire Doniger?"

"I've known Claire since she and Arnie first met—at the Decorator Show House a few years ago. She's a wonderful designer."

"Do you spend a lot of time with her?"

"I've called on her a few times since Arnie died, to make sure she was okay. Beyond that, we haven't really spoken; she prefers to keep to herself."

"How about before her husband died—you didn't see her socially?" Conrad asked.

"Not really," Rafferty said. "Why do you ask?"

"No reason," Sara jumped in. "Listen, Mr. Rafferty, we don't want to take up any more of your time. You've been a big help."

"Well, please let me know if there's anything else I can do for you," Rafferty said. "Did you get everything you needed from Business Affairs?"

"I think so," Sara said, standing and shaking Rafferty's hand. "Once again, thanks for taking the time to talk with us."

"Anything I can do to help," Rafferty said as he walked them to the door.

When the door closed, Kozlow peered out from the bathroom.

"Come on out, they're gone," Rafferty said.

As Kozlow stepped out of the bathroom, the door to the office flew open. "Just one more thing," Sara said. "I wanted to give you my card—just in case you need to reach us."

Kozlow stopped dead in his tracks. Standing in the middle of the office, Rafferty had Sara on his far right and Kozlow on his far left, in their respective doorways. As Sara was about to step inside, Rafferty quickly moved toward her, blocking her entrance. "Thank you," Rafferty said. "If anything comes up, I'll be sure to call."

"I appreciate it," Sara said. "And once again, I'm sorry to bother you."

"No bother at all. I'm glad to help." When Sara left the office, Rafferty closed the door behind her. Neither he nor Kozlow moved for ten seconds.

"She's mine," Kozlow finally said. "Enough of this."

"Shut up," Rafferty said, picking up his phone and dialing.

"Jared Lynch."

"Listen, you overpaid, egotistical talking head, what the hell are you doing over there?"

"What's wrong?" Jared asked. "Did something happen?"

"You're damn right something happened! I just spent the last ten minutes entertaining your wife and her pathetic staff!"

"You saw Sara?"

"I not only saw her; I was questioned by her. And I'm telling you, that was it. She's finished. I'm going to rip a hole in her so deep—"

"Please . . . just wait. Let me talk to her."

"I don't give a shit about your promises."

"I'll take care of her. I swear. Just give me a little more time."

"This isn't optional, Jared. If she doesn't back off, I'm going to reunite her with Barrow. Do you understand what I'm saying?"

"Of course," Jared said, sounding shaken. "I'm sorry it happened."

Rafferty readjusted his jacket and paused. He didn't like losing control, but he wasn't going to let them take it all away. "Now, do you have any good news for us?" he asked Jared.

"I think so—I just got word from the judge's clerk. The decisions on our hearings are coming down tomorrow. If we win a few of those, we'll be able to exclude some of the evidence from Sara's case."

"You better pray for a good outcome," Rafferty said. "Because if you stay on this path, she's dead."

"So what'd you think?" Sara asked Conrad as they left the offices of Echo Enterprises.

"My gut says he's a liar, but I can't prove it yet," Conrad said. "Even when I tried to provoke him, he never once started to sweat."

"Not only that, he seemed like he really wanted to help us."

"I wouldn't take anything from that," Conrad said, standing on the sidewalk. "Feigning assistance is easy. Keeping calm is an entirely different magic trick. Besides, no matter how polite he is, he's the only person who clearly benefits from Arnold's death. That alone makes him one hell of a suspect. I mean, he's about to inherit a fifty-million-dollar business, and he wants us to believe he doesn't know what's in the will?"

"Well, if anyone cares, I didn't like him," Guff said. "Anyone who has three telephones—that's not a good vibe."

"I'll make a note of that," Conrad said, hailing a cab. "Guff got a bad vibe; Rafferty must be a murderer."

"What's on the agenda for the rest of the day?" Sara asked.

"We prepare for tomorrow's hearing, we take another look at the will, and we do our best to figure out if Oscar Rafferty is a concerned friend or one of the best bullshit artists we've ever seen."

"I just wish we had a better way to nail down the exact day of the death," Guff said. "That might change the whole story."

As she was about to get in the cab, Sara stopped. "That's not a bad idea," she said. "You guys mind taking a ride to the East Side?"

"Can't do it," Conrad said. "I have some stuff to do back at the office."

"Just put it off for a—"

"I can't," Conrad said. "I have to get back."
Motioning for Sara and Guff to get in the cab, he
added, "You guys go ahead, though."

"Are you sure?"

"Stop worrying and get out of here," Conrad
said. "I'll see you when you're done."

As the cab pulled away from the curb, Guff
turned to Sara. "So where're we going?"

"To do exactly what you said. We have to nail
down the time of death."

"Wait a second," Guff said, trailing behind Sara
as she walked toward Claire Doniger's house. "That
psycho told you to check out Doniger's basement,
and you're just getting around to it now?"

"Yes, I'm just getting around to it now. I tried
getting a detective assigned, but they wouldn't
give us one, remember?"

"I thought detectives had to be assigned in
homicide cases."

"They do, but the budget cuts are streamlining
every department. That's the only reason we're
doing it ourselves." Sara walked up Doniger's front
stairs and rang the doorbell.

"Who is it?" a voice asked.

"It's Sara Tate, Mrs. Doniger. I want to ask you
a few questions."

Opening the door a crack, Doniger said, "I've
already spoken to an attorney, and he said I don't
have to talk to you. He said if you want to charge
me with murder, that's your right, but I don't have
to say a word unless he's present."

"That's good advice you got," Sara said. "But
did your attorney also show you one of these?"

Opening up her briefcase, she pulled out a single sheet of paper. "This is a search warrant. If you want me to, I can fill it out and call in a busload of cops, who'd love to help me embarrass you in front of your neighbors. Or you can be cooperative and let me in, which would make a lot more sense. The choice is yours."

Hesitating at first, Doniger slowly pulled open the door. She looked far more tired than the last time they saw her. Her once-perfect salon-styled hair was now flat and lifeless, and her usually well-rested visage was now bordering on haggard. Although she had tried to mask her pallor with a heavy layer of makeup, it was clear that Doniger was not having her best week.

As she stepped inside the lavishly decorated house, Sara turned to Doniger. "How's everything going?"

"Wonderful," Doniger said bluntly. "Now have your look around and be done with it. I'm very busy today."

Making her way toward the parlor room of the beautiful nineteenth-century brownstone, with its matched pair of Dutch landscapes, heavy brocade drapes, and Louis XIV furniture, Sara felt an awkward sense of déjà vu rush over her. For months, she'd been mentally walking through this place. To do it in person felt unnerving.

"Crazy, huh?" Guff whispered as they made their way to the living room.

"Like a dream," Sara responded. When they reached the kitchen, Sara once again approached Doniger. "So on the night you say he died, this is where you gave him his apple juice and granola bar?"

With a sour look, Doniger said, "I don't need your accusations. Kozlow was a burglar—nothing more."

"Whatever you say," Sara said. "Now can you point us to the basement?"

"Why do you want to see the basement?" Doniger asked.

"We just want to see if there's any other way a burglar might've snuck in," Guff said. "If there is, it'll help your story."

Doniger stared at Guff, deciding what to do. Finally, she offered, "It's the door right behind you. The light switch is on your right."

As they made their way down the stairs, Guff realized Doniger was no longer following. "By the way," he whispered to Sara, "you don't have the authority to sign a search warrant. You need a judge."

"I know that," Sara smiled. "But she doesn't. And now that we have her consent, we can search anywhere we want."

"Cute trick. Now what exactly are we looking for?"

"I'm not sure. All he said was to check the basement." When Sara and Guff reached the bottom of the stairs, they found themselves staring at what appeared to be Arnold Doniger's home office. On the far wall was a small wooden desk, a two-drawer file cabinet, and a personal computer. There was a Princeton reading chair in the corner of the room and a packed-to-capacity bookshelf on the right-hand wall. On the left wall was a perfectly preserved six-foot-long sailfish—apparently a trophy from a successful fishing trip—and a doorway that led to a storage room full of empty boxes and old furniture. The other two walls were covered with old photographs and other personal effects: pictures of Arnold Doniger when he was in the navy, photos of him on his sailboat, and one large portrait from his and Claire's wedding.

"Nice picture," Guff said, looking at the wedding photo. "They look really happy."

"It's sick, isn't it?" Sara asked. "One day you're wearing the white dress; ten months later, you're wearing the black."

"Welcome to the world of prosecution," Guff said.

Sara read through a framed article from *Avenue* magazine next to the photo of the couple.

"Anything interesting?" Guff asked.

"Define 'interesting,'" Sara replied. "According to this little society-page story, when Claire and Arnold were planning their wedding at the Pierre, Claire hated the curtains in the Cotillion Room so much, she had new ones made just for their wedding. Apparently, the Pierre refused to replace them, so Claire paid for them herself. Then, when the wedding was over, she just left them there— obviously they were too big to take home. The funny part is, the Pierre liked what she did so much, they left them up, and Claire's curtains are still there today—making her the talk of the town for at least a full ten minutes."

"So you're saying Claire's the type of person who enjoys a good roll in the dough?"

"If you're asking me if she likes this lifestyle, I'd say the answer is yes."

As Guff approached Arnold's desk, Sara suggested, "You take the desk; I'll take the rest of the room."

Fifteen minutes later, they hadn't found a

thing. Frustrated, Guff started lifting each photograph to look behind it. "What're you doing?" Sara asked.

"I'm not sure. Maybe I'll find a secret passage, or a used syringe, or something cool like that. You got any better ideas?"

"Not really," Sara said, stepping through the doorway that led to the other half of the basement. She saw an old, worn love seat, a set of four wooden kitchen chairs, and a variety of empty computer, stereo, and kitchen appliance boxes. She also saw a clear glass door that looked like it led to an industrial refrigerator. When Sara pulled the door open, a blast of cool air hit her in the face.

"What's that?" Guff asked.

Sara flipped on the light switch and stuck her head inside. At least three hundred bottles of wine were perfectly stacked in the cooler.

"Son of a bitch," Sara said. She eyed the back of the six-by-six-foot wine cellar, pulled a pen from her briefcase, and jotted a note to herself. She then stepped back into the storage room, a knowing glare lighting her eyes.

"What's the big deal?" Guff asked. "It's just a wine cellar."

"That's not all it is," Sara said, leaving the room. "Let's get out of here."

Sitting in Fawcett's office in the basement of the medical examiner's building, Sara waited for Guff to get off the phone.

"No, I understand," Guff said. "But do you think it's possible?"

As Guff waited for his answer, Fawcett walked

in and sat behind his desk. "Who's he talking to?" he asked Sara.

"Chillington Freezer Systems. They made the actual cooling unit for Doniger's wine cellar."

"Yeah. Yeah. No, I agree," Guff said. "Thanks again for the help." When he put down the phone, he turned to Sara and Fawcett. "Well, the wonderfully helpful customer-service people at Chillington said that a wine cellar is normally set at fifty-five degrees, and anywhere between fifty-five and eighty percent humidity, depending on the conditions of the room."

"I don't care about wine preservation," Sara said. "I want to know how cold their freezers can get."

"That's the thing," Guff said. "A wine cellar isn't a freezer. It's designed to chill, but not to get much lower than that."

"So how low—"

"Relax, I'll get there," Guff said. "According to the woman on the phone, you can manually turn the temperature down to somewhere between forty-five and fifty degrees. But if you turn off the dehumidifier and the reheat coil, and the room doesn't get any sun—"

"Like a basement."

"Exactly," Guff said. "In a room like a basement, you might be able to get it down to twenty or twenty-five degrees."

"I knew it!" Sara shouted, slapping Fawcett's desk. "I knew it the moment I saw it!"

"Would someone mind telling me what's going on?" Fawcett asked. "Why the sudden fascination with wine cellars?"

"Because of what you said in the autopsy," Sara explained, pulling out the preliminary draft of

Fawcett's report that she was keeping her notes on. "You said that Mr. Doniger had some tearing in the lining of the brain, and that it might be caused by intense cold or freezing temperatures. Here's our intense cold. That's how they kept the body from smelling up the entire house, and that's how they made it look like he died days after the burglary—they stuffed him in the wine cellar and turned the cold on full blast. Originally, I'll bet they planned to just call an ambulance the next morning and say that her diabetic husband had died. But when Patty Harrison called in a burglary and Kozlow got arrested, they had to improvise."

"What about the stuff in his pockets?" Guff asked. "The golf ball and the diamond watch?"

"My guess is Kozlow was being greedy. He probably grabbed them on the way out, hoping no one would notice. Clearly, he didn't know he'd be arrested minutes later. Then, when the cop brought him back to the Donigers' house, the cop asked Claire if she'd been burglarized. She had no choice but to go along with the burglary story. At that point, it was better than saying Kozlow was over there to kill her husband."

"It's certainly possible," Fawcett said. "A few years ago, there was a man who tried something similar with his dead wife. As I remember it, he put her in a meat freezer until his step-children left for vacation."

"See, that's why I love New York," Guff said proudly. "People are so conscientious."

To make sure that he always had an easy excuse to return home, Jared left most of his belongings in his apartment. Once a week, he would come home to pick up an extra suit, a few more ties, or whatever else he could come up with, so he could take a look around and, most important, see his wife. After their last fight, Jared was determined to stay away, but Rafferty's recent threat caused him to rethink his strategy. All he needed now was a little time in the apartment. To make sure that Sara wasn't suspicious, he called first. He said he'd be by at approximately eight o'clock. Hoping to catch her asleep, he didn't arrive until midnight. As quietly as possible, he made his way to the bedroom. Slowly, he opened the door.

"Where've you been?" Sara asked as soon as he entered. "You're four hours late."

Jared didn't respond. He leaned his briefcase against his nightstand, then went straight to the bathroom. For the past two and a half weeks, their conversations were becoming shorter and more sterilized, eroding to the point of near silence. Office news was clearly off-limits, but now, the tension had begun to extend to small talk as well.

When Jared came out of the bathroom, Sara was under the covers, her back turned toward her husband. Suddenly, she heard Jared ask, "Were you going through my briefcase?"

"What?" Sara asked, turning over.

"Were you going through my briefcase?" Jared repeated, pointing to the floor. "When I went into the bathroom, it was standing up straight. Now it's facedown on the rug."

Laughing, Sara said, "I know this may surprise you, but there's this thing we call gravity."

"Don't give me sarcasm!" he shouted. "I'm serious!"

Caught unawares by his sudden hostility, Sara asked, "What's wrong with you?"

"What do you think is wrong? I caught you—"

"You didn't catch anything," Sara shot back. "You're just pissed because you're finally realizing that you're going to lose this case."

"Don't say that!" he yelled. "I'm not going to lose!" His eyes were blazing with a look Sara had never seen on his face before. Gone was his usual unclouded confidence. In its place was pure desperation.

Trying to calm him down, she said, "Let's just call it a night and save the fighting for tomorrow."

"I'm serious, Sara, I'm not going to lose."

"I'm sure you won't."

"Did you hear what I said? I'm not losing."

"Jared, how do you want me to respond to that?" Sara asked. " 'You're right'? 'You'll never lose'?"

"I just want you to take me seriously."

Sara didn't reply.

"Don't ignore me like that," Jared said. "Do you take me seriously or not?"

"If you have to ask, the answer doesn't matter."

"Well, I have to ask. So give me an answer."

Turning away from her husband, Sara said, "Go fuck yourself."

When Jared returned to Pop's apartment, it was almost one in the morning. Still upset, he tried to keep his thoughts focused on the outcome of the upcoming motions. Even if only half of them went his way, he thought as he opened the door, he was still in good shape. Now well accustomed to the smells of Pop's apartment, Jared didn't pay attention to the mustiness that had seemed to be suffocating him when he first arrived. He didn't even notice the pictures of Sara that used to taunt him every night. But as he walked into the apartment, he did notice the 1946 vintage electric fan that was, for some reason, now spinning.

One of Pop's best old keepsakes, the powder-blue art deco fan had been built by General Electric in the years before they made the metal blades childproof with an adequate protective cage. "And it still works," Pop used to brag whenever the subject came up.

Watching the fan as it oscillated on the side table next to the couch, Jared knew something was wrong. When he had left this morning, the fan was turned off. And with the arrival of winter, only a lunatic would still be . . .

"Guess who?" Kozlow asked as he bolted out of the hall closet. Just as Jared turned around, Kozlow jabbed Jared in the nose with the palm of his hand. "They were in the office today!" Kozlow shouted as blood ran from Jared's nose. "They were in the office and then in the basement! How the hell did that happen?" Before Jared could answer, Kozlow gave him a knee to the stomach. "C'mon, hotshot, explain that one to me!"

Doubled over in pain, Jared noticed a broom that had fallen out of the closet when Kozlow jumped out. All he had to do was grab it. But before he made a single move, Kozlow followed Jared's gaze and turned around. "You were going to use this against me?" Kozlow asked, picking up the broom. With a quick swing, he smashed Jared in the ribs. "Answer me!" He hit him again in the shoulder. Then again in the ribs. Then again in the shoulder. "Why aren't you answering me?" Kozlow screamed as Jared dropped to the floor.

Standing behind his victim, Kozlow put the broom under Jared's neck and pulled tight. Choking for air, Jared fought wildly to wrench the broom from his neck. He dug his fingers against his throat, trying to get some leverage. It was no use, though. Kozlow wouldn't let go. Jared continued to gasp and his face flushed red.

With a sharp tug up, Kozlow forced Jared to his feet and pushed him forward. They approached the edge of the couch. On the nearby side table, the fan was still spinning. When Jared realized where Kozlow was heading, he went wild. In a roar of adrenaline, he planted his feet and pushed backwards, sending both himself and Kozlow crashing into a wall full of picture frames. Glass rained to the floor. The sudden fit of energy had clearly caught Kozlow by surprise, but within seconds it didn't seem to matter. Maintaining a firm grip on the broom, and holding it taut against Jared's neck, Kozlow was once again in control. He shoved Jared toward the blades of the fan. Jared was squirming and his hands grasped violently at every nearby object— anything to stop him from reaching the couch. He pulled over the lamp, kicked over the wooden coffee table, and pressed his feet against the sofa. But the more Jared fought, the harder Kozlow pushed.

With one final heave, Kozlow threw Jared facedown on the arm of the couch and pressed his knee into Jared's back. Kozlow picked up the fan and dropped it on the corner of the couch. Jared pulled his head back, his face only a few inches from the blades of the fan. Kozlow grabbed him by the hair and slowly pressed forward.

"You promised us that you'd win," Kozlow said.

"Isn't that what you said? That you'd definitely win?"

"Later . . ." Jared coughed. "The motions."

"Fuck later. This is for now," Kozlow said, pushing Jared's face even closer.

Jared turned his head to the side, buying himself the tiniest amount of space. Then Kozlow twisted him back, so that Jared's chin faced forward. He was so close to the fan, he could smell the dust on the spinning blades.

"Tell me when it hurts," Kozlow said.

Only millimeters away from the fan, Jared gritted his teeth and shut his eyes. Kozlow smirked. And Jared screamed.

The next morning, Conrad and Guff were standing outside the courtroom, looking for Sara. "I can't believe she's late," Conrad said. "This is the second time."

"Maybe something came up," Guff said.

"What could possibly come up? What else is she working on?"

"Her archery skills? Her tetherball game? How should I know?"

Looking at his watch, Conrad realized it was time to go inside. As he pushed open the swinging door to the courtroom, he saw Jared and Kozlow sitting on a bench in the back. Jared had a two-inch piece of gauze covering the end of his chin. Walking up to his opponent, Conrad said, "Nice to see you."

"You, too," Jared said flatly.

"What happened to your face?"

"None of your business."

"Have it your way. You seen your wife?"

"No. Why?"

"Because I need to speak to her, and I'm not sure where she is."

"You did fine without her last time," Kozlow said, laughing.

"That's funny," Conrad said. "I hope you're laughing like that at your sentencing hearing. It's a great way to show everyone what a hump you are."

"Okay, we get the picture," Jared said, standing up. "You're a real tough guy. Now get away from my client before I file harassment charges."

Standing face-to-face with Jared, Conrad said, "I guess you have no idea how hard it is to prove harassment."

"And you must have no idea how hard it is to be on the receiving end of the suit. Even if you win, it'll consume six months of your life."

Before Conrad could say another word, Sara came bursting through the door. Jared and Conrad looked at each other and fell silent. "What happened to your face?" Sara asked.

"Nothing," Jared said.

Five minutes later, the court clerk called case number 0318-98: *State of New York* v. *Anthony Kozlow*. With his angular jaw and perfectly trimmed beard, Judge Bogdanos cut a handsome but intimidating figure. As a prosecutor almost twelve years ago, he had been well known for his zealous, almost irrational belief that anyone who was arrested was guilty of something. To defense attorneys, Bogdanos was biased; to prosecutors, he was a hero.

"I'll keep this short and sweet," he said as the

parties sat down. "On the defendant's motion for a continuance for further fact finding, motion denied. On the defendant's motion to suppress the diamond watch, motion denied. On the defendant's motion to suppress the silver golf ball, motion denied. On the defendant's motion to suppress the testimony of Officer Michael McCabe, motion denied. On the defendant's motion to suppress the testimony of Patricia Harrison, motion denied. On the defendant's motion to suppress the testimony of the 911 operator, motion denied. On the defendant's motion denying probable cause, motion denied."

And so it went. All thirty-four of Jared's motions were ruled on, all of them denied. When Bogdanos was finished reading his decisions, he looked up and said, "Mr. Lynch, while I admire your persistence, I want you to know that I don't enjoy having my time wasted. In life, there are rare moments when quantity is more important than quality, but believe me when I say that this is not one of them. Understand?"

"Yes, Your Honor," Jared said, his eyes on the judge.

"Perfect. Then let's set a trial date. If it's possible, I'd like to do it next Thursday."

"That's fine with the People, Your Honor," Sara said.

Although tempted to ask for a later date, Jared kept quiet. Forcing a grin, he said, "The defense will be ready, Your Honor."

"Good," Bogdanos said. "I'll see you all then." With a quick flick of his wrist, he banged his gavel and the clerk called the next case.

* * *

"How'd it go?" Kathleen asked as Jared passed her desk.

Without responding, Jared headed straight for his office and closed the door.

In a minute, Kathleen followed. Expecting Jared to be at his desk, she was surprised to find him lying on the floor, his arms over his eyes. "Are you okay?" she asked.

Jared was still silent.

"Jared, answer me. Are you okay? What happened to your face?"

"I'm fine," he whispered.

"Where's Kozlow?"

"I'm not sure. He left the moment we got out of the courthouse. Probably went to tell Rafferty that I blew it."

"I guess that means the decisions didn't go your way?"

With his arms still covering his eyes, he added, "I should've seen it coming. I mean, except for one or two of them, all of those motions were worthless. I was just hoping that we could catch a break."

"From Bogdanos? You know better than that."

Shaking his head, Jared said, "Kathleen, I'm in trouble. I don't think we have a chance."

"Don't say that. The trial hasn't even started yet. In fact, when—"

"I'm serious," he interrupted. "It's completely stacked against us."

"Jared, you're a defense attorney representing a guilty party. It's supposed to be stacked against you." She sat down next to her boss. "It was stacked against you in the Wexler case, and you pulled it out. And the Riley case. And the Shoretz case."

"Those were different," he said. "Those didn't have—"

"They didn't have what? They didn't have your wife as the prosecutor? They didn't have the consequences of this case? Obviously, this case is bigger. But that doesn't mean we can't save her. Sara's not unbeatable—she's a new recruit who got a few lucky breaks. Otherwise, you're still the self-assured boy wonder. You know I'm right, Jared. Head-to-head, you have the advantage. She's going to be okay. She will. So don't shut down just because things aren't going your way."

Unconvinced, Jared continued to lie there, his arms still hiding his eyes.

"C'mon," Kathleen demanded. "Wake the hell up. You've been like this ever since Barrow died. Regain control. Isn't that what you're always telling the new associates? *Take charge. Take control.*"

"Listen, I appreciate what you're trying to do, but I'm not in the mood right now," Jared said. "Please just leave me alone. I'll come around when I'm ready."

"I wouldn't wait too long," Kathleen said. "The clock is ticking."

"Oh, man, how fantastic was that?" Guff asked when they returned to Sara's office. "I haven't seen such a slaughter since the dinosaurs encountered that cold spell. E-X-T-I-N-C-T. Extinct, extinct, extinct!"

"It wasn't that bad," Sara said.

"Are you kidding?" Guff asked. "Did you see Jared's face when Bogdanos announced the decisions? Denied, denied, denied, denied, denied. It started sounding like the synopsis of my dating history."

"If it's possible, it was worse than your dating history," Conrad said with a wide smile. "That was a full-scale massacre. Carnage, butchery, blood-bath, annihilation."

"Maybe I should give him a call," Sara said, reaching for the phone. "Just to make sure he's—"

"He'll be fine," Conrad said. "It's all part of the game."

"I'll tell you what," Guff said. "Insane as it sounds, today's the kind of day that makes me want to be a lawyer."

"Milk it for all it's worth," Conrad said. "Because now comes the hard part. Now we have to put together a trial."

At nine o'clock that evening, in Sara's office, Conrad watched Sara cross-examine Guff for the seventh time in the last two hours.

"So, Mr. Kozlow," Sara asked Guff, "why don't you tell the court exactly how you murdered Mr. Doniger."

"No, no, no, you're doing it again," Conrad interrupted before Guff could respond. "Don't goad him—lead him. Lead him to where you want to go and hold on to him the moment you get there."

"I feel like I've heard that philosophy before," Sara said. "I think it was in . . . the Gulag."

"It may seem extreme, but in life and in court, that's how you get what you want." Turning toward the sofa where Guff was seated, Conrad said, "Mr. Kozlow, you were in Arnold Doniger's house that night, weren't you?"

"No, I—" Guff began.

"And that's the only way to explain how you got Claire's watch and golf ball, isn't it?" He looked back to Sara. "Make sure every question counts. The jury is looking to you for their cues, and in their eyes, every stutter is a lie."

Getting up from the sofa, Guff said, "Speaking of which, I'd love to stay and get badgered some more, but I really have to run."

"Coward," Conrad said as Guff walked to the door.

When Guff was gone, Sara looked at Conrad. "Next victim."

"Fair enough," Conrad said, taking Guff's old seat on the witness-box sofa. "But I'm warning you, I'm not going to be tame like Guff. My Kozlow is far more ornery."

"Bring it on," Sara said as she moved into position in front of the sofa. She looked down at her legal pad, got into character, then faced Conrad. In a stern, commanding voice, she said, "So, Mr. Kozlow, you were in Arnold Doniger's house that night, weren't you?"

"Ms. Tate, why do you keep asking me that?" Conrad moaned, sounding wounded and weak. "I already told the jury the answer. See, that's the problem with lawyers today: You never listen. You just try to ram your point home, with no concern for the innocent souls you might be hurting."

Caught off guard by Conrad's response, Sara said, "That's not fair. You can't make him sympathetic."

"Really?" Conrad asked. "What do you think your husband's trying to do as we speak?"

* * *

Two hours later, Jared opened the door to his apartment. After Kozlow's attack last night, he didn't want to stay at Pop's, and he was longing to see his wife. For the past ten years, no matter what problems he'd encountered, no matter what pressures he'd faced, no matter what battles he'd fought, Sara had always been there for him. She was the first person he saw when he came out of his knee surgery, and she was the only person who said he did a good job when he lost his first case. For the past three weeks, Jared had found it easier to avoid her, but as he walked into the silent apartment, he knew that at this moment there was no one he'd rather see. He missed her laugh, and the way she made fun of his fashion sense, and the way she picked a fight when she disagreed with someone. "Sara?" he asked as he walked into the living room. "Are you here?" He went into the bedroom. "Sara? Honey, are you here?" Again, there was no answer. His wife was gone. "Please be okay," he whispered. For the past three weeks, Jared had been lonely; tonight, he was alone. Standing in the quiet of their empty bedroom, he felt every bit of the difference.

"One more time," Conrad demanded. "Start at the beginning."

"What're you, a robot?" Sara asked, collapsing next to him on the sofa. "It's almost midnight."

"If you want it to be perfect, you have to put in the hours."

"Screw perfection. For mortal beings, there's no such thing."

"I bet Jared's shooting for perfection."

"I'm sure he is. That's the difference between

us—he wants perfection, while I'm satisfied with doing it to the best of my ability." Pointing a finger at Conrad, she added, "And stop trying to use him against me. I don't like it, and it won't work."

"It's worked up until now," Conrad said.

"Well, stop it. It's annoying."

As he leaned back on the sofa, Conrad stared silently at Sara. Finally, he asked, "Have you always been so competitive with him?"

"With Jared? Of course. Since the moment we met."

"And how'd you guys meet again? As summer associates in a firm?"

"No way, we have a much better story than that. I met Jared during our first year of law school."

"Oh, God. Law school sweethearts. Is it possible to be more nauseating?"

"I doubt it. In this case, we've achieved perfection." As Conrad shook his head, Sara added, "The first time I saw him, he raised his hand to answer a question in our contracts class. When he was done, the professor called his response 'imaginative, but sophomorically implausible.' He was so obviously devastated, I knew he had to be mine."

"But that's not how you met, is it?"

"Actually, we met during the first few weeks of school, but I didn't get to know him until we were randomly matched as partners for moot court."

"I assume you hated each other."

"Of course," Sara said. "He thought I was too pushy, I thought he was a wound-too-tight know-it-all."

"So what finally brought you together?"

"I'm not sure. I think it was that I liked the word *penis*, and he had one."

"I'm serious."

"I know you are. You always are. But I'm not sure how to answer that. When I think about Jared, though, I know one thing: He's the person I aspire to be. Really. That's how I see him. And when we're together, he helps me be that person. Love has to be a complement."

"It certainly does," Conrad said.

"What about you? You ever been in love?"

"Of course I've been in love. I was even married for three years way back when."

"Huh," Sara said, looking at Conrad in a new light. "I don't see you as the married type."

"Me neither. That's why I left."

"What was her name?"

"Marta Pacheco. We met right after I got out of the marines and were married a year later. When I wanted to come to New York, she wanted to stay near her family in California. Really, it was just the straw that killed an already-overworked camel, but it was as good an excuse as any other to leave. We were way too young to hold it together."

"And now your love is the criminal-justice system. How romantic."

"This city is a vicious lover, but there's no one finer," Conrad said with a laugh. "Enough about my mistakes, though—I want to hear more about yours. Tell me why you got fired from your law firm."

"Still curious about that, aren't you?"

"Who wouldn't be? You've been hiding it since the day we met."

"And I'm hiding it today as well."

"Oh, grow up already. How embarrassing can it be?"

"Quite embarrassing. Very, very embarrassing."

"Just tell me. I won't tell anyone."

Sara was silent for a moment, then said, "Here's the deal. I'll tell you why I got fired if you tell me some equally embarrassing fact about yourself."

"What is this, fourth grade? Now we're trading secrets?"

"That's the deal. Take it or leave it."

"I'll take it," Conrad said. "Now let's hear your story."

"Age before beauty, daddy-o. You want to hear it, you go first."

"Your husband was right. You are pushy."

"Just tell the story."

"Fine, fine," Conrad said. "My story's easy. Have you ever heard of Plato's philosophy of the soul?"

"Is this some sort of literary tale?"

"Just listen," Conrad continued. "Plato believed that at birth, every soul received a unique demon or angel which defined that person's genius and destiny. In his view, on some level, we were all oaks in tiny acorns. When I was little, my mother was a firm believer in this. And without a doubt, she was convinced that I had the soul of an entertainer."

"You?"

"Believe me, I reacted the same way. Naturally, though, my mother wasn't really interested in my own pubescent opinion. So when I was fifteen years old, I was told that I had to get a part-time job to help supplement the family income. To maximize that venture, and to complete my destiny, my mom got me a job as a magician's assistant. At little kids' birthday parties, he did the tricks and I did all the assisting."

"That's not embarrassing. It sounds like a dream job."

"That's what I thought—until I saw my costume. For four years, I was forced to wear gobs of face paint, a rainbow wig, and giant shoes that—"

"You were a clown?" Sara laughed.

"That's me—the clown sidekick to Max Marcus, Cleveland's Most Overrated Magician."

"I can't believe you were a clown," Sara laughed.

"Laugh all you want, but I was really good at it. I even had my own clown identity."

"Really? What'd you do? Scare the little kids until they confessed? The two of you had sort of a good clown–bad clown thing going?"

"I have to admit I was a little weak on the personality side. But I did pick out a name. From the day I started, I was known as Slappy Kincaid."

Sara laughed out loud. "Slappy Kincaid? What kind of name is that?"

"It's a good name. In fact, for a clown, it's a great name." As Sara continued to laugh, Conrad said, "So now you have my embarrassing fact. Time for yours. Why'd you get fired?"

Sara finally caught her breath. "I'm warning you, it's not that big a deal. I mean, especially when you compare it to something like clown assistant . . ."

"Just get on with it."

"Okay, here's how it goes: Last year, when I went for my annual review, William Quinn, the head of the executive committee, told me that I wasn't going to make partner. Of course, the only reason I worked like a dog for the two years before was because of Quinn's reassurance that I was on the partner track. But things were obviously not working out as planned, and I was being asked to leave. However, since I'd put in a good six years of my life there, he said he'd let me stay on board for a whole four extra months if I needed to."

"How kind of him."

"Kindness is his middle name," Sara said. "So anyway, I smiled, said thank you, and calmly left his office. By the time I got back to my own office, I was ready to smack Quinn in the head with a tire iron. And that's when I saw the lovely little E-mail he'd sent me. According to the E-mail, the four extra months we spoke about had one small condition: I couldn't tell any of the other associates in the firm that I was being fired—I had to say I was leaving by my own choice. Apparently, they were worried about what the younger associates would think if they knew that the firm promised partnerships but didn't follow through. So in exchange for good morale, I was offered a better severance package."

"And the idiot sent it to you by E-mail?"

"He sure did," Sara sang. "Needless to say, I kindly responded with my thoughts on the subject. I politely declined his offer, and then, in my moment of blissful vindication, forwarded his letter and my response to the entire staff of Winick and Trudeau."

"I must say, that was incredibly mature of you."

"I was angry and hungry for revenge—it was a perfect time to regress. Besides, after throwing away six years, I couldn't let him do the same thing to the other lawyers. They were my friends. If you want to fire me, that's one thing, but don't expect me to hide your dirty secret."

Laughing, Conrad said, "So what'd you do when Quinn found out?"

"What's to do? When he came storming into my office, I told him that I held him personally responsible for wasting half a dozen years of my life. He called me an unseasoned, shallow-minded waste of space; I called him a bloated and domineering Boss Tweed. After lunch, I came back and all my stuff was conveniently packed up for me. Naturally, I didn't get the four extra months. Looking back, I guess it was a psycho move, but it really did seem like the best option at the time. And even if it is embarrassing, at least I—"

"Sara, you have nothing to be embarrassed about. You should be proud of what you did."

"You think?"

Conrad was flattered by the tone of her question. "You were looking out for your friends. That's what's important."

A tiny grin lit her cheeks. "I'm glad you see it like that."

"Of course, there are easier ways to protect them than by broadcasting your boss's private mail."

"Watch it, Slappy. Get on my bad side and I'll syndicate your memos, too. Vengeful pranksters are far more dangerous than lawyer clowns."

"But lawyer clowns are so much more fun."

"Don't flatter yourself," Sara said. "You're not my type."

"And what is your type?" Conrad asked.

"Let's see. I like astronaut clowns, doctor clowns, and political clowns. But I don't like lawyer clowns."

"Are you sure?"

"Why do you ask?" Sara asked coyly.

"Just answer the question: Are you sure?"

"I'm pretty sure. Why—" Before Sara could finish, Conrad leaned over, grabbed the back of her head, and gave her a long, deep kiss. Sara knew she should pull away. Instead, she just closed her eyes.

CHAPTER 15

"I can't do this," Sara said, pushing Conrad back after a couple of seconds. "It's not right."

"What's not right? My kissing or—"

"Any of it. All of it. The whole thing," Sara said. Her hands were trembling as she got up from her seat on the sofa. She shouldn't have waited. She should've pulled away quicker.

"I don't understand," he said. "I thought you—"

"Conrad, I care a great deal about you, but I'm still married. And while I may be annoyed with Jared, that doesn't mean I should betray him."

"But—"

"Please don't say anything else," she stuttered. Searching for people to blame, she was coming up empty. "I admit—I liked it, but I shouldn't have done it."

An awkward silence filled the room. Finally, Conrad said, "I'm sorry. I didn't mean to put you in that position. I was—"

"No, it's okay." She tried to sound as convinced as possible. "It's late. . . . We've been working hard. . . . We're both tired. You flirted with me and I flirted right back."

"I know, but that still doesn't make it okay."

"Nothing's going to make this one okay. Let's just call it a night."

Conrad stood from his seat and headed for the door. "If you want, I drove in today—so if you need a ride home . . ."

"Thanks," Sara said. Pausing a moment, she added, "Actually, maybe I should just take a cab."

"Are you sure?"

"Yeah," she said, her voice trailing off.

As he was about to leave the office, Conrad turned around. "Sara, I really am sorry. And I know this may seem like a lame excuse, but for that one moment, it truly did seem like the right thing to do."

"I know," Sara said, replaying the scene in her head. Being angry with Jared made it so easy. "That's what scares me."

Standing in the bathroom, Jared leaned toward the mirror above the sink and carefully removed the gauze pad from his chin. He winced when he saw the oval gash that Kozlow had left him. Although the bleeding had long since stopped, the cut was still extremely tender. Trying hard not to stare at it, Jared reached under the sink and took out some cotton balls and a bottle of hydrogen peroxide. This one's going to hurt, he thought as he wet the cotton with the colorless antiseptic. Holding his breath, he lightly dabbed his chin. In the mirror, he could see the yellow-white pus that was just beginning to form around the edges. And while that signaled the first step of the healing process, Jared knew the pain was just beginning.

It took Sara another half hour to realize she wasn't going to get any more work done. Conrad's kiss had shined the spotlight on something she'd never wanted to see, and regardless of how much she tried to focus her mind elsewhere, she couldn't stop thinking about every detail of the incident. As she hailed a cab, she kept asking herself the same question. How? How could she do it? She wanted to blame it on an external source: Anger. Loneliness. Frustration. But as her cab headed back uptown, past Carmine's, and Ollie's, and John's Pizzeria, and every other restaurant that reminded her of her husband, Sara finally faced the hard truth about her late-night encounter: While it was happening, she'd enjoyed it. And the only person she could blame was herself.

By the time she returned to her apartment, there was only one person Sara wanted to see— and when she entered her bedroom, she was surprised to find him on her bed. Fully dressed and lying on top on the covers, Jared was sound asleep. Sara kicked off her shoes just loud enough to wake him.

"Sorry," Jared said, rubbing his eyes. "I called, but you weren't here. If it's okay, I was hoping I could sleep here tonight."

Sara stared at her husband. On any other night, this would've been a fight. Tonight, though, she could only say, "Of course. Whatever you want."

* * *

When he woke up the next morning, Jared considered not going in to the office. He knew he had an imposing amount of work to do if he expected to be ready for trial, but he couldn't help but think that a relaxing mental-health day might be the best way to recharge his batteries. When he turned over and saw that Sara had already left for work, however, he kicked off the covers and jumped out of bed. Regardless of how tired he was, regardless of how exhausted, he couldn't let her win.

An hour later, Jared arrived at the office, briefcase in hand. As he rode the elevator to the forty-fourth floor, he thought about running on the treadmill in the gym. That was always the best method for clearing his head. But, once again, fear outweighed personal time, and anxiety outweighed relaxation. By the time Jared opened the door to his office, his mind was racing with trial strategies.

"You're late," a voice said as Jared stepped inside.

Jared jumped. It was Rafferty.

"For a man who's behind on points, you're getting an awfully late start on the day," Rafferty said, leaning back in Jared's leather chair.

"It's not even eight yet."

"Big deal. Sara got in by a quarter after seven."

Jared dropped his briefcase on his desk. "Is there anything else you want, or are you just here to threaten me after yesterday's debacle?"

"I don't need to threaten you anymore, Jared. You understand the consequences." Rafferty then put his hand on a sealed envelope and slid it across Jared's desk. "I'm just here to show you what else is happening while you're so busy drowning."

Jared opened the envelope, pulled out a small stack of photographs, and flipped through them. The first few photos were of Sara and Conrad talking, while the last few were of his wife and Conrad kissing. His face went white.

"And you've been wondering why she's spending so much time at the office," Rafferty said.

"Who took these?" Jared asked, his eyes still glued to the photos. "When were they taken?"

"Last night. An associate in their office took them for us. He does great work, don't you think?"

Jared rushed for the door.

"Where are you going?" Rafferty asked.

Jared didn't respond as he stormed out.

Jared barged through the metal detector on Sara's floor, ignored the sign-in sheet, and walked right past the security guard. "Hey, get back here!" the guard called. "Visitors have to sign in!"

As Jared marched down the hallway, he announced in a loud voice, "I'm looking for Sara Tate. Where is she?" A secretary pointed down the hall.

By the time Jared caught sight of Guff at his desk outside Sara's office, the security guard had caught up with Jared and seized him by the arm. "Do you know this guy?" the guard asked Guff.

"Yeah," Guff said nervously. "He's okay."

"Next time, sign in," the guard told Jared.

"Thanks," Jared said, pulling free of the guard's grip.

"I guess you want to see Sara?" Guff asked.

Without answering, Jared barreled past Guff and threw Sara's door wide open. As it crashed into the wall, Sara looked up from her desk, startled. "What the hell are you doing?" she asked, covering the papers on her desk. "I'm working here."

"I need to speak to you for a moment," Jared demanded.

Recognizing the gravity of her husband's tone, Sara shoved the papers back into their file folder. "Guff, can you leave us alone for a second?"

"Sure thing," Guff said, exiting the office and shutting the door.

Sara and Jared stared at each other. "Are you having an affair?" he asked in a low voice.

Sara's mouth dropped open and she looked away.

"Sara, please look at me," Jared said, his voice cracking. "We've always been honest with each other. Now answer my question: Last night, did you kiss Conrad?"

"Who said we kissed?"

"Who said we . . . ? I can't believe you!" Jared yelled. "You're lying! You're fucking lying to me!"

"Do you have someone spying on this office?" Sara asked accusingly. She looked out her window to see who could see in. Across the air shaft was a row of dusty windows to other ADAs' offices.

"Don't you dare change the subject," Jared said. "You betrayed me, and now you want to turn it around? *You're* the one who cheated on *me*!"

"First of all, lower your voice. Second, I didn't cheat on you. It wasn't like that. Conrad tried to kiss me, but I pulled away."

"So your lips never touched?"

"No," Sara shot back. "They didn't."

Pausing, Jared fought to contain himself. He felt a sharp pain at the base of his neck. Finally, he exploded. "Sara, I saw the damn pictures with my own eyes! I saw them! You were kissing him on *this* couch! This couch right here!"

"I don't know what pictures you saw, but I pulled away immediately! Nothing happened."

"First you say your lips never touched, then you say you pulled away. How the hell do you expect me to believe you?"

"Jared, I just do."

"Well, you can take that load of bullshit and sell it somewhere else. You're in no position to ask for trust."

"And you are?" Sara asked.

"I didn't cheat on my wife."

"No, you just rifled her briefcase last night."

"What?" Jared asked, forcing a laugh.

"I heard you, Jared. I heard every move you made last night. And when I turned over, I saw you. You must think I'm an idiot, though—after what happened last time, do you really think I'd bring important files home with me? I was testing you. You failed. So stop lying to my face."

His lips pursed in anger and his arms crossed, Jared just stood there. Eventually, he said, "Fine, I admit it. You caught me. But don't think this comes close to what you did with Conrad. This isn't some damn file, it's our marriage!"

"It's our trust! And when you went through my briefcase—"

"Your briefcase? You're equating this with your briefcase? Did you hear what I said? This is our marriage, Sara! Our marriage!"

"I know what's at stake, Jared! I'm not blind!" Sara shouted, getting up from her seat. "But I'm telling you, nothing happened! It was just a kiss—"

"Just a kiss?"

"And I pulled away! Now stop rubbing my nose in it!" Sara yelled, pointing a finger at her husband.

He grabbed her firmly by the wrist. "Get your hand out of my face."

"Don't touch me!" she shouted as she wrestled out of his grip. "I can have you disbarred! You're a thief!"

"Well, at least I'm not a whore!"

With a quick swing, Sara slapped Jared across the face.

Holding his cheek, Jared stared at his wife and saw something he had never seen. "You never should've done it, Sara. You ruined it."

"Jared, I swear to you. We never—" Before she could finish, Jared headed for the door. "Please . . . just listen." She reached for him and grabbed his arm. "I'm sorry."

"It's too late for that. Now let go." He tried to pull away, but Sara held fast. "I said, let go!" he shouted. "It's over!" With a sharp tug, he freed his arm, and the resulting momentum sent Sara smashing into a file cabinet.

Suddenly, the door to the office flew open. "What the hell are you doing?" Conrad asked Jared.

Without a word, Jared pulled back and took a swing at Conrad. Easily dodging the punch, Conrad grabbed Jared's arm and, in one motion, twisted it behind his back and slammed him facedown on Sara's desk.

"Get the hell off me," Jared said as people began to collect outside the office.

"Conrad, let him go," Sara said.

Releasing Jared, Conrad said, "Don't ever try to hit me again. Next time I'll break your arm."

"Next time I'll connect," Jared warned.

"We'll see."

Jared took one last look at his wife, then pushed through the small group of onlookers and made his way to the elevators.

"What was that about?" Conrad asked Sara.

"Nothing. I'm fine," she mumbled.

"I didn't ask how you were doing. I asked—"

"It'll be okay," she added, turning away from Conrad. "I'll get through it."

When he got out of Sara's office building, Jared headed straight for the Franklin Street subway. As he ran down the stairs, he could hear the rumble of a train pulling into the station. He cleared the turnstile just as the light chime sounded that preceded the closing of the doors. He made a mad dash for the train. "Hold it!" he screamed to one of the train's conductors, who was leaning out a window. But the doors shut in his face.

"C'mon," he said, hitting the doors. "Open up!"

The doors stayed shut.

"Please!" he yelled. He wedged his fingers into the protective rubber between the doors and attempted to pull them open. They stayed shut.

"No!" he protested, once again banging the doors with his fists. As the train slowly pulled away from the platform, Jared ran with it, hoping to somehow still climb aboard. *"C'mon!"* he screamed. *"Don't fuckin' leave!"* But the train plowed forward and picked up speed, even as the tears rolled down Jared's cheeks. It was no use. He couldn't stop it. In a flash, the train was gone, and Jared stood on the platform. Alone.

* * *

A half hour after Jared left, Sara called her husband's office. "Is he back yet?" Sara asked Kathleen.

"Not yet," Kathleen said. "I'll leave him a message you called."

Fifteen minutes later, Sara called again.

"Sorry," Kathleen said. "Still not back."

Hanging up, Sara called home. Then she called Pop's apartment. Nothing but answering machines.

Ten minutes passed before she tried his office again.

When Kathleen answered, she said, "Sara, I promise, the moment he comes in here, I'll have him call you."

A half hour later, Sara's phone rang. "Jared?" she answered.

"It's me," Kathleen said. "He just walked in."

"Please put him on."

"I already asked him, but he doesn't want to take your call. I just figured you'd want to know that he's back here safe and sound."

"No, I do," Sara said. "Thanks, Kathleen."

"Jared?" Sara called out when she got home that evening. "Are you here?"

When she didn't get an answer, she walked to Jared's closet in the bedroom and opened it up. It was cleaned out. All of his suits were gone. So were his shirts. All that remained were some bad ties and empty hangers. "No. No, no, no." She ran to his dresser and yanked the top drawer open. Empty, it came flying from the dresser, catching

Sara by surprise. Throwing it aside, she pulled open the next one. And the next one. And the next one. Socks, underwear, and undershirts were all missing. "You can't leave!" she yelled, slamming the last drawer shut. "Not now." She had never expected it to happen like this. Everything had been going her way. She had the research, and the evidence, and the motions, and even the judge. It was all supposed to work out. It was all supposed to be okay. But as Sara hid her head in her hands, she knew that when all was said and done, it wasn't going to be much of a victory.

Jared dragged his stuffed-to-capacity hanging bag through the stark white halls of New York Hospital. He took the elevator to the tenth floor and made his way to room 206. Leaving his luggage outside the room, he knocked on the door.

"Well, well, well, look who's finally decided to pay a visit," Pop said as Jared walked inside. "What brings you here? I mean, besides guilt."

"Can't I just say hello? Phone calls are fine, but there's nothing like a personal visit."

"Jared, that moonshine might work with those gullible, group-thinking juries, but I'm not buying a drop of it. The only reason you're here is either, one, Sara made you come; or two, you're in trouble."

"Don't say that, Pop. With my parents and grandmothers in Chicago, you're the only family I have in New York."

"Okay, so you're in trouble. How much money do you need?"

"I don't need any money," Jared said, pulling a chair up to Pop's bed. "Now why don't you tell me how you're doing. When are they letting you out of here?"

"When I'm better. Or if you want to believe my doctor, when they can get me walking again, which could be anywhere from two weeks to a month. There—now you've paid your moral debt. So why don't you tell me what's really going on?"

"It's nothing," Jared said, forcing confidence into his voice. "Sara and I are just struggling with this case we're both working on."

"The Kozlow case."

"Yeah, how'd you—"

"What, you think I'm not listening when my granddaughter speaks to me? My ears may be longer and hairier than yours, but they work just as well. And I knew from the moment this case started it would be a mess. You and Sara are competitive enough—you don't need a trial to put you at each other's throats."

"It's not the trial so much as what's going on around it."

"What else is going on? Is she sick? Pregnant? Are you finally going to wise up and have a kid?"

"No, Pop, she's not pregnant," Jared said, fidgeting with the nurse's calling device on Pop's nightstand. "She's just been pushing all the right buttons lately—for a while now, everything's been going her way."

Pop stared at Jared and smiled. Finally, he said, "You don't like the fact that she's beating you at your own game."

"No, you don't understand. It's about more than just winning—"

"Jared, you know that saying about bullshitting the bullshit artist?" Pop interrupted.

"Yeah."

"Well, let me put it to you this way: I'm Picasso. And if you think I believe you when you tell me it's not about winning, you're dabbling in finger paints. For as long as I've known you, you've been obsessed with success. You've been the golden boy, and Sara's been the one who's struggled. But now that the shoe's on the other foot, you're realizing that it's a bitch to wear high heels."

"This has nothing to do with ego. It's bigger than that."

"Son, you have to listen to what you're saying. If everything you've told me is true, it sounds like Sara's going to win this case—and the only person who isn't facing that fact is you. You may be a great lawyer, but in this instance, Sara has you against the wall. So now you have a choice: You can keep doing what you're doing and get your rear end handed to you, you can give up and admit defeat, which I know you'll never do, or you can talk to her and work out a resolution that leaves you both happy. The decision is yours."

With his eyes glued to the emergency call device in his hands, Jared knew that Pop was right about one thing: If he didn't take drastic action soon, he was going to lose the case. And if he lost the case . . . Jared looked up at Pop, unwilling to entertain the consequences.

"Want to tell me about it?" Pop asked.

"I do," Jared said. "It's just . . . I can't."

"Then you better tell her. Keeping it bottled up is only going to make it explode in your face."

As Pop's words sank in, Jared put down the emergency call device. "You may be right."

* * *

"Are you sure he wasn't at Pop's?" Tiffany asked, leaning on the edge of the plaza fountain at Lincoln Center.

"I went over there twice last night. As far as I can tell, he's gone," Sara said curtly as she stood next to her little sister. "Now can we please drop it?"

"You're the one who brought it up." Tiffany pointed at a man in a navy beret. "There's one."

Sara looked at the man with the beret. "He doesn't count. First, he doesn't look tortured. Second, that's not a black beret."

"On the Upper West Side, that's as good as you're gonna get."

"Are you nuts?" Sara asked. "You think all the good tortured artists are living in the Village? You just have to look harder in this neighborhood."

Staring at the crowds of people passing through Lincoln Center's vast esplanade, Tiffany stuffed her hands in the pockets of her pink winter coat. "I'm getting cold and the game's no fun."

"What do you want me to do? Set up a shuttle to the Guggenheim?"

"No, I just want you to be nice," Tiffany shot back. "It's bad enough that our visits are now every other week—the least you can do is enjoy being with me."

Surprised by the outburst, Sara put her hand on Tiffany's shoulder and pulled her in. "I'm really sorry, kiddo. I haven't been my best lately."

Tiffany looked up at her big sister. "Is it because you miss him?"

"Yeah, that's part of it."

"Then maybe you should do something about it. Maybe you can get off the case."

"You don't understand. It's not that easy."

"I don't care if it's easy," Tiffany said, still pressed against Sara. "I just want things back to normal. And the longer you two are mad at each other, the worse it is for the rest of us."

Later that evening, Sara and Tiffany ate dinner at Sylvia's soul-food restaurant in Harlem, home of Lenox Avenue's most famous smothered fried chicken. When they walked out of the restaurant, Sara looked up into the flat black sky. "I'll bet you a basket of corn bread that the first snow of the year hits in the next two days."

"If I didn't feel like I was going to vomit, I'd take that bet," Tiffany said as she held her stomach.

Smiling, Sara stepped into the street and hailed a cab. Out of the corner of her eye, she noticed a dark-blue sedan waiting across the street. She and Tiffany got into the cab, and Sara gave the driver Tiffany's address. As the cab took Sara and Tiffany deeper into Harlem, Sara turned around and noticed that the sedan was now behind them.

"Do me a favor," Sara said to the cabdriver. "Head down a few of these smaller streets. I want to know if the car behind us is following us."

Following Sara's instructions, the driver turned off Lenox Avenue and onto 131st Street. The sedan didn't follow.

"Who do you think it was?" Tiffany asked, staring out the back window.

"No one. Just my imagination," Sara said, relieved. "You can go back now," she told the driver.

For the next few minutes, as Sara and Tiffany sat in the back of the cab, Sara kept an eye out for the sedan. Without question, it was gone. The cab pulled up to Tiffany's apartment building on 147th Street. "If you don't mind waiting," Sara said to the driver, "I'll only be a minute." Sara got out of the cab and walked Tiffany inside—she always liked to check in with Tiffany's aunt at the end of each visit. After a brief conversation, Sara left the building and looked for her cab. It was gone. The only car in sight was the dark-blue sedan. The driver of the sedan, a pale man with a blond mustache, was leaning on the hood.

Sara reached into her pocket and pulled out her badge. "DA's office!" she yelled. "Who the hell are you?"

Unfazed, the driver of the sedan looked up and handed a folded sheet of paper to Sara.

"What's that?" Sara asked suspiciously.

"It's a new invention. We call it paper."

"Very funny," Sara said, grabbing it out of his hands. When she unfolded the piece of paper, she read the words GET IN THE CAR, POOH. Sara looked up at the driver. "Who wrote this?"

"No idea. All I know is where I'm supposed to take you. As long as I get paid in advance, I don't care."

She took a step away from the car.

"Don't be afraid," the driver said. "You'll be safe."

Sara still wasn't convinced.

"No offense, but if I wanted to hurt you, I would've done it by now. Especially in this neighborhood—no one would suspect a thing. Now why don't you get in the car?"

As she considered the man's logic, Sara noticed that Tiffany was watching the events from her apartment window.

"See, now if anything bad happens, you even have your own witness," the driver added.

To make sure Tiffany didn't worry, Sara shot her a strained smile and moved toward the car. "Where are we going?" she asked the driver.

"Not allowed to say," the driver said, looking over his shoulder. "But it'll be worth it."

Putting her faith in the message and taking one last look at Tiffany, Sara hesitantly got in the backseat of the car. For a half hour, the car headed downtown. The entire time, the driver kept his eyes on the rearview mirror. All through the Upper West Side, Sara thought they were going to Times Square. When they drove through Times Square, she thought they were going to the Village. When they drove through the Village, she thought they were going to her office building on Centre Street. And when they passed her office building, she said, "Where the hell is this place?"

"Ten more minutes," the driver said.

The car turned toward the entrance to the Brooklyn Bridge.

"We're going to Brooklyn?" Sara asked nervously.

"You'll see," the driver said with a smile.

Taking a sharp right onto the first exit off the bridge, the driver headed through the quiet historic neighborhood of Brooklyn Heights. Passing rows of classic town houses, traditional clapboards, and one of George Washington's houses, they headed straight for the riverfront Promenade, famous for its arresting view of lower Manhattan. The paved walkway was usually crowded with both locals and tourists, but the cold weather had a chilling effect on both the night and its population. "Last stop," the driver said.

Frantically looking around, Sara didn't see anyone.

"Get out of the car," the driver said.

"Here? You expect me to get out here? Are you nuts?"

"Get out of the car. You'll be thankful you did."

Following the driver's instructions, Sara got out and approached the window on the passenger side of the car. Leaning into the window, she asked, "Now what?"

"Wait here." With that said, the driver rolled up the window and sped off.

"Wait! Where are you going?" Sara asked, banging on the window as the sedan pulled away. Surrounded by nothing but some scattered benches and a concrete walkway, Sara felt the cold wind of the East River whip across her face. Looking around, she still didn't see anyone. She headed down the path toward the water. *"Is anybody here?"* she shouted. *"Hello!"*

"Sara," a voice said from behind her.

"Who the—" she yelled, turning around. It was Jared. She reacted instantaneously. "I've been worried sick about you," she said, embracing her husband. "Where the hell have you been?"

"Sorry," Jared said, pulling away. "I just wanted to make sure you were alone."

"I'm definitely alone. In fact, I've been alone since last night."

"You were the one who wanted me to move out."

"You know this is different," she said. "I couldn't even find you at Pop's."

"Sorry about that. I just couldn't face you after that thing with Conrad."

"Jared, I swear on my life, nothing happened

with Conrad. He went to kiss me, and I pulled away. Anyone who said it was more than that is lying."

"Fine, they were lying," Jared said, kicking at a random piece of nothing. "As usual, you're right."

"Don't shut down on me," Sara said.

Jared didn't reply.

"Jared, please. If you didn't want to get into this, why'd you call me out here?"

"I wanted to talk to you in privacy."

"So you have some nutjob pick me up with a cryptic note that uses my dad's old pet name for me? There are easier, less upsetting ways to get in touch."

"I figured you'd know the note was from me. Who else would know that information?"

"You'd be surprised what a stranger can find out about you." Sara sat down on a wooden bench, and Jared nodded silently in agreement. Carefully watching her husband, she added, "So if this isn't about yesterday, what else do we have to discuss?"

"The case," Jared said, his voice barely above a whisper. "We have to talk about the case."

Now Sara was annoyed. "Of course—the one thing in this world you actually care about."

"Honey, you know that's not—"

"It is true," Sara insisted. "But let me break it to you: The trial's in two weeks, the motions went our way, and when we've convicted Kozlow, we're going to go after Claire Doniger and anyone else we see as an accomplice."

Shaking his head, Jared pulled up the collar on his overcoat, trying to stay warm. The wind continued to beat against him. "Sara, I can't fight with you anymore. It's not worth it. I just want you to listen very carefully to what I'm about to say. I wouldn't even think of asking you this unless it was completely necessary." Moving toward her, he explained, "This may sound crazy, but I need you to take a dive. Lose some evidence, do a bad job on purpose—I don't care how you do it; I just need to win."

Laughing, Sara said, "Are you really that desperate? I mean, do you even realize how illegal that is? And that's without even considering the moral implications."

"Screw the moral implications. This is far more important than morality."

"Oh, that's right—I forgot your job is more important than everything else in the universe."

"Just listen for a second."

"I am listening," Sara interrupted, jumping from her seat. "And I can't believe what you're asking. When you had the upper hand, everything was fine and dandy. But the moment I'm finally doing well, you want me to roll over. You really have some set of balls, y'know that? This job has changed my life. For the first time in a long time, I feel like I'm back in control again. Things are going well; my confidence is strong; my anxieties are finally gone. This case has made me a new person. And if you think you can bully me into playing your game like you tried to do at the grand jury, you're living in fantasyland. I'm only saying this once, Jared. You're not taking this away from me."

"You don't understand," Jared pleaded. "You *have* to let me win."

"Have you been listening? I don't *have* to do anything."

"Yes. You do," Jared said flatly.

"I can't believe this. Is it an ego thing? Is that it? You can't stand seeing me beat you for once?"

"This has nothing to do with competition," Jared said, his forehead covered with sweat.

"Well, you can forget it," Sara said, turning her back to her husband. "The only person bringing home a victory is me. Hope you can live with it."

Jared grabbed Sara firmly by the arm. "Listen to me! It's bigger than you think!"

"I already heard you. Now let go of me."

Refusing to loosen his grip, Jared shouted, "Sara, I'm begging you one last time: You have to let me win."

"Why? What the hell is so important?" Sara shouted back, struggling to free herself.

Finally, Jared realized he had no other choice. Still holding on to his wife, he looked into her eyes. *"Because if I don't win this case, they're going to kill you!"*

Instantly, Sara stopped trying to pull away. "What?"

"You heard me. They'll kill you. The only reason I'm on this case is because they threatened to kill you if I dropped it. That's why I've been fighting so hard. That's why I've been pushing so much. And that's why I went through your briefcase. They've been following both of us since Kozlow was first arrested. They're the ones who broke into our house. And they're the ones who—"

"Oh, my God," Sara said, sinking back on a bench.

"This is serious, Sara. We're in trouble."

"The people who approached you—did one of them have sunken cheeks?"

"Sunken cheeks? No, I was approached by Kozlow and . . ." Jared paused.

"Kozlow and who?" Sara asked.

Jared glanced around to make sure they were still alone. Then he stared directly at his wife. "It's Oscar Rafferty. He's been there from the start. He's the one who—"

"That lying sack of shit!" Sara shouted. "We knew it—Guff called it the moment we left his office. Rafferty had you, and Sunken Cheeks had me."

"What're you talking about? Who's this man with the cheeks?"

Sara quickly related her encounter with Sunken Cheeks, explained how he had threatened to kill Jared, and described his untraceable fingerprints.

When she finished, Jared said, "So if you gave in, he would've come after—"

"That's why I didn't give in."

"But if he's the one responsible for hurting Pop, why didn't you arrest him?"

"I have no idea who he is. Besides, I was so nervous about what he'd do to you, I was terrified to touch him."

"I know how you feel," Jared said. He sat down next to Sara and brushed his fingers against the gauze pad on his chin.

"Who was it, Kozlow?"

"Took a pound of flesh on his own," Jared explained. "But it sounds like your guy was helping you. I mean, wasn't he the one who put you on Rafferty's trail?"

"Not at all. We found Rafferty on our own. He became a suspect as soon as we saw Arnold's will."

"Arnold had a will?"

"See, that's the problem with you defense attorneys. All you care about is getting your client off. We prosecutors are the only ones searching for the truth."

Ignoring the jab, Jared said, "Tell me about the will."

"There's not much to tell. According to our reading, Rafferty stands to inherit Echo Enterprises now that his near-and-dear partner is dead."

"Oh, you must be kidding me—Rafferty gets the business?"

"The whole thing," Sara said, noticing the look of disbelief on her husband's face. "Why? What does that tell you? I mean, besides the fact that he has a reason to kill his partner."

"That tells us why Rafferty was so intent on winning the case." Running his hand through his hair, he added, "Damn, that mean bastard is brilliant."

"Why? What'd he do?" Sara asked, slapping her husband on the arm. "Tell me already."

"It's actually pretty simple. Do you remember what a slayer statute is?"

"A what?"

"A slayer statute. Slayer. As in killer." When Sara shook her head, Jared explained, "A slayer statute prevents murderers from profiting from their own killings. Let's pretend you have a will. And the will says that if you die, I'm the main beneficiary. That means I get all your money."

"All twenty-five bucks?"

"Every last nickel. So now let's pretend that I try to get the money early by having you killed. Under the slayer statute, if it's proven that I had anything to do with your death, I'm not allowed to get a dime, a nickel, or a penny—even if your will says I get it all."

"Does New York have one of these statutes?"

"I don't know if there's an official statute, but the common law has the same rule."

"Then why didn't they just settle it?"

"As I remember it, you can impute foul play from any of the parties involved—which is why Rafferty couldn't let Kozlow accept a plea bargain or anything less than a full acquittal."

"So Rafferty is worried that if Kozlow is implicated in any way, and it's discovered that Rafferty hired Kozlow, Rafferty'll never get his nest egg."

"Not to mention the fact that he's nervous about his own murder charge. I mean, that's the only thing that explains Rafferty's concern with this whole mess. If he was innocent, he wouldn't care at all. And if he wasn't obsessed with the money, he would've let me plea-bargain it down."

"Do you think he could also be trying to protect Claire Doniger?" Sara asked, standing up.

"You're really convinced she's involved with this, aren't you?"

"C'mon, Jared. The woman's husband is killed and she doesn't shed a tear. More important, she doesn't lift a finger to help our investigation. Talking to her is like pulling teeth, and getting her to testify is like . . . it's like . . ."

"It's like pulling teeth," Jared said dryly.

"Yeah. Lots of teeth. A mouthful of teeth."

"Okay, so if she's involved, what's her motive? Does she get anything under the will?"

"Not a cent. But that doesn't mean anything. Our theory is that she and Rafferty are sleeping together. When they knock off Arnold Doniger, they get all the money *and* they get to play snuggle-bunnies every night. The only problem we were having was proving Rafferty's involvement. But it's clear that he's the man we're after."

"It's not a bad theory," Jared admitted. "And now that I think about it, he does get super-protective whenever she comes up."

"Is there anything else Rafferty's said that we might be able to use against him?"

Jared sat back on the bench and put his head in his hands. "Actually, you can't use any of this stuff against him. It's all protected by attorney-client privilege."

"I'm not worried about winning the case any-more, handsome. I just want to make sure you're safe, and get us out of . . ." Noticing that her husband wasn't moving, Sara stopped. "What's wrong? Are you okay?"

Without saying a word, Jared stood up and wrapped his arms around his wife. "I'm so sorry. I never meant to hurt you, Sara. I only did it because I was worried about you."

Feeling a wave of relief run over her, Sara held her husband tight. "It's okay. Don't worry about it. I was just as worried about you."

"But I—"

"Shhhhh, don't say another word," Sara said, still holding him close. "It's over. It's finally over." Leaning back just enough to look into Sara's eyes, Jared realized she was right. And for the first time in months, he decided not to argue. Instead, he pulled her in and lightly slid his hands across her shoulders and down her back. He loved the way their bodies fit together. Against her cheek, Sara felt the familiar scratch of his five-o'clock shadow. Closing her eyes, she took in the smell of the cologne she always complained about. And with her arms around his waist, she reached under his jacket and caressed the curve in the small of his back. She had forgotten how much she missed it all.

Silently pressed against each other, Sara and Jared didn't have to say a word. For too long, they had been at each other's throats. Now, finally, they were in each other's arms. And that was all that mattered. As reality slowly returned, Sara could feel Jared start to tremble. Moments later, his eyes welled up with tears. "It's okay," she reassured him as she struggled to fight back her own tears. But it was already too late—as was always the case, once Sara heard Jared sobbing, she wasn't far behind. Soon, both of them were overcome with emotion. "It's okay," she repeated as tears ran down her cheeks. "It's really okay."

"I know," Jared said, wiping his eyes with his jacket sleeve. "Until you were safe, I couldn't—"

"I know exactly how you feel," Sara said, wiping her own eyes. "But we have to keep the catharsis short. Neither of us is really safe unless we get out of this mess."

"No, you're right," Jared said, composing himself. He rubbed his eyes and cleared his throat. "Okay, now what's the next step?"

"Work the facts. Is there anything else that Rafferty or Kozlow might've said? Anything that might explain why Victor wanted the case? Or who Sunken Cheeks is? Is he a former employee? Does he have something against Rafferty? Has Kozlow mentioned any old grudges?"

"The only thing that caught me off guard is that Kozlow once said he was in the military."

"Really? Which part?"

"Army. Lenny told me he got kicked out, but that's all I know. Think there's something there?"

"Maybe. Victor's got a military background also. I'll look into it first thing tomorrow."

"Great. And can you also do a search on Rafferty's phone bills? I tried already, but you're the only one who can get his local calls. If your theory's right, we should see tons of calls to Claire and to Kozlow."

"And maybe to our mystery man with the cheeks."

"Hopefully," Jared said. "Maybe they're all working together." Looking up, Jared stared at the shimmering New York City skyline. It was beautiful, he thought. As beautiful as the first time he saw it from this spot, during a midnight biking tour he and Sara had taken at the end of their first year of law school. Jared took a deep breath and smiled. Finally, he was getting his life back. At that moment, he heard Sara laughing. "What's so funny?" he asked, turning back to his wife.

"Nothing," Sara said, her laughter a perfect mixture of nervousness and relief. "I just can't believe this happened to us. I mean, why us?"

"I'm not sure. Maybe it was just meant to be."

"Uh-uh. This problem didn't find us—I found this problem. If I hadn't been so worried about myself, I wouldn't have grabbed this case in the first place. And if I'd never grabbed it, you never would've been approached to——"

"Okay. That's enough. We don't need to play this game. You've had enough self-pity for one year."

"It's not self-pity. This is just me facing reality. If I'd never grabbed this case, we wouldn't be in this mess."

"You can believe whatever you want, but I'd never blame you for this. Now let's get back to the real question: What do we do with the case?"

Pausing, Sara eventually said, "I'm not sure. Obviously, we can't take it to trial."

"Maybe we can go to the judge and ask him to remove us because of a conflict of interest," Jared suggested. "Or maybe we can force a mistrial."

"We can do either, but that doesn't solve the problem."

"I really don't care about solving the problem," Jared said. "I say we get off the case and get our lives back. Let someone else play superhero."

"No way. This is our problem. Rafferty, Doniger, Kozlow, Sunken Cheeks, they're all our problem. And no matter how much you'd like to believe otherwise, they're not going to leave us alone until they get what they want."

"Fine, then all we need to do is figure out a way to stop the psychopaths from chasing us. How about we both bow out, and then we tell them that if anything happens to us, our lawyer will send out a letter that fingers Rafferty?"

"Jared, you're missing the big picture. Even if they leave us alone, we can't let them do the same thing to someone else."

"So now we have to forward Rafferty's E-mail to the entire firm?"

"Don't make fun—you know I'm right." As she let the logic of her argument sink in, Sara added, "Like it or not, it's our responsibility."

Jared nodded his head. "What do you propose?"

"I'm not sure. I want to talk to Conrad tomorrow. He knows his way around this world better than anyone."

"And what other worlds is he familiar with?"

"Oh, c'mon, Jared, why do you have to bring that up? I swear it was nothing. We kissed and I pulled away. That was it."

Jared didn't say a word.

Studying her husband's reaction, Sara felt awful. Without a doubt, that fleeting kiss would haunt her forever. As she tried to figure out what to say, she realized no apology would ever be enough. But if she expected to move forward, she also realized she had to start somewhere. "Jared, I'm sorry."

"You don't need to—"

"Actually, this is exactly what I need," she replied. "I really am sorry, honey. I'm so sorry I did this to you. I wish I could take it back. I wish I could just wipe the whole thing from existence. And while I know that's no excuse, I just hope you know one thing: The worst thing I can do in this world is hurt you. Nothing, absolutely nothing, causes me more pain."

"So you're not in love with him?"

"In love wi—Are you nuts? It was a moment in time—a misstep. *You're* my whole world, Jared. Nothing means more to me. I trust you with everything."

"If you trust me so much, why'd you spy on me with your briefcase?"

Sara reached over and tickled the back of his neck. "Baby, I was dead asleep the entire time. I only said that to test your reaction. Obviously, you failed, but I still trust you. And love you."

With a sly smile, Jared said, "You're ruthless, y'know that?"

"What can I say? Play with the best, you're bound to get beat."

"Sara, I swear I only did it because I was worried about—"

"I don't care about that," Sara said, taking Jared's hand. "Let's just have our make-up kiss and be done with it."

"Here?" Jared asked, looking around at the completely deserted Promenade. "In front of all these people?"

"Of course here. It's our perfect Hollywood moment. The intrepid heroes, the striking landmark, the windblown hair. It's all in place. All we have to do is—" Interrupting herself, Sara leaned forward, grabbed her husband, and gave him a forceful kiss. For a minute, they stood there, lips locked and arms wrapped around each other. Once again, everything else faded away. When they were done, she asked, "How was that?"

Jared smiled. "It's good to be home."

"Couldn't agree more. So you ready to get out of here?"

"Depends what we're doing."

"Well, right now, we're putting together a puzzle. And the moment the picture is crystal clear, we're going after the bastards who took it apart in the first place. If Rafferty thinks he's got problems now, wait until his ass meets my foot."

"I hope you're right. Because if Rafferty gets wind of this, he's not going to hold back—even if you are a DA."

"That's ADA to you. Now let's go home."

Standing behind a thick patch of overgrown shrubbery and shrouded by the low branches of

an oak tree, he silently watched the couple leave
the Promenade. He knew this would happen—
he'd said it from the beginning. When the pressure got too high, they were going to snap.

He watched them walk up the concrete path
toward Clark Street. They were coming directly at
him, but in the darkness he wasn't at all concerned. He didn't even duck when they got close.
He just leaned against the tree, his eyes tracking
them as they passed right by him. He was tempted
to reach out, but he fought the urge. Holding hands
and swinging their arms, Jared and Sara walked
with newfound confidence. They knew just about
everything now. That is, everything but the fact
that their secret wasn't safe.

CHAPTER
16

I knew it was him!" Guff said, rubbing his hands on his pants. "Wasn't I the one who said it? Wasn't I? I was the only one who said Rafferty was in on this!"

"Fine, fine, you were right," Conrad said. "Get over yourself." He turned to Sara, who was sitting on her desk. "What else did Jared tell you?"

"That's about it," Sara said. "Rafferty threatened Jared, he's been involved since the beginning, and if Jared doesn't win the case, he says he's going to have me killed."

"Do you think you can trust him?" Conrad asked.

"Who? Jared? What kind of question is that? He's my husband."

"He's also your opponent. Which means he could be using this to set you up."

"Sorry, but I think you've been smoking too much grassy knoll. This is serious."

"Hey, don't make fun of the knoll," Guff warned. "It's no joke."

Ignoring her assistant, Sara said to Conrad, "He even showed me pictures of us kissing. Not a pretty sight."

"Pictures? Where'd he get pictures?"

"My best guess is—"

"Whoa, whoa, whoa," Guff jumped in. "You guys were kissing? Was there sex going on in this office? Because if there was, I should know about it."

"It was nothing," Sara said. "A hapless accident between friends."

"Tell me about the photos," Conrad said.

"It looks like they were taken from over there," Sara said, pointing out her window to two offices across the way. "Both of them belong to other ADAs."

"Any idea who took them?"

"It had to be Victor," Sara insisted. "He may be working behind the scenes, but he's had his hand on the monkey wrench since this started."

"That may be true," Conrad said. "But until we can prove it, we don't have a thing on him. Even if he's suspicious, he still hasn't done anything illegal."

"That's why I want to start digging. Jared gave me Rafferty's private number, so I want to run a search on it."

"I can do that," Guff said. "I assume you want to see all the calls that've been made by that number as well as all the ones that have been made to it?"

"Everything you can get," Sara said.

Guff looked over to Conrad. "Can I—"

"I'm approving all of it," Conrad said. "If you have any problems, tell them to call me."

Sara nodded a thank-you. "Now, here's what I really need your help with. Jared said Kozlow spent some time in the military. I have this feeling that's where he met Sunken Cheeks. And since we can't do anything until we know who he is, I was wondering if we could—"

"Just tell me what you need," Conrad said. "Names of everyone in his division? Everyone at his base? Photos? Fingerprints?"

"Photos would be best. A name won't mean much, but I might be able to recognize him if I saw a picture."

"I'll have them here as soon as they can get them together. By the time the trial's over, we'll know the size of this guy's pinkie ring."

"No, no, no," Sara said. "I need it before the trial starts. If we wait until it's over, one of us'll be dead."

As Conrad and Guff were leaving Sara's office, Sara said, "Conrad, can I speak to you a second?"

"Uh-oh, lover boy, now you're in trouble," Guff teased.

Reading Sara's uneasy expression, Conrad shut the door behind Guff. "Let me guess what this is about."

"I know it's awkward, but we really have to talk about it."

"Sara, you don't have to say anything. I know how you feel about Jared. He's your husband."

"It's not just that he's my husband. He's—"

"He's the man you love," Conrad interrupted.

"No," Sara said. "He's more. Much more."

Conrad sat down on the sofa. "I'm sorry, Sara. I never planned for that to happen."

"You don't have to tell me. When you leaned in, I didn't exactly run away."

Leaning his elbows on his knees, Conrad kept his head down. "Damn," he muttered.

"Please don't beat yourself up."

"It wasn't right—I shouldn't have done it."

"Conrad, every friendship has a few awkward moments. This one's ours. And regardless of how much we apologize, I think the only way to get past it is to let it go."

"That easy, huh?"

Sara looked away. "I don't know . . . maybe."

Watching her reaction, Conrad knew there was no other choice. "I swear to you, I never—"

"No explanations necessary," she said, putting on her strongest face. "We'll live."

"I'm sure we will. But I truly am sorry, Sara. I read you the wrong way and I won't let it happen again."

"Deal," Sara said with a smile. She extended a handshake. "Onward and upward?"

Conrad shook her hand. "Sure can't get any lower."

"Are you ready for Thursday?" Rafferty asked when Jared answered the phone.

"I'm trying," Jared said. "I'm just having a hard time getting organized."

"You've been getting organized for weeks. What else do you have to do?"

"I have to finish my opening statements, I have to finish my direct examinations, I have to finish my cross-examinations, I have to think about jury selection, I have to decide what kind of juror is most likely to see Kozlow as sympathetic. All in the next three days. It's overwhelming."

"I don't care. Figure it out. Any other news from your wife?"

"Just that I'm back in the house. I told her I didn't like sleeping at Pop's, and after that disaster with Conrad, she felt too guilty to keep me out. Otherwise, there's not much to report."

"Are you sure?"

Jared didn't even pause at the comment. "Absolutely," he said. "And according to the notes in her briefcase, she's not calling Patty Harrison as a witness unless she needs her."

"Believe me, even if she calls her, Ms. Harrison isn't the same witness she used to be."

"Please do me a favor and stay away from her until we know what Sara's going to do. I don't want to have to add witness intimidation to the list of Kozlow's crimes."

"Don't worry. We have that side under control."

"I know you do," Jared said deferentially. "Now let me try and get some work done. I'll speak to you later." As Jared put down the receiver, he looked up at Kathleen, who had been listening to the entire conversation.

"Do you think he knows?" she asked.

"I have no idea," Jared said. "He's getting antsy, but I still think he's too nervous to suspect anything. I just hope Sara gets some answers before the trial."

At quarter past eight that evening, Jared arrived at home, slamming the door as he stepped inside. "Sara!" he barked the moment he saw her standing in the kitchen. "When the hell are you planning to hand in a witness list?"

"Whenever I'm ready," Sara shot back as she walked toward the bedroom. "And I'm not ready yet."

"Don't walk away from me," Jared shouted, following her. "You're turning this into a trial by ambush."

"Call it what you want, but I have until opening statements to finish my discovery work."

"Are you nuts? Nobody takes that long. Common courtesy says you should—"

"Common courtesy can kiss my ass. Those're the rules, and I plan to take full advantage of them. Now if you want to move back in, you better make yourself comfortable on the couch. Otherwise, leave me the hell alone." With a quick shove, Sara slammed the door in Jared's face.

A moment later, Jared carefully opened the door and tiptoed into the bedroom. Sara was already sitting in front of their computer, at the desk in the corner of the room, hunting and pecking at the keyboard. As he approached her, he read the words on the computer screen: *"How was your day, dear?"* Leaning over, he kissed the back of Sara's neck and took over the keyboard.

"It was fine," he typed back. *"Spoke to Rafferty. I think it went okay. I don't think he suspects anything. He's too nervous."* He let Sara use the keyboard again. As she laboriously typed, Jared pulled up a chair, so they were both seated in front of the computer screen.

"Why do this?" Sara typed. *"Conrad says we can have this entire place searched for bugs. They'll be in and out in two hours, and then we can speak as freely as we want."*

With a quick flourish at the keyboard, Jared wrote back, *"No way. If we have this place searched,*

Rafferty will know something's up. I say we play it safe until the trial."

Typing in her one-finger-at-a-time mode, Sara wrote, *"But my typing sucks."*

Jared laughed to himself. This was what he missed. He put his hand on the back of Sara's head and pulled her toward him. Ever so slightly, he kissed the side of her forehead. Then her cheek. Then her earlobe. With his lips brushing against her ear, he whispered, "I really do love you." As he worked his way down the side of her neck, he slowly undid the top buttons of her blouse.

Closing her eyes, Sara was ready to lose herself in the moment. Suddenly, though, it hit her. Pulling away, she typed, *"Forget it. Not while they're listening."*

"They'll never hear," Jared typed back.

"That's right," Sara typed. *"They won't."*

"Are you serious?"

Sara pounded out nothing but an exclamation point.

"Fine, I'll just sit here and suffer," Jared typed. *"Here I am suffering. I'm suffering. I'm suffering."* He paused. *"I'm still suffering."* When Sara slapped him on the back, he wrote, *"What else happened at work? Any news?"*

"Not yet," Sara typed. *"Tomorrow."*

When Sara and Jared had sat down to start typing, neither of them noticed that their desk had been moved about a quarter of an inch to the right. They didn't notice the additional upward tilt of their computer monitor or the brand-new splitter and extra wire that had been connected to the main monitor cable. And they certainly didn't notice the way the split wire ran behind the desk and into a perfectly drilled hole in their wall. Or how that wire snaked its way down alongside the gas furnace's vent pipe, which led directly to the basement. When it reached the basement, the wire connected to another monitor. And on that monitor, he read every word Jared and Sara typed.

Early Tuesday morning, Sara stepped onto the elevator with her shoulders back and her chin high. Darnell took one look and smiled. "My, oh, my, you must be eating those Wheaties," he said. "You got the look of a champion."

"That's my secret," Sara said.

As the elevator doors were about to shut, a young man wearing a short-sleeve dress shirt jumped inside. Sara instantly recognized him as the man who not only delivered the booking sheets to ECAB but had also originally suggested that she steal Victor's case.

"What's up, Darnell?" he asked. "Any good rumors I should . . . Hey," he added as soon as he saw Sara. "Nice to see you again."

"You two know each other?" Darnell asked.

"In a way," Sara said. Extending her hand, she added, "Officially, by the way, I'm Sara."

"Malcolm," he said as the elevator doors closed. "So how's that case working out? Was I right, or was I right?"

"You said it first: It certainly was a winner."

"Of course it was a winner. You wouldn't have gotten it if it wasn't."

Sara raised an eyebrow. "What're you talking about?"

"You know, the case."

"What about the case?"

Malcolm fell silent. Finally, he said, "I'm sorry. I thought you guys had already spoken."

"About what? Who're you talking about?"

Malcolm looked over at Darnell, then back to Sara. They were both staring at him. "Listen, I'm done with this one. My mouth isn't big enough for two feet."

"Malcolm . . ."

"No, no, no, it's not going to work. If you're having problems, go bother Victor." As the elevator doors opened on the sixth floor, Malcolm stepped out. "I'll see you later, Sara. Later, Darnell."

When the doors slammed shut, Darnell asked, "You okay? You look Casper."

"Just get me to the next floor," Sara said. "Fast."

Rushing out of the elevator and straight to her office, Sara pulled open a desk drawer and took out one of her old legal pads. Keep it together, she told herself. Don't get lost. Just figure out the hows and whys. Mentally replaying the conversation with Malcolm, she scrutinized every syllable. *You wouldn't have gotten it if it wasn't.* I wouldn't have gotten it if it wasn't. *I* would *not* have gotten it. She flipped through the legal pad and stopped on a clean sheet. Once again, she asked herself: Why would Victor want this case? Carefully and methodically, she went through all her old answers: Because he knows Kozlow, because he hates Kozlow, because he wants to punish Kozlow.

Damn, she thought. It was right there the entire time. From the very first day, he was preying on her weakness. Shutting her eyes, she tried to fill in the rest. Finally, it started to make sense. As her fists tightened, she could feel the rage working its way up the back of her neck. She didn't bother to fight it. *"You son of a bitch!"* she screamed as she threw her legal pad against the wall. "How could I be so stupid?"

Slamming the door to her office, Sara flew down the hallway, ignoring everyone in sight. Without knocking, she threw open Victor's door.

"Come in," Victor said, looking up from his desk.

Sara was fuming.

"I take it there's a problem?"

"You knew, didn't you?" Sara asked.

"I'm sorry, do you want to tell me what we're talking about?"

"Don't play bewildered with me. You knew the whole time, didn't you? That first day we met in the elevator, you knew exactly who I was. You knew my name, my background, everything there was to know about me. And most important, you knew how hungry I was for a case."

"Sara, I have no idea what you're—"

"It wasn't even that hard to plan, was it? Once you gave Malcolm a good enough excuse, all you had to do was find a big enough sucker. Someone who would do a good job, but still be easy to influence. Someone who was aggressive, but still too naive to suspect anything. Someone who was vulnerable. And desperate. And would take the case. Someone like me."

"You've got yourself quite a story there."

"This whole time I've been kicking myself for being so stupid. For being so greedy. But there's more to it than that, isn't there, Victor? I didn't steal that case on my own. You set me up and made sure I got it."

Sitting behind his desk, Victor let out the tiniest of smirks.

"I can't believe it," Sara said. "Why? Why didn't you keep it for yourself?"

"As I've always said, I don't know what you're talking about. But that Kozlow's quite a handful, isn't he?"

Sara clenched her teeth. "You're a real bastard, Victor."

"Even if I am, I'm one with far fewer headaches."

"Are you sure about this?" Conrad asked. "It doesn't make any sense."

"What's to make sense?" Sara said. "It's Victor."

"So let me get this straight—you're saying that when you were in ECAB that first day, Victor not only knew Malcolm was going to deliver that case, but he had already told Malcolm to *make sure* that you stole it?"

"Exactly."

"But if Victor didn't want the case, why not just give it away? And if he wanted it prosecuted, no offense, but why give it to you? Why not give it to me or someone with experience?"

"Because he never wanted Kozlow or Rafferty to know that he didn't want it."

"So now you don't think Victor buries cases?"

"No, I just think he didn't want to bury *this* case." Seeing Conrad's confused look, she added, "Let me start over. I'm still convinced that Victor's playing in some fishy ponds. I think he has a few wealthy clients who pay him a great deal of money to bury easy-to-miss cases, and I think he's as dirty as they come. Now what I'm willing to bet happened here is that one of Rafferty's big-shot friends told Rafferty about Victor. And when Kozlow got arrested in this case, Rafferty quickly went crying to Victor. The thing is, Victor's not stupid. He knows his little game only works if everything can be kept quiet. And as we know, Kozlow is to quiet as, well . . . as a raging maniac is to quiet."

"So Victor tells Rafferty to take a hike."

"Exactly. But Rafferty's also not stupid. Now that he knows Victor's dirty secret, he threatens to blow the whistle on Victor if Victor doesn't do a little magic. Naturally, Victor doesn't want to bury the case because he knows he'll be risking his own neck, but he can't give it away, because Rafferty'll play snitch. Now Victor's faced with a problem: How does he get rid of a case without looking like he's getting rid of a case?"

"He has someone steal it from him."

"Starting to sound familiar?"

Conrad stood from his seat and looked out his window. "It's actually pretty ingenious on Victor's part."

"The man's a power player. He's not going to risk his career on someone like Kozlow. This way, all he has to do is pretend he's pissed off. Then he tells Rafferty and Kozlow it's out of his control. Maybe he does a few more favors—like passing information and taking a few photos—and they're convinced he's on their side."

"So all the times he's been checking up on you . . ."

"He's either reporting it to Rafferty, or just making sure I don't stumble on his other cases."

Turning away from the window, Conrad said, "There's still one thing I don't understand. For Victor to know that you were coming in that afternoon, someone had to tell him. Besides you and Jared . . ."

"There was only one other person who knew where I was."

At that moment, Guff walked into Conrad's office. "What's wrong with the two of you?" Guff asked. "You look Casper."

"We're fine. I'm fine," Sara blurted. "It's nothing."

"Listen, if you guys want to touch tongues again, be my guest."

"Stop with that already," Conrad said. "It's not funny."

"Guff, can you actually excuse us for a moment?" Sara said.

"Why? What's the big secret?"

"Now," Conrad said.

"Okay, okay, it's a private moment—I understand." Guff headed for the door. "Just don't take it out on me. I'm on your side."

As the door shut, Sara looked over to Conrad. "Please don't tell me it's him."

"It's not," Conrad said. "I've known that kid since the day he started here. He doesn't have it in him."

"I don't care how long you've known him. Nothing else makes sense. He's the one who brought me to ECAB in the first place. I mean, I wouldn't have even walked in there if it wasn't for him."

"Sara, he was doing you a favor."

Now she was sweating. "Oh, God—then that means Rafferty knows Jared and I have been talking."

"Not a chance. No one knows anything."

"Then how do you explain—"

"I don't need to explain," Conrad insisted. "I know Guff. And more important, I trust him. He'd never do that to you."

"You can trust people all you want," Sara said. "It still doesn't mean they're not going to put a knife in your back."

Sara didn't get home until eight-thirty that evening. Heading straight for the bedroom, she could hear the quiet clicking of Jared at the keyboard. He had already typed, *"Hi, honey. How was your day?"* But when he turned around and saw his wife, he added, *"What happened?"*

Putting up a finger to signal *"Hold on a second,"* Sara, in her best annoyed tone, said, "Do you mind hanging out in the living room? I have some work to do in here."

"Do whatever you want," Jared shot back. He got up and stormed out of the room. He turned on the TV in the living room and then quietly returned to the bedroom. Over Sara's shoulder, he read, *"I think Guff may be on the other side of this. As far as I can tell, he took me to ECAB that first day for a reason."*

Taking the keyboard, Jared wrote, *"That's not a small accusation, Sara. If I were you, I'd double-check every detail before I wrecked that relationship."*

Realizing her husband was right, Sara wrote, *"Do we have a calendar?"*

"In my briefcase," Jared typed. *"My organizer."*

Sara opened Jared's briefcase and found his small electronic organizer. Pushing the button marked "Calendar," she saw the date as well as Jared's to-do list appear on the screen: *"Call jury expert. Finish direct. Call printer."* Using the "Up" key, she then scrolled back to Monday, September eighth—her first day on the job. But when the day came up on the screen, Sara's heart sank. There was only one item on Jared's to-do list for that day: *"Call V.S."* Under the initials was a phone number. Sara recognized the number's 335 prefix—it was a number in the DA's office. She took another look at the initials. *V.S.* Victor Stockwell.

Sara glanced up at Jared. Then back at Victor's number. It couldn't be.

By the time she turned back to Jared, he was staring at her. He silently mouthed the question "You okay?"

Sara nodded as she closed the organizer. It wasn't Guff at all. It was Jared. Feeling her legs go numb, she made her way back to the computer.

On the screen, Jared had written the question *"What did Guff do that made you so suspicious?"*

Fighting her hands from shaking, Sara typed back, *"Nothing. Just a feeling."*

CHAPTER 17

I told you it wasn't Guff," Conrad said the following morning. "I said it yesterday. I knew it couldn't be him."

"I don't really care about Guff," Sara said, her voice completely drained of energy. Her arms were folded on her desk and her head rested on them. She hadn't looked up since she told Conrad the story. "I need your help with Jared. I mean, maybe I'm wrong. Maybe it's not him."

"What're you talking about? Of course it's Jared."

She kept her head on her desk. That wasn't what she wanted to hear. Slowly, she felt her stomach start to turn. It wasn't possible. This couldn't be happening.

"Sara, are you okay?"

Feeling as if the wind were knocked out of her, she said nothing. This wasn't some distant friend. Or a new coworker. This was her husband. She was supposed to know everything about him. Everything. That was what she'd told herself last night to coax herself to sleep. And that was how she initially talked herself out of Conrad's conclusion. But the closer she looked, the more she found details she couldn't ignore. When he wanted to be, Jared was more manipulative than anyone she knew. In the last month alone, she had seen that firsthand. And the call to Victor—that was the only way Victor could've known she was coming. Over and over, Sara ran through the facts, and whether she trusted Jared or not, she knew there wasn't going to be an easy answer. "How?" she finally asked Conrad. "It doesn't make any sense."

"Sure it does," Conrad said. "I've seen Jared operate. He may act all squeaky clean, but he's as scheming as the rest of us. That's why he peeked in your briefcase. From the moment he told you about Rafferty, I said you should watch your back."

"You only said that because you're jealous of him."

Conrad glared at Sara as his voice took on a more serious tone. "I just think there's something he's hiding."

"Why, though? He hates Rafferty."

"I agree with that. But that doesn't mean Jared's not working with Victor. One thing has nothing to do with another."

Once again, Sara felt her stomach start to turn. "But why would he possibly do that to me?"

"Does he have anything to be embarrassed about in his past? Maybe he and Victor bury cases together—Jared lines up the clients, Victor makes them disappear. Or maybe he's being blackmailed. Maybe he's taking revenge for something you did to him. For all we know, he completely set you up in Brooklyn that night."

"Stop it," Sara said, raising her voice. "It's impossible. None of those things are true."

"Sara, I know this is hard, but you can't just shut your eyes and hope it all has a happy ending. Take off the blinders and deal with the problem."

"I am dealing with it."

"No. You're not," Conrad said. "If you were, you would've already stepped into his personal space and asked him why he was calling Victor in the first place."

Sara knew he was right. She should've asked as soon as she found the phone number. "It's not as easy as you think."

"Just call him. If he says he's never spoken to Victor, we'll know he's lying."

Sara reached across her desk and picked up the phone. Seven numbers later, she heard Jared's phone ring. "C'mon, I know you're there," she muttered. "Pick up the damn phone."

"Mr. Lynch's office," Kathleen answered.

"Hi, Kathleen. It's me. Is he in?"

"I'll check. Hold on a second."

Unable to stop fidgeting, Sara stood up. But Conrad grabbed her by the shoulders and sat her down again.

After a moment, she heard, "Sara?"

"Do you have a minute?" Sara asked, trying her best to sound calm.

"Of course. What's wrong?"

"Nothing. I just have a quick question. Do you know a guy named Victor Stockwell?"

"I told you before—only by reputation. Why?"

"Have you ever spoken to him on the phone?"

There was a short pause on the other end. "No. Why?"

Sara looked up at Conrad and shook her head. "Jared, is anyone in your office?"

"What's going on? Are you okay?"

"I'm fine. I just need you to answer this question. Have you ever spoken to Victor?"

Jared didn't say a word.

"Please, honey, you can tell me," Sara said.

"I haven't," he insisted. "Why do you—"

Before he could finish the question, Sara hung up. She felt a piercing pain in her chest.

"I'm sorry," Conrad said. He put his hand back on her shoulder.

Closing her eyes, Sara was reeling. Take it easy, she told herself. There're hundreds of logical explanations. But the more she thought about it, the more she realized she couldn't come up with even one. And when she realized that, she knew it was over. She didn't know him anymore. The phone rang, tearing through the silence. Sara didn't pick it up. It rang again. When it rang a third time, she reached for it.

"Don't," Conrad said.

"Jared, I don't want to hear your lame excuses," she answered.

"I'm sorry," Jared said. "I shouldn't have lied to you like that."

"So now the story's changing?"

"Sara, please, I'm telling you the truth—I spoke to him one time. That was it."

Sara covered her other ear and turned away. This was even worse.

"Sara?" Jared asked. "Sara, are you there?"

"I'm here," she whispered.

"Please don't be mad," Jared pleaded. "I know it looks bad, but it was for a good reason."

"I'm listening."

"Okay, here it is. Here's the story. Here's how it happened."

"Are you going to tell me why you did it, or are you going to make it up as you go along?"

"Sara, I swear to you, I only called him to get help. That night before your first day, you were so nervous, I had to do something. So while you were packing your briefcase, I went into the bedroom and called Judge Flynn. Now, I know you didn't want me to call in any favors, but you should've seen yourself—the article in the *Times* had you crazy. There was no way I could just sit on my hands. I told him what was happening and asked him if he had any suggestions. He said my best bet was to make sure you got a case. Then he made a few phone calls and told me about ECAB. He found out Victor was the next day's supervisor, and he gave me his number. The next morning, I called Victor. I explained the situation and said if he could help us out, Judge Flynn would really appreciate it. He said he'd see what he could do, but that was the last I heard of him. Next thing I knew, you had a case."

"Jared—"

"I know what you're going to say. I shouldn't have done it; I shouldn't have gone behind your back like that. I know it was wrong. I just didn't want to see you drown. It rips my heart out to see you like that."

"Then why didn't you tell me all this the other night?"

"I wanted to. I wanted to so bad. But I thought if you found out what I did, you'd slip back into self-doubt. I didn't want to see you lose that confidence. So I made the worst judgment call of all and decided it didn't matter. Obviously, I was wrong."

"And that's the truth?"

"I'm telling you, that's what happened," Jared said. "I wouldn't lie to you again."

"Twelve times were enough, huh?"

"I understand if you don't believe me, but that's the only reason I did it. When you called me before, you just caught me off guard."

"Then let me ask you one last thing: Why'd you let me suspect Victor all this time? You knew I was running crazy. Why not help me out?"

His answer was nothing but a long pause. Eventually, Jared stuttered, "I . . . I don't know. I just chose not to. I'm sorry."

Sara was shaken by his response. "That's it? You *chose not to*?"

"I swear to you, Sara. That's the real answer. I didn't mean to hurt you—I was only trying to help."

"Okay," she said, still attempting to discern if he was telling the truth. "We'll talk more about it later."

"Great, we'll do it later."

Unable to ignore the nervousness in his voice, Sara hung up the phone and looked at Conrad.

"Well?" Conrad asked.

She took a deep breath. "I'm not sure. Part of me thinks he's lying, but part of me really believes him."

"Are you out of your head?"

"You didn't even hear his explanation."

"Tell it to me." After Sara relayed the conversation, Conrad said, "Oh, c'mon, Sara. He lied to your face, let you hang up, and then called you back as soon as he thought of a good enough cock-and-bull story. I mean, all you did was read an article about budget cuts—do you really think that's enough to make him call Victor?" Before Sara could argue, Conrad added, "How about letting me do a search on your home phone? If Jared's story's true, we'll be able to see the calls from that night. One call to the judge; that's all we're looking for."

"I don't know," Sara said. "Except for one part, he gave me a good explanation. I think I have to trust him."

"Sara, don't be stupid. He didn't even—"

"Don't call me stupid! I'm not a moron, Conrad. And while you think you know everything about love and law, there's a chasm between the two. If I start searching our phone bills, I've train-wrecked the only thing we have left."

"So you'd rather be blind to reality?"

"Are you really that jaded? Is that what all those years here have done to you? This isn't about being blind. It's about having faith."

"I know what faith is, I just don't—"

"He's my husband."

Without knocking, Guff entered the office holding a thick manila envelope.

"Why don't you ask him?" Conrad said. "It's just another leap of faith, right?"

Sara didn't like Conrad's tactics, but she had to admit that Jared's story took the suspicion off of Guff. Favoring friendship over fear, she explained the story to her assistant. When she was finished, she was surprised to see Guff laughing.

"Me?" Guff asked. "You suspected me? That's the most absurd idea since Elvis carpeted his ceiling."

"So you're not mad?"

"Sara, I'm not in this because you're my boss. I'm in it because you're my amigo. If I got all huffy and puffy on you, I'd just be taking time away from that."

Sara couldn't help but smile. "Guff, if only everyone else were like you."

"The world would be a beautiful place, don't you think?" Guff said. "Now what're you going to do about Sunken Cheeks? The trial starts tomorrow."

"Forget about Sunken Cheeks," Conrad interrupted. "What're you going to do about Jared?"

"Conrad, can you please drop it already? I know it's under your skin, but it's not your life, it's mine. And if I plan to save it, I have to find out who this guy is in the next few hours."

Guff shook his head at Conrad. "Don't do this to her. She's running out of time."

Conrad crossed his arms and studied his colleagues. The conversation about Jared was going to have to wait until later. "Tell me what's in the folder."

Guff held up the manila envelope. "You want phone numbers? I got phone numbers. I got local, long distance, international, interstate, by the aisle, by the window." He threw the envelope on Sara's desk.

Flipping through dozens of photocopied pages, Sara struggled to read the dense report. "How do you—?"

"The calling log is in the back," Guff said.

When Sara read the log of Rafferty's phone line, she saw Claire Doniger's home phone number circled in red pen every time it appeared.

"If it makes you feel any better, Jared was dead on the money—there's no question there's a connection between them," Guff said as Sara continued to flip pages. "Rafferty may've said that they only spoke a few times, but there are almost forty calls made during the week of the murder. Four on the day of the burglary, when we think Arnold Doniger was murdered, and five on the day Claire says he died. Either way, these two are talking more than Lucy and Ethel."

"Good. Next up, where are we on Sunken Cheeks?"

"Same place we always were," Guff said. "Lost."

"When are the photographs supposed to get here?" Sara asked.

"Right about now," Conrad said, looking at his watch.

"Can you—"

"I'm on my way down." Conrad got up from his seat and headed for the door. "As soon as they hit the mail room, they're ours." Seeing that Sara looked more antsy, he added, "It's okay. It's going to work out."

"I don't know," Sara said. "What if they know about me and Jared?"

Conrad looked back at her. "Don't worry," he said. "They don't."

As he turned the corner and walked past the funeral home, Elliott noticed that a dark blue Town Car was waiting in front of his apartment. He headed straight for the car, and the window rolled down. When he leaned inside he saw Rafferty.

"Everything okay?" Rafferty asked.

Elliott didn't like the tone of the question. "Why wouldn't it be?"

"No reason. Just wanted to know if you heard anything new about Sara."

Now Elliott knew something was wrong. Rafferty either had something, or he was fishing for something. "Nothing out of the normal," Elliott said. "Why? You seen anything?"

"Nothing out of the normal," Rafferty said, his answer smothered in sarcasm. "But once the trial starts, I'm expecting a hurricane."

"Should be exciting. You have to let me know how it goes."

"Of course I will. I'd never cut you out."

"What's that supposed to mean?"

"Nothing," Rafferty said. "Just making sure we understand each other."

"Always have and always will," Elliott said. "So I'll see you when it's over?"

Rafferty nodded.

As Rafferty's car pulled away from the building, Elliott turned back to his front door. Don't let him rattle you, he told himself. It's all coming together. When he reached his apartment, he headed straight for the living room and unlocked the padlock on the storage trunk that served as his coffee table. Carefully, he lifted a box from the trunk and put it on the couch. He opened the box and pulled out one of six sets of plastic mannequin hands. At the base of the hands, written in thick black ink, was the name WARREN EASTHAM.

Elliott carried the hands back to the kitchen and stood them upright on his table. Then, carefully, he rolled up his sleeves and removed from his own hands the transparent, skintight latex gloves that held the sculpted fingerprints of a man who had been dead for almost eight months. And in that moment, as he slipped the gloves back on to their plastic holders, Warren Eastham once again returned to the dead and Elliott came back to life.

"Where the hell is he?" Sara asked, looking up from the outline of her opening statement. "It's been almost twenty minutes."

"You ever been in the mail room?" Guff asked as he assembled the witness files. "Pulling a package early takes at least a month and a half."

"I don't have that long—we're running out of time here."

"We're doing the best we can, Sara. You know that." Changing the subject, Guff picked up the wedding photo that was perched on the corner of Sara's desk. "Did you and Jared have a big wedding?" he asked.

"Monster. Jared's family doesn't do anything small."

"So you know all of his family? It's not like there're any secrets between you two?"

Sara stopped reading her outline and looked up at her assistant. "You're having second thoughts, aren't you?"

"They're not second thoughts—it's just that Conrad usually has a good hunch about this stuff. Plus, Jared's story . . ."

"I admit, it has a couple of holes. But each of them can be explained."

"No, you're right. Forget I said anything. You have to trust him."

Turning her attention back to the outline, Sara asked, "What about Conrad? You think I can trust him?"

"Don't even start with that. Conrad would never—"

"It's just a question. I mean, if we're going to raise the microscope, we might as well examine everyone."

"So you think Conrad's involved with Victor?"

"Actually, I don't think anyone's involved with Victor. But you do have to wonder why Conrad's so anxious to keep me and Jared from talking."

"I think we all know the answer to that one."

"Maybe," Sara said. "It's still something to think about. And speaking of which . . ." She flipped through her Rolodex and picked up the phone.

"Who're you calling?"

"Our favorite medical examiner," she explained as she dialed.

"Great," Guff said. "While you do that, I have a few more phone calls to make." Sara nodded to her assistant, and Guff left the room.

"This is Fawcett," he answered.

"Hi, Dr. Fawcett, it's Sara Tate, from the DA's office. I just wanted to remind you to send over a clean copy of the autopsy report before the trial—I need to submit it as evidence and mine's all marked up."

"Are you sure you haven't gotten it yet? I sent my final version over weeks ago. Messenger and all."

"Really," Sara said suspiciously.

"Yes, indeed. Of course, it's easy to make another copy, but—"

"Guff, did you send a messenger to Fawcett's office?" she called out, covering the phone.

Guff stuck his head back in the office. "Not me, boss."

Sara shook her head. "Let me ask you another question," she said, turning back to the phone. "Is it possible to fake a fingerprint?"

"Define 'fake.' "

"Do you need someone's actual hand to leave their fingerprint on something?"

"A few years ago, the answer would be yes. Not anymore. The beauty these days is that everything's possible. If I want to leave your fingerprint on something, I just need a copy of your print on a piece of paper. If I have that, I can make a photocopy of your print. Then, while the photocopy is still hot, I put a piece of fingerprint tape on the print and lift the tape."

"Off the copy?" Sara asked.

"Right off the copy," Fawcett said. "The toner from a copy machine is sometimes used for fingerprint powder. Once I have it on the tape, I can put that piece of tape anywhere. Bam—you're wherever I say you are."

"But what if there's no tape involved? Could someone do it by themselves? Maybe keeping someone else's fingerprints on top of their own?"

There was a prolonged pause on the other line. Eventually, he said, "If you wanted to, you might be able to do it with latex gloves. Of course, then you'd have to keep the gloves a little wet, but it's sufficiently possible."

"I don't understand."

"Real prints usually have remnants of sweat gland secretions or some other contaminant like grease or dust. But if you kept licking the gloves, or just rubbed them with a little bit of oil, you might be able to make it look like a real print. The real trick, of course, is copying the original prints, but as I said, it's not impossible. Why? Do you want to make a set of gloves?"

"No, I want to *find* a set of gloves."

* * *

Ten minutes later, Conrad returned to the office carrying a medium-sized box, which he dropped on Sara's desk. "Here's our new best option."

Sara got out of her seat and saw that the box was filled with thousands of neatly stacked photographs. Each of them was a portrait of a man in his army uniform, posed in front of an American flag.

"Kozlow was stationed at Fort Jackson in South Carolina when he first joined the army," Conrad explained. "He made it halfway through basic training, got in a fight with a fellow recruit and got the boot soon after. Apparently, he didn't want to face the consequences that went along with his attitude problems."

"So who's in these pictures?" she asked as she shuffled through the photographs. "Everyone on his team?"

"Team?" Conrad asked. "Do you know anything about military terminology? A team has two to three people, a squad has nine, a platoon is three to four squads, a company is three to four platoons, a battalion is five companies, a brigade is two battalions, and a division is three brigades, which is about five thousand people."

Sara looked down at the thousands of photographs on her desk. "So is that everyone in his brigade?"

"It's everyone who was at Fort Jackson while Kozlow was there. And the first pile is everyone in his basic training company. If you look carefully, you may find Sunken Cheeks."

Flipping through the first pile of photographs,

Sara said, "This is impossible. Look at these guys—they're all the same. Square shoulders and a crew cut, square shoulders and a crew cut, square shoulders and a crew cut. After the first bunch, it gets maddening. I might as well be looking through yearbooks or something stupid like that."

As Sara picked up the next pile of pictures, Guff came barging into the office, waving a fax. "Start writing your thank-you cards, ladies and gents, because Guff just saved the day!"

Conrad shot Guff a skeptical look. "This better be good."

"Oh, it is, Most Solemn One." He looked down at his fax. "While you were searching through the military past, I took the other way around and started searching through the present. I took the two names that came up from Sunken Cheeks's fingerprints and ran them through BCI. Sol Broder and Warren Eastham have almost nothing in common. They weren't born in the same cities, neither of them was in the military, they didn't live near each other, and as far as I can tell, they didn't even know each other. But they did have one thing in common: They were both criminals. So I ran a search on every piece of their criminal records—what their crimes were, when they were arrested, who their lawyers were, where they served their time—you name it, I searched it. Again, nothing came up. Both Broder and Eastham served their time upstate at the Hudson facility, but Broder was there four years ago, while Eastham was there two years ago. They were never there at the same time."

"So what's your great find?" Conrad asked impatiently.

"My great find is that a closer examination revealed the one thing Broder and Eastham had in common: When Sol Broder left the Hudson facility, Warren Eastham occupied his old cell."

"So?" Conrad asked.

"So that means they shared the same cellmate," Sara said.

"Exactly," Guff said with a smile. "And that cellmate is . . ." Guff held up the faxed mug shot of a prisoner. It was blurry, but it was definitely Sunken Cheeks. Sara's eyes went wide.

"That's him!" Sara said, grabbing the fax out of Guff's hands. "That's the guy who threatened me."

"Unbelievable," Conrad said. "You may get employee of the month for this one."

"I'm shooting for the whole year," Guff said.

"So who is he?" Sara asked, still studying the picture.

"His name is Elliott Traylor. That's all we have right now, but give me an hour and we'll have the rest."

"Here we go," Guff said, reading from a file folder as he stood in the middle of Sara's office. "The life and times of Elliott Traylor. He was born in Queens, New York, to Phyllis Traylor, who raised him on her own."

"What happened to his father?" Sara asked.

"There's no mention of a father," Guff said. "The family grew up relatively poor in Queens, and Elliott's mother used to work as both a secretary and a waitress. Here's the interesting part, though. According to their tax records, Elliott's mother used to work for a company called StageRights Unlimited. And that was the original name for—you guessed it—"

"Echo Enterprises," Conrad said.

"Are you kidding me?" Sara asked.

"Wait, it gets better. When she was at Stage-Rights, Phyllis Traylor was the personal secretary for Mr. Arnold Doniger. But according to her unemployment records, she was fired from Stage-Rights a few months before Elliott was born."

"That was at least twenty-five to thirty years ago," Sara said. "Is she still alive?"

"No, she died seven years ago from lung cancer. Elliott went to high school in Queens and then won an engineering scholarship to Brooklyn College. His test scores say he was quite the boy genius, but he apparently had a hard time when his mother passed away. He was only a sophomore in college at the time."

"What was he in prison for?" Conrad asked.

"Aggravated sexual abuse and aggravated assault. Seems he had a difference of opinion with a woman he was courting. She started screaming it was rape; he punched her in the face and broke her jaw. Luckily, someone heard and called the cops. From the file we have on him, he's a brutal bastard. Smart, too."

"That engineering degree might explain the fingerprints," Sara said.

"I still don't understand one thing," Conrad said. "What the hell does Elliott have to gain if Kozlow is found guilty?"

"Maybe he's holding a grudge from when his mom was fired all those years ago," Guff suggested.

"Too corny," Sara said. "And not strong enough to make him take all those risks."

"Maybe he's been hired by someone else who hates Kozlow and Rafferty for some other reason."

"No, now you're getting off track," Conrad said. "If Elliott is involved, he must have something to gain. There's a fifty-million-dollar business on the line here."

"Then let me ask you this," Guff said as he joined Sara on the couch. "If they take the money away from Rafferty, who gets it?"

"According to the will, it goes to Arnold Doniger's heirs."

"So Claire does get it?" Guff asked, confused.

"No, the will specifically states that Claire takes nothing, and since she waived everything else in the prenup, it goes to his other surviving relatives. First, they'll look to see if he has any children, then they'll—"

"Stop right there," Conrad said. "What if Arnold Doniger has a son he doesn't know about?"

"How do you have a son you don't—" Suddenly, a cold chill ran down Sara's back. "Oh, my God. You think Elliott—"

"Why not? It's the only thing that makes sense."

"Hold on a second," Guff said. "You think Elliott is Arnold Doniger's son?"

"Actually, I do," Sara said. "Look at the facts: Elliott's mother spends five years working as Arnold Doniger's secretary. Over time, a little office romance develops and Arnold starts having a little fun behind his first wife's back. Then the bad news hits—Elliott's mom is pregnant. Six months before the baby's due, Arnold tells her to hit the road. He may have tons of money, but he can't let an illegitimate child ruin his marriage, his reputation, and his lifestyle."

"I'm with you," Conrad said. "Six months later, Elliott is born. His mother has no job, no money, and, as the birth certificate says, no husband.

When Elliott is old enough, his mother tells him the story of his father, and for years, Elliott harbors nothing but hatred for the man who won't acknowledge his existence. So when the opportunity comes to get Dad's money—his rightful inheritance—Elliott wants to make sure he's first in line."

"See, I think he's more involved than that," Sara said. "Elliott has way too much information to just be showing up at the reading of the will."

"You think he took part in the murder?"

"That's the only way to explain how he knew about the wine cellar," Sara pointed out. "He and Rafferty could've plotted Arnold's death together. Rafferty would get the money; Elliott would get revenge. But when Kozlow got arrested and the plan fell apart, Elliott realized that he had even more to gain than the resolution of his I-hate-Daddy complex. At that point, he switched sides, turned on Rafferty, and pushed me to win." As the logic of her own argument registered, Sara slumped back in disgust. "Which means Elliott plotted the death of his own father."

"I know it's hard to fathom, but it happens all the time," Conrad said.

"But it's his father," Sara said, disgusted. "How do you kill your own parent?"

"By hiring Tony Kozlow to give him an overdose of insulin."

"There's only one problem," Guff said. "If Elliott's involved with the death, isn't he also covered by the slayer statute?"

"Of course," Sara said. "But that doesn't mean he's not a greedy little scumbag. Besides, the only way to prove Elliott was involved with Arnold's death is if Rafferty rats him out. And if he does that, Rafferty will be admitting his own involvement."

"Which he'll never do, because if he does, he'll never see a dime of Arnold's money," Conrad said.

"Exactly," Sara added.

"You think?" Guff asked skeptically. "It seems a little far-fetched to me."

"I disagree," Sara said. "You'd be surprised what people will do when their family's involved."

"Or what they won't do," Conrad said. "Like keep their mouths shut."

"But a bizarro Electra complex? What's the likelihood of—"

"Either way, it doesn't matter," Sara interrupted. "Regardless of what you believe, Elliott's clearly the man we're looking for."

"So what do we do now?" Guff asked.

"That's easy," Sara said. "Have you ever heard of a prisoners' dilemma?"

At nine o'clock that evening, Sara, Conrad, and Guff packed up their belongings. "You really think it'll work?" Guff asked as he put on his jacket.

"It can't miss," Sara said, stuffing two legal pads into her briefcase.

"Of course it can miss," Conrad said. "If you tell Jared, and Jared tells Victor . . ."

"Don't start with that."

"Then don't tell him. The plan only works if everything's kept quiet. That means no one should know about it—especially your husband."

"Why're you so convinced that Jared's involved with Victor? Why would he possibly do that to me?"

"I told you before, maybe you don't know him as well as you think you do. What if he and Victor are running this case-burying business together? Assuming Victor does it for money, he still needs some good way to find the richest defendants—and as an up-and-comer in a big-name law firm, Jared's the perfect scout. That's why he doesn't have any clients; they're all off the books."

"That's impossible."

"Is it? Are you sure? Think about it, Sara. Think carefully. People have lapses of strength all the time. All he needs is the tiniest push: He's not satisfied at work; he's sick of living in a tiny one-bedroom apartment; he needs the money; he's having trouble making partner—"

"I don't want to hear this," Sara said as she struggled to stuff a file folder in her briefcase. Realizing it wouldn't fit, she added, "Dammit, what the hell is wrong with this thing?"

"Take it easy," Guff said as he helped her with the folder.

"Sara, if you tell Jared, and he's on the other side, this thing'll blow up in our faces. We'll be sitting there thinking it's all going to work out, and then, out of nowhere, BOOOM!" Sara jumped at Conrad's sound effect. "Next thing you know, we're finished." Conrad let the silence of the room drive home his point.

"But if Jared doesn't know—"

"He'll be fine, Sara. It's not like I'm asking a lot. I don't need you to lie to him; I just want you to keep it quiet. Otherwise, we risk watching all our hard work slip away."

Sara turned to Guff. "What do you think?"

"I don't know. I see Conrad's point, but part of

me keeps thinking that once you doubt Jared, there's no going back."

"Don't be so melodramatic," Conrad said. "It's just one little secret—nothing more. Now what do you say?"

"I'm not sure," Sara said. "Let me see how tonight goes."

A half hour after she arrived at home, Sara was sitting in front of the computer, staring at a blank screen. When she had first walked in, she had expected to find her husband cooking in the kitchen or typing in the bedroom. But as she made her way to the back of the apartment, she was surprised to find neither. Determined to take advantage of Jared's absence, she'd quickly exchanged her business suit for sweatpants and a T-shirt, and pulled a chair up to the computer. Now was the time to decide, she thought. Before he gets home.

Carefully weighing each of the arguments in her head, she tried her best to reach a solution. Deep down, she wanted to believe him. It was the only choice. But the longer she sat alone in the silent apartment, and the longer she looked down at her watch, wondering where Jared was, the more she started to doubt him. And the more she started to doubt him, the more she saw the strength of Conrad's argument. She didn't have to lie to Jared—she just had to keep quiet.

Sensing the arrival of rationalization, Sara wondered what Pop would do in the same situation. He'd tell the truth, she thought. What about Jared's parents? They'd lie. What about her own parents? What would they do? Sara walked over to the row of pictures on her dresser, picked out the photo of her parents, and sat down on her bed. It was an old picture, taken on the day Sara got accepted to Hunter College. Her father was so proud that when they went out to a small nearby restaurant to celebrate, he brought the acceptance letter and showed it to the waiter. Then he took a picture of Sara with the letter. And his wife with the letter. And even the waiter with the letter. Finally, Sara grabbed the camera and said, "How about we get some people in the next one?" Within an instant, Sara's father had wrapped his arm around his wife and placed his hand so confidently on her shoulder. On the count of three, Sara snapped the picture.

Over a dozen years later, Sara loved the picture not because it was a great one, and not because it made her parents look beautiful. She loved it because every time she looked at it, she remembered that day—the acceptance letter, the pride, the waiter, the food, and most important, the people there.

The click of the front door locks jarred Sara from her memory. Jared was finally home. Brushing her thumb across the glass that covered her parents' image, she knew it was time to move past the lessons of death and to pay attention to the ones about life.

When Jared burst into the room, she could tell that he had already prepared his excuse. Racing to the computer, he was ready to type out why he was late, and where he'd been, and why she had to believe him about Victor. But before he even passed the bed, Sara stepped in front of him. Jared was biting at his bottom lip. He looked anxious, almost nervous. It would definitely be easy to keep the secret, she thought. Just don't say a word. She sat down at the computer, unclenched her fists, and fought her hesitation. Don't look back, she told herself. Only forward. And as her fingers danced across the keyboard, Sara Tate took her leap of faith. Over her shoulder, Jared read the words, *"Here's the plan . . ."*

Sitting on a discarded milk crate in the basement, he stared intensely at the monitor. It was propped up on two other crates, and it bathed the dark room in the artificial glow of blue light. When he saw the first few words flicker across the screen, he smiled at his own ingenuity. It hadn't been difficult to put in the splitter, but it did take some time to find the exact location of the gas furnace's vent pipe. Once he had that, though, he just dropped a plumb line from the hole in their wall down to the basement. That's what it took to get the wire down there: a washer on a string. All he'd had to do was make sure no one was home, which, for him, was as easy as finding out about their meeting in Brooklyn. He just had to know where to look. And who to speak to. Slowly, the screen was filled with Sara's plan. And as he read every word, Elliott nodded to himself. There was nothing to worry about. Sara, Rafferty, all of them—they'd never know what hit them.

CHAPTER
18

At six-thirty in the morning on the day of the trial, Sara and Jared sat at their kitchen table, staring silently at each other. Although Sara had made herself her favorite breakfast, a giant bowl of Apple Jacks and a tall glass of orange juice, she'd barely touched it. No matter how well prepared she was for this day, no matter how much thought she'd put into it, she couldn't shake the feeling that there was more to be done. As Conrad had warned her the night before, there was nothing like the anxiety of opening day. No amount of experience could appease it; no amount of preparation could allay it.

Sitting across the table from his wife, Jared was consumed by the same fears. Ten minutes ago, he had toasted two slices of rye toast without the crust. He still hadn't taken more than a bite. Since the day he'd arrived at Wayne & Portnoy, he'd been involved in at least twenty different trials. He'd personally been first chair on seven of them. And while he had already expertly faced dozens of doubting jurors, opening day was always the same: no appetite, upset stomach, striking pain in the base of his neck. That was the way every trial started, and that was what he felt as he stared across at his wife.

After shoving aside her cereal and orange juice, Sara pulled out a pen and scribbled a quick note on the corner of Jared's newspaper: "Good luck, my love. See you in court." Then, as silently as she could, she gave him a tender kiss on his forehead. A minute later, she was gone.

As Jared stood up to throw out his toast, the phone rang. "Hello," he said.

"She looks good today," Rafferty said. "Sharp coat, nice shoes, no jewelry. Clearly, she's dressed to impress."

"Stay the hell away from her," Jared warned.

"Don't make threats—they piss me off."

"Where are you?" Jared asked.

"In my car. Right outside your front door. I'm here to give you a ride to the courthouse."

"I don't need—"

"It's not an offer, Jared. Come downstairs. Now."

Jared quickly put on his overcoat and grabbed his briefcase. He'd expected Rafferty to offer a final bit of advice before the trial, but he hadn't thought it'd be this early.

Outside, the morning was typical for a New York winter: bitter cold, no sun, gray skies. When Jared opened the door to Rafferty's car, he saw both Kozlow and Rafferty waiting.

"Big day, boss," Kozlow said. "How do I look?"

"It'll do," Jared said, eyeing the suit they'd

bought for the grand jury. "Make sure to wear the glasses."

"I got them right here," Kozlow said, patting his breast pocket. "Safe and sound."

As Jared took a seat in the back of the car, he could feel Rafferty staring coldly at him. Attempting to ignore the nausea that was dancing in his stomach, Jared asked, "Everything okay?"

"I wanted to see how you were doing."

"Then you'll be happy to know that I hit pay dirt last night. I saw her questions for Doniger and Officer McCabe, I read her opening statement, and I got a look at her evidence list. We're in good shape—we're now prepared for everything she's bringing up."

"What about jury selection?"

"Do I look like a complete novice to you? I know exactly who I'm after: female, white, college educated—hopefully liberal. They take it easy on defendants. And they hate female attorneys."

"What about Sara? Who's she after?"

"Don't worry about Sara. She's never even done her own jury selection. I'm sure Conrad will have coached her, but she'll still be up there alone."

"So you think you've got it under control?" Kozlow asked. "You think the odds are you'll pull out a victory?"

"There are no odds in criminal-defense work," Jared said. "Either the jury buys your bullshit, or they see what you're selling and send you on your way."

"Well then, they better buy your bullshit," Rafferty warned.

"Listen, I don't need your—"

"No, you listen," Rafferty shot back. "I don't

want to hear that you can't give us odds. And I don't want to hear that you're not sure of the outcome. The only thing I want to hear out of your mouth is that you're going to win this waste-of-my-time case. In fact, that's what I want you to do. In your own words, I want you to tell me, 'Rafferty, we're going to win this case.' "

Jared was silent.

"Say it. Repeat after me," Rafferty said. " 'Rafferty, we're going to win this case. Without a doubt, I'm going to win this case for you.' "

Still, Jared didn't say a word.

"What're you, deaf?" Kozlow asked, digging his thumb into the cut on Jared's chin. "Say the damn sentence."

Glaring at Rafferty, Jared growled, "Rafferty, we're going to win this case. Without a doubt, I'm going to win this case for you."

"That's great news, Mr. Lynch," Rafferty said. "That's exactly what I wanted to hear."

Standing outside the courtroom, Sara nervously searched the hallway for Conrad. Although it was still twenty minutes before they were supposed to meet, she'd long become accustomed to Conrad being early. And if he wasn't early, in Sara's mind, he was late. Too anxious to wait around, she went to the women's rest room and ran the water until it was warm. She stuck her hands under the faucet, leaving them there for almost a minute. It was a trick Pop had taught her for her first law firm interview: the only known cure for sweaty hands.

As Sara held her hands under the water, she thought she heard a noise from one of the four stalls on the opposite wall. Shutting off the water, she looked in the mirror. No one was behind her. She bent over and took a quick glance under the stalls. No one in sight. Not again, she thought. Cautiously, Sara approached the first stall. She held her breath as she pushed open the door. Empty. Slowly, she pushed open the second door. Empty. As she moved to the third door, her heart was pounding. She carefully nudged it open. Again, empty. Finally, she reached the last door. She knew this was it. Over her shoulder, she thought she saw something behind her. Spinning around, she realized it was nothing. Just her imagination. Once again, she faced the door. With a quick thrust of her leg, she kicked it wide open. Empty. Shaking her head, Sara tried her best to pull it together. Don't let him do this to you, she told herself. But no matter how hard she tried to ignore him, she couldn't help but notice that her hands were once again covered in sweat.

After another regime of warm water on her hands, Sara returned to the waiting area outside the courtroom. Conrad still wasn't there. Finally, at ten to nine, she saw him turn the corner of the hallway. With his usual confident, determined pace, he brusquely marched toward the courtroom. "Ready?" he asked.

"I'm not sure. Am I supposed to feel like I'm about to lose consciousness?"

"It's your first case—and it's a hell of a case at that. It's okay to be jittery."

"Jittery's one thing. Vomitous is another."

"They're both normal. Now put it out of your head and move on," Conrad said. "Believe me, the moment the judge bangs his gavel, you'll get in your zone. Every great litigator has the same reaction. A trial makes you more decisive than usual; the emotion hits later."

"I hope you're right," Sara said as she opened the door and stepped into the courtroom. "Because if you're not, you're going to be carrying me back to the office." As she walked down the middle aisle, toward the front of the room, Sara looked around. Doniger wasn't there. Neither was Officer McCabe. The only people in the courtroom were the court clerk, the stenographer, and two court officers.

Approaching the prosecutor's table on the left-hand side of the room, Sara put down her briefcase and turned toward Conrad. "You don't think . . ." She stopped when she saw Jared and Kozlow enter the courtroom.

Shooting a cold stare at his wife, Jared made his way to the defense table and set down his briefcase. He then turned his back to Sara and Conrad.

"Aren't you going to say hello?" Kozlow asked.

"Shut up," Jared said, opening up his briefcase.

For the next ten minutes, both parties sat silently at their respective tables, waiting for Judge Bogdanos to arrive. Periodically, Sara looked over her shoulder, scanning the crowd. "This is bad," she said to Conrad. "I think we're in trouble."

Before Conrad could reply, the clerk of the court announced, "All rise! The Honorable Samuel T. Bogdanos presiding."

Rubbing his well-trimmed beard, Bogdanos took the bench and motioned for everyone to return to their seats. After checking to see that both parties were present, he asked if there were any final motions or anything else to discuss before jury selection took place.

"No," Sara said.

"No, Your Honor," Jared said.

"Then let's begin. Mitchell, please bring in the jurors."

The taller of the two court officers walked to the back of the room and stepped out to the hallway. He returned with twenty prospective jurors. As the prospects filed into the jury box, Guff came running into the room with a panicked expression on his face. He rushed to the front row of the spectator section and got Sara's attention. "I need to speak to you," he said.

"Why?" she said. "I thought you were going to—"

"Forget about that," Guff said, his voice deathly serious. "We've got problems."

Seeing that the jurors still weren't seated, Sara got out of her seat and approached her assistant. "This better be good. We're trying to make an impression on—"

"Claire Doniger is dead," Guff interrupted.

"What?" Sara asked, her mouth agape. "That can't be."

"I'm telling you, she's dead. They found her body early this morning. She's a real mess—throat slashed, knife jammed in her skull—she was completely mutilated."

"Ms. Tate, may I remind you that we have a jury to select?" Bogdanos said, losing his patience.

Sara turned around and saw that Conrad, Jared, Kozlow, the judge, the court staff, and all the jurors were staring at her. "Your Honor, may I approach the bench?" she asked.

"No, Ms. Tate, you may not approach the bench. I already asked if there were—"

"We have an emergency," Sara said.

Scrutinizing Sara with a penetrating gaze, Bogdanos said, "Approach."

Jared and Conrad followed Sara to the bench.

Sara leaned in toward the judge. "I'm sorry to interrupt, Your Honor, but my assistant just told me that one of our key witnesses was found dead this morning."

"What?" Jared blurted.

"Who is it?" Conrad asked. "Harrison?"

"Don't say another word," Bogdanos warned. He looked over at the jury. "Ladies and gentlemen, I'm sorry to do this to you, but we need a few more minutes before we begin. So we're going to ask that you continue to wait in the hallway until we're ready. Mitchell, if you don't mind . . ."

When the court officer was finished escorting the jurors out of the courtroom, Jared asked, "Who is it? What happened?"

"It's Claire Doniger," Sara said. "They found her murdered early this morning."

"What?" Kozlow asked, sounding shocked.

"Don't give us that innocent nonsense," Conrad warned Kozlow.

"Don't you dare make an accusation," Jared said, pointing a finger at Conrad.

"Enough," Bogdanos said. "Ms. Tate, what would you like me to do?"

Sara looked at Conrad.

"We'd like to ask for a continuance until we can get some more information," Conrad said. "Although we know the trial will have to go forward, we'll require at least a day or two to reorganize our case. Claire Doniger was a vital witness for us."

"Your Honor, there's no reason for a continuance," Jared jumped in. "This death may be a surprise, but her testimony was duplicative. I ask that the motion be—"

"A witness just died, Mr. Lynch," Bogdanos warned. "Even you should acknowledge that. Motion granted. We'll continue Monday morning."

"What'd he say?" Kozlow asked as Jared hung up the pay phone on the first floor of 100 Centre Street.

"I've never heard Rafferty like that. He was devastated. His voice was shaking. He kept asking me questions, but it was like he was lost." Jared picked up his briefcase and headed for the front door of the courthouse. "I have to be honest, though, I thought you guys—"

"Jesus, man, are you nuts? This isn't some crusty old neighbor—this is Claire we're talking about. Rafferty was crazy for her. If I even looked in her direction, he'd smack me in the back of the head."

"Maybe they had a falling-out or something."

"Not a chance. Man, did they really find her with a knife in her skull?"

"It sounds like she was really brutalized. Do you have any idea who might've done it?"

"Just one," Kozlow said. "And if it's him, I pity the poor bastard. Rafferty's going to rip him apart."

As he walked up the three flights of stairs to Elliott's apartment, Conrad tried to be as quiet as possible. He didn't think Elliott was home, but he wasn't taking any chances. That's why he had insisted on coming alone. With everything that had happened, it was the only way to make sure nothing got out. Secrecy guaranteed privacy. And once Conrad had privacy, the rest of his role was easy: Get inside and wait until Elliott shows up. Catching him unprepared would put him on the defensive. Then, as soon as he walked in, explain the situation—the fingerprints on the knife that killed Claire were traced back to Elliott, and everyone now knew he murdered her.

Of course, Elliott would deny it, but that wasn't the point. All that really mattered was that Elliott heard Sara's deal: If Elliott gave them a statement on Kozlow and Rafferty, they'd reduce Claire's murder to manslaughter. And if Conrad could get that, they were halfway home.

Reaching Elliott's front door, Conrad put his finger over the peephole and tapped lightly on the door. No answer. He knocked again. Still no answer. He reached into his pocket and pulled out the six skeleton keys that a colleague in Crime Scene had given him. Although most of the keys didn't work on new, more advanced locks, they still had a high success rate on old locks in run-down buildings. Like Elliott's. One by one, Conrad tried each key. The first three didn't work. But on his fourth try, Conrad heard the quiet click of access. Smiling to himself, he turned the knob and opened the door. He couldn't wait to surprise Elliott. He couldn't wait to pin him in a corner. And he couldn't wait to watch him squirm.

The only problem was, Elliott was home the entire time. He'd known Conrad was coming since late the previous night. And as he pulled back the hammer on his gun, he was fully prepared to deal with him. Stepping inside Elliott's apartment, Conrad didn't even see the first shot coming.

When the elevator doors opened, Jared and Kozlow stepped out and headed for Jared's office. "Are we done for the day?" Kozlow asked. "I'm getting tired of wearing this suit."

"Then take it off. I could care less."

As Jared approached Kathleen's desk, Kathleen said, "You better call Rafferty—he's been calling nonstop for the past . . ." Kathleen's phone rang. "There he is again."

"Put him through," Jared said as he entered his office. Picking up the phone, he said, "Rafferty, are you—"

"Where the hell have you been?" Rafferty asked, his voice racing. "I need to know what's happening . . . what's going on with the investigation . . . where they took her so I can—"

"Calm down a second."

"Don't tell me what to do!" Rafferty shouted. "This is *my* life! Do you understand? It's *my* life! Whoever did this, I want you to find that son of a bitch and tell him he's dead!"

"Listen, I'm sorry about what happened, but I need you to relax and control your temper. If they found her early this morning, we'll have some information by the afternoon. Until then, you should just—"

"Are you going to be able to get that information?"

"I assume so. Sara should have access to—"

"That's all I needed to hear. I'm coming down there." With a slam, Rafferty was gone.

* * *

Glancing over her shoulder, Sara checked to see if anyone was following her into 80 Centre Street. Seeing no one who looked particularly suspicious, she entered the building. "Hey, Sara," Darnell said the moment she stepped inside the elevator. "How's the trial?"

"A mess," she answered. "One of our witnesses was just found dead."

"Mob case?" Darnell asked.

"I wish," Sara said. "That'd be easier."

When the elevator reached the seventh floor, four people got off. Sara wasn't one of them.

"Your stop, Kojak. What'cha waiting for?"

"Damn, I forgot something in the courthouse," Sara said. "I have to get back over there." When the elevator doors closed, she was alone with Darnell. "Can you take me to the basement without stopping on the other floors? I don't want anyone to see where I'm going."

"Pretty sneaky, sis," Darnell said as he pulled down on the elevator switch. "Bottom floor, coming up."

When she reached the basement, Sara walked straight down the main hallway until she reached a door marked INTERROGATION ROOM. Passing it, she opened the next door on her right and quietly stepped in and took a seat. On the viewing side of a large two-way mirror, Sara watched as Officer McCabe stared down at his prisoner. All Sara could see was McCabe's back, but his body language revealed the rest: Things were not going smoothly.

His shoulders were tense and his fists were tightened. Clearly annoyed, McCabe pulled a rusty chair from under the interrogation table and took a seat. And at that moment, Sara got a good look at McCabe's prisoner.

"Don't tell me to be patient," Claire Doniger told McCabe, raising her voice. "I've been here since six this morning. You won't let me make a phone call, I'm not allowed to see anyone—you'd think I was the one under arrest."

"For the tenth time, Mrs. Doniger, the trial doesn't start until jury selection is done," McCabe explained.

"When that happens, you'll go across the street to testify. Until then, you're here for your own safety."

Sara leaned back in her chair. It was all going perfectly.

"No, I understand," Jared said into the phone. There was a long pause. "If that's what it says, we'll deal with it. And if I see him, I'll let him know. Yeah, I will. I promise."

"Well?" Rafferty asked before Jared could even hang up the phone. "What'd they say?"

"The good news is they lifted dozens of prints from the knife in Claire's body," Jared said to Rafferty. "The bad news is all the prints are yours."

"Oh, man," Kozlow said, laughing.

"They're wrong," Rafferty said definitively. "It's not possible. They don't even have my fingerprints."

"They do now—they got them from your office," Jared explained. "Sara has you down as her top suspect, so she sent Crime Scene over to Echo. They pulled perfect fingerprints from your coffee mug, from your desk, even from your doorknobs."

Seeing the instant change in Rafferty's complexion, Jared asked, "Are you okay?"

"It's not possible," Rafferty stammered. "I swear to God, it wasn't me."

"I believe you," Jared said. "But as an attorney, I have to warn you that—"

"I haven't even seen her for a week," Rafferty insisted.

"Then is there anyone else who might've had access to your fingerprints?" Jared asked. "Anyone who has something to gain if you take the fall?"

"You don't think . . ." Kozlow began.

"That scheming little toad," Rafferty growled. "If Elliott—" Cutting himself off, he turned to Jared. "Is there a warrant out for my arrest yet?"

"Not that I know of. But there will be by the end of the day."

"Good," Rafferty said. "Let them come for me then." Getting out of his seat, he stormed out of the room with Kozlow right behind him.

"Who's Elliott?" Jared called out as they left. Neither of them answered.

When Rafferty and Kozlow were gone, Kathleen came into the office. "So far, so good?" she asked Jared.

"I don't know," Jared said. "Ask me in an hour."

The first bullet hit him in the chest. The second one ripped through his stomach. But the first thing Conrad noticed was the taste of blood in his mouth. It came up almost immediately and reminded him of the bitter taste of black licorice. That's when the real pain set in. It wasn't like the pain when he broke his arm playing rugby. That was confined and sharp in focus. This cut to his core. As his body went numb, he felt less—but somehow, it hurt more. His vision started to blur, but he could still see his attacker across the room.

Elliott was sitting at the kitchen table, watching the event as if it were dinner theater. He was waiting for Conrad to fall, but Conrad wasn't giving in. "You better have more than that," he shouted at Elliott, barely able to hear his own voice.

Two more shots rang out. One hit Conrad's arm, the other his chest. His body was in shock now. But even as his thick legs started to buckle, Conrad staggered forward, lumbering toward Elliott with his arms extended. He tried to speak, but he couldn't.

Elliott fired another shot. It hit Conrad in the shoulder and pushed him backwards. For a second. Then he continued his march toward the table. He knew he was dying, but he was so close.

"What the hell is wrong with you?" Elliott shouted. "It's over."

Not yet, Conrad thought. Not until he—

A final shot exploded, catching Conrad in the throat. That was it. That was all he had. Grasping his neck, he felt himself losing consciousness. Everything turned white. He hit the floor with a thundering crash. His last thoughts were of his first wife and the day they met.

Still pointing his gun at Conrad, Elliott didn't move. Slowly, he circled around to the side of Conrad's body. Refusing to lower his gun, he used his foot to turn him over. Elliott wasn't taking any chances. With a quick shove, he got his answer. It was over. Conrad was gone.

* * *

When she returned to 80 Centre Street, Sara headed straight to her office, where Guff was waiting impatiently. "So?" Guff asked as Sara shut the door. "How'd it go with Rafferty?"

Double-checking to see that her blinds were closed, she answered, "I had to keep it short because I was on the pay phone across the street, but Jared said he went nuts. He and Kozlow tore out of the office before Jared could even pass along our offer."

"I still can't believe you told him," Guff said.

"How can you say that? He has the exact same incentive to catch Rafferty and Kozlow."

"And what about Victor?"

"Can you please stop? It's all working out. Jared hasn't said a word."

"So they definitely believe Claire is dead?"

"Who wouldn't?" Sara said proudly. "They pulled her out at six o'clock this morning, locked her in a room, sent Crime Scene to her house, and sent half a dozen people to Echo Enterprises to do fingerprint work. We even started a few office rumors. Except for an actual body, we have all the makings of a gruesome murder."

"You're not holding back, are you?"

"After what those bastards put us through? Not for a second," Sara said. "Why? You getting worried?"

"Just about the repercussions. Was Monaghan mad when you told him?"

Sara was silent.

"You did tell him, didn't you?"

Again, Sara didn't respond.

"Oh, man," Guff said. "I can't believe you didn't tell him. When he finds out, we're going to get reamed. Do you know how many resources we're wasting to pull this off? Not to mention all the potential ethics violations."

"I know," Sara said. "I just didn't want to risk a leak."

"You told Jared, didn't you?"

"You know that's different. It was okay to tell him, and it was okay to tell the ambulance drivers who picked up the imaginary body and a few of McCabe's cop friends, but that's where I want to draw the line. I figured the fewer people who know, the better."

"Are you reading my lips here?" Guff asked. Slowly, he whispered the words, "He's our boss!"

"And if he wants to ream someone, he can ream me," Sara said. "Otherwise, we're doing this the way we designed. It's a perfect prisoners' dilemma: If Rafferty and Elliott both stay quiet, they're safe, but if one leaks, the other knows he's going down. In a few hours, self-preservation's going to make one of them snap. All we have to do is wait for the fireworks."

"You really think it's going to be that easy?"

"Nothing's easy," Sara said. "But as long as we're the only ones who know the truth, it'll all work out."

After dragging the body into the living room, Elliott went back to the kitchen and picked up the phone. He dialed Rafferty's number and waited. Eventually, he heard Rafferty answer, "Hello?"

"How you doing?" Elliott asked. "Having a rough day?"

"You killed her, didn't you?" Rafferty asked. "I'm going to rip your head off, you gloating little—"

"Now, now, now, don't overact," Elliott interrupted. "Why don't you come down here and we can have a little talk."

"If you want to talk, I want you up here."

"Not a chance. We do it here, or not at all. Take some time and think about it—you'll be happy you came. I have something I think you'll want to see."

"What do you—"

Elliott hung up the phone. Turning back to the table, he opened a small box of bullets and re-loaded his gun. To his left was a set of plastic hands. At the base of the hands, two words were written in black ink: OSCAR RAFFERTY. This was it, he thought. All he had to do was wait.

"Why hasn't he called?" Guff asked, leaning his chin on Sara's desk and staring at the phone.

"It's only been two hours," Sara said. "Give him time."

"Maybe he's in trouble."

"He's fine. I'm sure he's just trying to make it realistic. You know how Conrad is: Can't rush perfection."

"How do you think McCabe is doing with Doniger?"

"When I saw him, she was driving him nuts."

"Then maybe we should go down there," Guff suggested. "Just to give her an update."

"If it'll make you happy, let's go," Sara said, following Guff to the door.

A few minutes later, Sara and Guff reached the basement. Hoping to get a look at how things were going, they entered the viewing room first. But as they stared out through the two-way mirror, all they saw was an empty room.

Before they could even react, Officer McCabe darted into the viewing room, his forehead dripping sweat. "Please tell me she's with you!" he said.

"What're you talking about?" Guff asked.

"Where the hell is Doniger?" Sara demanded.

"I don't know," McCabe said. "She asked me to get her some coffee, and when I got back, she was gone!"

"Oh, my God!" Guff shouted.

"What do you mean she's gone?" Sara asked, panic filling her voice. "She can't be gone."

"How long ago did this happen?" Guff asked.

"Not even ten minutes ago," McCabe said. "I was checking the bathroom, but when I heard the noise coming from here, I ran back and found you."

"Guff, watch the elevators," Sara instructed. "And keep an eye on the stairs. The two of us'll check every room down here. We're in a basement—it's not like she can crawl out a window."

Sara darted full speed down the hallway, entering every room she came to. The basement was mostly used as a storage area, so room after room was filled with nothing but industrial-sized file cabinets. How could she get out? Sara asked herself. Did she know it was a setup? Did someone tell her? Did McCabe let her out on purpose? At that moment, Sara stopped. What if Victor had something on McCabe? And what if Jared told Victor . . . No. No, he'd never do that. Get it out of your head. Within ten minutes, every room had been searched. Claire Doniger was nowhere in sight.

"I can't believe this," Sara said, trying to catch her breath. Turning to McCabe, she asked,

"How could you leave her alone? Were you even thinking?"

"Listen, honey, I did my best to watch her. It's not my fault."

"Oh, really? Then whose fault is it? It must be mine, because I'm the moron who thought you were up to the job of baby-sitting!"

"Calm down," Guff said. He pulled Sara away from McCabe. "It'll be okay."

"No, it won't," Sara insisted. "The moment Rafferty and Elliott find out she's alive, we're dead."

CHAPTER
19

You really think she's dumb enough to go to Rafferty's?" Sara asked as she sat next to Guff in the backseat of the speeding police car.

"She's got nowhere else to go," one of the two police officers in the front seat said. "Her house is a crime scene."

"But she doesn't know that."

"If she's really in love with Rafferty, that's where she's headed," the officer said. "Now, tell me about your husband. Were you able to find him?"

"There's no answer at his office," Sara said, trying to sound confident. "I called some of the partners he works with, but no one's seen him or his assistant since this morning."

Guff looked over at his boss. "Sara, what if he—"

"I'm sure he's just out of the office," Sara interrupted anxiously.

"But what if he's not? Maybe we should've waited for Conrad."

"We left a message at the office. He'll find it when he gets back."

"Try your husband again," the officer said. He handed her his cellular phone.

"Not now," she insisted, refusing to face the possibility. "Wait until we're done with Rafferty."

When they arrived at Rafferty's building, the two police officers approached the doorman. "We're here to see Oscar Rafferty in apartment 1708," one of them said. The doorman reached for the phone, and the officer added, "We'd prefer if you didn't call him."

The doorman ushered them inside and said, "I don't know anything, I don't want to know anything, I don't care."

"You're a real humanitarian," Guff said as they entered the lobby. No one said another word until all four of them were inside the elevator.

As they approached the seventeenth floor, Sara turned to Guff. "Obviously, Rafferty can't know we're looking for Doniger. So the story is that we're looking for Kozlow. Easy enough, yes?" Everyone nodded in silent agreement.

Reaching into the pocket of her pantsuit, Sara rechecked the gun that Conrad had given her before he left for Hoboken. Seeing what Sara was doing, Guff said, "Stop worrying about it. You don't have to use it—he just thought you should have it."

"It's fine," Sara said. "I can handle it."

At Rafferty's door, Sara rang the bell.

"Who is it?" Rafferty asked.

"Mr. Rafferty, it's Sara Tate from the district attorney's office. I spoke to you last week."

Suddenly, the door opened and Rafferty looked

out at his visitors. His features were drawn. His usually combed-back hair was a stringy mess. And his Brioni sportswear had been replaced by creased khakis and a rumpled shirt with the cuffs undone. "What is it, Ms. Tate?" he asked abruptly.

"Sorry to bother you again, but I was wondering if we could ask for a bit more of your time."

"If this is about Claire, I want you to know that I'd never—"

"We can deal with that later," Sara said. "Right now, we were hoping to take a quick look around your apartment. We have reason to believe that Tony Kozlow might be here."

"Why would—" Rafferty fought to keep his composure. "You're welcome to come in." As Rafferty stepped aside, Guff and the two officers made their way into the apartment and began their search. Sara stayed with Rafferty. Studying his tired eyes, she tried to figure out what he knew.

"I understand you sent a fingerprint crew to my office this morning," Rafferty said, breaking the silence.

"I did. And I was surprised to find out that you weren't at work today. Why'd you take the day off? Busy with other things?"

"Ms. Tate, your lack of subtlety is disgraceful. If you want to accuse me of murder, then arrest me."

"I plan to," Sara said. "Believe me, we're going to be speaking again soon."

At that moment, Guff returned to the living room. "No sign," Guff said. A minute later, the two officers followed.

"He's not here," one of them said. "The place is empty."

"Thank you," Rafferty said, showing everyone to the door. "Now if you don't mind, I have to make some funeral arrangements. Claire had no close relatives."

As she was about to leave, Sara turned around. "I thought you two weren't close."

"She's my former partner's wife. Good friends look out for each other."

"I'm sure they do," Sara said as Rafferty slammed the door.

Walking toward the elevator, Guff said, "I can't believe she wasn't there."

"Did you check everywhere?" Sara asked.

"It's a three-bedroom apartment in New York City. There aren't that many places to hide."

"I guess that means he doesn't have a wine cellar," Sara said as they stepped into the elevator.

"Do you think he knew?" one of the officers asked.

"Of course he knew," Guff said. "By now, the whole world knows."

"How can you say that?" Sara asked.

"Sara, I don't mean to stomp on your fairy tale, but I think it's time to take a second look at Jared. If you never would've told him—"

"That's not true," Sara insisted.

"It *is* true," Guff shot back. "Trust me, I agreed with you yesterday. I thought you were right to tell him. But you have to pay attention to what's going on here. I don't think Claire snuck out of the basement on her own—someone must have told her what was really happening. And the only way that could've happened is if someone knew what we were doing."

"No one knows, Guff! And even if McCabe let her out, that doesn't mean it's my husband's fault!" When the elevator doors opened, Sara burst through the lobby and headed for the police car.

"Where're you going?" Guff asked, chasing after her. "Don't run away."

"We have to go to Elliott's," Sara said. "He's the only other person who has a stake in this."

"But what if Conrad—"

"If Conrad's still there, we'll go along with his story. If not, we'll tell Elliott we're following up."

"That's great. I agree," Guff said. "But you have to start dealing with your husband. Let one of these guys check up on him."

"How many times do I have to tell you: Jared would never do that!"

Guff wiped his hands on his pants. He was torn. He didn't want to challenge her, but he was starting to get frustrated. In a softer voice, he said, "If you're so confident, why can't you find him? Why has he suddenly disappeared?"

Sara stared coldly at her assistant. "Give me your phone," she said to one of the officers. She quickly dialed Jared's number. Again, no one picked up. She shut the phone and handed it back to the officer.

"Now do you understand what I'm saying?" Guff asked. "It's not like you have to arrest him—I just think you should send someone to his office to check him out. With everything that's happening, we should know where he is."

Silently, she considered Guff's proposal. "And that's it? They're not going to question him? They're just going there to find him?"

"That's up to you."

Sara opened the door to the police car and got inside. "Okay," she said, slamming the door shut.

Turning back to the officers, Guff said, "Can you send someone to Wayne and Portnoy?"

"I'm on it," the taller of the two officers said, pulling out his walkie-talkie.

"And maybe one of you guys should stick around here," Guff added. "In case Claire decides to come by."

"I can do that," the other officer said.

As the first cop called in the instructions, Guff got in the backseat of the car. Sara was stoic. Her arms were crossed in front of her and her eyes were glued to the side window.

"Sara, you know it was the right thing to—"

"Don't bother," she said. "It's done."

Peering out his living-room window, which overlooked the front of the building, Rafferty watched to make sure that Sara and the rest were actually leaving. When he was convinced they were gone, he walked to his front door and stepped out into the hallway. He checked again for observers, then went down the hallway to the garbage room. Inside were Kozlow and Claire.

"Man, to get that warning, you must've given the doorman one hell of a Christmas gift," Kozlow said.

"Lucky for you," Rafferty said.

"No, lucky for you," Kozlow said. He left the room and walked back to Rafferty's apartment.

Rafferty and Claire embraced in the hallway. "Were there any problems?" Claire asked.

"Not at all," Rafferty said, still hugging her. "Not anymore."

"Can you two save the reunion for another

time?" Kozlow called out. "I want to get out of here."

"Relax," Rafferty said. He walked back to his apartment and put on his coat. "As long as we can avoid the cop Sara left behind, I want to have a little talk with the person who got her involved in the first place."

"There's a cop in the lobby? How're we going to get past him?"

"This building has twenty-four floors, a rooftop pool, its own gym, an underground garage, and a dry cleaner in the basement—you don't think it also has a side door?"

As Sara and company raced downtown, the officer driving the police car asked, "Where exactly are we going now?"

"Hoboken," Sara said from the passenger seat.

The car screeched to a halt. "No way," the officer said. "Not in this car. Hoboken's in Jersey. New York City cops have no jurisdiction over there."

"You have jurisdiction if you're in hot pursuit," Sara said.

"Does it look like this guy Elliott is directly in front of us? Does it look like he's avoiding us only by running across state lines? Does it look like we're in hot pursuit?"

"C'mon, there he goes!" Guff said. "I see him on the next block! Let's get him!"

The officer didn't move. "Listen, I agree the rules are stupid, but the Jersey cops raise hell if you break them. The last guy in my squad who crossed state lines without authorization was assigned to Port Authority for three months. Said the bus fumes were worse than the urine stink."

"C'mon," Sara said. "We're not doing anything crazy. We just want to find this guy and bring him back to the station."

"Do whatever you want. But unless you have the right paperwork, you're not doing it in this car."

"Fine," Sara said. She opened the door to the car. "Then let's get a cab. We'll go down there and pick him up ourselves."

"No," Guff said. "You can't."

"Why? This is bureaucratic bullshit."

"Maybe, but that's the way it goes. If we try to pick Elliott up without the proper authorization, we jeopardize the case and everything we find."

"But—"

"Sara, you know how it works. Don't let your heart get in front of your head. Break the rules and the judge will exclude your evidence."

"Take the ten minutes and call in the paperwork," the officer added. "They can fax it to the Hoboken police, and it'll be ready by the time we reach the Lincoln Tunnel."

"Are you sure?" Sara asked hesitatingly.

"Of course I'm sure," the officer said. "How long can a few sheets of paper possibly take?"

A half hour later, the police car was waiting in traffic at the entrance to the Lincoln Tunnel. "I can't believe this," Sara said, banging the dashboard. "I knew we shouldn't have called it in."

"Relax," the officer said. "Better we take the time now, instead of rushing in and regretting it later."

"What amazes me is that the entire criminal community isn't onto this trick," Guff said. "If I were going to break the law in this city, the first thing I'd do is move to New Jersey. No one can touch you there."

"I'm sure they know all about it," the officer said, trying to lighten the mood. "But who wants to live in Jersey?" When no one responded to the joke, the officer added, "C'mon, that was funny."

"Don't push it," Sara said. "Now's not the time."

"Who is it?" Elliott asked through the intercom.

"It's Rafferty. Buzz us in." The buzzer sounded and they made their way up the stairs.

As Elliott opened his door a crack, he saw Rafferty and Kozlow. "What're you so happy about?" Elliott asked. Kozlow kicked the door open, revealing Claire.

"Well, would you look at that," Elliott said. "They were lying to us."

"Actually, they were playing us against each other," Rafferty said, entering the apartment. "The only thing I can't figure out is how they knew to come after you."

"Why don't you ask him." Following Elliott's gesture, Rafferty, Kozlow, and Claire turned toward the other room. Conrad's body was still on the floor.

"Oh, God!" Claire shouted.

"Are you nuts?" Kozlow said. "You know what that's going to do to us?"

"I know exactly what it's going to do," Elliott said. "It's going to be my out."

With gritted teeth, Rafferty slowly turned around. "You son of a bitch."

"Is there a problem?" Elliott asked innocently.

"You knew all along, didn't you? You knew she was alive, and you knew what they were doing."

"I don't—"

"Don't play stupid, Elliott. Your lies are catching up with you. You've been threatening Sara since the beginning. That's how she knew you were involved, that's how she knew to come after you, and that's why she wouldn't take the dismiss and seal. You were supposed to stay away, and instead, you stuck your greedy nose back in."

Elliott backed his way into the kitchen, trying to get Rafferty to follow him. If he was going to make it look real, he needed everyone to be in place. "Oscar, I don't know what you're talking about."

"You lying piece of shit!" Rafferty yelled. "You think I'm a moron?" He shoved Elliott in the chest, sending him crashing into the kitchen table. "You think I'm blind? I know exactly what you're doing. You're trying to grab the money for yourself."

Just a little closer, Elliott thought. Near the window. Get the angles right. "I swear, I'd never—"

"*Stop your lying!*" Rafferty screamed, his voice booming through the tiny apartment. "I asked you one small favor: Find me someone to give the shot. That was your job. And what do you do? You turn on me! On *me*! I practically raised you, and that's how you repay me?"

Suddenly, Elliott stopped where he was. "You didn't raise me!" he shouted.

"Oh, I didn't? Who gave your mother money when Arnold fired her? Who sent her money every year until you were sixteen? Who—"

"You didn't give a shit about her—you were just afraid!" Advancing from the window, he stood face-to-face with Rafferty. "Until the day she died, you were worried she'd bring him up on charges. That she'd get vengeful and wreck his pathetic marriage. Or worse, that she'd get smart and sue your precious company. Rape accusations can be a real ugly mess, can't they?"

"Your mother wasn't raped," Rafferty insisted.

"*Yes, she was!*" Elliott yelled as a vein on his forehead flushed red. "He punched her so hard, he broke her jaw! I still have the medical records to prove it! And when he found out she was pregnant, he threw her in the street!" Noticing Claire's reaction, Elliott asked, "You didn't know that, did you? You knew he was ruthless, but you didn't know he was a monster. If you did, maybe you would've killed him sooner."

"That's enough!" Rafferty interrupted. "Leave her out of it!"

"Why? She's just as responsible as you are. In fact, she's more responsible. If she hadn't been so afraid of giving Arnold the shot, we never would've had to hire Kozlow. And if we hadn't hired him—"

"Hey, asshole . . ." Kozlow interrupted.

"Stay out of this," Rafferty growled. Standing in the middle of the kitchen, he turned back to Elliott. "We hired Kozlow because we wanted alibis—even you know that's true."

"That's true, but my mother's story's a lie?"

"Elliott, your mother was a degenerate who begged for it every day. I gave her money out of pity, not guilt. And if she told you she was raped, it was only because she was embarrassed by the truth."

"*You're a liar!*"

"No. I'm not," Rafferty said. He stuffed his hands in the pockets of his coat. "And if you want to join us in reality, you should start believing that and stop living in your mother's fantasies."

Enraged, Elliott reached for his gun. "You motherfu—"

Three shots rang out. Two hit Elliott in the chest, one went through the kitchen window on his right. Elliott fell to the floor and his blood inched across the linoleum. Ignoring his victim, Rafferty looked down at the hole he had just blown through the pocket of his own overcoat.

"No!" Claire screamed. She staggered backward until she hit the refrigerator.

"Oh, man, why'd you have to do that?" Kozlow asked Rafferty, throwing his hands in the air.

"Is he dead?" Rafferty asked, watching the blood seep across more of the kitchen floor.

"Of course he's dead—you shot him in the chest." Kozlow leaned over Elliott's body to be sure. "What're you doing, man? Are you even thinking?"

Standing behind Kozlow, Rafferty explained, "I'm doing what I should've done the moment this started." Rafferty pointed his gun at Kozlow.

"Are you crazy, Oscar?" Claire shouted.

Kozlow felt the barrel of the gun at the back of his head. "Oscar, if that's what I think it is, you're a dead man."

"No, I'm not the dead man," Rafferty said, his voice racing. "Look at the layout. You're the one who shot him. Not me. You. If you hadn't acted like such an animal, we could've walked away. It would've been perfect."

"Put down the gun," Kozlow said.

"Don't tell me what to do."

"Put down the gun!" Claire shouted.

Kozlow was nothing but pure rage. "First I'm

going to dance on your neck, then I'm going to dance on hers," he said. "It'll make Harrison look like a paper cut." Kozlow started to turn his head, hoping to look Rafferty in the eye.

"Don't move!" Rafferty yelled.

"Oscar, don't do this!" Claire pleaded.

Kozlow was tensed to jump. "I'm going to slice you open and—"

"Don't move!" Rafferty repeated. *"I mean it!"*

Kozlow wasn't stopping. He spun around and went straight for Rafferty's throat. But before he could make contact, another shot rang out. A crimson burst sprayed across the kitchen and Kozlow slumped to the floor. There was a dull thud as his head hit the ground.

"Oh, God!" Claire screamed. "Oh, my God!"

"Claire, don't flip out on me."

Shaking, Claire looked at Elliott, then at Kozlow. Both of them were now soaked in blood. She rushed to the sink and vomited.

"Dammit, Claire, what're you doing?!" Rafferty screamed. "You can't let them know we were here!" He pulled a pair of leather gloves from his coat and, as Claire continued to heave, turned on the faucet. He poured dishwashing liquid all over the sink, hoping to hide the smell. Then he grabbed Elliott's keys from the kitchen table, went into the living room, and opened the storage trunk. Rummaging through the chest, he found the contents of Sara's wallet and discovered the plastic hands with his name on them. The gloves were missing—which meant Elliott was wearing them. "Perfect. It's a perfect excuse," Rafferty said, throwing the empty hands aside. "Now he's me." He pulled out the Warren Eastham gloves and brought them back to the kitchen.

Knowing that the gloves would confound the investigation, he stuffed them into Kozlow's back pocket, grabbed Kozlow by the hand, and dragged him, facedown, toward the other side of the kitchen. Lifting the back of Kozlow's jacket, Rafferty found Kozlow's handgun. He took the gun from the back of Kozlow's pants. He then used his own gun to shoot Kozlow two more times in the back and once in the leg. When he was done, he placed his gun in Elliott's hand and shoved Kozlow's gun in his own pocket. "Now it looks like an argument," he said. "As Kozlow was leaving, Elliott shot him in the back. That's it. That's what makes sense." Rafferty looked over at Claire, who was still leaning into the sink. "Are you okay?" he asked.

"No, I'm not okay!" she cried. "You just put a hole in his head! You killed two people! What's wrong with you?"

"Don't say that, Claire! What was I supposed to do? Let them run around, hoping they don't ruin me?"

"We're already ruined. You think Sara Tate's going to—"

"Shut up!" Rafferty shouted. "I don't want to hear it! It'll work!"

Light-headed and still trembling, Claire looked like she was going to pass out. "Get me out of here."

"Shut up," Rafferty said, pulling her by the arm toward the door. "I need to make one more stop."

"I'm sorry about the delay," the Hoboken police officer said to Sara as they strode toward Elliott's building.

"Don't worry about it," Sara said, buzzing apartment eight.

When there was no answer after a few buzzes, the Hoboken cop rammed his shoulder into the door, which flew wide open.

When the group got to the top floor, they knocked on Elliott's door. Again, there was no answer. "Elliott, are you there?" Sara called out. "Conrad?" Trying the doorknob, she found it unlocked and pushed the door open. "Oh, God," she said.

"You know these people?" the New Jersey cop asked.

Sara didn't answer. She couldn't take her eyes off the bloody scene. This wasn't like the autopsy—she knew these people. And as much as she feared them, no one should die like this. "I can't believe it," she said. "Why would they . . . how the hell could he do this?"

Turning to the New York police officer, Guff said, "Hope the paperwork was worth it."

"Don't blame this on me," the cop shot back.

"Looks like a robbery," the New Jersey cop added as he examined the scene. "The guy in the leather jacket shoots the skinny guy, but as he's about to leave, the skinny guy sits up and shoots the leather guy in the back of the head."

"Are you kidding?" Sara asked. "Look at the streaks of blood on the floor. Someone obviously moved Kozlow's body."

"Or he was trying to crawl to the door," the Jersey cop pointed out.

"Oh, no," Guff said from the living room, his voice shaking. "Sara! Sara, get in here!"

Racing into the living room, Sara saw Guff

down on both knees. And Conrad's broken body lying in the corner. "Oh, no! Not him! Please, not him!" she screamed. She dropped down next to Guff and grabbed Conrad's head in her hands. *"Somebody get an ambulance! We need an ambulance!"* She wanted to cry, but the tears wouldn't come. She put her head to Conrad's chest and listened for a heartbeat. Nothing. "C'mon," she said, lightly slapping his cheek. "I know you're still in there. Don't give up!" Still nothing. She pounded his chest. "You heard me! You're not giving up! I'm not going to let you!" Again, she hit him. And again. But he still didn't move. As she squeezed his blood-soaked shirt, her hands were shaking and she started to hyperventilate. "Please, Conrad, don't do this. Please, don't leave. Please. Please, don't leave me. Not again." As the tears finally came, Sara wanted to shake him awake. She wanted to keep pounding his chest. She wanted to hear that pulse. But when it came right down to it, all she really wanted was to get him back.

When she turned around, Guff was still weeping. "C'mere," she said, opening her arms. Guff fell right in. For a minute, the two of them sat there, on their knees, silently consoling each other. "I'm sorry," Sara finally said, rubbing his back. "I'm so sorry."

"He was my friend," Guff cried.

As Sara listened to the rise and fall of Guff's sobs, she wondered how this had happened. Conrad hadn't just been caught unprepared. He was ambushed. And the only way that was possible was if someone had known he was coming. Climbing to her feet, Sara wiped her eyes with her sleeve. He'd warned her, but she hadn't listened.

She wouldn't make that mistake again. "Call the precinct and see if they picked up Jared," she said to the New York cop.

As the officer started dialing, Sara helped Guff up from the floor.

"You really think it's him?" Guff asked.

"I don't know what to think anymore. All I know is—"

"What?" the officer blurted into his cell phone. "When?" Silent for a minute, he answered. "She's with me. No, I got it. I'll bring her right in." He shut the phone and looked with shock at Sara.

"What?" she asked. "What's wrong?"

"They just got a 911 call from Wayne and Portnoy. The officer who went over there—he's been shot."

CHAPTER 20

The crowd outside the offices of Wayne & Portnoy was much calmer than Sara had expected, but it was still tenacious. Refusing to disperse, the evacuated workers gathered around the door, angling and elbowing for the best view of the action.

"Damn city turns every disaster into a spectator sport," the officer grumbled as the police car slowly made its way through the ever-growing crowd.

Even before the car came to a complete stop, the officer had his door open. When they were as close as they were going to get, about half a block from the building, he let it fly wide and jumped out of the car. Guff quickly followed. Sara didn't move.

Turning around, Guff stopped. "C'mon, let's go."

"But what if he—"

"Sara, you have to face it sooner or later. It's the only way to find out."

Nodding, she knew that Guff was right. As Sara got out of the car, Guff took off after the police officer, who was making his way toward the building. Following in the direction of her assistant, Sara fought her way through the tightly packed crowd. Within seconds, though, she lost Guff, who was too short to stand out. *"Guff, wait!"* she called out. It was too late. He was gone. Jumping up to get a better view, Sara caught sight of the police officer. He was holding his badge in the air and was almost at the front entrance of the building. But just as she moved toward him, she caught a glimpse of someone rushing away from the building and in the opposite direction from the crowd, approximately a hundred feet to her left. She could only see him from behind, but his athletic gait was unmistakable. Sara stopped dead in her tracks. "Jared?" she called out.

If the man heard her, he wasn't stopping. Craning her neck, Sara struggled to get a better look, but the crowd was too thick. *"Jared!"* she shouted again. He still didn't stop. Pushing through the crowd, Sara followed the figure. Forget about it, she told herself. It's not him. But as she watched his perfectly combed brown hair disappear in the sea of bystanders, she couldn't ignore the resemblance. At the top of her lungs, she let out one more scream. "JARED, IT'S ME!"

Suddenly, the man turned around and Sara's mouth went dry. Their eyes locked for an instant. That was all it took. It was him. Without a doubt, it was her husband. Before Sara could even register a response, Jared turned and ran. "Jared, wait!" she shouted as the crowd seemed to envelop him.

Using her outstretched arms to wade through the masses of people, she fought to catch up with him. He was weaving in every direction, seeming to use the confusion to his advantage. "Jared!"

she shouted, barely able to see him. "Please don't do this!" But Jared still didn't stop. And as Sara frantically collided with bystander after bystander, she realized she was starting to lose him. Between the endless crowd and the advantage of Jared's own speed, he was slipping away.

As Jared headed farther away from the building and down Seventh Avenue, Sara completely lost sight of him. Panicking, she pulled out her badge and waved her hand in the air. "Police!" she yelled. "Stop that man!" Although not a single person reached out to stop him, they did make it easier for Sara to maneuver through the crowd. Once they started stepping out of her way, she was able to fly through the wake of people Jared was leaving behind.

When she reached Forty-ninth Street, Sara stopped. Jared was gone. She looked down Seventh Avenue, but it didn't look like anyone was running there. Maybe he'd turned on Forty-ninth, she thought. Then she heard someone shout, "Watch yourself, asshole!" and spotted an angry man coming out of the entrance to the subway, looking over his shoulder. There. She darted down the concrete stairs, raced underground, and promptly encountered another mob of people. Judging by the size of the crowd, it appeared that everyone who was not still swarming in front of the building was trying to take the subway. Running past the long line that stretched out from the token booth, Sara hopped over one of the turnstiles.

She was stopped by a transit employee. "Sorry, not without a token," he said as he held her by the arm.

"Get the hell off me," Sara said, pulling away. "My husband—"

"Lady, I don't care who your husband is, you're not—"

She shoved her badge in front of his face. "You want to talk to my boss?"

"Sorry, I didn't realize you were a—"

But before the man could finish, Sara was gone, running down the subway platform. It took her only another thirty seconds to find Jared. He was forcing his way through the crowd toward the edge of the platform. Since most of the crowd was now standing still, waiting for the train to come, Sara could see that there were two other people running with him. When she was an arm's length away, she realized who they were. And when she realized who they were, she also realized why Jared had been running.

"You never give up, do you?" Rafferty asked. Standing behind Jared, he turned just enough to show Sara that he was holding a gun to Jared's back. Next to Rafferty was Claire, who looked miserable.

"Are you okay?" Sara asked her husband.

"Yeah," he said. Turning to Rafferty, he added, "Let Sara go."

"Not a chance. Now I get an extra hos—"

"He's got a gun!" someone shouted as chaos enveloped the crowd. Within seconds, everyone else on the platform scattered, racing for the turnstiles.

Using the confusion to her advantage, Sara reached for the gun in her right pants pocket.

"Don't do that," Rafferty warned. He shoved Jared out of the way and pointed his gun at Sara. "I'll decorate the walls with you." He was disheveled, sweating.

As Jared stopped himself at the edge of the

platform, Sara froze. Seeing the gun aimed at his wife, Jared did the same.

"Now give it to Claire," Rafferty said as people continued to scramble from the platform.

Claire reached out for the gun, but Sara hesitated. "You don't have to do this," Sara said.

"Shut up," Claire shot back. She took the gun and led Sara toward the edge of the platform, near her husband.

As Sara and Claire walked in front of Jared, Sara shot him a desperate look. They had to do something.

Determined to save his wife, and unable to get a clear view of Rafferty, Jared made his decision. Just as Claire passed him, he kicked her in the back of the knees, sweeping her legs out from under her. Hitting the floor with a jolt, she dropped her gun. Wasting no time, Sara lunged at Rafferty, whose gun was now pointed at Jared.

Rafferty got off a single shot, then turned his gun on Sara. But before he could pull the trigger, Sara plowed into him, connecting with a swift knee to the groin. The gun flew out of his hands, but she was too late—he had already shot at Jared. And as Rafferty doubled over in pain, Sara registered her husband's scream.

"*Jared!*" she shouted. She turned around, but he was nowhere in sight. She ran back to the edge of the platform. He was lying on the train tracks. Blood ran from his shoulder. "Jared, are you okay? Can you hear me?" she asked.

He didn't answer. From the vacant look on his face, she could see he was in shock.

Behind her, Sara saw Claire helping Rafferty to his feet. On her right, near the edge of the

platform, was Rafferty's gun. She looked back at
her husband. He was just starting to shake off
the effects of his injury. Get the gun, she told herself. Jared'll be fine. But as she moved for the gun,
she heard the jarring electronic tone that signaled
the imminent arrival of an incoming train. Leaning over the platform, she could see the train's
lights in the tunnel. There wasn't much time. Jared
was still lying there. So was the gun. She had to
pick one. The choice was easy.

She braced herself on the edge of the platform
and was about to leap down to the tracks when
she felt Rafferty grab her by the hair. As Sara was
yanked backwards, she managed to spin around.
She lashed out uncontrollably. *"Get off me! I'll kill
you!"* She clawed at his arms, then his face—
anything to make him let go. Taken aback by her
ferocity, Rafferty released her and crouched to get
his gun. Sara knew she had to be quick. At the
edge of the platform, she could see the incoming
train barreling toward the station. It was too close.
There was no way she'd be able to get in and out in
time. *"Jared! Stand up!"* she shouted.

Jared followed her instructions and tottered to
his feet. His legs felt like they were stuffed with
rubber bands, and as the pain set in, the smell of
his own blood made him nauseous.

"You'll be okay," Sara said. "Take my hand."
Dropping to her stomach, she extended her arm
down to Jared. The ground was vibrating from the
motion of the oncoming train, and as the noise got
louder, the nearby rats scattered.

Jared reached up and grabbed his wife's hand.
But before she could pull him up, Sara saw Jared
staring over her shoulder. Someone was behind
her. She turned around and looked up.

Rafferty pointed his gun at her. With a cold look in his eyes, he glared at Jared. "Let go of her."

"Don't do this," Sara begged.

Rafferty didn't answer. He could see the bright lights of the train as it emerged from the tunnel. "Say hi to Sara's parents for me."

The train was only seconds away. This was Jared's last chance to climb out. He didn't care, though. He wasn't going to put her at risk. Letting go of Sara's hand; Jared pulled away from his wife.

"What're you doing?" Sara yelled, her voice barely audible above the train.

"He'll kill you!" Jared shouted back.

"I don't care!" Sara screamed, still holding out her arm. "Get back here!"

The train was right there. As Jared searched the space below the platform, Sara knew he wasn't going to make it. They were out of time. It was impossible to hear anything but the shrieking of the train's wheels against the rusted tracks, but that didn't stop Sara from shouting one last "I love you" to her husband.

"Jared!" she pleaded. "Jaaaared!" At the last possible moment, Sara pulled her arm up and rolled away from the edge. And as he watched the train swallow Jared, Rafferty stepped back and smiled.

Claire ran for the doors when the train stopped. "Let's go!" she shouted at Rafferty.

"No."

"What are you talking about? Let's get out of here!"

"Not until I see his body."

"Not until you . . . Oscar, this is our chance! Let's go!"

"Forget the train. This is more important."

"Stop being so obsessed with them! We can—"

"Go if you want, but I'm staying. I'm not risking any more loose ends."

As the train doors chimed to close, Claire hesitantly returned to Rafferty. "We'll leave as soon as you check it out, right?" she said.

Without responding, Rafferty approached the edge of the platform as the train pulled out of the station. Leaning over and examining the tracks, all he saw was the blood from Jared's shoulder wound. Maybe the train had pushed him to the other side of the—But before Rafferty could complete his thought, he saw Sara charging at him.

"You killed him!" she screamed. When she smashed into Rafferty, he dropped his gun and, caught off balance by the impact, went flying over the edge of the platform. But as he fell, he managed to catch hold of Sara's jacket. Before either of them knew what was happening, they had plummeted to the tracks. Rafferty hit first, and Sara landed on top of him. Sara, wild with rage, was the first one up. As Rafferty struggled to rise, Sara grabbed him by his hair and rammed her knee into his face. *"You psychotic piece of shit!"* she screamed. *"Who the hell do you think you are?"*

Rafferty's answer came in the form of a single backhanded punch that hit Sara in the side of the face and sent her straight to the ground. Raising his hand to strike her again, Rafferty didn't see Jared's fist until it was too late. "Don't. Touch. My. Wife!" Jared growled as his knuckles crashed into Rafferty's jaw. Sara retraced her husband's steps to the narrow crawl space that had saved his life. Created by the pedestrian ledge that extended from the platform over the edge of the tracks, the tiny gap was just deep enough to protect her husband.

Using his good arm, Jared hit Rafferty in the stomach. And again in the face. And again in the stomach. For every restless hour, for every frustrated moment, for every ounce of fear he and Sara had suffered, Jared was determined to pay Rafferty back. Eventually, he grabbed Rafferty by the collar of his shirt and stared at his beaten face. Then a single gunshot sounded. Jared slumped to the floor.

Sara saw blood pouring from her husband's back. She wheeled around. Claire was standing on the platform and holding Rafferty's gun.

"Jared!" Sara screamed, rushing to his side.

"Oscar, are you okay?" Claire asked.

Rafferty nodded, struggling to catch his breath. He reached up and reclaimed his gun from Claire.

"Jared, speak to me!" Sara cried. "Please speak to me!"

Jared didn't say a word. But as Sara hunched over him, she caught a glimpse of the leather ankle holster that Barrow had given her husband. Carefully, she reached down, hoping to get her hands on the small pistol.

"Nobody move!" a police officer yelled as he raced down the platform. He pointed his gun at Rafferty. Guff followed behind the officer.

Rafferty pointed his gun at Jared and Sara. Claire picked up Sara's gun and did the same. "Let us out of here now, or I'll kill them both!" Rafferty shouted from the tracks. "I swear!"

"I don't negotiate," the officer said. He aimed his gun at Rafferty and inched his way farther down the platform. "And you're in no position to make demands."

"Oh, no?" Rafferty asked. "Between you and your sidekick, you have one gun. We have two. If you try and shoot one of us, the other's going to kill the happy couple. I'd say that's a damn good position."

Looking down at Sara and Jared, Guff saw that Sara was hiding the small pistol right below Jared's shoulder. "Don't listen to him," Guff said.

"I'm not joking," Rafferty warned.

"You do what you want," Guff said confidently. "But if you try to hurt them, he's going to blow both your heads off. He's going to start with her and end with you."

Unnerved, but refusing to budge, Claire kept her gun pointed at Sara and Jared.

Guff turned to the officer. "Can you make the shot?"

"I'll make it," the officer said.

"I'm warning you—don't fuck with me," Rafferty said. "You have three seconds to decide. One . . ."

Nobody moved.

"Two . . ."

Still nothing.

"Thr—"

"Her gun's empty!" Sara shouted.

"What?" Claire asked.

"It's empty. I emptied it before I left the office."

"She's lying," Rafferty said.

"No, I'm not," Sara insisted. "They wouldn't let me take it out until I emptied it."

Claire looked down at her gun. Her hands were trembling.

"Claire, fire it at me," Sara said. "There's nothing in there."

"Don't believe her, Claire!" Rafferty shouted. "She's a liar!"

But as the tears rolled down Claire's cheeks, she lowered her gun. Guff grinned at Rafferty. "Now what was that you were saying about one gun versus two?"

Rafferty kept his gun pointed at Sara, while the officer kept his gun pointed at Rafferty. "I'm not going to jail," Rafferty said.

"Actually, you are," Guff said. "The only thing you have to decide is whether you're going to be riding there in a cop car or an ambulance."

"That's not true," Rafferty said. "I'll hire the best lawyers in the city."

Sara knew he was right. He'd hire the best money could buy. And with the fingerprint gloves, they'd have plenty to work with. She looked down at Jared, who was still bleeding in her lap. No, she told herself. She couldn't let Rafferty walk.

"You can get any lawyer you want," Guff said. "All you have to do is give us the gun. You do that, and you'll be in a much better position to get out of this." Realizing he had Rafferty's attention, he added, "You know I'm right. It's the only smart thing to do."

"This isn't an easy case," Rafferty said as he took his finger off the trigger. "With the right defense team, I'm off the hook. I'll make bail by—"

"You think you're making bail?" Sara blurted. "The judge isn't going to allow bail for this. That cold-blooded murder of Conrad—"

"That wasn't me!" Rafferty shouted, once again raising his gun.

"And let's not forget what you did to Elliott and Kozlow, and Arnold, too."

"She's just trying to rile you," Guff said.

"Don't listen to him," Sara said, still hiding

Jared's gun. Jared's breathing became labored. She didn't have much longer. "Once we have you, you'll never see sunlight again."

"Oh, I get it," Rafferty said. "You figure if you enrage me enough, I'll actually try and shoot you. And if I do that, this cop gets to put a bullet in my brain." He shook his head. "I'm walking out of here, I'm making my one phone call, and I'm sleeping in my own bed tonight."

"Not a chance," Sara said, raising her voice. She could feel Jared shaking. "They'll never let you out!"

"Sara, shut up!" Guff yelled.

"It's a death penalty case!" Sara screamed. "You're getting the death penalty!"

"Good-bye, Sara," Rafferty said, lowering his gun. "It was lovely to make your acquaintance." As he approached the edge of the platform, Rafferty raised his arm and held out his gun to the officer. The officer reached down to take it. But before the officer could even react, Rafferty pulled the trigger and shot him in the stomach. He then turned his gun toward Sara.

In one fluid motion, Sara pulled her gun and fired. Three consecutive bullets ripped into Rafferty. Two in his chest, one in his shoulder. As he staggered backward, Sara fired another shot. And another. And another. She pulled the trigger again, but heard only a click. Click. Click. Click. Rafferty continued to stumble. When he lost his footing on the train tracks, he fell backward and his body crashed to the ground. It wasn't until that moment that Sara finally took a breath. The threats, the frustration, the angling and manipulation—they were all finally gone.

Hearing a soft moan from her husband, Sara

dropped her gun and cradled Jared's head in her arms. Right there: That was why she did it. *"I need an ambulance!"* she shouted. *"Please!"*

Blinking back into consciousness, Jared opened his eyes. "Did we win?" he whispered.

Her eyes welled up with tears. "Always the competitor."

"Just answer me."

She thought about Conrad. "Yeah," she sobbed. "We won."

"Terrific," Jared whispered.

"Are you okay?" Sara asked.

"I'm not sure. I can't feel my legs."

CHAPTER 21

"The district attorney will see you now, Ms. Tate," Monaghan's secretary announced.

Sara headed numbly for the door.

Monaghan was sitting with his hands flat on his desk, a grim expression on his face. "Sit," he demanded. "Let me get straight to the point. What you did yesterday was one of the most wasteful, egocentric, self-interested displays of power I've ever seen here in my seventeen years of prosecuting."

"I can explain."

"Explain?!" Monaghan hissed. "You killed one of my men! Conrad is dead!"

"Sir, I never meant—"

"It doesn't matter what you meant! I'm not interested in your intent. All I care about is the fact that he's dead. And not only is he dead, he's dead for a stupid reason—because as a self-absorbed neophyte, you were raring to pull off your own stunt!"

"But the circumstances—"

"I don't want to hear about the circumstances! I know you and your husband were both in danger. But if you had communicated your problem directly to me, we could've worked out a sensible solution. Instead, I have to deal with every reporter in the entire city, all of them wondering why I didn't know what was happening inside my own damn office. Do you know what that does to me? Oh, no, you didn't have time to think of that. Besides yourself, you didn't consider anybody. You didn't consider this office, you didn't consider me, and you didn't consider your buddy, Conrad, who you obviously cared nothing about."

Sara shot from her seat and slammed her fists against Monaghan's desk. "Don't you ever say that! That man was my friend! When you were ready to kick me out on my ass, he took me in for no good reason. And for better or worse, he trusted me with his life. So you can call me stupid, and inexperienced, and an incompetent novice, but don't ever, *ever*, tell me that I didn't care about him! He's the only reason I'm still in this office."

"Then maybe you should take the hint and consider leaving."

"Believe me, I was thinking about that all last night. There'd be nothing easier than for me to leave this place. I'd love to pack up my stuff, walk out that door, and wash my hands of the entire incident. Out of sight, out of mind—after this, I could leave the law behind in a heartbeat. But let me tell you: I'd never do that to him. He's going to get far better than that. Every day I step into my office, though, it's going to haunt me. *Every* day. I'm going to have to live with this for the rest of my life. But it's going to be worth every minute—because that man deserves a legacy."

Monaghan leaned back and crossed his arms, giving Sara a chance to calm down. "Tate, I hope the sermon made you feel good, because now it's time to listen to me. First, I don't give a shit about your whiny psychological consequences. This isn't a Ph.D. program, it's the DA's office. And I'm the fucking DA! Do you understand? I don't care that you saved yourself, or saved your husband, or caught the bad guy. I don't even care that those two officers are stabilized. And you want to know why? Because my man is dead! Period! End! That alone gives me the best reason to fire you!"

"If you want to fire me, fire me. I'm not quitting."

"Tate, get your ass up and get yourself out of my office. I don't want to see you, I don't want to know about you, and the only thing I want to hear about you is that the local news crews ate up your little fluff piece with the mayor."

"What're you talking about?"

"I'm talking about what you're going to be doing this afternoon. Lucky for you, the mayor's staff decided to make the most of it. He called me the moment the story broke last night: Wife ADA risks life and breaks rules to save defense-attorney husband. You couldn't write a better headline. So get to the hospital and practice your smile. The mayor'll be there at noon. He figures New Yorkers are going to feast on this."

"I'm not doing a photo op at Jared's bed."

"Yes. You are!" Monaghan shot back. "And you want to know why? Because I say so, because I'm the boss, and because you're going to listen."

"But that's not—"

"I don't care what you think, Tate! I'm not risking any more bad press. You're going to say cheese, and you're going to scratch the mayor's back, and hopefully, he's going to say thank you by looking the other way when he's slashing budgets. Otherwise, I'm going to have to revisit my list of expendable employees—where your assistant Guff is teetering on the edge."

"Tell the mayor I'll do it."

"I already did." Monaghan stood from his seat and pointed to his door. "Welcome to city politics," he added. "Now get out."

At the office, a small group of trial assistants clustered around Guff's desk. "If she did do it, she's a psycho," an assistant with horn-rimmed glasses said. "I mean, why else would you goad someone into shooting at you?"

"Can you please leave me alone?" Guff asked, annoyed.

"I heard she didn't want to give Rafferty even the tiniest chance to walk free," another assistant said. "Instead, she forced his hand and shut him down. Sounds pretty ballsy to me."

"I heard that was her plan all along," an assistant with a crew cut added. "That the whole thing was a setup to kill Rafferty."

"It wasn't," Sara said, pushing her way through the assistants. "It was a last-minute emotional decision that had no basis in rational thought. I thought my husband was going to die, so I wanted immediate revenge."

Startled, the group didn't move.

Sara looked down at Guff, then back at the assistants. "Go away. Leave him alone."

As the group dispersed, Guff followed Sara into her office. When he saw her packing up her briefcase, he said, "They fired you?"

"Oh, no," Sara said. "I got relegated to a far lower circle of hell: I'm doing photo ops with the mayor."

"You're kidding."

"Not a bit. Monaghan chewed me out for Conrad and for wasting resources, but the mayor loves the PR potential of the story. Anyway, Jared's the one they want in the photo—the mayor needs a good hospital bed to put his arm around."

"How's Jared doing?"

"Physically, he should be okay. The bullet just missed his spine, but it ripped open a lung. He also had some temporary paralysis in his legs, but the doctors said that was just from the shock of being shot in the back. Emotionally, though, he's on a different track."

"Did he decide what he's going to do about his firm?"

"What's to decide? Thomas Wayne personally called him up and told him to resign. The bastard didn't even wait until Jared was out of the hospital."

"I still don't understand why he has to resign. Can't he just—"

"Guff, to save the two of us, Jared told me confidential client information. More important, both clients wound up dead. The DA's office may have a public-relations wet dream, but Wayne and Portnoy has a PR nightmare. Every client of the firm is now terrified their secrets aren't safe."

"How's Jared dealing with it?"

"It's still too soon to tell. He was crushed when he first found out, but I think he's realized it had to be like this. Besides, any place that won't even give you a week to recover isn't the place you want to be for the rest of your life."

"Is that his rationalization or yours?"

"Last year, it was mine; now it's his. But I think he actually feels it."

"Great," Guff muttered. "Then at least one good thing came of this."

That was all Sara needed to hear. She had avoided the subject until now, but it was time to talk about it. "Guff—"

"We shouldn't have done it, Sara. We were out of our league."

"Do you really think that? Do you really think we didn't know what we were getting into?"

"But Conrad—"

"Conrad knew better than anyone. You remember what he said."

"Of course I remember—and thanks to this, I'll never forget. When we suggested sending a cop, he was the one who said we should do it ourselves, that that was the only way to ensure the secret. The thing is—"

"It doesn't make it any easier," Sara said.

"It doesn't make it any easier," Guff agreed. Sara had hit it right on the head. Just like Conrad used to. "Listen, I'm sorry. I don't mean to put the burden on you."

"It's not like that anymore—I don't mind the burden. And in this case, I deserve it. I just want to make sure you—"

"Don't worry, I'll get through it. Between the two of us, we'll have plenty to keep us busy: cases to prosecute, reporters to talk to, essays to write . . ."

"Essays?"

"Sure, if I'm going to get into law school, I'm going to need some good essays."

Sara smiled. "You're really applying to law school?"

"Would this face lie?" Guff asked, squeezing his own cheeks. "That was always the plan. This just gave it more immediacy."

"Good for you, Guff. I think he'd really like that."

"Of course he would. Then he'd have another disciple to brainwash."

Sara laughed. They'd definitely get through it. "Speaking of disciples, O Great One, in the rush to get out of there yesterday, I never got a chance to thank you for everything you did. Without you—"

"You wouldn't have stolen the case? You wouldn't have gone through this ordeal? You wouldn't have a sofa or a cool DA's badge?"

"I'm serious, Alexander."

"Uh-oh, first-name alert! First-name alert! Incoming serious discourse!"

"Make jokes all you want, but I really appreciate everything you did. You didn't make me take the case—I took it to help myself. And since neither of us could've known that Victor set me up for it, it's my responsibility."

"That's nice, but you don't have to—"

"Please let me finish," Sara said. "I promise I won't get mushy or sentimental. From the moment I walked in here, you were my . . . amigo. And as someone who doesn't get close to many people, that means a lot to me. No matter how bad things got, you were always there to help, and you always—"

"You're getting muuushy," Guff sang.

"Just take the compliment. Thank you for everything."

"Fine. You're welcome. I just hope our next adventure is a bit more pedestrian. Maybe we can get a cult massacre or something calming like that."

"We should be so lucky."

"Exactly," Guff said. "And speaking of lucky, Adam Flam wants to talk to you."

"Who's Adam Flam?"

"Head of the discipline committee. They just got out of the Victor meeting."

"They did? What'd they decide?"

"Go talk to him."

"C'mon, Guff, just tell me."

"I'm not saying a word. If you want to find out, talk to him. Room 762."

"Fine," Sara said, heading to the door. "But it better not be bad news."

"What do you mean you're not indicting?" Sara asked as she stood in front of Flam's desk.

"Just what I said," Flam replied calmly. He was a thickset man with tired eyes and a heavy Boston accent. "The committee decided there wasn't enough evidence to indict."

"Not enough evidence? If there wasn't enough evidence, why'd they put him on probation? Since the moment this thing started, Victor's had his hand in everything we've done. He was the one who asked for the case, and when he got it, he was the one who made sure I took it from him."

"Asking for a case isn't illegal. And last I checked, neither is putting your own name on a case folder."

"What about Doniger? She can testify that—"

"Doniger doesn't know anything. We questioned her until three in the morning, and she didn't give us a scrap. Whatever Victor was involved in, his ties were only to Rafferty and Kozlow, both of whom, as corpses, would be terrible witnesses. It's a simple proof issue—and until we can get that, the committee decided they didn't want to risk morale on an unsuccessful indictment."

"Morale? What the hell does this have to do with morale?"

"Everything," Flam answered. "Victor's one of the most respected ADAs in this office—he's part of the institution. So before you can take him down, you better be sure you have the evidence against him. If not, you're going to have half of the law-enforcement population screaming for your head."

"Are you telling me Victor's not getting indicted because he won last year's popularity contest?"

"No, he's not getting indicted because you don't have the evidence."

"I have some evidence."

"Tate, you don't have a case. And until you do, morality has to take a backseat to reality. Be thankful you went four-for-five and leave it at that."

"It's still not right."

"Neither was what happened to Conrad."

Sara refused to reply. It was something she was going to have to get used to. "Anything else?"

"We decided not to suspend you for goading Rafferty into shooting at you. And trust me, that was a gift—if you hadn't riled him up, that cop might've never been shot."

"I'm not saying it was a smart move, I just didn't want to give him another crack at exploiting the system."

"And what about Doniger's gun?"

"What about it?" Sara asked.

"I went down to the evidence room this morning. There were six bullets in it."

"So?"

"So it was supposed to be empty."

"What can I say? Some bluffs work, some don't. You should just be happy the rest of us are safe."

"No, you should be happy our committee overlooked that one," Flam said. "And just so there's no confusion, Conrad was our friend, too."

Sara realized that even when Guff went off to law school, she wasn't going to be alone. "Thank you," she said.

"Don't thank me. From what I hear, you're going to make a great ADA."

"I plan to," Sara said.

When she was done at Flam's, Sara walked back up the hallway to Conrad's office. It had been less than twenty-four hours since the last time she was there, but when she stepped inside, it already felt different. The sofa was still in the same place, the desk was still uncluttered, and the out-box still held more paperwork than the in-box, but something was clearly wrong. Despite the fact that it was filled with furniture, the room was empty.

Sara shut her eyes. Memorizing the smells of the office, she tried to picture his face. It was easy—easier than she'd thought. But she knew that that too would fade. And this was different from Lenny Barrow. She didn't have an old picture to fall back on. So she made one.

Sara moved toward the sofa and opened her briefcase. Inside was her portrait of Conrad—just like the ones she had done of Jared. Pulling it out, she stared at his face. And for that moment, he was back again. She could hear him yell, and rant, and teach, and scream. It had taken her all night to get it perfect, but he deserved no less. Carefully, she set it down on his spotless desk. She'd frame it later, but for now, it belonged here. "Goodbye," she whispered as she left the office.

As she closed the door behind her, she turned around and read the two quotations still attached to the translucent glass: *"Crimine ab uno disce omnes*—From a single crime know the nation"—Virgil; and "Fame is something which must be won; honor is something which must not be lost"—Arthur Schopenhauer. She pulled the quotes from the door, being careful not to rip the tape which held them there, and headed back down the hallway.

As soon as she reached her office, she slapped the quotes onto her own door and pressed them into place. Stepping back, she admired the new view. It wasn't nearly enough, but it was a start.

"He wouldn't have had it any other way," Guff said.

"Someone's got to do it," she replied. Without even opening her door, Sara walked down the hallway.

"Where're you going now?" Guff asked.

"To the hospital. But before I do that, there's someone I want to see."

When the elevator arrived on the sixteenth floor, Sara stepped out and walked up the well-lit hallway. Noticing the corridor's expensive carpet and intricate moldings, she made a mental note to herself. There was no way anyone on a government salary could afford this place without outside funding. At apartment 1604, she covered the peephole and rang the bell.

"Who is it?" a man's voice asked.

"Sara Tate," she replied.

When the door opened, Victor shot Sara a thin smirk. "Nice to see you, Ms. Tate. To what do I owe this pleasure?"

"I just want you to know one thing," Sara said bluntly. "I know you set me up. And no matter how long it takes, I'm going to eventually prove it."

"Prove what?" Victor asked.

Ignoring the question, she continued, "The committee may not be ready to indict, but that doesn't mean it's not going to happen. By the time I'm done, this suspension is going to seem like a—"

"I'm not suspended," Victor interjected. "I took an official leave of absence. And if what you're doing is threatening me, you better walk away before I file my own harassment complaint. You may think you're Super ADA just because you saved the day, but you still have a lot to learn about the game. And just so you know, I don't sweat rookies."

"Keep giving me that attitude," Sara warned, "I'm going to bury you with that cockiness. The truth isn't hard to find—even the best ADAs can't afford posh apartments on the Upper East Side without a little extra income."

"Sara, let me give you a free philosophy lesson. There's a subtle difference between truth and fact. Fact is objectively real, while truth must conform to fact. So if you can't find the facts, you can never prove the truth. Understand what I'm saying?"

"There's no such thing as a perfect crime, Victor.

If I can't prove it on this case, I'll find another. Either way, I'm never giving up. No matter what you do, or how much voodoo philosophy you spout, I will never, ever, ever stop. I'm annoying like that." Turning away from Victor's door, Sara headed back toward the elevator. "Enjoy the rest of your day, asshole. All the rest of them are mine."

Stopping by the nurse's station before she entered Jared's room, Sara asked, "How's he doing?"

"Just great," a short, bespectacled nurse answered. "With some love and a little physical therapy, he'll be back on his feet in a few weeks. He seems to perk up when he's getting attention."

"He's been whining to you, hasn't he? He's horrible when he's sick."

"All men are crybabies," the nurse said. "He hasn't been that bad, though. He's saving all the good whining for you."

"I'm sure he is," Sara said as she walked toward the room. She pushed open the door and saw Jared sitting up in bed. His left arm was in a sling, and his right arm was hooked up to an IV, but color had finally returned to his face. Although Jared had been told to take it easy, he was busy writing notes on a legal pad. As soon as he saw Sara, he stopped.

"How're you feeling?" she asked.

"I'm better. Now."

"And your back?"

"Don't worry about my back," Jared said. "How're you doing with Conrad?"

"I'll get there," she said. "It'll take awhile, but I'll get there." Sara noted the pained but concerned look on her husband's face. It was still a hard issue for him, and even as she tried to maintain a convincing facade, she couldn't bear to see him like that. In an instant, she was slammed by an onslaught of emotion. Through gritted teeth, she could feel it working its way up from the bottom of her stomach. Not for Conrad, but for Jared.

"I'm really sorry about him . . ."

"It's not him," she insisted as she wiped the tears from her eyes. "It's never been him."

Jared leaned forward, stretched his IV tubes to their limit, and embraced his wife. As he pulled her close, he knew he'd never let her go again. "Sara, I—"

"I know," Sara said, holding him just as tight. "I've always known." Resting against her husband, Sara slowly regained her composure. When she pulled away, she noticed the large jar of kosher half-sour pickles on the nightstand. "I see you got Pop's bouquet."

"Yeah, it just came."

"I was going to get you some balloons, but I didn't want to—"

"I don't care about balloons. I have everything I need," Jared said. Before Sara could reply, he added, "And in case there's any doubt, I never said anything to—"

"You don't have to worry—they found the splitter on our monitor early this morning. That's how Elliott got everything."

"So you're ready to trust me again?"

"Honey, you know the answer to that," Sara said. "I'm just sorry I got scared in the end."

"I'm the only one who owes the apology. If I had as much faith in you as you had in me, I would've never called Victor in the first place. And if I hadn't done that—"

"Let me interrupt right here," Sara said. "I don't want to play the if-then game anymore. As long as you're safe, as long as we're together, we'll get through the rest. Now tell me what else is going on."

"Nothing much," he said, looking down at his legal pad. "Just trying to figure out what I'm going to do with the rest of my life."

"On a legal pad? You can't do that. Legal pads don't work for creative thinking. They stifle imaginative thoughts."

"I'm not having imaginative thoughts. I'm just making a list of all the people who owe us favors. Hopefully, one of them will be able to find me a job." He looked down at the pad and reread the list of names. "Damn," he said, dejectedly tossing it aside. "I can't believe we're going through this again."

She sat on the edge of his bed and took his hand. "It'll work out."

"It's like riding a constant roller coaster: we're up, then we're down; we're happy, then we're sad; you have a job, then you're going to be fired; I get a new client, he turns out to be a psychopath; you shoot him, I get fired."

Sara laughed. "At least you have your sense of humor."

"I'd trade it for a job."

"I know exactly how you feel. But after everything we've been through, I'm convinced of one thing: There is a grand plan. If I hadn't gotten fired, I would've never been a prosecutor, which is right now the greatest thing that's ever happened to me professionally. If you didn't make partner, you weren't meant to work at that law firm."

"And if you weren't standing here next to me,

I'd have real problems to contend with. You're absolutely right. I just don't like having someone else make the decision for me."

"Never again, my dear. All the rest are up to us. Besides, once the mayor comes in here for his photo op, your phone is going to start ringing off the hook with offers."

"The mayor's coming here?" Jared asked, sitting up straight.

"Sure, now you're excited," Sara said. "You're going to be lapdog to the head honcho himself."

"What time is he getting here?" Jared asked, flattening out the covers on his bed. He reached for his legal pad and smiled. "This could really turn things my way."

Sara shook her head. "Let me give you a piece of advice: Play down the opportunism and play up the brave-but-injured hero. It's a lot more appealing."

Without answering, Jared flipped to a new page on his legal pad. "How much pull do you think the mayor really has?"

"I can't believe you," Sara said. "Why would you want to go back to a law firm? Even with the prestige factor, we both know that Wayne and Portnoy was terrible. Your hours stank, your work was unappreciated, you hated your bosses—the only reason you were there was for the money that comes with partnership, which was always promised, but never delivered."

"That's why I'm not looking at law firms."

Sara stopped, surprised. "You're not?"

"Nope."

"Then where're you looking?" she asked, raising an eyebrow.

"Well, if the mayor can pull some strings, I was

thinking of taking a look at the district attorney's office."

As a skeptical grin crept up her cheeks, Sara laughed out loud. "You sneaky son of a bitch," she said. "That's what that whole sad act before was about. You were trying to get sympathy so you could spring this idea in my face."

"What're you talking about?" Jared asked with a smile.

"See, I knew it. You never let up, do you? It's always competitive."

"What's competitive? I want a great job that's satisfying; you have a great job that's satisfying. Don't you think there's room for two prosecutors in a family?"

"There's certainly room for two prosecutors in a family—just not *this* family."

"And why's that?" Jared asked. "Are you jealous?"

"Of course I'm not jealous."

"Then what is it? Are you nervous? Intimidated? Worried I'll steal your thunder?"

"Listen, lover boy, you couldn't steal my thunder if you were knee-deep in a kiddie pool, sucking on a lightning rod."

"Do you realize how many Freudian references you just made in that one statement?"

"Don't try to change the subject. I'm not the pushover I used to be," Sara said. She grabbed the small device that controlled the positioning of Jared's hospital mattress. "If you're not nice to me, I'll fold you up in that Craftmatic adjustable bed before the nurses can even hear you scream."

"And that's supposed to scare me?"

Sara pushed a button on the control, and Jared's bed slowly moved into a V formation. "Okay, okay, you're not a pushover. I take it back. But that doesn't mean I can't be a prosecutor."

"I never said you couldn't. And if you really want to join my office, I'm not going to stand in your way."

Jared stared suspiciously at his wife. "You're not?"

"I already got what I want. We both did."

"So you'll love me even if I'm a prosecutor?" Jared asked.

"Yep."

"And you'll love me even if I go back to defense work?"

"Yep."

"Then I win either way, don't I?"

"It was never about winning."

"I know that—I just want to make sure we're back."